# VAMPIRE
# SURRENDER

# VAMPIRE SURRENDER

ALEXIS MORGAN
LAURA KAYE
LAUREN HAWKEYE
CARIDAD PIÑEIRO
VIVI ANNA

MILLS & BOON

Published in Great Britain 2014
by Mills & Boon, an imprint of Harlequin (UK) Limited,
Eton House, 18-24 Paradise Road, Richmond, Surrey, TW9 1SR

VAMPIRE SURRENDER © 2014 Harlequin Books S.A.

*A Vampire's Salvation* © 2011 Patricia L. Pritchard
*Seduced by the Vampire King* © 2012 Laura Kaye
*The Darkling's Surrender* © 2012 Lauren Hawkeye
*Her Vampire Lover* © 2012 Caridad Piñeiro Scordato
*Threshold of Pleasure* © 2013 Vivi Anna

ISBN: 978-0-263-91410-8

89-1014

Harlequin (UK) Limited's policy is to use papers that are natural, renewable and recyclable products and made from wood grown in sustainable forests. The logging and manufacturing processes conform to the legal environmental regulations of the country of origin.

Printed and bound
by CPI Group (UK) Ltd, Croydon, CR0 4YY

# A VAMPIRE'S SALVATION

## ALEXIS MORGAN

**Alexis Morgan** grew up in St. Louis, Missouri, graduating from the University of Missouri, St. Louis, with a BA in English, cum laude. She met her future husband sitting outside one of her classes in her freshman year. Eventually her husband's job took them to the Pacific Northwest where they've now lived for close to thirty years.

Author of more than nineteen full-length books, short stories and novellas, Alexis began her career writing contemporary romances and then moved on to Western historicals. However, beginning in 2006, she crossed over to the dark side. She really loves writing paranormal romances, finding the world-building and developing her own mythology for characters especially satisfying.

She loves to hear from fans and can be reached at www. alexismorgan.com.

# Chapter One

The sun had disappeared beyond the horizon more than three hours ago, yet the night air still hung heavy and damp with the day's heat. Cord ignored it just as he ignored everything except the rhythm of the work. As part of the prison's night crew, he'd been at it since sunset and had at least another six hours left to go.

Swinging the pickax up and over, his shoulders ached with the effort despite fifteen years of practice. On the downward slide, his vampire strength drove the steel blade deep into the asphalt, sending a jolt straight up the handle that jarred every joint in his arms and back.

Raising it up; slamming it down. Again and again, each swing of the ax marking another minute of Cord's life lost forever, wasted in this hell. The clank of his chains played in counterpoint to the sound of steel biting into stone.

"Break!"

The overseer barked the order a second time although there was no need. To a man, the entire crew had all stopped working as soon as the guard had checked his watch and opened his mouth.

Cord hobbled over to join the break line. Each man was

allowed two ladles of water. He drank the first one, poured half the second one over his head, and then gulped down the rest. The water helped cool him down and restore his energy, but only a little. What he really needed was blood, preferably straight from a pulsing vein.

He closed his eyes and tried to remember the spicy taste of fresh blood, rich and coppery and full of life as it poured straight from his lover's neck. It had been fifteen long years since he'd last had that particular pleasure, way back before his business partner Dwayne had gone missing, and Cord had gone to prison for his murder. Now he lived on outdated blood and old memories.

Cord slammed the door shut on that line of thought. To look back at the past made no more sense than looking beyond the next half hour. As a vampire with no future, nothing mattered other than losing himself in the monotony of the work assigned him. Life imprisonment had a whole different meaning when a man's existence could be measured in centuries.

"Break's over!"

Cord shuffled back to his place in line, automatically adjusting his gait to the length of chain that connected his ankles, always a few links short of a comfortable step. He retrieved his pickax and went back to work. Up and over and down, the clang of steel against stone. But before he could reestablish his rhythm, the closest guard stepped into Cord's line of vision and waved to catch his attention.

Cord stopped midmotion and lowered his tool to the ground. "Yes, boss?"

"Kilpatrick, you're wanted!" the guard yelled, jerking his head in the direction of where the jumbo prison transport was parked. "Report to the crew boss."

Cord nodded, doing his best to hide his shock. In all the

years he'd been loaned out for road work, he could count on the fingers of one hand the number of times one of the convicts had been allowed off the line except during breaks. Two of those times it had been because the convict in question had dropped dead while working. Twice prisoners had to be subdued by the guards when they lost control and tried to escape.

But it was the fifth occasion that still sent a shiver of cold fear straight up Cord's spine. The convict involved had been serving time for murder, found guilty even though the body had never been found. Under Coalition law, murder carried a mandatory death penalty. In cases where the corpse wasn't found, the execution was placed on hold only until such time as the body was eventually recovered.

Throughout the years, that night had played out over and over in Cord's mind like a 3-D horror movie. It started with the convict being called away from the line. He'd innocently approached the transport where the crew boss was waiting. At the last minute one of the Coalition's top executioners stepped into sight. As soon as the convict spotted the chancellor standing there, he'd frozen in place for a heartbeat before he broke and ran.

The chancellor caught up with him in seconds. At least the guy had made the execution quick and merciful. The worst part was how everyone had just gone on with their assigned duties as if death had meant nothing to any of them.

Maybe it didn't, but for Cord it was the stuff of nightmares, especially since he'd been tried and convicted on even less evidence. He wasn't sure exactly what he was feeling as he walked toward the transport, but he was very much afraid that it was relief. One way or another, his time in hell was about to end. Cord approached the crew boss, doing his best to look respectful and only mildly concerned about what was going on.

Sure enough, just as he reached the transport, the side door opened and a chancellor stepped out. Not just any chancellor, either, but Olivia McCabe, second only to Ambrose O'Brien, the top dog himself. What had happened to bring the biggest, baddest female chancellor in two generations all the way out here? A curiosity to be sure, and certainly not reassuring. Of course, if Cord were about to die, it was nice of the Coalition to send their very best to carry out his sentence. He supposed he should be honored.

He wasn't. To make matters worse, the mere sight of Olivia McCabe left him frozen in place, speechless and horny as hell. Thanks to her silver-blond hair, flashing pale green eyes and incredible body, she always had that effect on him.

Olivia walked toward Cord, her expression unreadable. When she got within arm's length, she stuck her hand out. Cord just stared at it, not knowing what to make of the friendly overture. After a second, Olivia let it drop back down to her side.

"Cord."

"Ms. McCabe, I wasn't aware that you were due for another visit. I'm sure there was no mention of it on my appointment calendar."

The chancellor smiled, her amusement genuine. "Gosh, Cord, I'd hate to think you weren't glad to see me."

"Any reason I should be?"

If Cord sounded bitter, they both knew he had reason to be. If the chancellor was there to end Cord's existence, he planned on meeting his end with dignity.

Olivia looked past him for several long seconds, focusing instead on the mixed bag of prisoners breaking up the asphalt behind them. What was she thinking? Pity for the poor bastards slaving away night after night? Satisfaction that justice had been served? Cord didn't know and frankly didn't care.

"Look, I don't mean to be unsociable, Ms. McCabe." He waved his hand in the direction of the work party. "But as you can see, I have pressing plans for this evening. Is this a social call or did you have a real reason for stopping by? I'm fairly certain this place isn't exactly on your way home."

Olivia's brows snapped down, her fangs flashing. "You used to be a better host, Cord, and since when does your voice sound like a pissed off bulldog?"

Cord's own canines dropped down in a defiant show of aggression. "My vocal cords were severed in a knife fight two months ago. They didn't heal right on the outdated blood they feed me, not that it's any of your business."

Cord was in no mood to play games. He forced himself to ask the hard question, his voice a harsh rasp. "Let's cut to the chase, Chancellor McCabe. Did you finally find Dwayne Delaney's body?"

Olivia's expression softened just a bit as she nodded. "We did indeed."

Cord straightened his shoulders. He had little left to call his own except for his pride. No matter what, he'd show no sign of weakness. "Then I guess you're here to end this party for me."

The chancellor nodded. "I am, but not in the way you think, Cord. Delaney's body was found two days ago. But here's the kicker—the coroner's preliminary report says he'd been in that shallow grave for no more than ten to fourteen days. The doc will be able to pinpoint the time of death more accurately when the tests are all finished, but that could take another week or more."

The chancellor's smile was more genuine now. "However, all things considered, I suspect you have an irrefutable alibi for that particular time frame."

# Chapter Two

Cord's knees melted away as the import of Olivia's announcement finally sank in. When he felt them start to give, he lurched over to lean against her transport, holding himself upright by the ragged edges of his self-control. Olivia opened the door and motioned him into the front seat. Inside, Cord laid his head back and closed his eyes, waiting for the world to quit spinning backward. Finally, he looked up at the chancellor who now held Cord's fate in her hands.

For the first time, he allowed himself to use his private nickname for her. "I'm sorry, Livi, but you're going to have to spell it out for me. What exactly does all of this mean?"

She squatted down so they were eye to eye. "It means that I drove all the way out here to pick you up and bring you home myself to make sure there weren't any glitches. I went to the judge who ruled on your case and had him order you remanded over to my personal custody before all the paperwork could be processed. That's not exactly normal procedure, but I convinced him I needed your help with this investigation."

Before Cord could ask another question, the chancellor's expression turned grim.

"By the way, when I contacted the warden about all of

this, I got the distinct impression that you're not his favorite inmate. That jerk wanted to keep you locked up until we catch the actual killer or at least until the coroner's report officially clears your name."

Her fangs were showing again. "I had to remind the bastard what the penalty was for unlawful imprisonment. After I pointed out that I could always order a complete review of all his records, he told me where I could pick you up. I'll be keeping an eye on him, though. I don't trust the little weasel not to trump up some bogus charge against you just for grins. As soon as you're officially in the clear, I *will* be launching that review."

She rose to her feet, her smile definitely looking deadly. "In fact, I've already frozen his files so he can't spend the next few days cleaning house. I'll teach him to mess with me or my clients."

Cord hated to feel grateful to anyone, especially someone who'd been part of the legal machine that had sent him to prison in the first place. But for her, he'd make an exception.

"Thanks, Livi. I owe you one."

"Like heck you do. We both know that if we'd all done our jobs right fifteen years ago, you wouldn't have ended up here at all."

He met her gaze head-on. "But you're here now, Livi. That counts for something."

The chancellor looked uncomfortable with Cord's gratitude; or maybe it was his pet name for her. "Let me get one of the guards to remove those shackles, and then we're out of here."

The ride back to New Eire took more than five hours, most of them spent in silence while Cord tried to come to terms with the abrupt change in his circumstances. Along the way, he devoured the cooler of fresh blood packs that Olivia had brought for him. Gods above, when was the last time he'd been able to drink his fill? Already he could feel his former strength returning.

As they left the guards and prisoners behind, Olivia had offered to swing by the prison to pick up any personal items Cord might want to retrieve, but he'd told her not to bother. He didn't want souvenirs from the total disaster his life had become. His ruined voice and the permanent scars on his wrists and ankles from the shackles would be enough of a reminder.

A couple of questions needed to be asked. "Does my family know? How about Francine?"

"Not yet. Ambrose thought we should keep this quiet for the time being."

That was all right with him. He didn't want to think about why the woman he was engaged to let him rot in prison for fifteen years without a single word, not even a notice that their engagement was officially over. Yeah, there was a thought guaranteed to warm a man's heart. The funny thing was that after fifteen long years, he could barely remember what Francine looked like.

Had he ever really loved her? He'd like to think he had. Maybe. After all this time, who the hell knew or even cared?

As they pulled up in front of an elegant brick home, he looked over at his escort. "Impressive. Definitely a step up from where I've been living."

Olivia shut off the engine. "It's Ambrose O'Brien's place. He wanted to talk to you, so we're staying here for the day."

Cord hadn't seen his old friend since the trial and wasn't sure he wanted to now. Looked like he had little choice in the matter, though, since the man himself was headed straight for them.

Cord rolled down his window. "That's quite a place you've got there, Ambrose. What did you do? Rob a bank?"

Was the big, tough chancellor actually blushing? "The place belongs to my wife's clan."

Okay, that was news. "I hadn't heard you'd gotten married. I guess congratulations are in order."

The chancellor smiled. "Thanks. Her name is Miranda Connor—well, Miranda O'Brien now."

Cord recognized the name. Her family's estate was in the same district as where his family lived. "Will she mind you dragging your work home with you?"

"It was her suggestion, actually, and she sends her apologies for not being here to meet you. She still has to spend a lot of time on family business, so she's back at the estate conferring with her mother."

Or maybe Ambrose was protecting her from a potentially violent vampire who'd just spent fifteen years in prison. If so, Cord really couldn't blame him.

Olivia walked around to open the passenger door of the transport for Cord since he hadn't yet managed to do that for himself. After living fifteen years in lockdown, it was going to take some time to get used to being able to open a door and walk through it anytime he wanted to.

He followed Ambrose up the steps to the porch. Before they went in, Ambrose turned back to face him. "I assume Olivia told you that we'll be needing your help in the investigation."

Suddenly all that blood Cord had chugged down wasn't settling all that well. "What are you not telling me?"

Ambrose frowned at his associate. "I thought you were going to explain everything on the way here."

"I thought it best to wait until Cord had a chance to get some rest."

Although she was talking to Ambrose, Cord was painfully aware of the fact she'd kept those intensely intelligent eyes pinned on him. He didn't need this, didn't need her pity, but apparently he was going to be stuck with Livi for the duration of the investigation.

"I don't mean to be rude." Although that was a lie. "Can we take this circus inside?"

She nodded and led the parade. "We'll only be here until we can leave for your place at sundown."

His place? He no longer had a place to call his own. His family had filed the papers to disown him about five minutes after the chancellors had hauled his unsuspecting ass off to jail. He hadn't heard from any of them since, which was just fine with him.

So what was his personal chancellor up to? Right now he was too tired to ask. Ignoring Livi, he spoke to Ambrose. "Look, I'm really tired. Could you point me to someplace I can crash for the day?"

"Sure thing. It's been an eventful night for all of us. Give me a minute to lock up."

But once again Livi stuck her pretty nose into Cord's business. "I can show you, Cord. I'm going to turn in, too, and your room is right next to mine. We need to get an early start because the drive out to your cabin will take most of the night."

He started up the stairs first, thinking about what she'd said. Last time he checked, he didn't own a damn thing, much less a cabin. He didn't want to rise to the bait, but he had to know. He looked back over his shoulder at her as they walked up the stairs.

"Okay, I'll bite. What cabin?"

"The one your grandmother left you in her will."

His grandmother had died? When? She had been his sole

supporter out of all of his extended family. And of course, none of the rest of the family would've thought to tell him of her passing. A dizzying wave of absolute fury mixed with grief washed over him.

Everything that had happened in the past few hours all hit him at once, short-circuiting his brain and sending him pitching headfirst back down the steps. He made a grab for the railing but missed. His last thought as he tumbled backward was, "This is going to hurt like a bitch."

# Chapter Three

"Cord!"

Livi caught him just before he took a header off the staircase. It was a struggle to stop his fall and keep her own balance. But thanks to her superior chancellor reflexes and strength, she managed to hold on to Cord's limp body and the railing long enough for Ambrose to give her a hand.

They each took one of Cord's arms and dragged him the remaining distance to the second floor. Luckily, his room was close by. They heaved him up onto the bed and then stepped back to catch their breath.

Ambrose gave her a narrow-eyed look. "He'd been holding up pretty well, all things considered. What did you say to him that sent him over the edge?"

She flinched under her boss's scrutiny. "He asked me about the cabin. Turns out he didn't know about his grandmother's death. I figured his family and the bitch wouldn't be bothered to tell him, but I thought the lawyers would have."

"Maybe you should have kept that particular fact to yourself until he had time to get his head around being out of prison."

At least Ambrose sounded more disgusted than truly angry

when he added, "But then it was probably only a matter of time before it all overwhelmed him."

She nodded her agreement. "Not to mention the prison had been feeding him only outdated blood for the gods know how long. There are laws regulating how much of that crap they can give the prisoners and how old it can be. It's just one more thing I'll be investigating once our boy here is completely in the clear."

Her boss's fangs flashed as he spoke, punctuating the anger in his voice. "Damn straight."

Her own were on display, as well, making her wish she could be alone with that scum warden for five minutes. He'd think twice about mistreating someone like Cord again.

"Do you want help getting him out of those clothes?"

Ambrose shook his head. "I'll take care of it. You go get some sleep. You're going to need to be at your sharpest to deal with his clan. I can stay with him awhile to make sure he's all right."

"Okay. I'll be next door if you need me for anything." Or if Cord did. Especially if Cord did.

She wanted to be the one to stay, but couldn't risk giving her boss any more reasons to suspect that her interest in Cord's case was anything more than professional. The truth was she'd been fascinated by Cord Kilpatrick from the very beginning. Fresh out of training, she'd been one of the investigators on his case fifteen years before when he'd first been charged with murdering his business partner. Unlike the head investigator, Olivia hadn't believed Cord was guilty even then, but hadn't been able to prove any different.

Once he'd been convicted—sentenced to death but with the mandatory stay of execution—she'd volunteered to oversee his case. For the past fifteen years, she'd visited him in prison four times a year, twice the norm required by law.

At first she'd been hoping that he'd remember something, some small detail that would either break the case wide-open or at least convince her that he was actually guilty. Watching his hope for a reprieve slowly die over the years was one of the hardest things she'd ever had to do.

Later, she visited because she suspected that she was the only one who'd ever bothered to make the effort. He never seemed particularly happy to see her, but at least he accepted the few things she'd brought him—cookies, books, magazines. It got harder to face him each time knowing that she only served as a reminder of the world that had turned its back on him.

Normally she took pride in her job, knowing most of the time the Coalition legal system worked. Her clients who were sentenced to prison deserved to be there, with Cord being the sole exception.

He'd been different from the very beginning. All through the trial he'd held his head high, cooperating to the fullest, depending on the legal system to give him justice.

Yeah,and look where that got him. That trusting expression in his eyes was long gone, replaced by bitter suspicion, except for a small hint of warmth whenever he called her Livi. His face, while still handsome, was all sharp edges now, carved that way by the brutal life behind bars. His body was muscular, but too lean for his frame, thanks to the poor prison diet.

He moved wrong, too. Even with the shackles gone, fifteen years of shuffling along in chains might be a hard habit to break. Some things he'd get back, like his natural born grace, but some were gone forever.

She made quick work of getting into bed and turned out the light. As she drifted off to sleep, her last thought was that the man who'd haunted her dreams for fifteen years was just on the other side of the wall. Maybe now that she'd gotten him out of prison, she might finally get him out of her system.

Cord jerked awake. What the hell? Habit had him forcing his body to relax while he assessed the situation. Something had torn him out of deep sleep, but the question was what? His fangs ran out, his fists clenched, and his instincts were running on full alert. It finally hit him: the sounds were all wrong.

Cord's heart banged around in his chest while his brain tried to come to terms with his surroundings. Slowly, the details came into focus. He wasn't in his cell on his cot. Instead, he was sleeping in a regular bed, one with clean-smelling sheets and a real pillow. That's right. Livi had brought him here to Ambrose's house.

The quiet that surrounded him was disturbing. No one was snoring; no one was crying in their sleep; no one was screaming for help that rarely got there in time. Violence had quickly become a way of life in prison, to the point it became normal to wake up at night to find out his next-door neighbor had been killed during the day.

Sitting up, Cord ignored the lamp by the bed, preferring the darkness protected by the lockdown shades on the windows. He sensed it was bright daylight outside, but obviously Ambrose had put him in a room that was safe for a vampire to sleep in.

He didn't remember going to bed, much less stripping off his prison clothes. There was a gap in his memory starting about the time he and Livi had started up the steps. What had happened after that?

Finally, it all came flooding back. His grandmother had died, leaving Cord her cabin on the family estate. He bet the relatives loved that, but then maybe they didn't care. Once he died, it would revert back to the family and they probably hadn't foreseen a day when he'd come strolling home a free man.

He was a free man. How was he supposed to get his mind around the idea? He crawled out of bed, needing to walk off some of the weirdness. The thick carpet felt foreign to his bare feet, his toes digging into the plush fiber. The prison was concrete and iron bars with nothing soft to ease life inside. He paced back and forth in the room, never quite reaching the far side.

It dawned on him that in his head he was back in his cell with only seven feet between one wall and the other. Not only that, his steps were the exact length of his shackles. He stopped moving for a few seconds, and then forced himself to take a long stride and then another until he reached the farthest point in the room. His fingers trembled as he touched the wall before turning around to make the return trip.

After a few rounds, he felt better, more relaxed and in control. He'd give himself another few minutes and then maybe see if he could get back to sleep.

A soft knock on the door froze him in place, waiting to discover who it was.

"Cord, are you okay?"

Damn it, it was Olivia. "I'm fine. Just restless."

"Okay, good night."

He listened to the soft sound of her bare feet padding back into her room next door. His mind filled with images of her climbing into bed, her pretty hair mussed and her eyes sleepy. Just what he needed. Wasn't it bad enough that he'd wasted hundreds of hours thinking about her over the years? Wondering what kind of lover she was. How she'd feel under him in bed, calling his name as their bodies joined and he drove them both hard and fast. Now she was only a few feet down the hall, but it might as well have been concrete walls and iron bars.

Exonerated or not, he'd be the last man on earth she'd take to her bed. Livi probably had dozens of men standing in line to date her, not to mention she had her career to think about.

He stared at the door for a few seconds more before he started walking again, taking another handful of laps just for good measure. By the clock, he still had several hours before he had to be ready to leave with Olivia—or Livi, as he preferred to think of her.

It made her seem more of a woman and less of the Coalition executioner she really was, like maybe she'd made some of those long treks to the prison to visit Cord the man, not Cord the convict. His hands itched to know if those short, silvery curls were as soft as they looked, if her skin was as satin smooth as he'd always dreamed it was.

Damn it, he shouldn't be thinking of Livi—no, make that Olivia—at all. It only screwed with his mind, and he'd need all his wits about him to get through tomorrow and all the days after that.

He crawled back into the bed, tugging the covers up to his chest and breathing in the scent of fresh sunshine and soap. As the silence settled around him again, he could almost swear that he heard Livi's soft voice call out, "Sleep well, Cord."

"You, too," he whispered and closed his eyes.

# Chapter Four

"So what are you thinking about so hard, Cord?"

Livi passed a slow-moving truck before glancing over at her silent companion, wondering if he'd even heard her question or was just choosing to ignore her. As if feeling her gaze, he slowly turned to face her.

"I'm thinking maybe we should rethink this whole mess. I appreciate my grandmother's gesture of support, but it's not like anyone else will be throwing a welcome home party for me. Yeah, you've already put through the paperwork to clear me of the murder, but you know how the clans are. Understandably, vampires have long memories. I'm not guilty of murder, but I am guilty of dragging the family name through the dirt. That taint is probably only just starting to fade. They won't appreciate me stirring it all up again."

Wow, that was the most words he'd strung together at one time since she'd first picked him up.

She changed lanes again. They were only a few miles from the turnoff to his family estate. It was understandable that he was starting to have a few qualms about what lay ahead for him. That didn't change what she had to do.

"Cord, I can't worry about what your family thinks. I

have an investigation to run, even if I step on a few toes along the way."

She shot him a quick look. "Besides, once we've nailed the killer, none of this will be hanging over your head anymore. Then you can do what you whatever you want, even make a fresh start somewhere."

Maybe even with someone, but she left that part unspoken.

The lights of the dashboard cast Cord's face in eerie relief. She wished there was something she could do to ease the pain and hurt behind his grim expression.

He sighed and looked out the side window. "I'm assuming you've got a suspect in mind."

Rather than tell him her own suspicions, she changed the subject. "We're almost there. You'll have to give me directions to the cabin."

The level of tension coming from Cord's side of the car ramped up big-time. He leaned forward, staring out into the night at the entrance to his family home. One glimpse of the pure hunger in his eyes had her looking away. It was a private moment, not one meant to be shared.

His voice was low and rough. "Turn right and then stop. I'll have to see if my old code still works. If not, we'll have to push the buzzer. Somehow I can't imagine them opening the gate once they know it's me."

She pulled up to the keypad. "Do you want to get out to enter your number or do you trust me enough not to go blabbing it all over the district?"

She'd meant that last part as sort of a joke, but his only response was to rattle off a series of eight numbers.

When the gate immediately rolled open, his shock was obvious. "I would have thought they'd have deleted me five minutes after the jail door closed."

It was odd. "Or maybe they don't hate you as much as you think they do."

"Yeah, right. That's why I haven't heard a word from any of them in fifteen years."

She winced. "Sorry, Cord. I wasn't thinking."

"Not a problem. Follow the road to the right when it splits. Drive on for another mile, and the cabin will be on your right. It's set back off the road quite a distance, but you can't miss the pair of gargoyles at the end of the driveway."

His smile looked a bit rusty. "Grandmother always said they watched over her. I used to climb on them and pretend they'd fly me anywhere I wanted to go."

Then he settled back against the seat again and closed his eyes. He was so quiet she almost thought he'd drifted off to sleep, but then he spoke.

"And for the record, Livi, you're the only person I trust right now."

All was quiet when they reached the cabin. Cord climbed out of the transport, but made no move toward the front porch. Too many memories and too many nightmares had him all tied up in knots. Luckily, Livi didn't push him, instead letting him take all the time he needed.

"I spent most of my childhood in this cabin. My parents preferred the nightlife in New Eire to living in the country. Me, I was always happier here. Maybe if I'd never left, my life wouldn't have gone to hell so quickly. The clan's finances were a wreck, though, and I had to live in New Eire to stay on top of things."

He didn't want to know what Livi thought about that. "I'll grab the bags."

She followed him around to the back of the transport and popped the trunk. After he retrieved their suitcases and headed for the front door, she followed behind him with the box of groceries they'd brought. He made a second trip back for the big cooler of blood that Ambrose had provided for him. It wouldn't last Cord more than a few days, but then he didn't plan to be there that long.

Inside, he stood back to watch Livi's reaction to his grandmother's home. It was just as he remembered it, which surprised him. According to what Livi had told him, it had probably been vacant for at least two years.

"Somebody's been taking care of the place."

The chancellor blushed. "You'll find out anyway, but just so you know, your family contested your grandmother's will. When the judge turned them down, he also ordered them to maintain the cabin until you decided what to do with the place."

"I don't suppose you had anything to do with that."

She didn't respond, which was answer enough. Instead, she asked, "Which way's the kitchen?"

"Through that door."

He set the luggage down by the stairs that led up to the loft and followed Livi. While she put the perishables in the refrigerator, he checked the cabinets for supplies.

"If you're hungry, I make a mean omelet." Then he frowned. "Or at least I used to. It's been a while."

"Sounds good."

While he busied himself getting the ingredients together, he was painfully aware of Livi watching his every move. Thank goodness his grandmother never rearranged anything, so it didn't take him long to have bacon frying and the eggs ready for the skillet. When Livi seemed relaxed, he pounced.

"So you think Francine is behind Dwayne's murder?"

The chancellor merely smiled. "I wondered how long it would take you to figure that out."

He turned the bacon. "There were only three people directly involved in the finance business Dwayne and I started. He's dead, and I didn't do it. That leaves Francine. I don't know if I believe she would be capable of murder, but you must have your reasons for suspecting her. What are they?"

Livi sipped the tea he'd made. "She never broke the engagement contract. I kept wondering why when most vampires would have done so at the first hint of a scandal."

Cord had wondered the same thing himself. "The last I heard, her clan had almost died out. Maybe her clan leaders pressured her to maintain the connection to mine."

Livi stared at him over the rim of her mug. "Sorry, but from what I've heard about Francine, I don't see her as the type to martyr herself for her clan. Besides, there isn't a court in the Coalition that wouldn't have declared the contract null and void if she'd wanted out, with or without her clan's approval."

After giving him a few seconds to mull that over, she did some pouncing of her own. "Did you know that she's now the CEO of your clan's business holdings?"

Okay, he wouldn't have seen that one coming. "How the hell did that happen?"

"After they found Dwayne's body, I finally read the fine print of your betrothal papers. Seems there was a clause inserted in the standard contract that would only come into play if you were to die before the marriage was…um, consummated after a legal marriage ceremony."

Livi blushed, her eyes dropping down to stare at her tea before she continued. "Seems Francine would retain the same rights she would've had as your wife. Once you were convicted and sentenced to death, she invoked that clause. The bottom line was that it gave her control of everything. Not just your private business holdings, but also your controlling percentage of your clan's financial dealings."

When she looked up at him again, her pale eyes were ice-cold. "Seems your loving fiancée has a real cutthroat talent for getting rich, especially when she does it using other people's money. There have been complaints in the clan, but legally there was nothing anyone could do to stop her."

He thought about that as he cooked the omelets. "That's such a different image of her than I remember. But you're right, something doesn't jive. I would never have agreed to a clause like that. Are you sure it's part of the original agreement?"

The badass chancellor side of Olivia's personality was definitely at the forefront right now, her fangs showing when she smiled. "We're checking into that. I wonder how she'll react when she learns her long-lost fiancé is back among the living and therefore legally back in control of the Kilpatrick finances. By the way, that ruling is part of the official decision by the judge who remanded you to my tender care. Things could get interesting."

Cord's own fangs ran out to full length. "Interesting is one word for it."

The truth was he was less interested in Francine and the clan's money than he was in the amazing possibilities of being in Livi McCabe's tender care.

An hour later, the dishes were done and the sky was getting lighter in the east. Too late for any of the dear relatives to come calling, which was an immense relief. They were probably huddled together trying to figure out how best to banish him from their midst. Tomorrow would not be any fun at all, and he'd need to be at full strength to face that bunch, not to mention Francine. It was time to go to bed, unfortunately alone.

His grandmother was never one for fancy technology, so closing the shutters meant cranking each one shut by hand. Sunlight was no danger to Livi with her mixed human-vampire blood, but she helped him secure the cabin.

He also double-checked to make sure both doors were bolted and barred shut. Even if someone else had a key, they still wouldn't be able to get in. If Livi was wrong about Francine, or even if she wasn't, there could be a wild card out there who wouldn't be happy to have Cord out of prison and out to regain his position in the clan.

When everything was secure, he met Livi at the steps. "You can have the bed in the loft. I'll take the couch."

The thought of Livi in that big four-poster, curled up under one of his grandmother's hand-pieced quilts had him hard and hurting. It had been more than fifteen years since he'd last had sex. As prison life had weakened him, he'd eventually lost the urge. But now, after two days of fresh blood and fresh air, all those desires were coming back with a vengeance, due in large part to the woman standing in front of him.

She looked puzzled. "There's only one bedroom in a cabin this size?"

He kept his eyes focused on the lumpy couch where he'd be spending the long daylight hours alone. "Yeah, my grandmother didn't want to encourage unwanted visitors. She turned my old room into an office as soon as I moved out. When I came back for a visit, I always used the couch."

Livi started up the stairs, but stopped on the first step and turned back to face him. "We're adults. We could just share."

Gods above, he so didn't need that image burning in his head. The woman had to have more sense than that. But then again maybe not, considering her skin was flushed rosy with heat, her heart was racing and those beautiful fangs were peeking out over her lower lip.

"Livi, go upstairs and go now."

He grabbed on to the newel post with both hands and held on for dear life to keep from tossing her over his shoulder and pounding up the stairs as fast as he could. "Because if you don't go right this minute, we'll be doing a lot more than sharing a couple of blankets. It's been too long for me. I have no control."

She didn't budge. "And what if I want you out of control?"

## Chapter Five

Gods, she was treading on the far edge of a major breach of chancellor ethics, but right now she simply didn't care. She'd been craving this man's touch for fifteen years. If he thought his control was shaky, well, so was hers.

When he didn't immediate answer, she backed up a step and then another, forgetting that retreat would likely trigger a male vampire's predatory instincts. Cord's dark eyes flared wide, and his head tipped back as if to better scent her arousal.

When he lunged for her, she retreated up two more steps before he caught her. Her brain might not be functioning all that well, but her body knew exactly what it wanted—demanded, and right that minute.

His hands, rough and callused from years on the road gang, grasped her arms, pulling her back down the steps to slam up against his rock-hard body. The jolt fed the growing ache inside of her. Sweet gods, yes, she wanted this, wanted him.

Cord's mouth ravaged hers with exquisite thoroughness, his tongue sweeping across hers, only to move on and trace the length of her fangs. She reciprocated, imagining how it would feel when he took her vein at the same time he took her body, impatient to experience it for real. She wrapped her legs around his hips, bringing the center of her need in direct contact with the bulge of his erection. It wasn't nearly enough.

Then Cord ripped his mouth from hers. "Livi, we've got to stop this now. Please."

Why? He clearly wanted her as much as she wanted him. He made no effort set her down, to back away, but the pained expression in his eyes made it clear he meant business.

A bolt of pain, born of both bitter disappointment and acute embarrassment ripped through her chest. She let her feet drop back to the floor, determined to regain her dignity and to ignore the burn of tears in her eyes.

Cord allowed her to put a small distance between them. But when she would have run up the stairs, he stepped in front of her.

"Livi—"

"No, Cord. No explanations necessary. You made yourself clear."

He reached out to wipe a tear from her cheek with the pad of his thumb. Gods, even that little touch was enough to rekindle the craving she had for more of the same.

"No, I didn't."

His big hand cupped her cheek, lifting her gaze up to meet his. She blinked when she saw the heat reflected there. Okay, maybe she should hear what he had to say.

"I'm listening."

The tension his stance eased just a bit. "I'm still not a free man."

That was so not true. There was no way she'd let him go back to prison. "But, Cord—"

He shut her up by swooping in to brush a soft kiss over her lips, stealing her breath away.

"You said it yourself. According to the law, my engagement to Francine still stands. That's true, isn't it, Olivia?"

His use of her real name was like a bucket of cold water in her face. "Yes, Cord, that's true."

And honorable man that he was, even after all he'd been through and everything Francine had done, he was going to stand by his word. She had to admire his integrity. Damn the man, anyway.

"Look, I just need to go to bed."

Although she'd rather run back to her transport and put far more distance between the two of them than a single flight of stairs. She picked up her suitcase and started climbing the steps again. At least this time, he didn't try to stop her.

But when she reached the top, he called her name.

"Livi, there's one more thing you should know."

He didn't speak again until she relented and looked back down at him. "What's that, Cord?"

"Come sundown, I have every intention of getting to the bottom of Dwayne's murder, whether it was Francine or someone else. I'll need your help with that."

"That's why I'm here. I'll do my job."

His eyes had taken on that predatory gleam again. "But regardless of how that turns out, I'll be ending my engagement with Francine. I need to make sure she has no legal recourse against me or my family other than what was spelled out in the prenuptial agreement."

Where was he going with this?

"I can help with that. If I don't have the clout, Ambrose will."

"Good. I just thought you should know what my plans were because you have a vested interest in all of this getting resolved fairly and fast."

"Why is that? So I can get back to my job?" How considerate of him.

"No, because once I'm in the clear, I'll be coming after you with everything I've got, Chancellor McCabe, and I intend to finish what we started a few minutes ago."

He actually licked the tips of his fangs and grinned up at her. "I'm going to be all over you, Livi, and I don't plan on stopping for a very long time. If you've got a problem with that, you'd better let me know now."

She swallowed hard and studied the determination radiating from the alpha vampire staring up at her with pulsing heat in his gaze.

Finally, she shook her head. "I've got no problem with that, Cord. No problem at all."

Feeling much better than she had only seconds before, she smiled back at him and headed for the bathroom to get ready for bed. The sooner they got to sleep, the sooner sundown would come.

Cord was awake long before darkness fell. He'd slept better than he had the prior night, but still had some problems with the silence. He'd paced the floor a few times, once again having to practice taking full steps and ranging around the room in random patterns. Eventually he'd leave the limitations of prison life behind, but it would take time.

He stared up at the ceiling. Livi had been stirring around up in the loft for some time. Was she staying up there because she didn't want to wake him or because she wanted to avoid him?

No, his Livi wasn't afraid of much and especially not him. She'd take on his entire clan single-handed if that's what it took to clear his name once and for all. He liked that about her; in fact, there was a whole lot about his chancellor that he liked, maybe even loved.

He'd always known there was a surprisingly strong connection between the two of them, but he'd never let himself name what it was he was feeling for her. Gratitude for all her visits and caring had been part of it, but it had grown to be so much more than that.

When the top step creaked, he threw back the old afghan his grandmother kept on the back of the couch and sat up. It was tempting to meet Livi at the bottom of the steps, but he didn't want her think he was about to pounce. Not yet, anyway.

Her smile was a bit shy. "Oh, you're up. I wasn't sure and didn't want to wake you."

"I've been awake for a while."

She came closer to where he sat. "Trouble sleeping again?"

"Not as much. Mainly it was because tonight promises to be eventful."

He stood and stretched, taking pleasure in the way her eyes followed his every move. Truth was, he added a few more moves just to bask in her approval a bit longer.

"Want some breakfast?"

"You stay." She started for the kitchen. "It's my turn to cook."

He followed her anyway. "I'll make the coffee."

After he set the coffee to brew, he zapped a pack of blood in the microwave. Normally, he'd take it in the other room, but Livi didn't seem to be bothered by watching a vamp feed. It fact, the whole scene felt surprisingly comfortable. Cozy, even. Definitely a far cry from eating slop at a battered and scarred table with two dozen other inmates.

Livi plunked a plate down in front of him. "I don't know where you were just then, Cord, but it wasn't a good place."

He shook off the effects of the memories. "Sorry, I was just thinking about how weird all of this is. You know, in just two days going from swinging a pickax to sleeping on my grandmother's couch."

Her soft green eyes looked at him with sympathy as she came around the counter to where he sat. She brushed her fingers over the short stubble of his buzz cut.

"I imagine the memories will hit you at odd moments for a while to come."

Even knowing he was playing with fire, he tugged her down on his lap. "A kiss might help ward them off."

"You think so? Maybe we should test your theory."

Rather than the explosion of their last kiss, this was a coffee-flavored seduction. His hands ignored all his orders for them to behave, instead learning the curve of her hip, the way her breasts fit his palms, the round fullness of her backside. All perfect, all too tempting.

He pulled back slowly, not wanting her to feel rejected, not again. His smile was rueful as he nuzzled her neck, tasting her skin right over a pulse point. "So much for my good intentions. I swear, Ambrose shouldn't let you out in the field without posting a warning label on your uniform."

She laughed as she stood up. "I'll be sure and pass along your suggestion. I'm sure he'll get right on it."

Before Cord could respond, someone pounded on the front door. Just that quickly, Livi, the warm, willing woman disappeared. In her place stood Olivia McCabe, Senior Chancellor for the North American Coalition, her strong features radiating authority and determination.

"Cord, are you ready for this?"

They both knew things were going to get ugly before they got better. Someone he knew had let him rot in prison for fifteen years for a crime he hadn't committed. His fangs dropped down, ready for a fight.

"Oh, yeah, Madam Chancellor, I'm more than ready."

# Chapter Six

Before turning the final lock, Cord took a deep breath and searched for some calm. His blood was running hot from kissing Livi, and there was a very good chance his soon-to-be ex-fiancée was waiting on the other side of the thick oak door.

For a brief second, he was tempted to leave the world shut outside while he dragged his chancellor upstairs to bed. Getting naked with Livi would be a lot more satisfying than getting down and dirty with Francine over the clan's finances and rehashing the past fifteen years.

But he wanted more than a one night fling with Livi, and he needed to sever all contact with Francine before that could happen. It all boiled down to the fact he had no future with Livi until he faced his past.

He flipped the lock and yanked the door open. As soon as he did, the vampire standing on the porch launched herself straight at him.

"Cord! Sorry to arrive unannounced, but when they told me you were back, I just couldn't wait."

He backed farther into the room, Francine still clinging to his neck. Her performance would've been more convincing if he hadn't seen the absolute fury in her eyes just before she buried her face against his chest.

Olivia stood across the room in full chancellor mode, with her fangs out and her arms crossed over her chest. He shot her an apologetic look as he worked to break Francine's near choke hold on his neck.

Livi wasn't as patient. "Ms. Clark, I hate to interrupt this little reunion scene of yours, but I'm here on official Coalition business and would like to get started."

Francine stiffened and finally let go. When she stepped back, a single tear trickled down each cheek as she smiled at him. If not for the reptilian chill in her blue eyes when she glanced in Olivia's direction, he might have even bought what she was selling. Had she always been such an accomplished actress?

The two women stared at each other, obviously sizing up the competition. Neither looked impressed.

Francine finally broke the silence. "Excuse me, but you would be?"

Cord would've hated having that particular smile of Olivia's aimed at him. Certain parts of his anatomy were sensitive to that much cold. Luckily, for the moment, it appeared both women had forgotten he existed.

"I would be the chancellor in charge of the investigation into the recent murder of Dwayne Delaney. Also, I'm here to oversee the immediate transfer of control of all clan assets back to Mr. Kilpatrick and to ensure the transition goes quickly and smoothly. I'm sure you would agree, Ms. Clark, that would be in the best interests of everyone."

If Olivia was all ice and cold, Francine was fire and flames. On the surface, she was every inch the elegant highborn vampire female, from her tailored clothes down to her designer shoes. Cord might be years behind on current fashion, but money always showed. But all of that was simply surface trappings meant to disguise her sharp mind and even sharper fangs.

Francine glanced in his direction, clearly trying to assess where he stood in all of this. He spread his feet wide and crossed his arms over his chest, an unspoken declaration that he wasn't going anywhere soon.

"Cord, darling, I don't want to hurt your feelings, but I feel I must be blunt."

He shrugged his shoulders. "Go right ahead, Francine. There's not much that's going to hurt my feelings after the past fifteen years."

She flinched. "What happened to your voice?"

"My throat was slit." He kept his face impassive. "Thanks for asking, but you were saying?"

Francine was having trouble trying to decide which of them to look at. Her eyes flickered from one to the other before finally settling on Cord. Did she think he was the softer touch? If so, she was in for a surprise.

"I was just saying that you've been out of the loop on the clan's business affairs for fifteen years. You can't possibly expect to transition back into your previous life and pick up all the pieces overnight. I understand that you will want to become more active, but these things take time. Ask anybody."

Olivia stepped forward and held out a folded sheet of paper. "Actually, Ms. Clark, I did ask somebody—Judge Willard, to be specific. When he set aside Cord's conviction, he also set aside the clause you invoked fifteen years ago. If you read this court order, you'll see that as of yesterday morning, all of Cord's previous holdings and any moneys that have accrued in the interim have reverted to his control."

Francine's mouth was working, but nothing was coming out. Finally, she snapped it shut and snatched the paper from Olivia's hand. As she read it, her face flushed hot, and she stamped her foot in pure frustration.

"You'll understand that when dealing with this amount of

money and complicated business affairs, I will be consulting with my own attorneys before I accept this as valid."

Then she smiled at Cord. "Of course, now that you're finally out of prison, we can proceed with our wedding plans. Once we're married, all of this will be moot."

She sidled closer and looped her arm through his, probably hoping a physical connection would nudge him over to her side of things. Not so much. He removed his arm from hers and stepped away.

"I'm sorry, Francine, but I can't in good conscience hold you to our marriage contract. I'm not the same man that you agreed to marry."

Or the same fool.

Once again, she backed away and regrouped. She was nothing if not resilient. "Well, you'll be hearing from my attorneys on that, as well, Cord. I've stood by you all this time. I can't believe that you'd abandon me now."

Olivia entered the conversation again. "Your definition of standing by your fiancée is certainly an odd one, Ms. Clark. According to the prison records, you didn't make a single trip to visit Mr. Kilpatrick in all of that time. Nor did you write him a letter, send an email or make a phone call. I know. I checked. The judge concurs. He's willing to entertain a petition from Mr. Kilpatrick for a dissolution of the contract with no penalties. You should have read the fine print."

Francine looked as if she'd just gotten a whiff of something disgusting. Then she shot a look in his direction.

"You understand why I couldn't come, Cord. It was bad enough the family name had been dragged through the papers, but there were also some…irregularities on the clan accounts. If we'd continued our association with you, our clan's reputation would have been utterly destroyed."

Olivia actually laughed and applauded. "Good one, Ms. Clark. That was quite a performance, although I doubt Cord enjoyed it as much as I did. After all, he's the one you cut adrift for all those years."

Francine went on point. "Tell me, Chancellor, do you always take such a personal interest in your clients? Or was it just Cord? How often did *you* visit him in prison?"

Okay, he'd been prepared to be civil, but he wasn't going to let Francine sharpen her claws on Olivia. "Chancellor McCabe worked with Ambrose O'Brien to oversee my incarceration, Francine. You'd have known that if you'd ever bothered to ask."

He deliberately crowded her, letting her taste his fury. "Obviously, you were more concerned about the clan than you were me. But let's just make this clear—The Kilpatrick Clan is my family name, not yours, and it never will be. Now, you need to leave."

She still wasn't ready to give up. "But Cord, think of how things used to be between us."

Suddenly it was too much—the past tangling up with the present, all of it painful.

He pinched the bridge of his nose, fighting a blinding headache. "Look, I'm sorry, but just go."

The walls were closing in on him, threatening to crush him. There wasn't enough space to breathe and no air even if he could. He had to put some distance between himself and the rest of the world. Without waiting to see if Francine actually left, he headed for the kitchen.

Damn it, Olivia was following him, the last thing he needed at the moment. He glanced back at her, hoping she'd take the hint. She'd already stopped, but tossed him a phone.

"Here, take this with you. Ambrose is number one on speed dial, and I'm two. You know, just in case."

He snatched it out of the air. "Thanks."

Then he walked straight out the back door and into the night.

# Chapter Seven

It took every ounce of self-control Olivia could muster not to shackle Francine and drag her skinny ass back to New Eire in chains. Unfortunately, her rational mind knew that would only make a complicated situation even worse. Right now she didn't have enough evidence to charge the vampire with anything more than being a total coldhearted bitch.

But it was only a matter of time before the law came down hard on Francine, and Olivia would be there to make sure there were no loopholes, no mistakes. Once that cell door slammed shut, maybe Cord would finally really be free.

To come after her. She couldn't wait.

Francine stared toward the kitchen, a calculating expression on her face. Without glancing in Olivia's direction, she spoke.

"I have no intentions of letting him go, Chancellor. I suggest you turn those hungry eyes in another direction. Cord Kilpatrick still belongs to me."

Olivia called on all her years of dealing with the dregs of society for control. "Sounds like Cord has a different opinion on the subject. He also said you should leave. Since this is his home now, I'd suggest you not give me an excuse to arrest you for trespassing."

The word *haughty* didn't do Francine's obnoxious attitude justice. "You wouldn't dare."

No, she wouldn't, but the vampire didn't have to know that. Rather than argue the point, Olivia simply opened the door and waited for Francine to flounce her way out.

"I'll be back with my attorneys. You can tell Cord that I won't give up without a fight. I've spent fifteen years of my life building up the Kilpatrick enterprises."

"And he spent fifteen years in hell."

Olivia followed her outside. "By the way, you might also want to tell your attorneys about who Cord has on his side, starting with me and Ambrose O'Brien, not mention Judge Willard, the senior most member of the judiciary. Now go."

Livi stood on the porch and watched Francine drive away gunning her engine to send up a spray of rocks and dust. Good. It meant that her control was shaky. As long as her emotions were in the driver seat, there was a greater chance the woman would make a mistake.

Back inside, Olivia debated about what to do next. Her first instinct was to go after Cord, just to make sure he was all right.

But she had a feeling he'd been crowded enough for a while. She'd give him a few more minutes and then go after him. She understood that he'd had a lot thrown at him in not very much time. But any long delays would only give Francine that much more time at the helm of his business interests. Even now, the woman was probably trying to siphon off even more of the clan's funds into her private accounts.

Of course, Francine didn't know that Ambrose had the Chancellor's cyber squad watching for the first sign that she was going take the money and run. The woman wouldn't know what hit her. That thought had Olivia smiling again.

To keep herself busy, she cleaned up the kitchen. By the time she was done wiping down the counter, there was still no sign of Cord. She pushed the chair they'd been sitting in back up to the counter, savoring the memory of the kiss they'd shared and the way his hands had felt on her body.

Most men found her too intimidating, thanks in part to her job, but also because of her athletic build and that she was as tall or taller than most of the male species. Not so with Cord. He treated her as if she were fragile, something to be cherished.

That was okay. She had some pretty strong protective instincts when it came to him. Without letting herself think too hard about what she was doing, she tossed the dish towel on the counter and stepped out on the back steps.

Where would he have gone? Not far, she was betting. Maybe someplace out of his past when he roamed these woods as a boy. She could almost picture him running through the night, playing under the stars and moon.

Closing her eyes, she breathed deeply, trying to catch his scent. There, off to the left, just the faintest hint of Cord mixed with the damp smell of water. If she remembered correctly from the map she'd studied of the estate, there was a small lake or pond near the cabin.

It didn't take her long to spot an overgrown trail into the woods. Her chancellor night vision wasn't quite as highly developed as a vampire's would be, but it was good enough to get her where she was going.

She slowed down when the trees started thinning out, stopping completely when she reached the clearing surrounding the pond. Her heart pounded at the stark loneliness in the silhouette of the man standing at the edge of the water. She had no doubt that he'd heard her coming. Most likely he was also aware of the way her pulse raced at the sight of him.

"Is she gone?"

"For now, but she'll be back. On her way out, she made sure I knew that you still belong to her."

"She's wrong about that, but it's really the money she wants, not me."

"Then she's a fool."

Cord finally turned toward her, smiling at her in the darkness. "Ah, Livi, you're good for my soul."

She took that as invitation to come closer. As soon as she was within reach, he gave her hand a quick squeeze and then let go. She wanted so much more from him, but the simple touch would do for now.

"This is where I used to come to do all my hard thinking when I was a kid." He picked up a stone and sent it skipping across the shiny black surface of the water.

"My grandmother didn't like me wandering too far, so this was the compromise we made. I was far enough to be out of sight, close enough for her to keep track of me from the kitchen door."

"You two were close."

"Yeah, well, she was always there for me when no one else was. You would have liked her." He looked at her out of the corner of his eye. "You remind me of her."

Livi had to laugh. "You're such a smooth talker, Cord. For future reference, most women don't like to be told they remind a guy of their grandmother."

His own chuckle was rough, but sounded genuine. "Well, I am a little out of practice in these things. Most things, in fact."

Just that quickly, all the humor drained out of his expression. "I've made a decision, Livi, and it's not going to make you happy."

"What kind of trouble could you have gotten into out here?" She'd thought he was joking, but now she suspected that wasn't the case.

"I called Ambrose and asked him for another chancellor to take over the case. He's coming himself."

"But why? Is it because of what happened last night?"

He stared out at the water. "Yes."

"I know I've crossed the line. I'll get my things packed and be ready to leave when he gets here."

She should have known that a man like Cord wouldn't have wanted her; she was just the first female he'd been near in fifteen years. Before she'd gone three steps, Cord caught her by the arm and spun her around to face him.

"Damn it, Livi, I knew you'd take it wrong. The last thing I want is to send you away. You're the only thing that's keeping me anchored right now."

His voice was little better than a growl, but it still sent shivers up and down her body. "Then why?"

"I don't want you stuck in the middle of this mess."

"It's my job, Cord. I'm here to see justice done. I'd do the same for anyone."

Well, not exactly the same, and they both knew it. Especially when he pulled her close for another one of those incredible kisses, the kind where she melted right into him. They shouldn't be doing this, but she suspected he needed her touch as much as she craved his. It was a promise of what the future might hold for them.

"We'd better go inside. I want to show you what I've been following on your family's finances."

Cord stopped to stare out at the water again. "Truth is, I'm not sure I want to take over again. Don't know that I can. I've lost so much."

He threw another rock, sending it pinging off a rock just

offshore. "I can still feel the chains around my ankles. I even walk as if they're still there."

She rested her hand on his shoulder. "Give yourself some time, Cord. You've only had your life back for two days."

He glared at her, although she sensed the anger wasn't directed at her. "I'm never going to get that life back. I'm never going to be that naive fool again. He's gone, dead and buried just like Dwayne."

"Tell me about your friend."

"He was human, not vamp or chancellor, but we were born on the same day. His parents were killed in an accident, so he grew up with an aunt who used to live right down the road. We spent our childhoods living in each other's back pockets. We did everything together."

The words kept pouring out. Maybe he had just needed someone to listen.

"We went to different colleges, but kept in touch. On breaks we'd get together and hang out. We planned all along to go into business together. Heck, he even introduced me to Francine."

"Really." Now that hadn't been in the files. "How well had they known each other?"

Cord's eyes narrowed. "Looking back, I'm guessing a hell of lot better than I had thought. They had to have been in on this together somehow. What I can't figure out is what he got out of faking his death and making it look like I did it."

"I can answer that."

Olivia spun around to face Francine. How had the woman managed to sneak up on a chancellor and a vampire without either of them noticing? The answer was obvious. They were too focused on other things. Cord was lost in the past. She was lost in him.

Cord didn't seem to be at all worried about the gun she

had pointed at the two of them. "Do tell, Francine. I'd really like to know."

"He loved me, and I suppose I loved him as much as I can love anyone. If he'd been a vampire or even a chancellor, there might have been a future for us, but I couldn't settle for a human mate. My clan would've never allowed that to happen even if I were stupid enough to contemplate the idea. When he introduced me to you, we both saw the possibilities. You were too busy trying to stabilize your new company and pour some money back to the Kilpatrick coffers to notice that your fiancée and your business partner spent so much time together."

She came closer, stepping out of the shadows. "I have to admit, you might have been a whiz with money, but between sheets Dwayne had you beat hands down. Unfortunately, once you and I got engaged, he became unhappy. Seems he didn't want to spend his short life settling for... How did he put it? Oh, yes, table scraps."

Her lips curled up in disgust. "And you, Cord, kept postponing the wedding. I have to wonder if on some level you knew something was wrong. Anyway, when I started pushing you to set the date, Dwayne threatened to tell you about us. I offered him a onetime deal, and he took it. He'd fake his death and make sure you were blamed. I gave him enough money to live on until the dust settled."

She laughed. "The idiot really thought I'd give up all of this to live with him. When he came back demanding more money, I had to eliminate the problem."

The whole scene became almost surreal. At least he was learning the truth that he'd been searching for. He never expected to be standing in the darkness with the two women in his life, both his past and hopefully his future. If he and Livi managed to survive the night.

To keep the conversation going, he said, "So you did kill him?"

He couldn't bring himself to say his friend's name. In a lot of ways, Dwayne's betrayal was the worst.

Francine rolled her eyes. "Of course I did—I had to. It was a simple business decision. He would have kept draining the money I'd worked so hard to earn."

"Well, it's nice to know that you had the clan's interests at heart."

As he spoke he shifted slightly, putting himself in front of Olivia. Stubborn woman that she was, she immediately moved back beside him. He liked the symbolism of having her at his side, but wanted her out of danger. However, now wasn't the time for a shoving contest.

"So, Francine, what's next on your agenda?"

"Well, you both have to die. I would have thought that was obvious." Her smile was a little sad. "I'm actually sorry about you, Cord. You gave me the opportunity that made me what I am today. Even if you were willing to honor our betrothal, I really don't think an ex-convict is the appropriate mate for the CEO of the Kilpatrick clan. Once the world knows you died at the hands of an obsessed chancellor, all the sympathy will be on my side."

Francine shot Livi a nasty look. "You first, bitch. I told you Cord was mine, but you were out here kissing him anyway even after I warned you. You shouldn't have thrown yourself at him. Do you really think he'd settle for someone like you?"

With no warning, she pulled the trigger. Cord screamed Livi's name as he threw himself forward.

Burning pain in his upper arm didn't stop him from reaching Francine before she could get off another shot. His hands, powerful from years of hard work, fit around her neck perfectly. She fought with every ounce of her vampire strength, but she was no match for a male vampire in his prime.

Within seconds, Francine's movements weakened, her eyes bulging out as she struggled for the breath he wasn't about to let her have. The bitch had to die. She'd killed his friend, stolen Cord's heritage and fifteen years of his life. But her ultimate sin was threatening Livi, his mate.

Someone was pulling on his arm. "Cord, let go of her. We don't want her dead."

Yes, he did.

"Cord, we need this done right. She needs to stand trial. Let justice finally have its day. Don't let her steal any more of your soul. She's not worth it."

Slowly, the words began to make sense. "Francine will be tried and convicted. Let Ambrose and his people do their jobs."

Olivia, his Livi, managed to get in his face, her pale eyes sparking hot with emotion. "Please, Cord. For me. For us."

His fingers unclenched, leaving Francine gasping on the ground like a fish out of water. He tossed her gun out of reach and then flipped her over on her back to yank her arms behind her, taking a bit of mean pleasure in her small gasp of pain.

"Here."

Livi dangled a pair of cuffs in front of him, the kind strong enough to hold the strongest vampires and chancellors. He should know. He'd worn them often enough himself. When Francine was trussed up, he rose to his feet, turning his back on the furious woman on the ground.

As soon as he did, his arms wwere full of Livi, and all was well.

Cord threw the dead bolt in total disgust. "Damn, I thought they'd never leave."

Livi didn't answer. In fact, she was no longer in the living room. Maybe she was in the kitchen fixing yet another fresh pot of coffee. Between Ambrose and his people and Cord's own family, there'd been a steady stream of visitors wandering in and out for hours.

As frustrating as things were, at least they'd accomplished a lot. Ambrose had staged a raid on Francine's corporate headquarters back in New Eire and followed that up with another on her home here on the estate. Between the financial records and Olivia's newly recorded testimony and report regarding Francine's confession, it was unlikely that Cord would have to take the stand during Francine's trial. He didn't want to think about what would happen to her if they convicted her of Dwayne's murder, but then he didn't really care, either.

She was dead to him, one way or the other.

The handful of family members who'd showed up had been a mixed bag. A couple seemed genuinely glad to see him. A few were nervous about what was to come next. It seemed Ambrose had frozen a great deal of the family assets until it could all be sorted out. Cord had spent a lot of time and effort reassuring his blood kin that he wasn't out to ruin the clan for having abandoned him fifteen years ago. Finally, they'd left. He doubted they were convinced, but only time would prove his intentions were honest.

Right now he had more pressing matters on his mind. A certain chancellor to hunt.

Hmmm. No sign of Livi in the kitchen. He tried the back porch, closing his eyes and reaching out with his other senses. No, she wasn't in the woods, either. Odd.

He finally caught the faintest trace of her scent near the staircase. It was too early for bed.

Or was it? He grinned.

He'd made her a promise that once he was free of his past he'd be coming after her with everything he had. It was hard to chase a woman if she didn't hide.

Smiling around his fangs, he started up the steps. By the time he made it to the top, all worries that certain parts of his body might have forgotten what they were designed for after years of doing without had totally disappeared.

Even so, this would be different. It had to be because he'd never done this before. Yeah, he'd had sex. But he'd never truly mated with a woman who felt like the other half of his soul.

Livi stood at the window, staring out at the stars. She glanced his way, looking far calmer than he felt, but the pulse point at the base of her throat gave her away. Her emotions were running full bore, even if she was trying to hide it.

He was glad. He didn't want to be the only one in the room who feared he might disappoint.

"Olivia McCabe, if you don't tell me to leave now, there'll be no turning back, not for either of us."

He prowled forward, unbuttoning his shirt and flashing his fangs. Her smile was all woman and temptation and her eyes followed his every move.

"Last chance, Chancellor McCabe. Once I touch you this time, you're mine and I'm yours. Period. Got that?"

She nodded, and her tongue darted out to lick the corner of her mouth, the tips of her fangs flirting with him.

"I'm going to strip you down, Livi my love, and taste every inch of you."

She backed up a step, clearly gauging if she should try to run, not that she'd get far. While she mulled it over, he tossed his shirt over the chair in the corner. After toeing off his shoes, he reached for the buckle on his belt. A quick jerk left it unfastened. Next, he undid the snap of his jeans. Her gaze tracked the slow slide of his zipper, her breathing speeding up when she saw that he'd gone commando. Soon there would be nothing between them except for her clothes.

That wouldn't last long.

Finally, Livi broke and ran. He caught his lover before she'd gone more than a handful of steps. That small skirmish was over, but the major battle was yet to come.

He swept her up in his arms and tossed her into the middle of the four-poster that dominated the room. It felt so damned right to tumble into a tangle of arms and legs with his Livi in the big bed where he'd been conceived and born. It was only a matter of time before the next generation got its start there, as well. Or maybe on that old couch downstairs. He wasn't picky as long as he got to spend as much time as possible locked in his lover's arms.

"You have too many clothes on, Livi."

She yanked him down for one of her bone-melting kisses. "You didn't give me much of a chance to take them off."

"If I had, this might have been all over before we actually reached the bed. The only way I've made it through today was imagining you naked—" he kissed her forehead "—and how well we were going to fit together—and in how many different ways."

His mate blushed, but looked pleased. She arched an eyebrow as she studied the part of him that made it all too obvious how badly he wanted her. "Looks like it will be a tight fit, big guy."

Okay, now he was blushing. He tugged her uniform shirt up and spread his fingers over her soft, warm skin. "I'm sorry my hands are so rough."

She caught his hand in hers, brought it up to her mouth and pressed a soft kiss on his palm, a healing benediction. "No apologies necessary."

Then she traced a line of callus with the tip of her tongue. "These are just a sign of how incredibly strong you are. Fifteen years would have broken a lesser man."

He closed his eyes and soaked up the warmth of her breath against his skin. Time to do some more touching of his own.

Seconds later her shirt hit the floor and her lacy bra decorated the lamp on the bedside table.

Her pretty breasts deserved odes of praise, but they struck him speechless. He offered homage with his teeth and tongue. From the way she writhed beneath him, she clearly understood what he was saying.

While he savored the peach-sweet taste of her nipples, he unsnapped her uniform pants. The zipper cooperated. It was a good thing because otherwise he'd have used every ounce of his vampire strength to rip the cloth out of his way. He loved the sound she made as he slid his fingers down and down and down.

Ah, yes, finally, he found the damp heat he sought, slipping deep to test her readiness for him. This was going to be so damn good. As much as he loved her breasts, he needed so much more right now. He kissed each one in apology, a promise that he'd get back to them and soon. Then, he stared down at the woman who'd been his touchstone of sanity for fifteen years.

"Livi, you have no idea how long I've dreamed of this very moment."

Yes, she did because she'd been having those same dreams herself. With any other man, she might have been self-conscious as he looked his fill. But right now it was all she could do to make sense of the all the sensations flooding through her. Cord's mouth was so hot as he'd kissed her breasts. The cool of the quilt on her back. The rough but gentle touch of his hands. All of it building and building until all she could do was whimper.

"Cord, please, I need you on me." She captured his erection with a gentle squeeze. "I need you in me. Take me now."

"Yes, ma'am."

He sat up and stripped away the rest of Livi's defenses right along with her clothes. He settled between her knees, running his fingertips up her legs, starting at the arch of her feet and straight up to the hungry center of her need. She was on fire.

His dark eyes glittered, and she was pretty sure his hands were trembling. That was good because hers were, too.

"Honey, I can't be gentle about this. It's been too long, and I need you too much."

She flashed her fangs at him in invitation. "I want you to take me hard, Cord. I've been waiting too long for this to want it any other way."

Then he covered her, crushing her down into the mattress. With a near growl, he pushed hard to settle deep inside of her. She'd been right. Oh, yeah, he was a big man all over. The fit was tight, but absolutely perfect. The first thrusts skated the sharp edge of pain and pleasure, but her body quickly adjusted as she held on with every ounce of her strength.

The pounding rhythm intensified until nothing existed beyond the sweat-slick slide of skin against skin. He rose up, supporting his weight on his arms, his face contorted with pleasure as he rode them both hard. She wrapped her legs around his, holding him tighter, claiming him for her own.

Finally, he focused on her throat, his gaze a caress in itself. She arched her head back and to the side, offering him her throat, her life's blood.

A vampire's primitive nature was never more obvious than in bed. Cord struck fast and hard, his fangs finding and penetrating her pulse. His mouth closed over the wound, pulling hard on her vein in counterpoint to his cock's thrusts deep within her. Just that quickly, it was too much. She couldn't hold back another second as the combined assaults on her senses drove her over the edge.

But at least she took Cord racing along with her, shuddering as he pulsed deep within her.

As he licked the wound closed on her neck, she knew nothing would ever be the same again.

For the first time in a decade and a half, or maybe in his whole life, Cord was at peace. Staring down at the woman tucked in at his side, her long legs still tangled with his, he toyed with her hair. He finally knew its texture, and it was every bit as soft as he'd imagined.

"I thought you were there to kill me."

Livi rose to look him straight in the face, a taste of temper in her eyes. "You thought I'd do that? After everything, you thought I'd execute you right there on that dirt road?"

He smiled at her outrage. "No, I *hoped* you would, Livi. You were the only bright spot in my life for a long, long time. I know I never acted grateful for your visits, yet I was. But I had become so damned lost in that hell. When I saw you, all I could feel was relief that it was going to finally be over. That you were going to show me mercy and end it all."

A hot tear dripped off her chin onto his chest. Damn it, he hadn't meant to make her cry.

"I'm screwing this all up, Livi. I'm trying to thank you."

She frowned and rolled on top of him, straddling his hips. That little move almost derailed the whole conversation, but he managed to keep his focus.

She poked his chest with her finger. "It's not your gratitude I want, Cord."

He caught her hand and kissed it. "Well, you've got it, not to mention my heart, my love, my life."

He'd finally found the right words because her pretty face lit up. "I love you, too, Cord."

"Show me."

He flexed his hips to suggest exactly how that could be done. And bless this woman who saved him, she took the hint.

* * * * *

# SEDUCED BY THE VAMPIRE KING

LAURA KAYE

Voted Breakout Author of the Year in the 2011 GraveTells Readers' Choice Awards, **Laura Kaye** is a bestselling and award-winning author of paranormal, contemporary and erotic romance.

Laura grew up around a large extended family who believed in and regularly told stories about their own personal encounters with the supernatural. Family lore involving angels, ghosts and evil-eye curses cemented in Laura a lifelong fascination with the supernatural and the world of fantasy. Laura was an avid reader and writer from childhood—at fourteen, she handwrote a fifty-notebook-page paranormal take on *The Secret Garden*; at sixteen, her time-travel historical short story, *Peter Save the Tsar*, won an award from the county Board of Education.

As an adult, new dreams and pursuits overshadowed these earlier interests in fiction writing, and it was years before the storyteller in her soul demanded to be heard. Since awakening, Laura's inner muse has insisted on making up for lost time by whispering ideas for new stories and characters into her ear faster than she can write them—but she wouldn't have it any other way!

A published nonfiction author, Laura's day job as a historian and training as an archaeologist help her create vivid portrayals of other times and places. Laura lives in Maryland with her husband, two daughters and a cute-but-bad dog, and appreciates her view of the Chesapeake Bay every day.

# Chapter One

Nikolai Vasilyev was right in the middle of the shit, and it was exactly where he wanted to be. Shots erupted from two positions ahead of him and ricocheted off the abandoned cinder-block streetscape he'd been patrolling. Ducking into an alley, he felt a telltale whiz of air buzzing his ear and went flat against the concrete wall of the old factory. Inhaling the frigid, early winter night air, Nikolai's hackles rose and his fangs stretched out. His enemies were close enough he could feel their evil.

He wanted trouble. And he found it. Or it found him. Semantics.

Somewhere ahead, concealed among the long-neglected buildings, a band of Soul Eaters apparently had a sniper's roost. Those demented murderers jeopardized the hidden vampire world by caving in to the lure of exsanguination. All vampires drank from humans, but only the Soul Eaters consumed human souls by drinking through the last beat of their hearts, then removing and eating it. Their addictive recklessness threatened to expose them all to the broader human world, and escalated the ancient war between the two rival strains of immortals.

Nikolai plotted out a plan of attack, the street taking shape in his mind's eye like a 3-D simulator. Dark satisfaction pooled in his gut. Sending these little birdies flying from their nest—permanently—was going to turn this night from a miserable waste to decently tolerable. It didn't get any better than that for him. Not anymore. Not since he'd dishonored himself, and the Soul Eaters killed Evgeny and Kyril.

The hushed, efficient chatter of his warriors sounded in his earpiece and drew Nikolai from his thoughts. Torturing himself over his brothers' deaths had no place out on the street. There was plenty of time for that while the sun kept him inside cooling his heels. He peeked over his shoulder and around the corner of the building. A volley of shots rang out and Nikolai growled a curse under his breath, his gaze swinging around to the rusted industrial street lamp illuminating his position. He sighted the bulb and squeezed off a single bullet that solved that problem, then turned, fell to a crouch and took another light out farther down the street.

"Who's got a lock on that gunfire?" came Mikhail's voice through the earbud. His second-in-command was a consummate soldier and the only thing holding his kingdom together at the moment. Nikolai was man enough to admit that. "Report in."

One by one, six of his finest warriors gave the all clear and confirmed their locations. Nikolai sighed. He didn't want to share this one. He didn't want to have to rein himself in. When he found the Soul Eaters' position, he wanted to unleash the inhuman monster within, to surrender to the grief and rage boiling inside him as he tore his enemies to pieces with his bare hands and fangs. No fucking audience required.

As if they all didn't worry about him enough. He hated the weighted silences and sidelong glances that seemed to follow him wherever he went these days. Christ, he needed to release a little of the volcanic agony expanding in his chest, making it hard to breathe, hard to think. Hard to care.

An awkward silence passed before he heard, "My lord, what's your area of operation?" Mikhail's tone no doubt sounded level and professional to everyone else, but Nikolai recognized the wariness and exhaustion in his oldest friend's voice. Guilt soured his gut. "I say again, my lord, what's your AO?"

Focusing on the task at hand, and not the way he was failing Mikhail—hell, failing all of them—Nikolai did a quick ammunition check and ran through his mental plan one more time. He took a deep calming breath and centered himself, using his memory of the last time he saw his brothers, expressions frozen in death, to fuel his resolve.

"Son of a bitch, Nikolai, answer me. You're there, aren't you?"

With indecipherable words still ranting from the speaker, Nikolai tugged the unit from his ear and yanked it from around his neck. He dropped it to the ground and crushed the receiver with his boot, insuring no one could come behind him and eavesdrop on his warriors' movements.

With an apology to Mikhail and a vow to Evgeny and Kyril, Nikolai moved out onto the street, staying low and tight to the building. He set his sights on the general location from which the earlier shots seemed to originate and ducked into doorways and alleys whenever he could. Twenty meters ahead, a third street lamp posed an insurmountable problem. Whether he got rid of it or left it intact, he would reveal his position to the enemy.

He voted for the cover of darkness and took it out with a single shot, only the sudden blackness and sprinkling of glass against the concrete sidewalk revealing what he'd done. It was enough.

A barrage of gunfire erupted, the snaps and crackles of high-speed projectiles close enough to make him dive for cover. The enemy fire brought something useful with it, too—the Soul Eaters' muzzle flashes gave away their position and told Nikolai precisely where he needed to go.

Release and relief were so fucking close.

The break in the gunfire meant they'd likely lost his position in the dark, so he bolted from his place behind a car and flashed across the street at preternatural speed. Closer now. He was so close he could smell their fear. He reveled in it. Drank it down into his belly like the sweetest nectar. Soon, he would gorge himself on it.

Reconnoitering the new side of the street, Nikolai shoved out of his hiding place and darted across the intersection to the block that housed the Soul Eaters' fortified position.

Victory lured him forward, out into the open.

Bullets rained down around him, but he ducked and twisted, plowing onward. His fangs pinched his bottom lip as he hauled ass to safety. A doorway loomed ahead, one that should be shielded from the nest above.

A new barrage of gunfire clattered and echoed in the space between the wasted buildings. The sound hurt his head and disoriented him. Nikolai couldn't place its location.

And then searing fire tore into his shoulder, the side of his neck, the back of his thigh.

Fuck, somehow they'd gotten behind him. And no one was covering his six. Because he hadn't let them.

He was hit. Hit bad.

Howling more from the agony of defeat than the pain of the tainted bullets, poisoned with the blood of the dead, Nikolai flashed down the side street before the blood loss and infection drained his powers, his life. He pushed himself to keeping moving and lost track of the distance he covered as he retreated from the abandoned industrial quarter toward the general direction of Moscow's city center.

His breathing was loud in his own ears, a mix of a rasp and a gurgle that told him the neck wound was critical.

Son of a bitch. Mikhail was going to kill him. Assuming he survived.

The poison hit his heart as the industrial area gave way to apartment buildings and shops. He crashed against the brick wall of a building and his vision blurred and twisted. The world went sideways and he hit the ground so hard it rattled his brain in his skull. Between the blood loss and the poison, moving took herculean effort, but he had to get off the street.

Gun still tight in his grip, he dragged himself on his forearms, pulling the dead weight of his body toward a gravel path that ran alongside the building. His muscles screamed, sweat stung his eyes and his gasping breath scorched his throat. A thirst more intense than any he'd ever felt made his tongue feel thick and his fangs ache.

As the building's shadow covered him, Nikolai could move no more. He hoped the kingdom he'd refused to lead these long months would survive the succession crisis his death would leave behind.

Regrets. Oh, so many regrets.

Bitter cold bent his bones until he was sure they would snap. He shivered, sending his teeth and fangs clattering against one another. How wonderful it would be to have the warmth and companionship of a mate right now.

He had not strength enough to even chide himself for the thought.

A black fog descended, stealing first his sight, then his hearing. Tortured thoughts remained to the end until, mercifully, they too faded to nothing. Just like him.

# Chapter Two

One question kept repeating itself in Kate Bordessa's mind: *What the hell am I doing here?*

She stuffed her gloved hands in the pockets of her parka and ducked her face against the cold night air. It was one-thirty in the morning and the street was empty, except for her. Unanswered questions and a sense of anxiety had kept her awake until she'd finally given up on sleep, thrown on some clothes and hopped the underground metro at the university. She thought walking around Red Square and seeing the cathedrals, palaces and towers there would cheer her, would remind her why she had come to study in Moscow. But not even the vivid colors of Saint Basil's or the festively lit outline of the GUM department store had made her feel any less like something wasn't right.

So she'd walked, hoping physical fatigue would drive away the unfounded anxiety. Though she remained firm on the reason she'd fled the States—her parents wanted a destiny for her she could never accept—Kate couldn't escape the restlessness that always left her feeling she wasn't doing something she was supposed to do. Under the surface, a sense of unease, as if she'd forgotten an important appointment or a commitment, nagged at her. In quiet moments, a gloom of foreboding descended over her, setting her heart to racing and making her momentarily sure some tragedy had unfurled— and *she* might've stopped it.

It was all making her crazy. And homesick. Maybe it was her looming birthday that was causing her unease. Though you wouldn't think turning twenty-one would be traumatic.

Pausing at an intersection, Kate swept her gaze in a circle around her. The can of mace in her pocket boosted her confidence to be out here, but a woman still had to stay aware of her surroundings. Finally, the light changed and she tugged her hood snug to her face as she crossed the street. Shops, businesses and office buildings gave way to apartment buildings. She didn't know this neighborhood well, but she was familiar enough with the city after living here for five months to be certain if she kept going a few blocks, she'd come to a metro stop on the line she needed. Hell, maybe she'd even pass the closest one and keep walking until the one after.

A couple tucked against each other passed her on the sidewalk. Their low voices and laughs heightened her loneliness, unleashing a deep-seated fear she'd never find that sense of belonging others seemed to develop so effortlessly. It was as if she was a square peg in the round hole of life. Never had a boyfriend. Barely been kissed. Parents urging her to join them in something she couldn't fathom. And the closer it got to her birthday next Friday, the more acute all these confusing, ridiculous feelings became. It was almost as if a clock was ticking down to…something? What, she just didn't know.

Suddenly, her scalp prickled and the hair on her neck and arms rose. Her stomach clenched and flip-flopped. What the hell?

Sure someone was stalking her, Kate shook her hood off and whirled, but the street was empty. Still, the ominous feeling was so convincing, it took every ounce of willpower to restrain her desire to run..

Finally, she stopped trying to resist, and broke out into a jog, relief flooding into her when the squat red M of the metro came into view up ahead. Gloved hand grasping the mace, she passed one apartment building, then another,.

"Shit." Her ankle twisted off the edge of a broken curb she hadn't noticed. Thankfully, the height of her boot prevented her from rolling it enough to cause a sprain. Damn thing still hurt, though. She paused and leaned a hand against the corner of the building, her exhalations fogging on the cold air.

*Take a freaking breath, Kate.*

She rotated her foot and stretched her ankle, reassuring herself it was fine. She just needed to go home and go to bed. Everything would look better in the morning.

The breeze kicked up and…Kate froze. What was that smell? Something spicy and warm. She couldn't begin to place it, but all at once she forgot her panic. Swallowing the saliva pooling on her tongue, she inhaled more of that enticing smell like a lioness scenting the most delicious meal on the wind. She looked up at the apartments, but everything was dark. Behind her, the street remained empty. To her left, a driveway disappeared into darkness…

And the darkness concealed the source of that scent.

She wasn't sure how she knew it, but she did.

One step. Another. Lured into the darkness. By something that called to her very soul, that appealed to her on a primal level. She had to…what? She wasn't sure. Find it? See it?

Taste it.

The urges were so instinctual she didn't even think about questioning them.

Shaking off the odd haze, Kate removed her smartphone

from her jeans pocket and woke up the screen to provide a bit of light. A series of selections turned on her flashlight application and cast a brighter, broader illumination.

Boots. The first thing she saw was a pair of big black boots.

She gasped so hard and unexpectedly, the cold hurt her throat.

The man attached to those boots was huge, unmoving, and facedown in the dirt and stones of the driveway.

Without question, he was the source of the scent.

She had the oddest sensation of being sucked through a tunnel, or of seeing her life replayed in fast-forward behind her eyes. And, either way, the end led her here. To this moment. To this alley. To this man.

Weeks and months of foreboding and worry and dread all culminated right here.

*Pomogite mne. Help me.*

At the sound of the distant voice, Kate spun, wielding her flashlight phone like a weapon and shining the light around. "Who's there?" But the alley was otherwise empty.

Trembling, she cut the glow back to the man and scanned his body with it. Blood soaked through the dark fabric of his pants on his right thigh. A lot of blood. A hole tore through his coat near his right shoulder. Long strands of blond hair peeked out from underneath a black knit cap.

She stepped to the other side of him, the dull ache of her ankle forgotten, and crouched near his head. Her light shined on the side of his face, but between his position and the cap she couldn't make out much except… "Oh, shit."

Blood coated his jaw, neck and the arm he'd collapsed on, and it had dripped to the ground beneath him, not soaking in but pooling on the frozen surface. Heart in her throat, she gingerly peeled back the lapel of his coat. Her stomach turned. His neck was literally torn apart.

Thoughts shot through her brain in a rapid-fire barrage. *Is he alive? Oh, God, he's gotta be dead. Could the shooter still be here? That blood...that freaking blood is what I smell. But how? Help him. Help him!*

Kate dialed 03 on her phone and waited, eyes still on the man's form, trying to discern movement. Gently, she laid her hand on the middle of his back. There! Her hand felt the soft rise and fall her eyes couldn't perceive.

Relief rushed through her.

The operator answered in Russian, inquiring about the nature of her emergency and her location, and Kate had never been more glad for her fluency in the language. "I found an unconscious man. I think he's been shot. He's bleeding really badly from his neck and leg."

"Did you see the shooting? Is the shooter still in the area?"

She whipped her gaze to the right, then the left. All remained silent and still, except her. But what if whoever did this was hiding? Watching her. Watching him. Rage shot up Kate's spine, almost stealing her breath. She was nearly disoriented by the emotion's intensity and unexpectedness. *No one will hurt him again.* Dizziness threatened at the bizarre thought. She shook her head and struggled to be present in the moment. "Uh, no. I...I didn't see anything. And I don't think anyone else is here."

The dispatcher fired off a stream of questions Kate did her best to answer. At the woman's suggestion, she yanked off a glove and sacrificed it to the cause of applying pressure to his neck wound.

Anything to help him.

She turned down the offer to stay on the line until the ambulance arrived. The flashlight feature drained her cell battery quickly and it was already running low.

*Nuzhna pomoshch'. Need help.*

Kate fumbled her cell phone at the reappearance of the voice. Her nerves were just frayed. That's what it was. Must be. There was no one else here.

She set her phone on the ground next to them, light shining where she was working on his neck, and blew out a breath that failed to calm. "Come on, mister. Hang in there. Help's on its way."

Blood saturated her glove and Kate gasped as the warmth kissed her palm. She jerked back and scrubbed her right hand against her thigh. The oddest tingling erupted in her other hand as she rubbed against the denim. Ignoring the sensation, Kate tossed the ruined glove away and pulled off her left one. Her gaze scanned him as she murmured in low tones for him to hold on.

His hat. His hat was thicker than her glove. Gently, she pulled the cap off the back of his head, spilling blond hair mostly pulled into a ponytail. She slid her palm under his forehead to provide some cushion against the cold hard ground as she removed the front of the hat. Securing the thick folded knit against the crook of his neck, she eased her hand out from under him.

His head rolled enough to reveal his face in profile.

Kate gaped and moaned.

She scrabbled backward until her spine slammed into the brick wall of the looming building.

Between his parted, anguished lips, two sharp teeth protruded.

Fangs.

He had fangs.

# Chapter Three

Vampire.

Her heart pounded in her chest, forcing her blood through her veins so hard and fast the roaring whoosh of it filled her ears.

He was a freaking vampire!

But...*oh, God*...what kind?

Kate had to look. Either way, she had to know what she was dealing with. Light-headedness threatened from her rapid breathing, but Kate forced herself to creep onto her knees and reach out a shaking hand. Shining her flashlight on his face, she flinched as her thumb pressed to his eyelid.

*Please, please, please.* The light quivered as she lifted the thin membrane of skin, hoping against hope it didn't reveal the soulless black iris and sclera of a Soul Eater. Her whole body sagged in relief. A perfectly white sclera and bright sapphire-blue iris shined out at her.

*Oh, thank God.*

Not one of the evil ones, then. She dropped her head into her hands and sucked in deep breaths that did little to ease her.

She'd traveled five thousand miles to get away from vampires—from studying them, preparing to serve them, from the possibility of a future involving them—and here she sat, in a pitch-black alley, with an unconscious one at her feet.

And, *holy shit*, she wasn't even going to let herself think about why the vampire's blood had affected her that way. Why it still affected her body and instincts and reactions even now.

Everything she'd been running from had just caught up to her. Her parents were members of the Electorate, a group of influential humans who knew about the presence of vampires in the world, hid their existence and worked with them in their fight against evil vampires known as Soul Eaters. For their efforts, the humans reaped benefits from the alliance—including earning the vampires' protection and access to their blood, which cured disease and slowed the aging process significantly.

When she'd turned sixteen, Kate's parents had shared their secret and encouraged her to enroll in a program that would immerse her in the history and culture of vampires, preparing her to one day take their place on the Electorate Council. The program also entered her in a training class to become what they called a Proffered, a virgin human woman trained to serve the blood needs of the vampire warrior class—and possibly become a lifelong mate. Apparently, all vampires were born male, so the perpetuation of their species could only be achieved through the joining of the races, a joining that cemented their alliance through kin ties and not just diplomacy alone.

In the beginning, Kate had been interested. She loved medieval history and was intrigued by her discovery of this world within a world. Her parents' enthusiasm and pride also drove her. And, as she learned of their prominence within the council, she felt the weight of familial obligation, too.

But the whole Proffered thing…it scared her as much as it fascinated her.

The idea of it felt objectifying and exploitative. When she gave someone her virginity, she wanted it to be because they liked and cared for her—she didn't even have to have full-out love. But she certainly didn't want it to be because she happened to have the ability to fulfill some biological need. And the idea of becoming a vampire's lifelong mate—what did that even mean? The whole thing raised so many questions.

So, as she'd neared her twentieth birthday—the year in which human blood apparently became particularly powerful for a vampire—she'd known she would never be able to go through with it, and she'd withdrawn from her training early.

She stared at the man—the *warrior*, probably—in front of her and had to admit that, despite her jaw-dropping surprise at encountering the very thing she'd believed she could never accept, that fierce strain of protectiveness from before still flowed through her.

She gasped. The ambulance would be here soon. *Oh, my God. They can't find him.*

Kate flew upright, her back ramrod straight. She might not want to become a vampire's mate, but that didn't mean she had any intention of revealing their existence to the broader world. Between her training and her family, she understood very well how important the good vampires were to humans' survival against the evil ones, and thus how vital it was to keep the secret. They had to get out of here. She had to get them out.

Though she'd never seen it firsthand, she'd learned vampires could heal, so her concerns about moving him alleviated a little. But she couldn't even attempt it while he remained facedown.

Silently apologizing, she braced both hands on the shoulder closest to the neck wound and entry hole in the back of his coat. Digging the toes of her boots into the gravel, it took all her strength to get him moving, but finally she rolled him onto his back. Pulse racing, her gaze raked over his features, but they were hard to make out through the dark and the loose strands of hair and smears of dirt and blood that covered his face.

She frowned. The left side of his hair bore no braid. Not a warrior after all, then, as braids represented the fraternity and bond of the warrior class.

Her thoughts scattered as her eyes caught a glint of metal on his chest. His bloody hand gripped a gun, a semiautomatic SIG Sauer, if she wasn't mistaken. Some introductory weapons training had been her father's idea.

Frowning, she inhaled a deep breath and reached for it, surprised at how much effort it took to pry his fingers free from the grip. "If you can hear me, I'm not stealing it, I promise. I'm just going to hold it for you. I don't want to try to move you with it loose."

A growl sounded in her head. Her gaze flashed to his unconscious face. The voice she'd heard, this sound—could they be coming from him? She'd never learned of such a thing, though, she'd also never met a real living breathing vampire—or wanted to.

"We have to get you out of here," she said in a hushed voice. "Please."

His fingers relaxed. Or so it seemed. She finally pulled the weapon free.

With the help of her flashlight, she engaged the decocking mechanism on the side of the gun's frame, making it safe to stow. But it was too big for her coat pocket. Feeling ridiculous, she holstered it in the waistband on the back of her jeans, grimacing at the feeling of the cold metal digging into her skin.

Stepping to his shoulders, Kate reached under his arms and gripped the fabric there. Her hands were so cold that she had to fight for purchase against the material. She rose into a crouched position and tugged.

Nothing. Not even a budge. Oh, no. "Come on, mister. We have to go before the ambulance gets here."

This time she tried hooking her arms under his, and that worked, but it placed so much strain on her back she had to keep pausing. Thank God the authorities moved slowly in Moscow. Her ears strained to hear the far-off sound of sirens that would tell her she was out of time.

As she dragged him in uneven starts and stops over the gravel, her hunched-over position brought her face close to his. A warm thrill zinged down her spine and settled into her stomach like a shot of vodka. His spicy scent was so strong and appealing up close she had to resist leaning in farther, pressing her nose to his cheek, his hair. His throat.

*Jeez, Kate, get your freaking head together.*

They rounded the back of the building and victory flared in her gut. Now to find a place to conceal him while the ambulance came and went. Kate straightened to a standing position and pressed her palms into her lower back, stretching and soothing. A street lamp on the other side of the building's rear revealed a small parking lot with a half-dozen cars parked against a chain-link fence and a Dumpster close to where she stood. Maybe she could hide him behind the line of cars. Maybe the ambulance crew would assume it was a false report. Maybe they wouldn't see the disturbed gravel where she'd dragged him. That was a lot of damn maybes, but what else could she do?

"We're almost there, now," she murmured as she bent again and hooked her arms under his. "Hold on." Pushing herself harder, she tugged him toward the row of cars. But what was she going to do with him after this crisis passed? She shook her head and focused on pulling him. She could only worry about one thing at a time.

A wet, throaty groan sounded from the vampire.

Kate's gaze dropped to his face, only dimly illuminated by the distant light. "It's all right," she said. "You're gonna be all right."

Her foot went down farther than she expected. Kate stumbled, her boot wedged in some kind of hole, and struggled to hold her balance. She failed.

She landed so hard her breath exploded out of her. The way she'd had her arms wedged under his kept them hooked together, and the vampire's dead weight landed on her aching legs.

Her tailbone throbbing from the impact with the ground and the way the gun's barrel dug into her skin, Kate groaned and fought to pull herself free of him.

Another, louder growl rolled out of his chest, like the low rumble of thunder, and he stirred, his head jerking against her thighs.

If he regained consciousness, this would be so much easier. "Hey, are you—"

A tearing pain ripped into her wrist.

Kate cried out and tried to wrench away, but— *Oh, my God! He bit me!* She gasped and moaned, "No!"

She threw every muscle into escaping the iron grip of his hands on her forearm and his impaling fangs in her radial artery. Her boots scrambled for purchase against the loose gravel but his weight held her down. With her free hand, she grabbed a fistful of blond hair and yanked.

The sound that ripped from his throat issued an animalistic warning her body recognized. Her heart raced in her chest, her scalp prickled and the hair rose on her arms and neck.

Clutching her arm, he rolled onto his side and settled most of his big body within the cradle of her thighs, one shoulder pinning her hips tight and hard.

*Pozhaluĭsta, pozhaluĭsta. Please*, he begged over and over, wearing down her resistance as his tone became more desperate.

Blood rushing behind her ears, the sound even louder for the deep, sucking draws exiting through her wrist, Kate went still.

*Please*, he groaned in her head. *Dying.*

The abject need in his voice sucker punched her. Her hand slackened in his thick hair, but didn't fall away altogether.

Dying. The possibility made her feel dizzy and weak. Or maybe that was just the blood loss. For sure, though, injured as he was, he must require a lot of blood. Could she really deny him what he needed to survive? Did she even want to? His tongue laved over her skin, and her body knew the answer even if her brain resisted.

As she acquiesced, the hard metal digging into her sacrum captured her attention. The gun. Kate debated and rejected the idea in the blink of an eye. He was one of the good ones. And he wouldn't kill her. As soon as the thought passed through her brain, her heart knew the truth of it.

*I give...my word.*

His being in her head felt inexplicably right. She fell back against the ground and gave in to his desire.

He unleashed an anguished whimper. *Thank you.*

Kate sucked in a breath at the way he seemed to respond to her thoughts. Without conscious thought, she stroked his hair and turned her head to watch him. The darkness and the angle of his face concealed the feeding, but Kate didn't need to see it.

She felt it. In every cell of her body.

## Chapter Four

The more Kate gave in to his need, the more she perceived the movement of blood where they were joined. And the longer he sucked the lifeblood from her, the more she became almost inebriated with the feeling of his hands and tongue and fangs on her. In her.

Arousal spiked through her body, hot and unexpected.

Kate arched under him. Her fingers tightened in his hair, but not as before. This time, her grip encouraged and embraced him. A moan tore up her throat. She wasn't even sure what she needed, she simply knew her body yearned for something more. From him. With him.

What was happening to her?

A big hand squeezed her hip and Kate jolted at the pressure. He shifted his position again, bringing the weight of his chest hard against the increasingly sensitive nerves at the junction of her thighs.

She thrust her hips upward, helpless to resist her body's growing need. The heat between her legs was all the more noticeable for the cold air surrounding them. But the longer he fed, the hotter she got, as if there was a cocoon surrounding and protecting them. All Kate could feel, all she knew, was the two of them intertwined in a moment more intimate than any she'd ever experienced.

Over the sound of her panting breaths and his wet sucking, she swore she could almost hear something like purring, a low growl of deep satisfaction. The soft rumble added to the electricity building between her legs.

Around her, the world spun until it blurred. Within her, a white-hot energy pooled low in her belly. Never, ever had her body threatened to go to pieces this fast. It was as if his very presence had flipped a switch inside her. He shifted between her legs again. Oh, God. Oh, God, if he didn't stop, she was going to explode.

He whimpered, trembled. Kate shook off the heavy haze of her arousal and forced herself to lean up onto an elbow. His head shook on his shoulders, as though he struggled to hold it upright.

She remembered the shredded appearance of his neck and winced in sympathy. "You could—" Kate swallowed thickly "—let me sit up and lay with your head in my lap. It'll be easier for you that way."

His mouth stilled against her, but didn't release.

"It's not a trick," she said. Kate pushed herself into an awkward sitting position, and the vampire moved ungracefully to allow her. His head lolled back onto her thigh, one hand still forming a manacle around her arm. She looked down into his face, burning with the desire to see him more clearly. His eyelids fluttered and sagged as if they were too heavy to lift, and ultimately fell closed.

When she was as settled as she could be with him sprawled over her legs and lying in her lap, she stroked his forehead back over his messy hair. "Okay, just hurry. You need to get out of here. And leave me some."

His mouth and tongue moved languorously against her

skin. The sensation ricocheted up her arm and through every vein, spiking the fire raging within.

*My guardian angel*, he intoned in solemn Russian in what she now knew without question was his voice.

Her heart squeezed at the reverence of his thought. "Well, I don't know about— Oh, shit." Warmth flooded over her thigh. His blood. His neck seemed to leak as fast as he drank. Icy fear snaked down her spine. "You're bleeding really badly."

Her gloves and his cap were long gone.

Kate only had one thing left: she unzipped her parka and shrugged it off her free arm. Frigid air flooded into the bubble of warmth she'd imagined surrounded them and made it hard to breathe.

A scuff, from the far end of the alley.

Kate froze and tilted her head, listening.

It sounded like… Her ears strained. Footsteps?

Fear erupted in her gut. Couldn't be the ambulance. There had been no sirens. No vehicle noise. And why would the paramedics be so purposely quiet?

Brilliant red rage displaced the fear and set her senses on high alert.

All her calm disappeared and morphed into stone-cold protectiveness and fierce possessiveness. *He is mine. And no one will take him.*

Operating on instinct, Kate's hand found and removed the SIG from her jeans, a dark satisfaction flooding her as she returned the decocking lever to its live position. She was so damn glad he'd gone for her left wrist, leaving her dominant hand free to shoot. If necessary.

Holding the gun out over his body, she aimed for the darkness of the driveway. Her heart lodged in her throat, but her hand held steady.

Three hulking shapes stepped into the dim light behind the building.

"Jesus, we found him," one of them said.

"Fuck. The human's armed," another called.

Before she'd even blinked, they'd disappeared. "Drop your weapon," a deep male voice barked.

As if. She whispered, "You have to wake up now, vampire. There are others here. And I don't know if they're friend or foe. Please. Wake up."

"Drop your weapon," the unseen man barked again. "Last chance."

"No way. Leave us alone. We're not your business," she said with more bravado than she felt.

"The hell you're not—"

"Enough," someone commanded. "I'm coming out," the same voice continued. "And I'm unarmed." Hands raised, he stepped where she could see him.

The man—the vampire, she assumed—was huge. Same dark paramilitary dress and black cap as her vampire wore. Didn't mean they were on the same side, though. He pointed with his chin. "He's hurt."

Kate glared at him, refusing to be distracted. Her shooting hand remained ready. She had no idea how she was going to get them out of this.

"I'm Mikhail."

"I don't want to shoot you, but I will."

He nodded. "Won't you put the gun down so we can talk about how to help him?" he asked in accented English.

The vampire's sucking pulls slowed against her wrist. He groaned and his mouth went slack.

Kate wanted nothing more than to divert her gaze and check on him, assure herself he was still breathing. For the first time, her hand trembled around the gun. Over her frozen cheek, a single tear trickled, leaving a hot saline trail that burned against the cold air.

"His neck," she whispered in English, forcing her eyes to hold Mikhail's gaze.

He nodded. "We will help him."

She shook her head, not daring to believe he was a friend. If she was wrong...

A thought came to mind and she gasped. "What color are his eyes?" she asked. Her plan wasn't foolproof, but it was better than nothing.

Mikhail cocked his head to the side. "Blue."

Kate narrowed her gaze. They were hardly any old blue.

"Bright, like a sapphire," he continued.

Kate sucked in a breath to respond. A hand clamped over her mouth. Another grabbed her wrist. Her finger squeezed and a single gunshot rang out into the night.

"Get him!" a male voice ordered. Commotion erupted around her. Growling. Cursing. Barked commands and replies.

Her own muffled screams added to the fray. "No! No! Don't hurt him!" Fighting the hold that wrapped around her, she kicked and flailed and squirmed to get free.

"Clear!" someone called. "Oh, shit, Mikhail. It's bad."

Kate's body screamed at the separation from her vampire. The palm of her hand burst into pins and needles. Her throat went tight and dry. She had to get to him.

He was hers. *Hers!*

"Damnit, Leo! Get control of her. I hear sirens," a voice demanded.

"Stop fighting. Damn it. Be still, human."

She slammed to the ground and the weight of a knee fell on her chest. Big hands pinned her arms to her sides. Barely able to breathe and her eyesight blurred from the blow to her head, Kate went limp.

A harsh masculine face appeared right before her, his gray

eyes—*good-guy eyes*—boring into hers. "Calm. Sleep. Now," he intoned.

Her mind went foggy. Darkness closed in around her.

Deep sorrow surrounded her. She'd lost him. She'd failed. That old feeling of foreboding and looming tragedy returned.

And that was the last she knew.

Nikolai floated on the edge of consciousness, not wanting to wake from the dream. In it, he was no longer alone, but had a mate who walked at his side. He didn't know what she looked like, but the sound of her voice, the smell of her skin, the taste of her blood. Those he could never forget.

Sated by the sacred crimson nectar that flowed from her veins, Nikolai covered her body with his. Entered her. Howled his masculine satisfaction. Moving in her was a revelation of ecstasy and belonging. She clutched at his shoulders and murmured in his ear, *You're gonna be all right. You're gonna be all right.*

His angel, always taking care of him.

"My lord? Wake up. You are safe," came a deep, familiar voice.

He didn't want to leave her, to leave that place where he wasn't alone.

"Come on now. Wake up."

Nikolai surfaced as if he'd been trapped under water for days. Brain sluggish, eyes bleary, mouth full of cotton. He gasped and choked as he tried to make use of his thick tongue.

"Nikolai?" Mikhail's voice sounded as if from a distance.

In the dim light of the room, Nikolai struggled to make sense of the shapes around him. Slowly, *too damn slowly*, his eyes regained the ability to focus.

Elbows braced on his knees, Mikhail sat in a chair by the side of his bed. Or, *a* bed, anyway. White walls and blankets.

This wasn't his room. The infirmary, and not the one in their city headquarters. They'd brought him to Vasilievskoe, his ancestral estate about an hour outside Moscow.

In that moment, as their gazes met, his friend's brown eyes looked as ancient as he actually was. His head sagged on his shoulders and he clasped his hands where they hung between his knees. "I want to kill you."

Nikolai chuffed out a breath. "Mishka," he said, infusing an apology into his friend's nickname.

"Don't Mishka me."

He deserved the other man's anger. What could he say? "I'm sorry."

Mikhail cursed and shoved out of his seat, the chair screeching against the tile floor. He paced and muttered under his breath. The other man still wore his fighting gear from the night before, twisting Nikolai's gut with guilt.

"How long have I been out?" Nikolai managed to say, pushing himself into a sitting position with a groan. The movement made him aware that IVs were attached to the crooks of both arms. And, damn, but everything hurt.

"It's early afternoon. About ten hours." Mikhail whirled on him. "Ten goddamn hours I didn't know if my king, my friend, would die or live to see another night."

He winced at the volume of his friend's outrage. "I was stupid."

"You were fucking moronic." He braced his hands on his hips and glared.

The situation wasn't funny, not in the least, but Nikolai felt the corners of his lips rise. "I'll concede the point." Few others had the balls to talk to him this way, but he and Mikhail had always been close, almost like brothers. His stomach plummeted. Kyril and Evgeny were gone, but Mikhail was here, and Nikolai was going out of his way to piss on his friendship. "Look, Mishka—"

"Save it. I know, all right? I lost them, too. I loved them, too. They might not have been brothers of my blood, but they were still my brothers. Like you. Since we were young. So I get it. I do. But I swear to Christ—" He covered his mouth and turned away.

Nikolai cleared the lump from his throat, cursing himself for failing Mikhail exactly as he knew he would, and dragged them back to safer ground. "So, give me the rundown on my condition."

Mikhail turned and crossed his arms. "Broken femur and scapula. Bullet passed through the former, lodged in the latter. Doc got it out on the table. Hit to the right side of your neck took out your jugular and nicked your carotid. Lost half your volume of blood. He patched you up, though, and set up the transfusion before we brought you here. Says you'll survive to be a pain in the ass another day."

Ignoring the gibe, Nikolai frowned. How the hell had he survived such injuries? No doubt about it, Anton was a master surgeon, but the blood loss alone…not to mention the poison. A deep sense of something like déjà vu came over Nikolai. He frowned, suddenly certain he'd forgotten something important. He scrubbed a hand through his hair, hampered some by the connected tubes. "Jesus. What a mess."

Mikhail sighed. "Yeah. Understatement of the century, my friend. Even more complicated by the girl. We need to decide what to do with her. She's seen a lot."

Nikolai narrowed his gaze and tried to decipher the words, but he had no idea what Mikhail was talking about. "What girl?"

Staring at him, Mikhail dropped back into the chair beside the bed. "What girl? The one who saved your life."

# Chapter Five

Kate woke up disoriented, hurting and pissed off.

She eased into a sitting position, the back of her head throbbing harder as she rose, and tried to make sense of her dim surroundings.

Small, spartan cot, rough stone walls, an empty wooden table. She looked to the right and gasped. Bars. An iron-barred door.

Was she in jail?

She flew to her feet and moaned. The small room spun around her. With her head in her hands, she sucked deep breaths until the dizziness passed. Clenching her eyelids, she prayed she'd been having a nightmare. She opened her eyes.

*Oh, shit.* No such luck.

Outrage bubbled up from Kate's gut. Surveying the room, she located a high-tech security camera in one corner. Old-looking cell paired with modern surveillance equipment. The vampires had her. Had to be.

Kate glared into the camera. "Let me out of here, damn you. Do you hear me? You have no right." Her voice rose with each word until she was shouting, the sound echoing off the stone.

Trying the door next, she shouted, "Let me out of here!" Holding a bar to hold herself steady, she looked down at her body. Coat gone. Mace gone. Cell phone gone. Her hand flew to her lower back. Gun gone.

But her clothes…they were the same. And they were covered in blood. Her jeans were red and stiff from hips to knees. Smears of blood ruined her pale blue sweater, and the sleeve of it was shredded. She sucked in a breath. Gauze circled her forearm from the heel of her thumb to nearly the crook of her elbow. Spots of maroon seeped through the layers.

The details of the night flooded back to her in vivid color.

Her vampire.

His attack.

Her acceptance.

The arrival of the others.

Kate slid down to her butt, wincing as her tailbone eased against the stone floor, and sagged against the bars. Eyes stinging and throat tight, a confusing maelstrom of emotions washed over her like rough waves in a storm, swamping, tumbling, turning her round and round.

Fear and bewilderment released her tears onto her cheeks. A vampire had fed from her. And she'd let him. She hadn't fought, not really.

Worse. In the end, she'd liked it, craved it, wanted to give him everything he needed. She'd wanted more.

How could she have so easily turned her back on everything she'd believed? Sitting there on the dirty floor of a freaking dungeon, Kate didn't even know who she'd been in those long minutes in that alley.

Rage also flowed through her and tensed every muscle in her body until she trembled. *She'd* found him. *She'd* helped him. *She'd* saved him. He was *hers*. And *they'd* taken him away, ripped him from her arms, literally.

The emotions completely contradicted each other, but that didn't make them any less true, any less real.

And if that wasn't enough, Kate's mind struggled with another set of feelings she would rather just pretend didn't exist. Desire. Hot and torturous. His scent clung to her, concentrated as it was on her clothes, her skin. It made her... want. What? Everything. She thirsted. She hungered. She felt an urgent emptiness between her legs like nothing she'd ever before experienced.

What was happening to her?

Heaving a deep breath, Kate shook her head. No. Enough. She fisted the wetness off her face and wiped the useless tears on her sweater. *Shit.* If only her head didn't hurt so bad she could think more clearly.

In the distance, a door clinked as if a lock was disengaged. Footsteps echoed against the stonework.

Using the bars, Kate pulled herself up and stepped back from the door.

A vampire in all black appeared on the other side. Tall, lean, dark blond hair to his shoulders. The left side bore a braid—the mark of a warrior. His features were no less attractive for how unfriendly they were. He had familiar gray eyes.

They stared at each other until the warrior finally threaded his hand through the bars and held out a bottle of water.

Kate crossed her arms. "Like I'd trust that."

"If we wanted to kill you, you'd be dead already. Besides, the cap is sealed." He thrust the bottle closer. His voice confirmed he was the same one who had hypnotized her in the parking lot, except it was gentler now. He shrugged and placed the bottle on the floor inside the bars. "Suit yourself." His gaze looked her over from head to toe, and then he turned.

"Wait," she said. "The vampire...where is he? How is

he?" The questions were out of her mouth before she'd even thought to ask them. But then, she burned to know.

The man's expression darkened, his eyes narrowed. This look she remembered from earlier. "He is of no concern to you."

Kate scoffed and stifled the more confrontational response on the tip of her tongue. "Like hell. I saved him." She held out her arm. "And I've got this nice little memento to prove it." Actually, she had no idea what the wound looked like, but it stung and ached like crazy.

He grunted. "That doesn't make you special. That makes you convenient."

His words struck her like a punch to the gut. Wasn't that the very thing she most feared as she'd once considered the possibility of a future with vampires? Dizziness returned and made her eyes throb, but Kate held her stance. No way she was letting him see how much pain she was in, how much his words had affected her. "When can I go?" she asked, voice softer than before.

The vampire shifted feet. "I don't have that information. I just have water. Drink it or don't."

Glaring, Kate threw out her hands. "What is your problem? What did I ever do to you?"

His gaze narrowed and dark light seemed to flare behind his eyes. He stared as if debating, then shook his head. "Drink the water. You lost a lot of blood."

Cursing under her breath, Kate watched his retreating form through the bars, totally bewildered by the exchange.

Nikolai stared at Mikhail, his brain churning on the words *The one who saved your life.*

His dream came back to him, only…it wasn't a dream. Was it? Not all of it, anyway.

Ignoring the hit-by-a-bus pain that racked his body, Nikolai flew forward and swung his legs off the bed. He ripped the IV from his right arm and reached for the left.

"My lord!" Mikhail grabbed his wrist, stilling him. "What are you doing?"

Nikolai ignored his friend's use of the title. Despite refusing to lead his kingdom, he couldn't get his warriors to treat him as if they were all the same. And they *were*. Hell, the others were arguably better—they hadn't dishonored themselves, and across the board had handled losing two of their comrades far better. After a while, he'd mostly stopped making an issue of the "my lord" crap. He shrugged off Mikhail's grip and glared up at him. "Take me to her."

The warrior shook his head. "You're hours out of surgery, still low on blood volume, and now bleeding again." He sighed and gestured at the crook of Nikolai's arm. "She can wait."

His tone regarding the girl rankled Nikolai. "She saved me," he said, mostly to himself, trying out the idea. He struggled to wade through the pain and disorientation to remember what had actually happened. He could hear her voice, feel her arms embracing him… "No… Fuck, no. I attacked her." He looked to Mikhail. "Didn't I?"

"I don't know." He scrubbed his face. "When we got there, she was holding you. Defending you with your own gun. Her wrist was a mess, though."

Nikolai tore out the second IV and rose to his feet before Mikhail had a chance to react. She'd not only saved him, but held him, protected him. He had to see her. To put a face to the deeds, to the jumble of emotions roiling within. "Get me some clothes."

"Nikolai—"

"Clothes, damn it." Mikhail nodded and left, and Nikolai sagged against the mattress. Why the hell was he acting this way? So she'd fed him. So what? Feeding from humans wasn't remarkable, though none had ever rearranged his insides the way the mere idea of this one seemed to. He just needed to put a face to the actions. Appease his curiosity. That would drive away this incessant yearning to get to her, to be with her.

He pushed off the bed and crossed to the sink. Aw, he looked like hell. Blood-matted, tangled hair. He peeled back the thick gauze on the right side of his neck. The crisscrossing black of the stitches stood out in sharp relief against the angry red of the healing wound. A few more hours and he could remove them altogether. He dropped the bandage to the trash can.

The cold water he splashed on his face made him yearn for a shower. Well, since Mikhail was taking his sweet-ass time. A small bathroom in the corner had a shower stall his body filled completely. But it did the job. The water ran red around his feet—leftover blood, nothing fresh. His lineage was strong, virile, granting him the ability to heal quickly.

And the girl's blood out in the field, when things had been do-or-die critical, didn't hurt, either. In fact, it had been the difference between life and death.

He whipped a towel off the rack and scrubbed it over his hair and skin, wincing as he passed over his neck. He wrapped a second towel around his hips. When he walked back into the infirmary room, he found Mikhail sitting in the chair waiting. He jutted his chin toward the bed, directing Nikolai's gaze to a pile of clothing with a manila folder sitting on top. He picked it up. "What's this?"

"Information. On the girl. She had a passport and cell phone. Leo ran them."

Nikolai flipped the folder open.

Katherine Ann Bordessa. From Washington, D.C. American exchange student at the Moscow University for the Humanities. Fluent in English, Russian and French. He scanned farther down. "Oh, goddammit."

"Yes," Mikhail said as he rose from his seat.

"Her parents sit on the North American Electorate Council." His desire to speak to her went from curiosity to necessity. He needed to learn what happened between them and ensure it didn't escalate into some sort of diplomatic incident. For now, he knew enough. He chucked the papers to the bed and grabbed some clothes.

"Will there be anything else, my lord?"

"Stop calling me that?"

Mikhail just stared at him, mouth shut but posture speaking volumes.

Nikolai stepped into black pants, part of his typical street-fighting uniform, and yanked them to his waist. He reached for the little leather pouch he always carried on him. That his friend thought to bring this to him made his throat go tight. He cleared it as he tucked the bag in his front pocket. "Where is she?" he asked, tugging a T-shirt over his head. When Mikhail didn't answer, he turned.

The warrior's expression had him bracing for bad news. The man pursed his lips, then said, "The dungeon, rear cell."

## Chapter Six

A series of metal clinks preceded the pounding of boots down the corridor outside Kate's cell. Weighed down by exhaustion, hunger, an oppressive headache and a sore butt, she stayed seated on the cot, back against the wall, knees drawn up in front of her.

A low, terse exchange echoed off the stonework a moment before two big bodies filled the doorway in front of her.

*My vampire!*

She flew forward on the bed, her feet settling on the floor. She fought a groan and gripped the metal edge of the frame to keep her balance. *This damn headache*. But it didn't matter, because her vampire was standing before her. Conscious. Healthy. More gorgeous than any man she had ever seen.

Those eyes. Those bright sapphire eyes. That's what she noticed first—not just their incredible color, but their haunted intensity, the way she could almost feel them raking over her in return. Golden-blond hair flowed past his broad shoulders, though it wasn't braided like that of the black-haired warrior who stood at his side.

She sucked in a breath and glared at the other man. *He*

was the one who had pretended to want to talk, but had really just distracted her so the gray-eyed vampire could jump her.

Her vampire cut his gaze back and forth between them. He bit out a question Kate couldn't understand because he asked it in German. She frowned.

The exchange went on for a moment, and Kate pushed off the bed and took a step toward the door. Another. She just needed to make sure he was really okay. After everything. And the closer she walked, the farther her body wanted her to keep going.

Both vampires turned to look at her and she froze.

Heart kicking up in her chest, she met her vampire's bright eyes and asked, "Are you okay?"

Light seemed to flicker behind his gaze, which dragged down her body and focused for a long moment on her blood-covered legs. He cocked his head as if not understanding her, though she knew she'd spoken in flawless Russian. Finally, he met her eyes and nodded. "I am well. And I understand you had something to do with that."

Kate's stomach flip-flopped at the sound of his voice, deep and much more commanding than what she'd heard in her mind. She felt it like a physical touch. She shrugged. "I tried."

"Katherine—" the other one interjected "we are in a bit—"

She groaned at his use of her name. She'd never made introductions—had never been given the chance. "My passport. Right? You took my passport?"

The man nodded. "It was necessary. Your belongings will be returned to you."

Kate crossed her arms, not sure whether to trust his words or assume they were simply a ruse, same as he had done in the alley when he'd distracted her. "And you're Mikhail, right? Since you know so much about me, it's only fair I know a little about you in return." Her gaze shifted from the dark vampire to the one she'd saved, who wore an expression that appeared almost amused.

"Yes, I'm Mikhail—"

"Nikolai," her vampire blurted. "And you, your name is Katherine."

A thrill shot down her spine. She loved the sound of her name on his voice, as if his tongue caressed the letters. "Yes. I go by Kate, though."

He shook his head. "Katherine is a beautiful name."

"My lord—"

Nikolai held up a hand. The gesture was full of an authority the other vampire responded to immediately.

*My lord?* What was that about?

The blond vampire scowled. "Leave us, Mikhail. And give me the keys."

Intrigued, she watched the warrior obey and depart with a final glance her way.

Alone again, Kate wasn't sure what to say. God, he was tall and broad. She remembered the muscular feel of those shoulders. She wanted to run her hands over him and prove to herself he was well. She wanted to press her face into his neck. Instead, she stood there watching, waiting, hating the iron bars that separated them. But maybe it was better to have the barrier. It would keep her from caving into his allure as easily as she'd done before.

What she couldn't tolerate anymore was the awkward silence. "I was worried about you. I'm glad you're better." That odd tingling returned to her palm and Kate fisted her fingers without thinking about it. The movement pulled at the wound on her arm. She winced.

Standing firm and still on the far side of the door, he said, "Your concern…" He shook his head. "Thank you." His gaze dropped to the movement of her hand. "I am better, but it appears you are worse for our meeting."

Heat bloomed on Kate's cheeks. She wrapped her arm behind her back. "Oh, well…" A dozen responses vied for airtime, but that's all she could manage. The deep reverence of his words and his raw masculine beauty, all rough edges and hard angles, stole her breath. And she was so conflicted about the feeding she could hardly think straight. How could she both cherish and regret the memory of it? She ducked her head.

He released a breath and recaptured her attention. "I have to ask you, Katherine, how did you come to find me?" His voice was low and deep, his intense gaze studying her.

Maybe she imagined it, but he seemed fixated on the bloodied parts of her clothing. She shifted feet, self-consciousness making her want to squirm. She tucked her hair behind her ear. "It was a complete coincidence. I was walking to the metro—"

"In the middle of the night?"

She frowned. Was this some kind of interrogation? The thought squeezed her heart. After everything she'd done, he didn't trust her? And why was it she cared? "I couldn't sleep. I thought a walk would help."

"The university is twenty kilometers away from the city."

"Which is why I was taking the metro." She sighed. So tired. "Why all these questions?"

"We need to understand what happened tonight."

His distance and dispassionate tone left her feeling empty and bereft. And so stupid. As if anything unique had happened between them. As if he would think she deserved any special consideration. "Well, here's what you need to know: I found you unconscious and bleeding, tried to help you, got bit for my trouble—" she pulled her arm from behind her back and thrust it toward him "—and then got tackled, kidnapped and dumped in a dungeon. Does that help?"

The volume of her accusations hurt her own head. On top of the pain and the blood loss and the adrenaline let-down, it was more than she could take. She swayed, hating that she was showing weakness in front of him, but unable to hold herself together any longer.

Nikolai was completely enthralled by the woman standing before him. Beautiful in her assertiveness. Bravery proven over and again. Wearing so much of his blood he went hard between his legs. She appealed to his body, intrigued his mind. His right hand tingled and twitched. He fisted against the foreign sensation.

Katherine went unsteady on her feet even as her angry words still echoed against the stone walls. Her uncharacteristic display of weakness put him into motion.

He unlocked and opened the door as she turned for the cot, and wrapped a steadying arm around her shoulders before her knees buckled. Nikolai sucked in a breath at the warm feel of her in his arms, at the soft brush of her hair against his hand, at the feminine scent of her skin, infused as it was with the remnants of his blood. Her voice, her touch, her scent—all these he remembered. Now having seen her beautiful face—the long chocolate waves and ice-blue eyes were a killer combination—his memories of the night became clearer and crisper in his mind. He was mesmerized, fascinated. And she was…she was shaking.

"Sit," he said, guiding her down and resisting the urge to press her back against the bed, to feel her under him. Instead, he crouched at her knees.

"I'm fine. Just have a headache."

Nikolai frowned and shouted for Leo, knowing he was

manning the security booth and would hear him on the camera's audio feed. Katherine jumped and cringed at the sound of his voice. "Damn, I'm sorry."

She shrugged and licked her lips, those pale blue eyes not quite meeting his. "Just a bump on the head. I'm fine."

There was something she wasn't saying. He sucked in a breath and was about to ask, when he heard a voice from behind .

"My lord," Leo said.

Katherine's eyebrows flew up at the appellation. She narrowed her gaze as if questioning him. "She needs pain medicine. Yes?" He tilted his head and scanned her face. High cheekbones, full mouth, creamy pale skin. Too pale.

"Yes, please."

"And food, I suspect." It was more than a suspicion, he could feel the hunger rolling off her. This connection to her needs and emotions was unexpected, and unwelcome. Still, he owed her. "When did you last eat?"

Her eyes flicked over his shoulder, then back to him. "I'm not sure. What time is it?"

"Pushing three in the afternoon."

She looked down and slid her clasped hands between her thighs. "Dinner, last night."

Nikolai sucked in a breath and whirled on Leo. "Has she not been offered any food?"

Leo's eyebrows flew to his hairline. His mouth dropped open, and his gaze cut to the floor by the door to the cell, where a bottle of water sat untouched.

"She has had nothing at all?"

"I'm sorry, my lord." Leo bowed his head. "I'll get something, uh, now. I'll just—" He thumbed over his shoulder and left.

Nikolai crossed the room and retrieved the bottle, then returned to his crouch before her. He removed the lid and held the water out to her. "Drink it. I know I must've taken more from you than I should've. You are probably dehydrated."

Katherine eyed the bottle, swallowing hard enough to be audible. "Why do they all listen to you?"

"Because I'm a pain in the ass if they don't." Saying any more would lead to conversations there wasn't a chance in hell he would have. With her. With anyone. "Now, drink."

She arched an eyebrow at him, and the commentary regarding his command was crystal clear. He almost smiled, except it was obvious she wanted the water, so why didn't she take it? All at once, he knew. It was the same concern he would've had in her position. He put the bottle to his lips and took a long sip, then offered it to her again.

Her shoulders sagged and she accepted the bottle, drinking nearly half of it at once. Twin reactions coursed through Nikolai—regret that she didn't trust him enough to take the water before he'd proven it clean, and satisfaction at seeing one of her needs sated. And at having a hand in that.

Truly, he couldn't blame her for the mistrust. Hadn't he approached her the same way? Wary. Questioning. Not to mention his brethren had thrown her in a dungeon. The satisfaction, though, that was a whole other animal. In and of itself, something to be distrusted. Because the root of it lay in his fascination with her, desire for her—a desire he needed to ignore. If the past six months taught him anything, it was that he could never again tolerate such loss. No way he would ever put himself in the position of feeling this kind of pain again. Evgeny's and Kyril's deaths had left a gaping hole in the center of his being.

Shit. Why was he even thinking about any of this?

Katherine rested the nearly empty bottle on her thigh and glanced up at him. A glossy sheen covered her bottom lip.

Nikolai's mouth fell open as his respiration increased. The plump, wet skin called to him, beckoned. To taste it… All at once, his mind went blank and he could focus on nothing else. Unconsciously, he leaned in, watching as her lips parted and her tongue snaked out to wet her top lip, too. Their eyes met. Hers were hooded and intense, heaven in a stare. He held her gaze as he moved closer. Her scent added to her allure, surrounding and confusing him. The smell of his own blood, on her, followed fast behind, building within his chest a deep, hot feeling of male satisfaction. Christ, he loved her wearing his blood. Were it on her skin, he wouldn't be able to stop himself from devouring it. Devouring her. Warm, quick exhalations fell against his lips. He shouldn't do this, he really fucking shouldn't, but he had to, he had to know—

"My lord, I brought—" Footsteps ended abruptly in the doorway behind him.

Nikolai wrenched back and rose to his feet, his heart hammering against his breastbone. Disappointment warred with relief in his mind. What the hell was he doing? He fixed a glare on Leo and nodded to the table.

Eyes down, the young warrior crossed the room and dropped the tray to show his displeasure.

"Something on your mind, Leo?"

"No, my lord," he said, gaze still averted.

"Didn't think so." Skin prickly, muscles tense, fangs aching, Nikolai was pissed off now and not sure why. "Is Anton here?"

Leo shook his head. "Stayed in the city once you were stabilized."

Nikolai didn't miss the unusual gruffness to the kid's voice. "Call him and tell him to come. And let me know the minute he arrives. Now, go." Leo lifted his eyes enough to communicate understanding and gave a single nod. Feeling edgy and restless, Nikolai watched him leave and then grasped the tray and placed it on the bed.

Wide, leery eyes peered up at him. The sound of her heart was thunderous in his ears. "Examined?"

Nikolai crouched again. "You're hurt. We have a doctor on staff. I would like him to look at you. Will you allow it?"

"Um. I'm just a little banged up." Her gaze dropped to the tray.

Her implicit refusal stoked the fire of his mounting anger. "Christ, Katherine, you're a little more than banged up." Before he'd even thought to do it, he yanked her wrist from her lap and tore the gauze free.

She gasped and pulled back, but his grip on her elbow held her in place.

Holy Mother of God. He was an animal. A fucking animal. Chewed. It was the only word to describe what he saw. From wrist to midforearm, her arm was a landscape of red and purple. One, two, three times his fangs had penetrated her flesh—and not cleanly, and at least twice had his other teeth broken her skin, too. Angry bruises in the form of fingers—his fingers—circled her arm in several places.

"Stop. You're hurting me."

Her words slapped him. He released her, suddenly aware of how hard he'd been gripping her elbow and hand. She cradled her arm against her stomach, remnants of gauze still clinging, and hid the worst of the injuries from his gaze. But the image was seared onto his brain. His throat went raw, as if he'd swallowed glass.

His head sagging on his shoulders, he tugged his hands through his hair. He couldn't stop hurting others, could he? And to hurt *her*, of all people. Maybe they'd all just be better off if he—

"Hey," she said softly. The light touch of her hand landed

on the back of his head. After a moment, she stroked him. Slow. Gentle.

Out of nowhere, a hazy memory slammed into his brain. The soft drags of her fingers in his hair, when he'd been injured, when she'd given him permission to feed from her vein. How shaken she must've been, how much pain he'd clearly inflicted, and yet she'd shown him tenderness, compassion.

"I'll see the doctor, okay? You know, as long as he's a real doctor, and all." The soft cup of her hand petted over his hair again.

For a long moment, Nikolai absorbed the incredible warmth and gentleness of her touch. It had been so long since he'd allowed himself the smallest pleasure. He didn't deserve it, but that didn't keep him from wanting it, from needing it, like air, or blood.

Resigned to see fear or hatred or disgust in her eyes, Nikolai lifted his head.

She smiled at him, her eyes filled with what looked like understanding and concern. "Okay?"

Nikolai's chest flooded with a foreign warm pressure. The hand that he rubbed against his sternum ached and the meaning of that sensation niggled at his consciousness. What was she doing to him? He swallowed, hard, and nodded, the flash fire of his rage dying as quickly as it had roared to life. "Okay."

# Chapter Seven

Feeling that odd pull to her again, exacerbated by a deep and growing need to heal her, to care for her, to make her better, Nikolai turned his attention to the tray. Next to the plate of grilled sashlyk was a pill bottle. He handed it to her. "Will this work for you?"

She read the label and nodded, then set about removing the plastic safety wrapping securing the cap. Her cheeks pinked, intensifying her luscious scent and making Nikolai realize he was watching her every move. He sat back on his ass, knees drawn up in front of him, and put a little distance between them as she swallowed the pills.

Eyeing the tray, she licked her lips. "Do you, uh, do you want some? Or, oh, maybe you don't eat..."

"I do, but it's for you." Nikolai's mouth went dry at the offer. After everything she'd given him, she was willing to offer more?

"I can share."

"Please."

Shrugging, Katherine picked up a sashlyk skewer and pulled a piece of marinated, grilled beef from one end.

"I hope this is to your liking. The only human foods we

eat are meat and spirits, and I'm sure the staff didn't have time to prepare for our arrival."

"It smells great. Anyway, I'm so hungry anything would taste good, so…" She ate the beef from her fingers, and sucked the juice from her thumb.

Her teeth, sinking into the rare flesh. The pink juice on her lips. The little, throaty sounds of pleasure and satiation. Nikolai's erection turned to steel. Each bite taunted and seduced him. It was everything he could do to sit still and let her finish her meal.

Maybe diverting his attention from her mouth would help. His gaze dropped to the shapely fit of her sweater over the round fullness of her breasts. His palms ached to feel the heavy warmth of them, his fangs throbbed at the thought of penetrating the perfect mounds with his bite while his cock filled the cleft between her thighs. He heaved a breath and forced his eyes to keep moving, but there was no place safe to look. The blood—his blood—smeared across the hem of her sweater and coating the front of her jeans from waist to knees unleashed a deep yearning in his gut. He *wanted* her to have his blood, but not accidentally. He wanted her to have it because he'd knowingly offered and she'd willingly, wantonly accepted.

He sucked in a breath. There was only one way that happened. If they were mates.

Which was something he could never have.

Jesus, but she was making him think, making him consider. Making him want.

*No.*

"How old are you?" he asked.

She swallowed the bite she was chewing and wiped her mouth with a napkin. "Twenty."

Nikolai dropped his head to his knees with a groan.

"Almost twenty-one," she said, cracking open a new bottle of water Leo had brought in with the tray.

His gaze cut back to her. "When?"

She wiped her wet lips with the back of her hand. "My birthday's on Friday."

What kind of fate would lead him to this brave, beautiful creature, a woman who had saved and protected him, at the height of her blood power for just four more days, when he could never claim her, never have her? Not for keeps.

She rose from the bed and stepped around him to return the tray to the table.

Her scent wrapped around his heart, his cock. Heat flickered across his right palm. "Goddammit," he snapped. All the signs were there.

"What?" she said.

He couldn't let himself be seduced by an impossible idea. He sprung to his feet and made for the door, still open from his earlier rushed entry. "I have to go."

"Why?" She followed after him, the alluring beat of her heart and intoxicating femininity revealing her place within the room.

He couldn't stop, couldn't reply, couldn't look at her. If he did, there'd be no going back. He grasped the edge of the door.

Small hands fisted in the back of his shirt. "Wait. Why are you leaving? I mean, did I—"

He halted, heart slamming against his sternum, fangs stretched out and aching. "Release me," he rasped.

She heaved a shaky breath he felt against his arm. "I… can't."

"Release. Me," he said louder. Competing emotions warred within him until he thought he might split apart.

"Nikolai—"

It was his name rolling off her tongue that did it.

He whirled and buried his hands in her hair. He pulled her to him, causing them both to stumble, and he backed her into the ancient bars of the door. It clicked shut, sealing them in and cutting off the last of his restraint.

Tilting her head back, Nikolai devoured her mouth. His lips sucked, his tongue explored, his fangs rubbed against her moist flesh. *Oh, God*, she was so sweet and warm and wet. He stepped into her, forcing their bodies together from chest to thighs. And, goddammit, she was soft everywhere he was hard.

Her hands curled around his neck and climbed into his hair, fingers tangling and tugging. She pulled him in tighter and surrendered to the kiss. She met him stroke for stroke, their tongues curling and twining together.

And Nikolai no longer knew who was surrendering to whom.

Kate was adrift in sensation. She felt engulfed by the heat rolling off Nikolai's big body, which was hunched around her possessively. His hard muscles flexed and bunched against her, setting her on fire everywhere they touched. His warm, spicy smell invaded her brain until it was the only thing she knew. His tongue in her mouth, his hands all over her—she couldn't fight it. In truth, she didn't want to. Earlier, when it seemed he planned to kiss her, she'd resisted the idea, kept her body from succumbing to the instinctual pull and leaning toward his. But now, even though he represented everything she'd never wanted, she could no longer deny that something about him spoke to her body, her psyche, her very soul. She was totally and completely seduced by her vampire.

A groan sounded from deep in his throat, conveying pure, desperate need, and he pressed harder into her. Against her back, the iron bars formed an inescapable cage. In front of her, his body towered over and confined her, emphasizing the thick ridge of his erection straining against her belly. She'd never felt more free than she did in that moment, utterly trapped by Nikolai.

And if his preternatural power wasn't prominent enough in the sheer strength of his body around hers, the hard edges of his fangs against her lips and tongue wouldn't let her forget it. Fascinated despite herself, she wrapped her tongue around a fang and flicked at it. Nikolai growled and ground the steel length of his cock into her hip.

Kate went hot and wet between her legs, completely overwhelmed by her body's ecstatic reaction to his. Never had she imagined she'd be capable of such euphoria. She'd certainly never felt it before. Maybe she wouldn't again. The thought unleashed a current of panic into the lust flowing through her, because what she was feeling for Nikolai was so much more than physical.

Her heart tripped over the pain he seemed to carry in the cast of his eyes and the set of his shoulders. He unleashed every protective and nurturing instinct in her body—*she* wanted to be the one to take away whatever hurt him, or to comfort him, at the very least. And there was absolutely no denying that all the angst and restlessness that had been making her feel unsettled in her skin lately, that had been getting worse and worse these past weeks, mostly disappeared in his presence.

There was no refuting the physical attraction, either. As close as they were, it was miles too far apart. She embraced his big shoulders, pulling, tugging, needing him closer. Her body remembered her unfulfilled need from the night before, spiking her arousal and creating an urgent ache between her legs. God, she wanted him…wanted him…in her.

Her hands fell to his waist and gripped at the fabric of his tee, burrowing under. His skin was warm and smooth over hard, flexing muscles. She pushed the shirt higher, needing to feel more, explore more, to know if he was this amazing everywhere.

Abruptly, Nikolai wrenched back from the kiss, and he looked every bit of the creature he was. Lips red, mouth open, fangs protruding, eyes aglow. Unease flared in her stomach. He was going to pull away. Like before. She dug her nails into his sides, willing him to stay. He reached back with one arm and tore the shirt over his head.

Relief crashed through her and she moaned in admiration of the artwork decorating his skin. A massive stylized black eagle spread its wings across his pecs and its tail curled down over the carved muscles of his stomach. Its golden claws wielded swords, and its regal head bore a crown. It was a fascinating, beautiful play on the Russian coat of arms. Symbols she didn't recognize adorned his right arm, from wrist to biceps, the black ink against his fair skin such a stunning, attractive contrast.

Inexperience be damned, she was drawn to taste him. Pushing onto tiptoes, Kate pressed an openmouthed kiss over his nipple and sucked him in. Oh, he tasted of that incredible spice he wore on his skin. She couldn't get enough. She kissed and licked across his chest, and his hands fisted in her hair—holding her or tugging her away, she couldn't be sure.

He grasped her chin and nudged her mouth up, then kissed her eyes, her nose, the corner of her lips. "So beautiful."

Each kiss, each touch, each word washed away the last of her uncertainty until she knew she would give him anything he wanted. That didn't mean she wasn't scared, because she was, but everything in her, down to the very marrow of her bones, told her he was worth the risk.

"May I...I want to do something for you," he said around a kiss.

"Anything," she whispered, her lips trailing down the hard angle of his jaw to his neck. Tight crisscrosses of black thread were the only evidence of his terrible wound. Taking care to be gentle, she pressed a featherlight kiss atop his stitches.

"Oh, angel," he groaned. The sound rumbled against her breasts, adding to the electric tingling making her pussy slick and needy. He grasped the hem of her sweater, then his whole face slid into a scowl. "Goddammit." Looking over his shoulder, he barked. "Camera off. Now."

As she watched, the red blinking light on the unit went dark.

Her sweater was up and over her head as the heat of a blush warmed her face, but she was so deep into Nikolai, she found she couldn't think long on her embarrassment that someone—some *vampire*—had been watching them together. She gasped at the sensation of the cold bars pressing stripes into the skin of her back. Big hands cupped the sides of her breasts and his mouth fell to her cleavage. He kissed and nibbled, dragging the tips of his fangs across the mounds in a tantalizing threat. She threw her head back against the door and silently begged him to do it.

Oh, shit, she was so far down the rabbit hole with him. And, God help her, she wouldn't have it any other way.

She carded her fingers into his hair, loving the thick silkiness of it, and embraced him as he sucked her nipple through the thin satin of her bra.

He gripped the back of her left wrist and pulled it to his mouth. "This is what I must..." He trailed off and laved his tongue against the red marks on her arm.

She moaned as his saliva tingled against the cuts and abrasions. It didn't hurt. Just the opposite. It brought such maddeningly beautiful relief. The sensation ricocheted through her and had her writhing against him. He hummed something that sounded like satisfied approval and slid a thick muscled thigh tight between her legs. She cried out at the glorious friction and couldn't help but rock her hips against him.

He cut his gaze to hers as he licked her forearm with his healing saliva. His eyes were a blazing blue. She could fall into those eyes and be so happy there… The thought brought another with it, and suspicion sent her heart slamming against her breastbone: *he* was the cause of her angst. Somehow, needing to find Nikolai, protect him, be *with* him was the source of the restlessness and confusion plaguing her all these long months. She'd left the service of the Proffered, and soul deep her body had known that decision put her on the wrong path.

The truth of her revelation spiraled through her body and settled itself in every cell. Combined with his tongue, his thigh, his eyes, those little sounds of masculine appreciation—it was all too much. "Oh, God, Nikolai. You have to…" She shook her head, unable to control her breathing, or her body. "You have to stop, or I—"

"Not yet." He pulled his leg away.

She whimpered and flexed off the bars.

The corner of his mouth curled up as he healed her with one last long, languid stroke of his tongue.

"No, no. I have to. Please." She squirmed and ground her belly against his cock. Despite her general inexperience, her body acted on its own instinct, seemingly knowing what, or whom, would bring her the relief and release she nearly screamed for.

"You have to what, angel?"

She hesitated for a few short, quick heartbeats. "I have to…" The word on the tip of her tongue, she clenched her thighs together, burning for the friction he'd given to her moments before. "Oh, God."

"You have to come, yes?" he whispered against her ear. Kate nodded, her stomach flip-flopping at his tone, full of sin and satisfaction. One hand fell to her jeans, tugged at the zipper, ripped the denim open. "I want to wear you on my skin," he said.

Gently but firmly, he slid his fingers under the band of her panties.

The rough pads of his fingertips slid into the soft hair at the top of her mound, and Kate moaned and grabbed the closest bar with her free hand to keep from falling. He kicked at the inside of her shoe. "Open."

Pressed against the iron bars of her dungeon cell, Kate spread her legs. Nikolai's fingers dipped into the slick folds of her pussy, rubbing, flicking, pressing tight circles that stole her breath. He lingered a kiss to the healed skin over her radial artery, then dropped her arm and brought his mouth back to hers. The movement of his lips was deep, reverent, just the beginning of something she knew she'd never forget. She grabbed a bar with her newly healed hand and just let herself feel the incredible ecstasy he drew from her body.

Forehead resting against hers, he pushed one finger inside her and met her gaze. She gasped, his finger so much bigger than her own, which until this moment had been the sum total of her experience.

"Come on me, Katya. I want to feel it. I want to see it."

"Nikolai," she whimpered, holding his gaze. His finger simultaneously eased the ache and escalated it as he penetrated and thrust, his palm providing more of that glorious friction against her clit. Panting, she couldn't keep from moving her hips and urging more. Inside, her body tightened around his finger.

"Mmm, yes." Licking his lips and drilling his intense, flaring gaze into her eyes, he added a second finger.

Kate moaned at the fullness, reveled in it, wanted more—even if her desire scared her. The thought was fleeting. His fingers moved in and out of her in a shallow quick pattern that rocketed all her energy downward, then detonated in a brilliant explosion of light and heat that sent her flying, falling, floating outside herself.

Hanging on the bars, her whole body sagged against him, her weight falling onto his hand between her legs and his chest. She was dimly aware of the approving growl rumbling from deep in his throat.

He wrapped an arm around her back and tugged her hair, gently pulling her head back so he could claim her mouth. The kiss was slow and sensual, full of the promise of more to come. And despite the fact that the room spun around her and she couldn't control the pace or volume of her breathing, more was exactly what she wanted. She couldn't wait to have the chance to bring him the same incredible ecstasy he'd given her.

Nikolai pulled his hand from between her legs, but didn't leave her skin. Still under the stretched fabric of her panties, his big, warm grip slid around to grasp the naked curve of her hip. His fingers were wet where they dug into her ass, but she couldn't feel embarrassed about it, not after he'd shown her the pleasure her body was capable of experiencing. He broke the kiss with a gleam in his eye. A cocky smile played around the corners of his mouth. As infuriatingly smug as it was, he wore the good humor so well she could only find it sexy.

"Katya, I—"

An exaggerated cleared throat sounded from just down the stone corridor outside her cell. "My lord, Anton awaits you in the security booth."

Kate sucked in a breath. But neither the voice nor the intrusion of the reality that others probably *knew* what was going on in here were the most alarming thing. Not by far.

Nikolai flew back from her, eyes and head averted as if he'd done something wrong. Breathing hard and scowling, he bent down and retrieved both their shirts. When he stood up, he held her sweater out to her, but didn't look her in the eye.

In almost slow motion, Kate released her hands from the bars, just now realizing Nikolai's actions had frozen her into a spectator as she tried to decipher the marked change in his mood. The moment her hand clutched the soft blue of her sweater, tears pricked the backs of her eyes. She clutched the cotton to her chest. "Nikolai—"

"Don't," he snapped, his voice low and tight. He yanked his shirt over his head, hiding those beautiful tattoos, hiding himself, from her gaze. "For God's sake, clothe yourself."

Blinking repeatedly to pinch off the threatening tears, Kate slipped back into her sweater. She tugged at the zipper to her jeans, but it wouldn't budge. Had he broken it? She buttoned the top and stretched her sweater downward to make herself decent.

For the first time since her orgasm, when he'd worn that beautiful little smile she'd thought so appealing, Nikolai met her gaze. His was cold, distant, disgusted. He stepped up to her and glared. When his eyes flickered to the door and back, she realized she was standing in front of it. He was waiting for her to move so he could leave.

Her face flamed hot and her heart thundered mortification through her veins. Biting her tongue to restrain the apology she almost uttered, Kate took three steps backward, clearing the door and putting lots of space between them. Space he apparently wanted.

Nikolai reached through the bar and turned the key hanging in the lock. He pulled the door open and, without looking back, without another word, stalked out of the cell.

# Chapter Eight

Nikolai needed to punch something. Repeatedly. Anything to distract himself from the hurt and humiliation he'd seen in Katherine's pale blue eyes. The hurt and humiliation he'd put there. What the hell had he been thinking?

He glared at Leo, standing with his arms crossed at the end of the hall, and dared the young warrior to give him a reason to lose his shit right here and now.

Leo dropped his gaze. "Anton's in the security booth."

The king—for it was the first time in a long time he felt so deadly serious about an order—got right up in the blond's face. "After the doc's done with her, you get her out of that cell. Back to Moscow. Out. Of. Here. We clear?"

"My lord—"

Nikolai fisted the man's T-shirt and dragged him in closer, flashing his fangs in warning. "Are we crystal fucking clear?"

Leo's gray eyes flared a silver light that hinted at the man's own building anger, but he kept his mouth closed.

"Nikolai," Mikhail said, stepping from the security booth. "Let him go."

He released Leo with a shove and stalked past his friend into the booth.

Anton dropped his phone into his pocket and smiled. "My lord, you're looking better. Want me to examine your n—"

"There's a human woman in there who got banged up earlier and was complaining of headaches." He pointed in the direction of the dungeons. "I want you to examine her. And then I want her out of here."

Anton shook his head, his good nature not dampened at all by Nikolai's lack of niceties. "I'm afraid that's not possible."

"Why the hell not?"

"Been snowing all day. Must be two feet of snow out there. Roads are a mess."

"You made it here okay."

"I made it as far as Poreche and hiked in the rest of the way until Leo rode out with the snowmobile. The roads back to Vasilievskoe are completely impassable."

Nikolai stared at him a long moment, then paced the room. He couldn't get rid of her. Just perfect. The weight of the other males' eyes settled on his shoulders like an anvil. He paused at the computer panel, his gaze falling on the controls to the security cameras. Heaving a breath, he hit a series of keys and buttons, bringing the monitor displaying the feed from Katherine's cell to life.

A pang his heart had no goddamn business feeling squeezed his chest. She sat on the floor, in the exact spot he'd left her standing, her back against the bars and her arms hugging her legs in front of her. Her face rested sideways on her knees, so he couldn't make out her expression.

Damn it all to hell and back. He wanted her. He wanted more of the way he felt when he was around her. Lighter, freer, relieved just the smallest, life-giving amount from the constant suffocating press of his grief. She made him believe it was okay to take a breath, a single in and out of his lungs, without thinking of how he'd utterly failed his kid brothers.

And damn, she was so strong. Despite being locked behind dungeon bars, the first thing she'd asked was if *he* was okay. Her compassion overwhelmed him again and again. He kept trying to imagine the scene Mikhail had earlier described. Her, feeding him and holding his warriors at gunpoint at the same time. Of course, his men were there for him, but to think he'd met a woman with the mettle to do what she'd done, to stand up for him in a do-or-die situation. He wanted to melt into her, to crawl into his bed with her in his arms, to lay his head on her chest and sleep his pain away.

She was his equal, in every way. No, not true at all. She was so much better than him.

Yeah, and that kind of woman would never want a male so grossly tainted by dishonor.

He dragged his hand through his hair, and the movement of air carried her scent to his nose. Jesus, she was fire wrapped in satin and silk. She touched him and he burned. But it hadn't been enough. With her, it would never be enough.

And that meant she had to go.

With the Soul Eaters so numerous they were nearly an infestation in Moscow, Saint Petersburg, Nizhny and Perm—not to mention the south of Russia, where cities like Saratov were actually losing population due to the evil ones' destructive addiction—he couldn't divide his attention enough to even consider a relationship.

*That's a goddamn lie and you know it.*

He could never have someone like Katherine Bordessa, and lose her. Simple as that. And the war was too volatile to chance it.

What a fucking coward he was. No hero material here, that was for sure.

He heaved a sigh. "Fine. Get her out of that damn cell, though. And get her some clean clothes." With a final glance at the monitor, Nikolai offered a silent apology for the way he'd treated her, then turned his back on her image. "You—" he glared at Leo "—sparring ring, ten minutes."

Voices echoed down the stone hall, but Kate couldn't really make them out. Well, not since Nikolai had growled out his command to send her back to Moscow.

She thumped her fist against her forehead. Stupid, stupid, stupid. How had she been so stupid? Man, she'd heard of vampires' allure, how everything around them felt so much more intense. And now she understood it firsthand. He'd made her believe he liked her, cared for her, wanted her. The reverence in his gaze as he healed her arm, the deep rasp of need in his voice as he encouraged her pleasure, the pet names that seemed to communicate affection and familiarity—she'd fallen for every last bit of it.

Worse, she'd thought it all *meant* something. As if. She thunked her head against the wall behind her and immediately regretted it. The medicine Nikolai had brought had dimmed the ache, but the bump on the back of her head was still sore.

*Wrong path, my butt.* Leaving the service of the Proffered was the smartest thing she'd ever done. Tonight confirmed it once and for all.

*Then why does it hurt so much?*

Footsteps approached, diverting Kate's attention from her self-examination.

Mikhail pushed through the still-open door and looked down at her with those analytical dark brown eyes. Another man entered behind him, thin and kind-faced. "Katherine, I understand Nikolai talked with you about seeing Anton, our doctor." He gestured to the other man, who smiled and nodded. "So, I'll leave you—"

"No."

Mikhail tilted his head. "I don't—"

"I won't see your doctor." She pushed up off the floor, grinding her teeth against the ache in her head.

"Nikolai said you were complaining of a headache after some sort of injury." Anton said in a calm, even voice. "Can you tell me what happened?"

"Skull versus frozen ground. Okay? I'm fine." She glanced at the man, then back to Mikhail, hating her rudeness but needing desperately to leave from where she wasn't wanted. "I know he wants me gone, so just give me my things and I'll be on my way."

Anton raised his hands. "The king was very clear," Anton said, apparently leaving it to Mikhail to decide. "He wants me to give her a clean bill of health, but I can't examine her against her will. I won't."

The doctor's words faded out as her brain focused on the first two that had so casually fallen from his lips.

*The king.*

Who was he talking— *Oh, God, no. No, it can't be. No braid. No jewels. How can he be the king?*

"He hasn't worn them in a while," Mikhail said.

"What?" Kate asked, the room doing that spinny thing again.

"I said he hasn't worn them in a while."

Oh, jeez, had she been thinking out loud? Hoping to hide the blush heating her cheeks, Kate scrubbed her hands over her face, torn by conflicting desires: to know more, to know why Nikolai, the Vampire Warrior King of Russia, apparently, didn't wear the symbols of his rank and title, *and* to get the hell out of here. Now. It wasn't just any old beautiful, sexy vampire who didn't want her. It was the freaking king.

Shit. What if word of this got back to her parents? Nikolai seemed so disgusted with her when he left. They had her passport and cell phone. Surely it wouldn't take that much research on the vampires' part to determine her family's association with the Electorate Council. Bordessa wasn't that common a name.

As if a man being repulsed by bringing her to orgasm wasn't bad enough.

Anton broke the awkward silence. "Well, if you change your mind, just have someone come get me. It's not like we're going anywhere any time soon."

Kate frowned. "What's that supposed to mean?"

"Go ahead, Anton. I'll get you if we need you," Mikhail interjected. The man nodded and left. "It's snowing, Katherine. The roads are closed."

She groaned, and her stomach dropped to the floor. "Tell me you're not serious."

"I'm afraid so." He sighed. "Look, I know you don't want to be here, but if you'll let me, I'd like to show you to a room where you'll at least be more comfortable."

"Why?"

"Because there's no need for you to be imprisoned. I'm sorry we did that in the first place."

Kate hugged herself and shrugged. What the hell. A real room would be nice, especially if it was near a bathroom. Or a shower. "Okay."

He held out his hand. "After you."

Without a backward glance, she stepped out of the cell.

"If you'll follow me," Mikhail said.

Down the stone hall, through some sort of empty high-tech office, Kate followed the warrior. The hallways leading through the downstairs were dark, rough-hewn, and she was fascinated despite herself. Wherever she was, this place was old. How she wished she could explore.

They came to a flight of wide stone steps and made their way up. On the top landing, Mikhail entered a code into a pad on the wall, releasing the heavy door in front of them with a metallic click.

In contrast to the dim lighting of the lower level, this floor was all white-painted cinder blocks. The bright light revealed midnight-blue tones in Mikhail's jet hair. Along the long corridor, most of the doors were solid with only a single small square window at the top, so Kate could only get the most cursory of glances into her surroundings. In the distance, music with a driving bass beat caught her attention. The farther up the hall they walked, the louder it got.

A warrior—the young one who had manhandled her out in that parking lot—rounded a corner and made for the closest door. His gaze scanned down the front of her before meeting her eyes, and she couldn't read his expression. He pushed a door open, letting the screaming guitars and pounding drums blare out into the hallway full force.

"You're late," someone shouted from within.

"I'm still in time to kick your ass. *My lord.*"

Kate and Mikhail walked past the door as it eased shut. Through the narrow gap, Kate had just enough time to see Nikolai's shirtless broad back, the cut muscles decorated with more beautiful designs she couldn't fully make out. His gaze cranked her direction and their eyes met in the split second before the door closed between them.

God, every time she saw him, he was more gorgeous than the last.

Butterflies took flight in her stomach. "He's a warrior," she said, eyeing Mikhail's braid and trying to engage him for the first time since they'd departed her cell.

"Yes. A great one."

"Then, why no braid?"

"It's not my story to tell, Katherine." He started up a second set of stairs. "This way."

At the top, there was another keypad, and then they stepped into a modern-looking vestibule. When the door they'd come through clicked shut behind them, another door sprang open ahead of them. The room on the other side was like a huge family room. Massive leather sectional sofa, several leather recliners. A screen for a projection television. Behind a pool table sat several pinball machines, and a carved wooden bar lined a far wall.

She chuckled, taking in the liquor and beer bottles and empty glasses on the coffee and end tables. "Is this the vampire man cave?"

The side of his mouth quirked up.

She shrugged. "My dad has a room like this. My mom calls it his man cave."

Mikhail smiled, just revealing the tips of his fangs. "I suppose so. We half live in this room."

For some reason, his smile made her sad. "None of you do that very often, you know that?"

"Do what?"

"Smile."

The jovial expression dropped from his face. "Not been a lot to smile about lately."

"I'm sorry to hear that."

He shook his head. "Just through here, then up one more flight."

Kate didn't fight him on the change of topic, and followed him out of the den. A central staircase came down to a wide foyer, flanked on the far side by a set of ornate doors with medieval Cyrillic characters in gold leaf forming an arch over the top.

Mikhail continued up the steps, but Kate hung back at

the bottom, admiring the incredible painting all around the doors. "What's this room?" she asked, drawn to inspect the artwork more closely. When he didn't answer, she glanced over her shoulder.

He stood in the middle of the steps staring at her. "It is the Hall of the Grand Princes."

"Oh," Kate said, stepping back from the wall. She didn't know exactly what that was, but by the room's name and the tone of Mikhail's voice, she knew it was important. An image sprang to mind, of Nikolai—King Nikolai, apparently— standing on a dais wearing a rich robe and gold crown. She didn't know whether to be amused or awed by the thought. "It's very beautiful."

He cleared his throat. "Thank you."

This time, when he turned, she followed him up the stairs. At the top, the decor changed yet again. Arched doorways, exposed buttresses in the ornate foyer, a tarnished but still striking cut-glass chandelier all framed lush carpets, vibrant wall tapestries and thick, heavy curtains covering the windows. Antiques sat chockablock to one another, and portraiture and other framed art vied for space on the crowded walls. The color scheme was rich and masculine—deep reds and dark blues, and appealed to her very much.

After several turns down a twisting hallway, Mikhail stopped outside a door. "This is one of the sixteen bedrooms in the house." He turned the brass knob and pushed into the dark, crossing the room to turn on a lamp next to a wide sleigh bed. "There's a bathroom through that door. I hope this will serve."

"It's great. Thank you." Her words were a complete understatement—the room was stunning, with wallpaper that gave her the impression of sitting amidst a great garden. But now that they were here, she didn't really want to be alone. Not as if she could ask him to keep her company, though.

He scratched his jaw and said, "I will try to find you some clothing."

"Right. Thanks."

"Okay, then." He left, pulling the door shut behind him.

Kate released a long breath. This was the most surreal night of her life. Or, wait, the most surreal *two* nights, she guessed. After a quick trip to the bathroom, she poked around the large space, finally making her way to one of the windows. It took a minute to dig through the layer upon layer of heavy velvet curtains to finally get to the glass. Her efforts were rewarded with a ledge so wide she could sit on it.

Half sitting, she gazed out at the winter night, snow falling in a silent blanket on the dense forest. There was no view, really, but that didn't keep it from being beautiful, peaceful. She sighed.

She wasn't sure how long she'd been resting there, when a knock sounded at the door. Wading through the miles of fabric made her laugh, and she was still grinning when she found Mikhail standing in the hallway with a thick stack of clothing in his hands.

"This is all going to be too big on you, so I brought several things for you to choose from."

Kate reached out for the pile.

Mikhail gaped. "Your arm." The tattered ends of her sleeve hung loose, revealing the smooth, unbroken surface of her skin. "He healed you?"

Heat exploded over Kate's face. She pulled the pile from his arms and hugged it against her chest. "I'm sure something will work. Thank you, Mikhail."

He stood there at loose ends, eyes wide, clearly wanting something else but not saying what it was.

She gestured at the clothes. "Well, thanks again."

His shoulders sagged. "Katherine?"

The hair rose on her arms and neck. "Yes?"

"Thank you for saving him. He's been my best friend for over five hundred years. I would've…well, we all would've been lost without him."

*Five hundred years?* The idea of it made her light-headed. She shook off the sensation. "Anyone would've—"

"No. What you did was special, and I stand indebted to you."

She watched him retreat down the hallway, looking every bit the warrior he was.

Kate turned again to the empty room, her hands trembling. Ridiculously, part of her felt so comfortable here, as if she belonged, and already felt the heartache of leaving them, of never seeing any of them again.

Never seeing Nikolai again.

## Chapter Nine

Nikolai bumped fists with Leo and gave him a shove. "Good match."

He chuckled. "You weren't half bad, for an old man."

The king barked out a laugh, the fighting having beaten some of the raging frustration out of him. "Says the two-hundred-and-twelve-year-old vampire."

He flashed Nikolai a grin.

"Thanks for sparring, Leo," he called as he reached the door.

"Yeah. Hey, my lord?" Twisting his shirt in his hands, Leo looked to the floor. "I didn't mean to, but I hurt her. I knocked her to the ground too roughly, and she hit her head."

Stomach clenching, heart pounding, Nikolai didn't need to ask which "her" he was referring to. "Why are you telling me this?"

Leo lifted his gaze, met Nikolai's head-on. "She really fought for you. Even got off a shot before I could disarm her. I've never seen anything like it. Well, except for mated—" He clamped his mouth shut. "Just thought you should know."

Nikolai turned and wrenched the door open.

"Nikolai?"

Red flags waving in his mind, he froze but didn't look back.

"I see the way you look at her. They would want you to be happy."

He bolted from the room. No way he was having that conversation. Didn't matter that Leo had been Kyril's best friend—the two had been thick as goddamn thieves. Didn't matter that he meant well. It only mattered that he got the hell out of there, away from that wary look on Leo's face. Away from his encouragements that he go after something he could never have.

Down the hall, up two staircases, through the meandering turns of the main floor. He knew the house like the inside of his own mind, and could've navigated it blindfolded, which was good since all he could see was *that look* on Katherine's face. As if he'd slapped her.

Well, hadn't he? No doubt the coldness in his words and actions had stung just as much.

He pressed his hand into the ache that settled under the bare skin of his chest.

Nikolai turned the corner into the wing that housed his private quarters, a series of rooms that formed a virtual apartment. His brothers' rooms had been in this part of Vasilievskoe, too, and their deaths had left the Vasilyev wing particularly still and quiet except for his own movements. Which was just fine by him.

Except…

Nearby, the plumbing whined. Someone was running the water. He backtracked and turned down an adjacent hallway. Light shined from under the door of the lone guest room in this part of the manor.

He was going to kill Mikhail.

Before he even thought to do it, he found himself standing in front of that door. *Her* door.

Oh, what the hell was he doing?

He should apologize. Rationale squarely in place, he rapped his knuckles against the heavy panel of wood. Again. No answer. "Katherine?"

He knocked his head against the door. Deep need rose within him, to lay eyes on her and reassure himself she was okay. She'd been attacked, bitten, kidnapped and imprisoned. Not goddamn likely she was okay. And that wasn't even considering what had happened between them, which had been phenomenal until he acted like a son of a bitch. The urge to see her made it hard to breathe.

He pushed through the door and called her name again. Two things struck him simultaneously: soft splashes of water from the direction of the open bathroom door and a stack of clothes on her bed.

Inside the room, her sweet-blooded scent infused the air and reawakened his cock, reminding him of his unsated arousal from before. Each breath pulled more of her into him, until he ached to penetrate her in return, in any way she'd allow. In every way she'd allow. Prickles on the skin of his right palm made him fist his hand.

His breath coming faster, shallower, Nikolai stepped over her discarded clothing to the bed and quickly flipped through the pile of fabric—robe, T-shirt, sweatshirt, sweatpants. All Mikhail's.

An image flashed into his mind. Katherine, wearing Mikhail's shirt and sweatpants, so big on her she had to roll them at the waist and ankles. Katherine, wearing *Mikhail's* clothes.

*Another. Male's. Clothes.*

Nearly blind with a possessiveness he had no right to feel, Nikolai grabbed all the clothes and stalked out of the room. Bursting through the door to his apartment, he chucked everything in the general direction of the nearest trash can. He whipped his robe off the back of his closet door and ripped a few articles of clothing from a drawer. He wasn't even aware he'd returned to the guest room until her scent invaded his brain.

Nikolai glanced up, and found himself looking into Katherine's startled pale blue eyes.

"What are you doing?" Kate asked as she clutched the plush white towel tighter against her breasts. Her heart took off at a sprint as she drank him in. He radiated a dark energy that wrapped around her and resurrected that maddening ache in her left hand. Maybe something wasn't fully healed after all.

"I brought you clothes," he nearly growled.

Kate glanced to the empty bed and pointed with the hand not holding the towel closed. "I had clothes."

Light flashed through the sapphire and his jaw ticked. "Those didn't work."

Staring at him, trying to make sense of his completely confusing pronouncements, Kate couldn't help but notice the prominent bulge filling up the front of his workout gear. Good God. She hadn't finished toweling dry, but there was really no arguing that the slick wetness suddenly between her legs was from the bath. She shook her head. "How can clothes not work? Mikhail just brought them for me."

He growled. Literally growled. She blinked and found him standing right in front of her, the ball of wadded-up clothing the only thing separating them. She gasped, breathing in the mouthwatering scent of his male spice, and stepped back. Nikolai followed, kept pace with her as she retreated until she was trapped between him and the bed. "*His* clothes don't work. *His* clothes will *never* work."

Damn it, her left hand tingled as if it had fallen asleep. She shook it, and Nikolai's eyes tracked the movement. His tongue rubbed against the tip of a fang. Kate swallowed as she watched the sinuous movement of his pink tongue. She clenched her thighs, a tormenting throb blooming deep in her pussy.

"What do you want?" When he didn't answer, she braced herself and looked him in the eye.

"I want…" He turned on his heel and crossed to the door.

Brilliant, white-hot anger pounded through her veins. Every muscle strung tight, she leaned back against the bed. Not a chance in hell she was chasing after him, not again. No matter how much her body screamed for him to stay, for him to crawl on top of her and claim her as his.

No way.

In the silence between them, a tinny click sounded out. Despite herself, Kate glanced through the hanging threads of her damp hair to see him standing at the door. He dropped his hand from the lock. Ancient Cyrillic letters spelled out two male names across his mountainous shoulders.

He tossed the clothes he'd been carrying to the floor. With leonine grace, he walked back to her, his eyes boring into hers. Her body screamed in victory, more of that tantalizing moisture gathering on the sensitive lips of her pussy. She narrowed her eyes at him and arched a brow.

In front of her again, he stroked his knuckles over the hand holding the towel. Once, twice. Her nervous system sprang to life and set her to trembling. He dragged his gaze from their hands to her eyes. "I want you, Kate. I shouldn't, because my head's a freaking mess. And I don't deserve you, after what I did to you before. But none of that changes the fact that I can think of *nothing* besides the idea of having just one perfect night. With you."

Kate shook her head. "You don't want me."

Dark blue light flashed in a wave behind his eyes. "I *do* want you. I ache for you." He pushed his hips into her thigh, grinding his cock against her.

Kate couldn't seem to get enough oxygen into her lungs to clear her head. "That's not what you said," she whispered, almost gasping from the muscle spasm that rocked through her core.

He tilted his head and frowned. "You heard me?"

"Kinda hard not to."

The muscles in his jaw clenched. "I'm sorry. I was pissed at myself. Not at you. You, Katherine, you deserve only the best. And that's not me."

"Then why are you doing this?"

He licked his lips, flashing the tips of his fangs again. "Because, God help me, I am driven to distraction by the very thought of you." He cupped her face and caressed his thumb over her cheekbone. "By your beauty, by the fire in those lovely pale eyes." Stepping in closer, he bought them into contact from ankle to breast. "I am humbled by your compassion, proud beyond measure of your courage." He leaned his face into hers so that his breath tickled her lips. "I want you on my skin, in my mouth." He feathered his fingers down her bare arm, sending her into a shiver. "I want to see you naked, explore you with my hands, part your knees and bury myself in you. I want to hear you scream my name as I stroke deep and hard inside you. That's what I want."

Nikolai's unbridled honesty struck her like a match. A flame roared up inside Kate, melting the reserve she'd built up after what happened earlier, making her body crave his so intensely she hurt. Tentatively, a part of her afraid he'd change his mind again, she reached out and weaved her fingers into his silky blond hair, where his braid should be. "But you're the king."

He leaned into her touch. "I'm just a male, like any male."

It was such a lie. No man had ever turned the blood in her veins into flowing lava. No man had ever made her ache. No man had ever made her feel this...*alive*. It was all so overwhelming—she just had no experience feeling the things she felt, wanting the things she wanted. And he should know.

Taking a deep breath, she said, "I've never done this before, Nikolai." As her cheeks heated, she watched her fingers drag through his hair. Oh, he was so beautiful.

He tilted his head to force her to look at him. "Done what?" A range of expressions played out across his face. "You mean..." His eyes went wide. "Are you saying you're a virgin?"

## Chapter Ten

Heart triple-timing in his chest, Nikolai soaked in the beautiful flush on Katherine's cheeks and waited for her answer. What had he ever done to find someone like her? Someone so beautiful, so strong, so damn perfect in every way, for him.

She nodded, her eyes flickering to his and away again.

And Nikolai's thinking brain went offline.

Triumphant euphoria flooded into every cell. He locked his hands around her neck and pulled her in for a kiss so deep, so intense, it drove everything else from his mind. His tongue explored her mouth, his hands massaged her neck and tugged her hair. Needing to be closer, to drive away every molecule of air separating them, he pushed between her legs and ground himself against her mound. Kate cried out and threw her head back.

"Oh, God, angel," he rasped. Her body was like a feast spread out before a starving man. His lips fell to her throat, kissing, sucking, drawing the heated flavor of her skin onto his tongue. He laved long strokes against the throbbing pulse of her jugular, reveling in the drag of his fangs against her tender flesh. "I want you so damn much."

He scooped his hands under her thighs and lifted her atop

the high bed. She wrapped her legs around his hips and her heels dug into his ass. He rocked his cock against her pussy, fascinated as the towel parted and rode up, inch by tantalizing inch.

Light fingertips fell on his chest and traced down the center of him, making his stomach muscles flinch and clench. At the waistband of his pants, she stopped. Nikolai nearly groaned in need, but he didn't want to push her. He wanted her to want him in return, so he had to let her go at her own pace.

His brain refused to let him think through everything that her still being a virgin could mean.

After the briefest hesitation, Kate's hand slid between them and gripped his cock over the thick cotton. That time, Nikolai couldn't restrain the groan the incredible contact drew out of him. "Christ, how you make me feel…"

His words seemed to encourage and embolden her. She massaged and squeezed, until he couldn't help but thrust into her hand.

Nikolai rubbed his fingers over the knuckles still clenching the towel in front of her breasts. "Katya, let me see you. Let go."

She dropped her hand, and the towel slipped behind her.

Pressing his palm to the valley between her beautiful breasts, Nikolai met Katherine's heavy-lidded gaze and counted the rapid thumps of her heart. Vitality thrummed through her and into him, tempted parts of his soul back to life he thought long gone. Dragging his hand down her body, over the curve of her belly and into the soft brown hair of her pussy, Nikolai watched her watch him.

"What do *you* want, Katya?"

A deep blush roared over the flush already staining her cheeks. He leaned over her and rubbed his nose along her jaw. The blush strengthened the scent of her blood on the air. "You are so lovely. I have to know what you want."

She ducked her head against his. "I don't have the words," she answered. "I just want you."

Her words eased the ache in the center of his chest. Oh, what was she doing to him? With slow, gentle thrusts, he rolled his cock against the nerves at the top of her pussy. "You don't know the words," he asked, "or it's hard to say them?"

"Oh, my God," she whispered. "Nikolai."

The desperation in her voice rocketed into his balls. Cupping her breasts, flicking her nipples with his thumbs, he nipped his fangs down the long column of her graceful neck. "Tell me," he rasped. Her throat worked at a rough swallow under his worshipful lips. Hoping to deaden the hot ache in his palm, he lowered his right hand to the wet lips of her pussy and rubbed slow, tight circles.

She released a high-pitched cry. "I need you," she whined.

"My what? My fingers?" He eased his middle and ring fingers into the depths of her cunt. His fingertips found the swollen glands he hoped would give her pleasure and massaged, reveling in the new flow of moisture over his palm. He breathed the scent of her arousal into his very soul. Starting slow, he rocked his hand up and down. Her whimpers and gasps spurred him on. He fingered her faster, making sure the heel of his hand rubbed her clit, until the wetness of her juices around his moving fingers formed a raw, decadent sound track. "Is this what you want?" he bit out as the walls of her pussy tightened.

"Yes," she cried. "No. No, I want…"

"What? Say it, angel."

"I want you to…oh, my God, Nikolai…I want you to fuck me. I want your c-cock inside me."

Damn it all to hell, this shy innocence together with what he knew of her courage and bravery was a combination so appealing, so arousing, it nearly took him to his knees. Bracing himself on the mattress beside her, he pumped his hand faster, harder, willing her body to let go.

The velvet walls of her cunt clamped down on his fingers. Katherine screamed and went boneless, falling back against the bed. He stroked her through the orgasm, milking out every last ounce of pleasure for her.

Katherine lifted her head, her eyes coming back into focus, and licked her lips. Her toes curled into the waistband of his pants. "Off."

"Yeah?" He pushed them to the floor, then crawled onto the bed between her knees. Hands under her hips, he guided her body higher on the mattress. A small soft palm wrapped around his cock. "Fuck," he said, surprised and pleased by her firm, sure grip.

Goddammit, he needed in her. He *wanted* in her. Hand aching, fangs throbbing, dick leaking in her grasp, Nikolai stared wide-eyed at the incredible site of her jacking him off.

He was about to cross some cosmic line. He knew it. He felt it in his gut. But he couldn't pull back, couldn't resist the incredible seductiveness of Katherine Bordessa. He pulled her hand away and brought it to his mouth for a long kiss on her palm. That she smelled of his maleness caused his cock to twitch against his stomach.

"Katya, there's something you need to know about what is going to happen between us."

She tilted her head against the mattress, strands of her chocolate hair spread in a dark halo across the plush comforter, and stared at him a long minute. "You're going to bite me."

Hands braced on either side of her shoulders, he leaned over her. "How did you know that's what I was going to say?"

"Nikolai, I trained as a Proffered, but, more than that—"

she released a shaky sigh "—I want you to bite me so damn bad I can barely lie still."

"You…what?" His brain was so scattered he couldn't pull his thoughts together to respond, to absorb the significance of her revelation. On top of everything, she was a Proffered? Groomed to be a vampire's mate? Emotion barreled through his veins—that dark rage from before reemerged at the thought he might've lost her to another, soul-deep gratitude warmed his chest as each new evidence of her rightness for him filled his heart, convinced his brain. All this, it felt so much bigger than him—magical and fated, even. "But you didn't serve?" he finally managed to say.

"I…no." She shook her head. "The whole thing scared me. I don't know."

"And now?"

"Come here," she whispered, cupping his face in her hands. The touch was so gentle, the voice so sweet, she lured him in as surely as if magnets resided in the center of their chests. "Before, it was an abstraction. Now, it's just you. And, everything else aside, I want you, Nikolai." She lifted her hips and rubbed herself against him.

"Jesus," he said, taking his dick in hand. He was so hard, so sensitive, his own touch was nearly painful. "It may hurt, Katya, for a moment, but I will make it go away. Yes?"

She nodded. "I need you in me, Nikolai. The emptiness hurts already."

"I will take care of you," he murmured, his heart making plans his brain hadn't yet approved. But, in that instant, none of that mattered. Her words beckoned him in, welcomed him home, seduced him to believe they could have a chance.

Kate moaned and dug her fingers into the muscles straining with leashed power all down his sides. The steel length of his erection pushed into her, filled her with a heavy pressure that made her hold her breath.

"Angel, I can't—" He shook his head, blue eyes blazing, pleading.

She tugged at his back, urging him down. "Let go, Nikolai. I want it."

With a growl that ricocheted out of his throat and down her spine, Nikolai's weight covered her as he thrust forward, burying himself deep inside her in one hard stroke. Hunched around her, his hands curled under her shoulders and clasped tight. Kate cried out at the stretching invasion, but then his fangs sank into her throat, cutting off her voice.

His hips drew back and hammered home at the same time his tongue and teeth sucked a long, hot draw from her veins. The friction and the rush of blood worked together, easing her, melting her, making her hot, tense and needy all over again. Inhaling precious air, Kate surrendered to the dark ecstasy brewing between them. As soon as she did, arousal reignited within her body, erasing every care that didn't involve pleasing him over and over.

Her body was on fire, but her mind was calm. All the angst, all the restlessness, all the questioning—it disappeared the moment they became one.

She buried her hands in his hair and cradled him against her throat. "Take…take all you need," she said. He was so thick, so long, and filled her so perfectly, like a missing piece of her very soul she'd searched her whole life for and finally, miraculously, found.

As he fed from her vein, her palm erupted in a new sensation. An ache, to be sure, but this time, it was the burn of a need nearly fulfilled. Any discomfort that remained resulted solely from the incompleteness of her relief. She had no idea what any of this meant, but she knew it the way she knew she needed oxygen, or water. That was how she needed Nikolai.

*So good, Katya, so good, so good. I can't get enough.*

She gasped and awe-filled joy brought tears to her eyes. Emotions built up in her cells, barreled through her veins, until she was certain he must taste what she felt for him, what she would always feel for him, no matter what. Electricity spiraled through her and settled low in her belly, building, charging, threatening an explosive release she didn't think her body could possibly handle.

Stroke after delicious stroke brought his pelvis against her clit. She chased the maddening friction, lifting her hips, meeting his thrusts. Everywhere she reached out, her hands found hot, hard-bodied male flesh. Each breath sucked that incredible male spice—stronger and more attracting than she'd ever smelled it before—into her lungs until her toes curled against the bedding.

*Forgive me, brothers. Wanting her doesn't mean I've forgotten you.* The desperate lamentation of his thoughts was so different from her own ecstatic pleasure, the pain behind the words urged a single tear to spill from her eye.

"Oh, Nikolai," she whispered through a tight throat, her hands stroking his hair. His words confused her—what had happened to his brothers? And were those the names on his back? But that didn't stop her protectiveness over him from rearing its head. "It's okay. You're okay. I've got you."

A strangled moan rang out of him. His fangs withdrew. He laved that healing tingle over his bite before lifting his gaze and meeting her eyes. The sapphire burned with emotion.

Kate cupped his face. "I can hear you," she whispered. "I don't know how, but I could out there in that alley, and I can now."

He opened his mouth to speak, and Kate's eyes went wide.

Dark red ringed his lips, coated his tongue. A demanding, foreign hunger erupted in Kate's gut. She arched up, her mouth crashing into his, and sucked his tongue hard and deep, driven by a relentless need she'd never before experienced. It wasn't enough.

She shoved at his shoulders, and he let her flip them over. Kate's hips took over their frantic dance, rising and falling over his cock, sucking him deep inside again and again. His big hands gripped her ass, grinding her down and lifting her back up. Her body was poised on the edge of a cliff, ready to fly to the heavens, to free-fall into space. She just needed more of that red.

Clutching the hard angle of his jaws, Kate kissed him, sucked at him, whined that it wasn't enough. "What's happening to me?"

"Jesus, Katherine, talk to me."

She moaned against his lips. "I don't know, I don't know." Around the parched tightening of her throat, she swallowed, trying to ease the urgent thirst making her nearly insane. "Oh, my God, Nikolai. I want…I feel…"

His hands dug into her hair and forced their gazes to meet. "What, my sweet angel?"

"I want your blood," she said so quietly she barely heard the confession leave her own lips.

Within her clenching cunt, Nikolai's cock grew harder, thicker. "Fuuuck, Katya, I think you are…." His words died in a groan as he rolled them in a messy tangle of limbs. Her head ended up right on the edge of the bed. "Oh, please," he begged, "if there's a God above."

With a roar, her king buried his fangs into the yielding flesh of her breast and erupted within her, igniting her own spasming release. His hips jerked and pressed as his mouth sucked her boneless.

It was the most glorious, peaceful, contented moment of her life.

She had nothing to compare the experience to, of course, but she already knew nothing would ever compare to Nikolai. He'd proven himself a giving and passionate lover, and in a few short hours had turned everything she'd thought she known about herself on its head.

Their bodies calmed, their panting breaths the only sound in the room, Nikolai licked closed his bite on her breast and lifted his head to meet her gaze. Out of nowhere, a starburst of tingles exploded where their bodies were still connected. The sensation raced through her, fast and foreign, and left her insides feeling like a puzzle put together all wrong. Kate gasped and clutched to Nikolai, and only held her panic at bay by focusing on the sheer and utter joy reshaping her new lover's face.

## *Chapter Eleven*

Nikolai threw back his head and shouted a warrior's cry of victory. Katherine screamed, the nails on her right hand digging marks into his back. He grasped her left, interlocking their fingers. "Hold on, angel," he gritted out.

All at once, the sensation disappeared, and Nikolai's gaze cut to their joined hands.

Delicate black markings formed an overlapping pattern of endless square knots that wrapped around his right hand and continued onto her left. His heart expanded in his chest until he was sure it would burst.

For the love of all that was holy, he'd found his mate.

As he stared at the mating mark in awe and wonder, the dream he'd had upon waking after surgery came back in vivid detail. On some level, he'd known. Her blood in his veins had revealed the truth. No matter how much he'd fought the idea, tried to deny what he'd been feeling these last long hours, she was meant to be his. And he, hers.

"Nikolai, our hands," she whispered, eyes wide and beautiful as she lifted their hands and studied the marks. "Is that—"

"Yes. It's a mating mark, Katya, and the mark of good mating, too. See how small the knot work is?" She nodded, her gaze meeting his before returning to their hands. "The blood magic between us is strong. It tells me things I already suspected, though I resisted them, and now I know for sure."

"And what's that?" she asked, dragging those beautiful baby blues away from their joined grasp.

"That you were meant for me. In every way, you are my equal. Hell, my better. I admire you greatly, Katya, and not just for saving my life. Me, my warriors, we put you in an impossible situation, one you handled with grace and courage. I hate that we met in this time of war and chaos in my world, but there's no denying that the mere idea of you standing by my side through the good and the bad of it makes it all so damn much easier to bear."

Reaching out to stroke the hair off her face, he shifted, reminding him that he remained buried in her sweet pussy. Despite the incredible, mind-bending orgasm, his cock was still as hard as she was wet. He rocked his pelvis, slow and gentle, and hummed his approval when she released a small moan and lifted her hips to meet his.

"What happened to your brothers?" she asked, her voice so full of that compassion he already associated with her. "On your back, it's their names, isn't it?"

He nodded. "They were killed in a battle with the Soul Eaters. Six months ago. They walked into an ambush, were outnumbered, and I couldn't get to them in time."

She squeezed his hand. "Oh, Nikolai, I'm so sorry."

"Don't be. It was my fault, and I will never forgive myself."

She tilted her hips, just the littlest amount, and he couldn't remain still. The soft give-and-take of their actions, of this new round of soul-bearing lovemaking, provided as much comfort as pleasure.

"No, I don't believe that. How could it be your fault?"

He scoffed. "We call the part of the city where they died

the meat grinder, because all the abandoned buildings provide nests for the Soul Eaters. We used to play poker to see who got that sector on patrol. Kyril and Evgeny died because I bluffed my way through a hand of seven-card straight."

Swallowing roughly, she dragged the fingers on her free hand through the left side of his hair. "Is that why you refuse to wear the marks of your position?"

"I dishonored myself, Katya. As a warrior, as a ruler, by playing games with men's lives, with the lives of my only living blood relatives. I lost the right to call myself warrior, or king."

"Do you want to know what I think?"

He kissed her hand, still intertwined with his, and rocked his body into hers in an easy, gentle rhythm. "Always."

"I didn't know your brothers, of course, but I have brothers of my own. And though sometimes we want to kill each other, they have always been my greatest defenders, and the first ones to call me out when I acted like a brat. And I just think…I think your brothers wouldn't want you to turn your back on something so important, Nikolai. Kings rule, warriors fight. That's who you are, and who you should be." She licked her lips and offered a small smile. "They wouldn't want you to stop living just because they no longer do."

Her words lodged a knot in his throat. Oh, God in heaven, he was falling in love with this woman.

"Will you tell me about them sometime?" she asked, wrapping an arm around him and pulling them closer together.

"Will you stay long enough to hear all there is to tell?"

She glanced at their hands and squeezed. "Isn't that what this means?" Her pale eyes went wide and a light blush colored her cheeks. "Oh, I guess I just assumed—"

"Shh, angel, yes, it's what it can mean. It's what I *want* it to mean." His heart rate kicked up in his chest. "The mark will last three days, then disappear forever if the mating is not consummated."

He rolled onto his side and pulled Katherine to him, holding her thigh open so he could maintain their intimate connection. Even as his hips moved, he spoke words he never thought he would: "Will you be my mate, Katherine? Will you stand at my side, serve as my queen and share in my life, my blood, my immortality?" Now that he'd surrendered to the blood magic so clearly working between them, he felt the rightness of it down deep.

She gasped and grasped her throat, as if surprised. "Oh, Nikolai, are you sure? You said one night. Just one perfect night."

"Angel, I'm more than sure. I didn't dare hope for more than that. And, now…now that I have the chance for a lifetime of perfect nights, a chance at a lifetime with you, I want it more than anything I've ever wanted in my very long life."

She smiled. "I do want you, Nikolai. I truly do. I left the service of the Proffered and fled five thousand miles around the world to get away from it, I thought. But, really, something in me just knew that, had I stayed, I'd have been in the service of the wrong king. How fast this has all happened is crazy, but I want you, a life with you, all of it." She bit down on her bottom lip and rubbed hard at her throat.

Her words were like the sweetest salve, knitting up the raw edges of the psychic wounds he bore deep within. But still, he frowned. Unease stirred in his gut. Something wasn't right… "Are you okay?" He grasped her hand before she marked her neck .

She trembled. Nodded. "I…I don't…I'm *so thirsty,* Nikolai."

The world went still around him. They weren't mated.

Not yet. But every instinct told him she was hurting for the want of his blood.

Jesus. How could he make her wait until the ceremony to feed? Even if they held it at tomorrow's nightfall, that was hours away. He couldn't. He didn't want to.

An idea came to mind. Maybe he didn't have to, either.

Withdrawing from her body, he squeezed her hands. "I want to ease you, angel." He reached over the side of the bed and found his pants. From the pocket, he retrieved a small leather pouch. He returned to her and pulled the drawstring open. "Hold out your hand."

Four faceted gemstones poured out into her palm. She gasped and leaned in, turning her hand this way and that to catch the light.

He smiled, knowing just how fascinating they were to look at. "They're alexandrite. Our sacred stone. Very rare. It changes color in different lights." Just then, they appeared red with flashes of pale purple.

"Oh, they're beautiful. I've never seen anything like it. But, how will this help—"

"If you'll allow it, I would like to share a private con-summation with you. Right here. Right now. I still want the formal ceremony, Katherine. I want to stand before you and claim you as my own, but I can't watch you suffer, not when I can take the pain away."

"Oh, Nikolai, yes."

Deep satisfaction pooled in his gut. The thought of her feeding from *his* vein seduced him with the rightness of the plan. "But I need you to hold on a moment longer, if you can, because you deserve a male doing his duty, shouldering his responsibilities. And I want to be that kind of a male, for you. So—" he lay on his back next to her, his marked hand settling on his chest "—it doesn't have to be perfect, but if you could braid three of those into my hair…"

"You want *me* to do it?"

He looked at her and smiled. "Who else would I ask, my angel?"

"Okay," she whispered. As her fingers grabbed and tugged thick strands of his hair, Nikolai closed his eyes and imagined all there was to come. Her mouth filled with the flavor of his blood. The consummation mark adding color to the black of their hands. Standing within a circle of his warriors and publicly claiming her, and being claimed in return. A new blooded family. Maybe even a newling, someday. She'd brought him back to life, and now she was giving him the world.

Trembling fingers stroked over his hair. "It's done," she said, voice tight with need. "What should I do with this one?" She held the last jewel between her fingers.

He drew her down for a single slow, deep kiss, then took the stone from her. "This one is going to bring you ease." Placing a faceted edge against his throat, he pressed the jewel hard into his flesh until it felt the burn of the laceration, and then he scored a long line. Warm blood bloomed over his skin, pooled and ran down the side of his neck.

Her eyes went wide, her mouth dropped open. Her heartbeat thundered in the quiet of the room.

"What do you want, Katherine?" he said in a tight voice, his cock reawakening against his belly.

He didn't have to ask twice.

She fell over him, her mouth finding and licking the crimson stream, her body writhing and shifting until she lay atop him.

Masculine satisfaction roared out of him, pounded through

his dick, made his balls grow heavy with need. But this wasn't just about him.

Nothing would be, ever again. Thank God.

For, he was meant to serve. And while, by lineage and all that was just in the world, he had a duty to serve as king and commander, by choice he would also serve his mate, his angel, his...love. Always and first, for however many nights he had left.

Her mouth sealed over the cut and sucked the lifeblood directly from his body. Five hundred years of living and fighting all came down to this moment, and he could wait no longer. Lifting his head, he struck his fangs into the soft tendon where neck met shoulder, and completed the bonded circle of blood between them.

The first swallow of her nectar brought her thoughts into his mind.

*Oh, God, I love him I love him I love him.*

The words reassembled him into a new male, a better male, *her male*, tonight and forever. Feasting on her blood, and feeling the connection cycling through and between them, Nikolai thought in reply, *As I love you, Katherine. Now, take whatever you need, take everything, because we have all night, and I am yours. Forever.*

\* \* \* \* \*

# THE DARKLING'S SURRENDER

## LAUREN HAWKEYE

**Lauren Hawkeye** is a writer, yoga newbie, knitting aficionado and animal lover who lives in the shadows of the great Rocky Mountains of Alberta, Canada. She's older than she looks—really—and younger than she feels—most of the time—and she loves to explore the journeys that take women through life in her stories. Hawkeye's stories include erotic historical, steamy paranormal and hot contemporary.

# Chapter One

Aubrey pressed the cold metal against her heart and heard nothing.

She knew that she'd placed the stethoscope in the right place because she could feel the chill of it against her skin, right over her left breast. But there was no comforting *thump-thump* of her heart, no *whoosh* of warm blood as it moved through her veins.

She'd played this game before, as a resident at the local hospital. *Thump*—the stethoscope found her warm, human heartbeat. Remove the metal, remove the sound.

Now it didn't matter if the device was against her skin or not. All that she could hear either way was silence.

Yet the silence was different with her new undead senses. It had a sound, of sorts—a never-ending reverberation, as if she could hear the very molecules of the air vibrating.

It wouldn't have surprised her. She could hear everything else, from the tiny, scurrying steps of the spider creeping up her slick bathroom wall, to the beating heart of the human walking by outside.

Bored of the game, Aubrey let the stethoscope fall to the floor. Listlessly she pulled herself to a sitting position, and she could have counted the threads in her sheets, so sensitive was her skin against them.

They were the same sheets that she'd had two weeks earlier, when she'd still been alive. They covered the same bed that she'd slept in, which sat in the bedroom she'd had for over a year.

Not that she'd actually slept in the bed that much. She'd been almost finished her residency at the local hospital, had almost been fully accredited. Dr. Aubrey Hart—she'd had the title already, but hadn't felt like a real doctor, not yet. She'd been so looking forward to it.

Instead, she was dead. Undead.

Undead and starving.

Malcolm, her maker, had come by earlier that evening. He'd peeled the covers away from her newly translucent skin and eyed her with disgust.

*Get up,* he'd told her. *Go out. Feed. I won't bring you blood any longer.*

Aubrey knew that he wasn't lying, just as she knew that he wasn't sorry he'd turned her. To be sorry he needed a conscience, and that was something that Malcolm didn't have.

Not all vampires were jerks, just like not all humans were good.

It was her luck that she'd been turned by an asshole.

His voice berated her as she sat there, staring blankly across the room at the mirror. The woman that looked back at her was familiar, and also looked like a complete stranger.

Gone was her golden tan, the one vice that she'd allowed herself throughout med school. In its place was skin the color of milky cream, threaded through with a webbing of amethyst veins.

Her hair was still flaxen, and her eyes still sky blue. But both were brighter and better now, despite how worn she felt.

It was the allure that came with her new life, or so Malcolm had said. She now had the power to draw the unsuspecting in, to draw them close, without them ever knowing why.

Not to mention that she was very nearly gorgeous. She would have considered herself plain at best, before.

But even with all these advantages, she was unable to adjust. She'd hidden in her bed for weeks, poking her head from beneath the sheet only when Malcolm visited. He'd taped aluminum foil over her window the second day, when streaming sunlight had burned a vivid ruby stripe across her arm.

She hadn't known any better.

He'd also brought bags of blood, viscous cardinal-red blood, and had pinched her nose closed and poured it down her throat when she'd rebelled at the thought of drinking. He'd awakened the hunger, and now she had two choices—feed or die.

She still wasn't sure which she'd choose.

She had to choose before sundown tonight, or she'd grow too sick, too weak to make the choice. And if Malcolm didn't come back—and she'd believed him when he'd said he wouldn't—she'd slowly wither away to nothingness.

Aubrey's new, sharply tuned eyes fell on the framed photo that sat on her dresser across the room. Though the gleam of the brassy frame was brighter than ever before, and though the grain of the dark wood swirled in an intricate dance that she'd never before noticed, it was the girl in the photo that caught her attention. With a mortarboard on her head, and pale hair falling in a curtain around rosy cheeks, the young woman looked fierce—ready to take on the world.

Aubrey felt that that young woman was a million miles away from where she was right now.

But the longer she looked at the picture, the more she could feel a sense of dissatisfaction growing. She'd sat here for nearly two weeks, stewing in anger and misery. Anger at Malcolm for thrusting this life, or unlife, upon her when she hadn't wanted it. For stopping her dead when she'd almost achieved her dream.

The girl in the picture would have simply crinkled her nose and crunched the anger and misery into submission if they stood in the way of her goals.

Aubrey wondered if she had enough gumption left to channel that girl back into her empty shell.

Suddenly wanting a closer look, Aubrey pushed back the sheets that had tangled themselves around her legs. Shifting her weight, she placed one foot flat on the prickly carpet, then the other. Then she tried to put her weight on those feet for the first time in two weeks.

She wobbled and nearly fell. And it was the struggle that awoke some of the old Aubrey in her.

If she was going to wither and die, it would be by her choice. Not because Malcolm had made choices for her.

She hadn't sampled this new existence yet, hadn't seen if she could bear it.

Tonight, she decided, she would. She would hunt. She would drink.

*Then* she could make an informed decision.

Though she'd pretended not to listen, Malcolm's words *had* actually sunk through the undulating waves of grief, when he'd bothered to talk at all, that was. He'd given her the most cursory of explanations of her new life, the minimum that he could get away with without setting some council down upon his head for abandoning a newborn.

As she walked down the street, the soles of her boots clicking decisively on the wet pavement, Aubrey was suddenly grateful for the bits of information that he *had* imparted.

*Go hunting someplace where you won't know anyone*, he'd told her. It was harder to take what you needed when the victims were a part of your old life. Bite from the neck, the wrist or the inner thigh. That was where the blood flowed hot and rich.

And most important, don't drink too much from one person. If you drank too much, the person either died or was turned. And then either the humans fell into an uproar, or you were responsible for a newborn vampire.

Like many a person who'd had an unplanned child and hadn't had the grace to accept it as a gift, Malcolm had been disgusted with the responsibility of an infant. Aubrey had had no idea that he was a vampire—she'd thought he was simply the man who made her mocha latte at the coffee shop she frequented every evening. His shift had ended; he'd asked if he could walk her to the hospital. Though she had been reserved around many people, Malcolm had been both unassuming and sweet, and she'd enjoyed his company—at least, she had until he'd bared his fangs at her.

He hadn't meant to turn her—he'd simply taken too much from her wrist

He'd made it quite clear to Aubrey that siring a newborn was the worst thing that could happen in a vampire's life.

Like a child feeling the sting of rejection from a parent, it had hurt Aubrey to hear it. And perhaps that was why she decided to disobey the first of her maker's orders.

Instead of going to a place she'd never been, she went to the hospital where she'd been a resident. With every step closer that she took, the weaker she felt.

The hospital smelled of blood. Old blood, new blood. The bittersweet smell saturated the area for the entire city block, and Aubrey inhaled deliberately to draw the scent in.

It made her thirsty. It made her hungry. It made her want.

The thirst warred with longing as she stepped close to the automatic double doors of the front entrance. She'd spent so many hours there, closed inside the building where the smell of acrid antiseptic tried to wash away the delicious tang of blood. She'd spent more time here than she had in her own home.

The snaking hallways, the small, windowless rooms. She knew them all.

The people, too. So many familiar faces. It was comforting, a soothing balm on her grieving soul.

If she even had a soul anymore.

But surely amongst all the new faces that appeared in Admitting and the emergency room, she could find someone she didn't know. Someone whose scent appealed to her in the way that cinnamon rolls and freshly brewed coffee once had.

Maybe she could even find someone who was sick, sick enough that their fate was already decided. Then it wouldn't matter how much blood she took. She could drink and drink, drink until this dreadful, ever-growing thirst was finally assuaged.

"Dr. Hart!" Slowly, Aubrey turned her head. She'd just reached the front doors of the hospital, and the fluorescent lights that were placed around the perimeter of the musty brick building cast everything with a minty-green tinge.

A man sat on a dilapidated wooden bench that was set back into the grass. Huge goose bumps prickled his skin from the kiss of the chilly breeze—he wore nothing overtop his flimsy hospital gown. An intravenous line carried something that smelled sickly sweet to his hand from a clear plastic bag, and Aubrey could smell the blood that was crusted around the tiny wound.

She recognized the man, but it was as if she was seeing someone she'd once known a very long time ago. He had been a patient that she'd tended a few times, and she couldn't remember his name.

She stared at him openly, fascinated with the changes in him. Or rather the changes in how her new eyes saw him, she supposed.

More than anything, she saw the flow of blood through his veins, moving with every beat of his heart.

"Dr. Hart?" The man lowered his contraband cigarette from his mouth slowly, and Aubrey admired the beautiful tangerine ember of the lit end. She cocked her head curiously, studying the man as he studied her.

He seemed to be growing uncertain, and slightly embarrassed with it.

"I'm sorry." He stubbed out the cigarette on the wood of the bench with nervous fingers, the lit stick burning a round circle into the grain. "You just…you look like someone that I haven't seen in a while."

Aubrey nodded. The mirror had told her how different that she now looked, but it was still surprising to have it confirmed. But more curious was the knowledge that she could bite this man here, could drink from him, and it would be easier than anything she'd ever done in her life. He was here, waiting, like a gift.

But she didn't want him. Something in the smell that wafted off of him was slightly distasteful to her senses, and she knew that she couldn't—wouldn't—drink from him.

Dismissing the man, she turned, walked away from the entrance to the hospital and instead found herself compelled to walk around the side of the building to the poorly lit loading dock where the staff of the hospital made their way to and from work.

The concrete beneath her shoes was damp, and its dark

tone seemed to swallow the flickering robin's-egg light of the fluorescents and the silvery gleam cast by the moon.

She liked how things looked through her new eyes.

More, she liked the smell that intensified with every step that she took. There was someone back here. Someone who smelled like chocolate, rich, silky chocolate.

She could hear the steady thump of the person's heart, and the quiet fizz of that chocolate-infused blood as it was pumped through iridescent veins. She could already taste it, that first taste of blood from the vein, and she wanted it like she'd never wanted the disgusting, congealed sludge contained in the plastic bags that Malcolm had brought her.

"Could I get a hand with this?" The voice attached to the cocoa smell was irritable. Aubrey was taken aback.

She recognized the voice. Unlike the fog that had clouded her memory of the man at the front entrance, this remembrance was like a scalpel through soft flesh.

"Gavin Thibodeau." She didn't realize she'd spoken aloud until the man himself whipped around and squinted through the night in her direction.

"Hart?" His voice sounded like metal shards, scrubbing away at the quiet din of background noise of a hospital at night. "What the hell are you doing lurking around in the shadows? And where have you been? Do you know—"

He cut himself off as Aubrey stepped closer, and was more easily seen. The last time she'd seen him, her locks had been lank and habitually in a long tail, and she'd never bothered with makeup or jewelry. There had been no point when she wore scrubs all the time.

Now she was vivid, a colour image in a black-and-white picture, something that she had made an effort to accentuate, though she wasn't entirely certain why.

She felt like a different person. She was a different person, one who could attract someone like Gavin.

Yes, she could attract him. She could have Gavin if she wanted him.

She found that she did. That, at least, hadn't changed when she'd died.

"Hello." Even her voice sounded different than it had. It was warm and smooth, like thick, creamy honey.

Gavin—she'd never thought of him as Dr. Thibodeau, though she'd always called him that to his face—had been her preceptor, her supervisor, at the hospital. He was tall, had spiky hair the color of espresso and eyes of glacial ice. A silver bar pierced his eyebrow, one that he took out when on duty, and she knew from the clothes that he wore to and from work that when not in scrubs he preferred skinny, low-riding denim, studded belts and fitted T-shirts.

She'd had a yen for him even before she could smell the intoxicating aroma of his blood.

"Where the devil have you been, Hart? It's bloody unprofessional to just take off without a word. You've screwed up your residency but good." Aubrey watched as he raked a hand with long, skilled surgeon's fingers through the gelled spikes of his hair. He was wearing a pair of those skinny jeans and a long-sleeved black T-shirt.

Her mouth watered, and she felt the sting of her fangs as they began to descend. They pricked her tongue, and she tasted the salt of her own blood, but it held no appeal.

It lacked the essence of life that Gavin's did.

She wanted his blood, wanted it spread out on her tongue, in her mouth and down her throat.

She wanted more than that, too. She could feel arousal spreading over her like the warmth of the sun that she could no longer worship. It was a sensation that she was familiar with, only intensified with her new senses.

"I've been sick." She took a slow, deliberate step toward him, and then another, and saw his pupils dilate and his nostrils flare just the tiniest bit.

Interesting. She hadn't used any of her new vampire allure—at least she didn't think she had. Malcolm had told her that it was a force that had to be released consciously, but who knew if he'd been telling the truth.

"You work in a hospital." The tempo of Gavin's heartbeat quickened, and it sounded musical to Aubrey's ears. "If you were seriously sick, you should have come here."

"I couldn't go to a hospital." Aubrey stepped closer still. She understood now what Malcolm had meant when he'd spoken of hunting. She was the predator, and she'd locked in on her prey. "It wasn't like that."

Gavin's stare fell to her lips, which she licked. His voice was shaky as it uttered his next words.

"What was it like, then? Do tell." She liked that he hadn't lost his sarcasm, even in the face of his confusion. And he was confused, she knew that, even before she'd done anything more than talk.

She was different now. She was confident, she was sexy. She was beautiful.

She was going to have what she'd been dreaming about for months. And she was going to have blood, too.

"Do you really want to talk?" Closing the rest of the distance between them, Aubrey leaned in a calculated inch. If she'd had any breath left, she would have been able to exhale on his lips and have him feel the warmth.

"You're…different." Gavin closed his eyes and breathed in deeply. "What's different?"

Aubrey placed her rear at the edge of the van floor that

was now at her back. Gavin had been moving a box, it looked like. A large, heavy box. She pushed at it with a hand, and it slid back into the vehicle as if it was empty.

She saw Gavin blink at the ease with which she moved the item, when he'd grumpily asked for help...and he was no weakling. She'd seen the muscles of his arms under the short sleeves of his scrub shirt. He was lean, but he was also ripped.

Leaning backward so that her weight rested on her elbows, Aubrey stared at Gavin, unabashed. "I've had to reevaluate my life. Being sick...changed me. And now all I can do is work with what's left."

She wanted him to come closer. Wanted him to touch her. She could've just grabbed him and torn her teeth into his neck, but she wanted him to come to her willingly.

She wouldn't do this, wouldn't do any of this, unless he was at least partially willing. Which was probably why Malcolm had told her to hunt only those who were strangers to her.

It was too late. She'd caught the scent of her prey, and like a decadent fudge brownie to a dieter, she could think of nothing else.

She would have him inside her, just as she'd wanted him for months. And while he was inside her, she would taste his blood. She'd drink, she'd grow strong.

And then she'd make him forget that any of it had ever happened.

Gavin was horribly confused. Dr. Aubrey Hart, the resident who'd abruptly dropped out of her residency weeks earlier, was lying against the back of his van with a confidence he'd never seen even a hint of before, and her body language was screaming at him to take what he'd tried not to think about taking from her before.

He wasn't sure that he believed that she'd been sick. It was more like she'd had a complete personality transplant. But if he'd found her skittishness cute before—in a forbidden, can't-ever-act-on-it kind of way—he found her new seduce-me attitude sexy as hell.

He liked strong women. They were difficult, they were demanding and they were a hell of a lot work, true, but they also challenged him.

What kind of man would he be if he wanted some sweet young thing who would just acquiesce to his every desire?

That was why he'd never understood his attraction to Aubrey. But now, with the memory of the sweet girl and the reality of the new woman in front of him, the two swirled into a delicious mix that made his mouth water and his cock thicken. Like whiskey and beer, the combination seemed as if it shouldn't work.

But oh, how it did.

But something still seemed off to him, and that something had him holding back from simply climbing into the back of the van with her and covering her body with his own.

"We should go inside and discuss your residency." He tore his eyes away from the curves clad in tight denim and reminded himself that he was her preceptor. This was not appropriate.

His glands screamed at him in response, and his hands actually twitched with the need to put them on her, to feel her skin.

She simply blinked, continuing to watch him brazenly with that direct stare. He decided that that was what had him unnerved.

The Aubrey Hart that he knew rarely made eye contact with anybody.

"Come here." He was completely taken aback at the words

that left her mouth, and even more so at the subtle movement that accompanied them.

As she spoke, she sat up slowly and at the same time opened her legs, just the slightest bit.

There was no doubt in his mind as to what she was getting at. But he didn't know how to respond.

He wanted her. Oh, he absolutely did. This newfound brazenness that she was displaying all but made him drool. But at the same time, he was used to being the aggressor. The initiator. Part of him fought against the idea of being reeled in with suggestive body language and a sexy stare.

Not to mention that he was her boss. Even if that fact was rapidly fading away.

He found himself taking a step closer to the van—and Aubrey—and then one more.

Could he do this? He wanted her so badly that he didn't feel like he had a choice. Was it possible that she wanted him as much? Or was this some strange kind of power play?

His cock pressed painfully against the zipper of his jeans, demanding an answer.

He made up his mind.

"No. *You* come *here*."

## Chapter Two

Aubrey was so thirsty that she could barely speak. But she managed to murmur assent over the thickness in her throat as she slithered down from the van and moved to where Gavin stood.

This was it. She was about to make her first kill—in figurative terms, of course. She wouldn't *kill* him, she'd simply wipe his memory after it was all done.

But the thought of killing, of how very easily she could accidentally take his life, brought feelings from her old life foaming to the surface.

This was *Gavin*. Dr. Thibodeau. The hard-assed preceptor who nonetheless had comforted her when she'd lost her first patient. The one who was always on her case to be better, because he knew she could be.

The one with the smile that made her weak in the knees.

If she could have walked away at that point, she would have. But she was too far gone, both with the thirst and with lust.

She had to have him, and so she snugged her body up against his own. She could feel the outline of his arousal pressing against the flesh of her belly, and it pleased her immensely that she hadn't yet had to use her new vampire allure.

At least, she didn't think she'd used it. Again, she couldn't be sure.

"Aubrey." Her name falling from his lips sounded like a curse, and she savored it as well as the rich smell of his blood. She'd never heard him say her name before, not her first name. It had always been "Dr. Hart," and it was usually barked at her in disgruntled tones.

She shushed him, the soft *shh* slithering into the night. His frame was tense as she closed the last whisper of space between them, tense with what she thought was confusion.

Tilting her head up, she let their gazes meet. She'd been intending to try using some of her new allure, but instead found herself feeling weak in the knees. Though she assured herself that it was just due to the hunger—though lust for Gavin made her hunger fade from the forefront of her mind, she was starving—in her gut she knew that it was likely because of the intensity in his icy-blue eyes.

The roles had suddenly been reversed, and she found it ridiculously exciting as, in the time it would have taken to snap her fingers, Gavin clasped his strong hands at her waist, lifted her an inch off the ground and claimed her mouth with his own.

The thirst grew exponentially, and at the same time was the furthest thing from her mind as she found herself being seduced, instead of the other way around. Gavin's kiss—the first kiss she'd had in over two years—was hot and possessive. It had taken more convincing than she'd thought she'd need to get him here, but now that he'd acquiesced, she felt as if she was the one about to be taken.

His tongue teased her lips until she parted them. It took conscious effort not to let her new fangs extend. She could have bitten him right then, she knew that, but lust was over-powering thirst. She wanted him, all of him, before she drank.

She felt a twinge of unease at the thought of drinking from him now, of stealing his life force without his knowledge, but she shoved it away, pushed it down, and let herself be carried away by the rising tide of pleasure.

Gavin slowly lowered her back to the ground, his hands sliding from her waist to splay over her back. He was hot against her flesh, which now tended to be cool. It wasn't an unpleasant coolness, but the contrast of his heat was delicious.

"Van," she murmured against his lips. At his silence she drew back far enough to look at his face. He'd cocked an eyebrow in amusement at her bossiness, which she knew was a far cry from the woman she'd been before.

Well, this Aubrey was just fine with saying what she wanted. She tugged backward, and with that same look of amusement on his face Gavin allowed himself to be pulled back toward his vehicle.

The amusement was burned from his expression in a blast of heat when Aubrey hitched herself up so that her ass rested against the edge of the open van, just as she'd been earlier, and wrapped her legs around Gavin's hips.

They both exhaled at the contact, though Aubrey's was an expression made of habit, not need for air. His now-rigid cock was pressed against her soft center, denim straining against denim.

It was the moment of no return. She knew it and he knew it. Gavin's breathing was ragged, and Aubrey went still with the intensity of the moment as they both contemplated what they were about to do.

Then they lunged.

Gavin laid her back on the floor of the van, her legs still wrapped tightly around his waist. As he leaned forward, Aubrey thought that her mouth was about to be claimed again, but instead Gavin placed the lightest of kisses on her lips, then on each cheekbone and her forehead. Just the slightest brush of lips, a butterfly touch.

When he stared into her eyes she felt as if he could read all her secrets. She'd always felt like that, but now she actually had secrets. She squirmed—even though she was so thirsty, so full of need.

The squirming only served to press their flesh together in interesting ways. Gavin hissed, and Aubrey closed her eyes and relished the sensation.

Then she reached up and drew him down until he lay on top of her.

She'd had enough of the play, of establishing dominance. She'd come here for a purpose, and she needed to recall Malcolm's advice. Though she hadn't heeded his warning, and had chosen to prey on someone she knew, she needed to finish what she'd come here for.

Her morality was having issues with using him, but she assumed that she would get past the feelings. Malcolm hadn't told her one way or another, but judging by him, vampires were selfish creatures who existed only to support their own needs and desires.

Gavin moved his lips from her face and slid them down over the pulsing cord in her neck. She felt her fangs prick at her lower lip as she pictured doing the same to him, right before she bit.

Not yet. Oh, not yet. She wanted more, much more from him first.

His tongue flicked out and tasted the hollow in her collarbone then ran a seam over to the edge of her tight T-shirt. His lips stayed pressed there as his hand moved tentatively from the floor of the van, where it had been splayed, to toy with the hem of that same shirt.

The old Aubrey would have frozen at the thought of Dr. Gavin Thibodeau running his hand up under her shirt. *This* Aubrey took her own hand and guided his hand up to cover the cotton of her bra, then moved her hand back to tangle with the other in his liquorice-black hair.

She heard Gavin groan as his hand found the mound of her breast. She felt the sound vibrate through her.

Tilting her head back, she let the white gold of her hair fall in a stream down her back. She rocked her hips forward, and Gavin's hand squeezed in reflex, massaging the tender flesh of her breast.

She couldn't handle it anymore. Her new senses were clearer than they'd ever been, and every touch of Gavin's fingers on her flesh made her skin sing. It caused need to churn greedily in her gut, and the cleft between her legs to pulse with heat.

Moving her hands from his hair to his shoulders, she tugged at the long-sleeved black cotton that covered his torso. She meant to simply tug the shirt up and over his head, but her tug ripped the shirt in a jagged seam down the back. Gavin looked back, astonished.

Making sure that her teeth were again fully retracted, she bared them like a predatory cat.

After a long moment in which Gavin simply blinked at her, stunned, he grinned with his trademark sexy smile that had always driven her crazy.

Then he took the hand covering her breast and moved it to the collar of her shirt. With another grin and a flash of his own teeth, he twisted his wrist until her own shirt split. Something dangerous seemed to pulse in the air, and Aubrey breathed in its darkness.

She'd found a match for her new self here, though she never would have guessed it. Whatever she gave to Gavin, whatever she took, she knew that he would match it. It was a relief.

She wouldn't hurt him. She wasn't sure that she could. He was just as strong as she, though he was still just a human.

The hunt was on, and she was no longer completely certain that she was the predator and he the prey.

Like animals mating, they clashed their bodies together. Aubrey pulled open the fly of Gavin's jeans with one hand, pushing them down until all he wore were the tattered remains of his shirt. He undid the button of her denim with only slightly less speed, and as soon as the pants were past her hips he moved his kiss to her stomach and then down.

Her panties were black cotton, simple and practical. But they felt like the most decadent of lingerie when Gavin took the side of them in his teeth and tugged until the flimsy fabric snapped.

Aubrey felt the need begin to rise and coil in her veins when he moved his teeth, his lips to the hot, wet, needy area between her legs.

He kissed her clit, and she nearly screamed at the contact. But instead, she bit her lip, tasted the blood and stayed as silent as he as he began to slowly stroke her with his tongue.

If she'd still been the mousy Dr. Hart, she wouldn't have been able to handle the situation. He clearly had some experience with this. But all she could do at the moment, all she wanted to do, was enjoy.

An impending orgasm began to well up in her belly, making her muscles begin to shake. When Gavin saw that she was about to unravel, he slid his lips from between her legs and up her naked torso in one smooth movement.

"Bastard." She cussed at him in a heated whisper as the need receded the slightest bit.

He leveled her with that cocky smile again, then pulled her bra down so that her breasts were bared to the night air and to his touch.

His hot mouth sucked in her erect nipple to be teased with a circling tongue. She ran her fingers through his hair again, pulling at the thick strands when the sensations became too much to bear.

When he crawled the rest of the way into the van, it put some momentary space between them. Aubrey took advantage of it by reaching between them and wrapping her fingers around his cock.

He hissed in a breath, and Aubrey held in a chuckle as he struggled, clearly torn between enjoying the sensation of her fingers on his erection and closing the door behind them.

Finally he wrenched himself away from her touch and, fumbling with the handle, pulled the door closed. The seats in the back of the vehicle had been removed, but even still it was close quarters.

Aubrey liked it. There was no escaping.

It seemed escaping was the last thing that Gavin had on his mind.

"That wasn't very nice of you," he murmured into her ear as he flipped her over onto her stomach. She let him, both because she was curious and because something about the commanding way he spoke made her feel as if she had no choice.

"What wasn't? This?" Crawling to her knees, she pressed the globes of her ass into his pelvis, gasping at the feel of his erection as it brushed her skin.

"Yes." Gavin placed his hands on her shoulders, then slid them down her arms until his surgeon fingers braceleted her wrists. "That. Now I'll have to teach you a lesson."

Aubrey was amused. He had no idea that she was past lessons. She was the one in control here, even if he didn't know it.

She was proven wrong when a moment later she found her hands bound together with some kind of cord.

"Huh." She assumed she could break the cord, could get free…if she wanted to.

She found that she didn't. She was under his control, just the control of his raw will.

It was the hottest thing she'd ever encountered.

Or the second hottest, she amended when her sight was suddenly gone. Soft cotton was wrapped around her eyes, and she concluded that he'd used his torn T-shirt as a blindfold.

It smelled of him, was infused with him.

With her sight and her ability to touch gone, the thirst again came to the forefront. It warred with the need for Gavin to stop teasing and to hilt himself inside her. She couldn't have said which she wanted more.

"There." Gavin's breath was hot as he whispered into her ear. "Now you'll behave."

Aubrey would never have guessed that Gavin had a kinky streak.

She never would have guessed that she did either. And she wasn't about to admit how much she liked being restrained, being controlled.

But she couldn't hide her arousal when he bent her over the box that she'd moved earlier, then cupped her ass in his hands and squeezed.

"Is this what you want, Aubrey?" She remained silent.

But it was. This, and his blood.

Then he pressed his cock against her entrance, and all she wanted was him.

It was delicious torture to have him there, right where she

wanted him, yet not. She rotated her hips, and felt him quiver against her in response.

"Now." He spoke as he thrust forward. She would have gasped had she needed to as he buried himself inside her tight, wet channel. She heard him hiss air in through his teeth as she closed around him, and when he began to move, she understood what it was like to be taken completely.

She braced her knees on the rough rugs that covered the floor of his van, holding herself as still as she could so that he could move inside her with all his force. Being so physically restrained excited her, as did the knowledge that when it was all over she would bite, she would taste him in her mouth, down her throat.

She only wished that he would enjoy it as much as she would.

The tidal wave of the orgasm she'd been denied earlier began again to rise. They rocked together, his front pressed to her back, and she felt full for the first time since she'd been turned.

She sensed that he was close to coming when his breath began to hitch and his thrusts became uneven. Though she could have ripped herself free, she began to struggle, just enough that he slowed his movement long enough to untie her wrists and remove her blindfold.

Though she hated the loss of the restraints, she needed her hands—and her eyes—for what she was about to do. Rolling and maneuvering until she had moved Gavin to the floor of the van, she picked up the rocking where he'd left off.

The pleasure began to spiral in her, and she knew that this time there was no holding it back. His movements told her that he, too, was on the cusp.

Throwing back her head, letting her hair fall down her back, she let both her desires take over. She slowly lowered her incisors until they were fully extended, then dipped her head back down until her face was right in front of Gavin's.

Lost in his impending orgasm, he opened his eyes hazily only when her lips brushed his. He took in the sight of her new teeth slowly, as if the vision was filtering through a dream.

Then she placed her lips just under his left ear and took her first bite of live flesh.

Beneath her he jerked. With the first taste of red chocolate on her tongue, she licked her lips and moaned. She moved back until she could see his face, and intended to try to use some of her allure to make it pleasurable for him, too.

But though he looked stunned, he also looked as if he was still as aroused as he'd been before she'd bitten. She felt his cock jerk inside her, and he groaned, and it seemed like a sound of pleasure.

He liked it. He was scared, but the fear was mixed with desire.

It undid her.

Lowering her lips, she again sank her extended teeth into his neck. Sealing her lips around the bite, she suckled his neck as she would have his cock.

She felt his life force enter her body, surging through her veins and restoring her vitality. She felt alive in a way she never had after drinking from one of the sealed plastic bags that Malcolm had brought her.

This was magical. This was *life*.

As her belly filled, pleasure spilled over. She released Gavin's neck, arched her back and rode them both into climax. She stayed silent, but drank up the noises of shock and pleasure that Gavin let spill from his lips. When he was finally silent, she ceased movement and revelled in the sensation.

When she again opened her eyes, she saw Gavin staring up at her with that same shock and pleasure, but also with something that she couldn't quite read.

Was it fear? It should have been fear.

"Thank you." Though it had been easier than she'd ever imagined to stop drinking from him before she took too much, what she had to do next wasn't at all.

She had to wipe his memory. She knew she had to. She couldn't let him remember that she'd bitten him, that she was no longer the girl he'd known.

She was remarkably sad that he wouldn't remember the girl she now was, though. Placing a hand on either side of his head, she caught him in her stare, hoping that she was doing it right. Without breaking eye contact, she willed from the bottom of her soul that he not remember anything from tonight. His muscles tensed against the invasion into his mind, and when he relaxed she knew that she'd done it.

Easing back, she quickly slid back into her jeans and tied her torn bra between her breasts. She shoved her torn panties in her pocket.

He'd be confused when he came to, and would surely wonder why he was naked in the back of his van.

But he wouldn't know, wouldn't have a clue. He'd have bite marks, marks that looked like a vamp bite, but the average human didn't believe in vampires. He'd find something in the ordinary workings of the world to explain it away.

As Aubrey slid from the van and eased the door shut behind her, her veins were full of new life, her thirst slaked and her limbs weak from sex.

But as the coolness of the night air stole Gavin's heat away from her skin, it was harder than she could have imagined to walk away.

Malcolm had been right. She should have chosen someone

she didn't know. Her feelings were now invested in something that the other person would never remember.

Damn it.

# Chapter Three

The pounding on the door sounded like an entire army practicing drills in her head. Aubrey surfaced slowly from the depths of her sleep, as if floating gradually to the top of a pond after being submerged for hours.

Vampire sleep was far deeper than that of a human. It took time to rouse a vampire out of it, particularly when rays of light were still shining in the sky, though the clock on her bedside table told her that they were about to fade again.

She'd slept the entire day.

As Aubrey blinked to clear the cobwebs of lingering dreams—and yes, she'd discovered that vampires *did* dream—from her mind she thought grumpily that the person thumping at the door must have been a giant if they were able to wake her from a sound sleep.

She padded quietly on her bare feet to peep through the Judas hole.

She'd hadn't yet learned not to question her sharpened eyesight, so she blinked deliberately to get a second look at what she saw through the glass. Gavin stood on the other side of her door, and she was at a loss about what to do.

"Um… just a minute." He would be here to discuss her

residency, she knew, because he wouldn't remember anything of their encounter the night before. No, he wouldn't remember a thing, never mind that it was burned into her mind forever.

She remembered at the last minute to grab some pants before she opened the door. It seemed silly, since he'd seen all of her the night before—tasted all of her, too—but again, he wouldn't remember.

The door screeched as she wrenched it open. After the initial tug to get it past its swollen frame she swung the heavy wooden slab back, revealing herself to Gavin slowly.

"Yes?" She attempted a smile, attempted to look normal. And sick, since that was her story.

The scent of his blood hit her again, and it was all the more potent because she now knew what it tasted like. She could hear it rushing through his veins, and was happier than she should have been to make out his pulse picking up at the sight of her.

Gavin swept his gaze very obviously up her body and down, lingering on the peaks of her nipples, evident through the thin cotton of her shirt.

He shifted a bit, his pulse skipping a beat, and Aubrey was startled that she was having any kind of effect on him. As far as he was concerned, she was still the mousy little resident.

She hadn't known he'd been attracted to her then.

"After last night, I don't think I count as company." Without waiting for an invitation, Gavin pushed past her, letting himself into her apartment.

She stared after him, confused.

He remembered last night?

"I…I'm not sure what you mean." Gone was the confidence of the night before. In the light of day, and with the brusqueness in his tone, Aubrey again felt like a resident with her preceptor.

Except that she wanted to impale him with her fangs while he thrust into her with his cock.

She shook her head to clear it of that memory as she followed him quickly to a tiny living area, where he began pacing .

"I think you do." He wheeled around to glare at her when she approached him from behind. The marks she'd made in his neck were virulent red, and made her thirsty.

With no idea how she should respond, she decided to be cautious and play dumb.

"Why don't you just ask instead of hinting?" she asked once she'd sat down.

Gavin snorted, and she realized that, instead of being scared of his sarcasm and temper the way she's once been, she was turned on by his contrariness, and also by the way he looked with his dark hair all rumpled from sleep.

"That's how we're going to play it, then? Fine." He approached her—*stalked* her might have been the better word—placing an arm on either side of her and leaning in, effectively caging her in place.

"Last night we had the best sex that, to my surprise, I've ever had. Then I blacked out and woke up naked in the back of my van, with two nasty puncture wounds on my neck."

Aubrey squirmed at his words. When he put it that way, it sounded as if only an idiot wouldn't figure out what had happened. Though she still wasn't sure why he would have remembered the sex.

Though it *had* been pretty memorable, and she was more pleased that he'd thought so, too, than upset that her mojo hadn't worked.

"And then. And then!" Gavin moved forward until his nose was nearly pressed against her own. "After I stumbled home, confused and disoriented, I discovered a little something extra that you'd left me. I spent the entire night and day in disbelief, but it's real. And you are the common denominator in it all."

Aubrey licked her lips. He was so close, and she could see the pulse throbbing in his neck faster than usual because of his agitation.

"Are you listening?" He sounded every bit like her preceptor and nothing like the lover who had bound her hands and caressed her body.

"How could I not be?" Aubrey tried to sound flippant, but she was focused on his neck. She wanted to lick it, to kiss it. To drink from it.

"Don't you want to know what that little something extra is?" His lips were now just a whisper away from her own. She wanted to close the distance, but didn't think that he would respond too kindly to it, not in his current mood.

"Do tell." She hoped her words didn't sound nearly as unsure as she felt.

His lips brushed her own, just a whispering tease before he backed a full five paces away. She nearly groaned aloud at the tiny taste, which she knew he'd done just to be cruel.

"What is *this*?" With her vision on his face, it took her a minute to notice what he was talking about. But he'd thrust his hands away from his body, holding them palms up, and when she finally looked at them she felt her jaw drop.

They were glowing. Blue light, sapphire blue, deep-sea blue, emanated from his flesh, tinting the air around him the color of the sky.

"What? What?" Aubrey moved to her feet in a movement so swift she saw Gavin blink.

"Oh, that's not all, sweetheart." She ground her teeth together at the endearment, which she knew was not used because he felt like being sweet. But her irritation was forgotten in the next minute.

Pulling a small blade from the pocket of his jeans, Gavin slashed a shallow cut across the underside of his forearm. Aubrey couldn't help the moan from escaping her lips when the scent of the hot, fresh red blood hit her nostrils.

She watched, mesmerized, as a fat drop trickled over Gavin's pale skin and fell wetly to the ground, where it tinted her carpet carmine.

Gavin took his free hand and passed it slowly over the cut, an inch above it.

When his arm again came into view, the skin was smooth and unblemished. There was no cut.

"How did you do that?" She nearly forgot about his blood as she stared in wonderment. She looked up into his face, forgetting that she was now supernatural herself. "What are you?"

He was in her face again before she could blink. How had he moved that fast? He cupped his hands under her elbows and lifted her until their faces were level.

"That's what you need to tell me, Aubrey." His stare was fierce. "I was a normal man last night. Just a normal man. Then you came along, and now I don't know what has happened to me."

"I…" Her voice trailed off. She'd been about to repeat her story, that she'd just been sick, but the look on her face told her that he wasn't going to buy in, no way.

And she wanted to tell him the truth. If she'd done this, though she had no idea how she could have, then she owed him at least that much.

"You'd better sit down. Which involves, ah, putting me down." He did, slowly, and she had no question that he was in control of the moment.

How was it that she was now a vampire, was now stronger than ever before, and still she acquiesced to him?

He stalked past her and sat, slowly, on the couch. Resting his elbows on his knees, he leaned forward and stared at the floor. "Talk."

She sat beside him gingerly, not just because he was in a volatile mood but because she wanted so very badly to taste him.

"When I said I'd been sick, it wasn't a lie." This seemed like the safest place to start. "But it wasn't anything…it wasn't a human sickness."

"You're a vampire." His words were flat, and though somehow she knew that he'd guessed, she still felt compelled to ask him how he'd known.

"The marks on my neck were my first clue." His laugh had no trace of humour. "And I've always wondered if they were real. We get a lot of victims into emergency with trauma to the neck, the wrist. The inner thigh. All places with major arteries."

Arteries. Veins. Blood. She was thirsty. She wondered if Malcolm had caved and left any plastic bags of it in the fridge. The bags of congealed liquid were revolting, especially now that she'd tasted it hot and from the vein, but it would satisfy her hunger.

"Yes. I'm a vampire. I was sick because I'd been turned." She held out her hands, which were pale and cool, the skin nearly translucent.

"Did you turn me?" Gavin's voice was quiet.

"No!" She turned to look at him then, but he kept his gaze fastened to the floor. "No. I couldn't have. You can only turn someone if you drink too much. And I didn't. I'm sure of it."

"Why did I pass out then? And why am I so thirsty?" His

voice was flat, but she heard in it the undercurrents of his turmoil.

"You're thirsty?" She swallowed past her own dry lump. "You can't be. I know I didn't turn you. You passed out because I wiped your memory. At least, I thought I did. I don't know why you still remember everything."

"Did you do it right?"

Aubrey was insulted for a moment. Who was he to question if she was doing her vampiric things properly? But she supposed, after a moment, that he had a right to ask.

"I'm pretty sure." Her words were soft, for she wasn't actually all that sure. "I have no idea why you're thirsty. And I don't know why you can…why you can do whatever it is you just did. I can't do that."

"Are you sure? Have you tried?"

Aubrey was taken aback. No, she hadn't tried, but surely Malcolm would have told her about any fancy powers that came along with vampirism.

Then again, Malcolm wasn't the most reliable of guys in general.

"Give me your knife." When he failed to produce it, she snaked her fingers into his hip pocket and pulled it out for herself. She felt the jut of his hipbone as she did so, and it made her mouth water.

Palming the blade, she took a deep breath—not that she needed it—and dragged the point of the knife across her own forearm. Blood welled up just as it had in Gavin's, though hers was thicker, darker and sluggish.

Narrowing her eyes, she focused on the cut. Not entirely sure of what she was supposed to do, she tried to will it to heal. But no light shone from her fingers, and the cut continued to ooze blood.

"Am I doing it right?" She turned to Gavin, brow furrowed, and found him transfixed by the sight of the blood welling from her sliced arm.

He dragged his gaze from her arm to her face with difficulty, and swallowed thickly.

"You're thirsty." He nodded after a long pause. "Thirsty... for blood?"

He nodded again. "It repulses me. It's disgusting. But...I can smell it. Smell you. And I want it so bad."

Aubrey sat still, her mind frantically working. This was new territory for her. But she accepted her gut reaction and held out her arm.

"Here." She saw his pupils dilate as the blood drew close to his nose. "Bite."

Gavin took her wrist, encircled it with his fingers. Eyeing her warily, he moved the tender skin of her wrist to his lips.

She melted a bit when he brushed those lips over the flutter of her pulse before moving down the length of her arm to where her skin had been sliced open.

He opened his mouth and then bit.

Nothing happened. He didn't have fangs; he couldn't break her skin.

"I don't understand." He narrowed his eyes at her. "How did you bite me?"

Aubrey closed her eyes slowly, then forced her teeth to extend. It wasn't hard to do, not when she was so thirsty and his delicious smell so close. Lifting her upper lip, she showed him her teeth, the teeth of a predator.

To his credit, he didn't appear frightened, or even fazed. He merely cocked his head and then bared his own teeth. She assumed he was trying to make his teeth do the same.

"Anything?" He sounded hopeful, and from the look in his eyes she could tell that it was because the thirst had hit him.

She shook her head. Frustration painted his features.

Without thinking, she drew a finger through the blood on her arm, then lifted it to his lips. His tongue flicked out, tasting, then licking her finger clean.

He moaned as the taste hit his tongue.

"I need more." A shiver shimmied down Aubrey's spine. He was asking, but she had no doubt that he could take if he wanted to, even with her new strength.

She was confused, so confused about the whole situation. But the bloodlust needed no explanation. They each had a thirst, and they each had the means to quench it.

"Here." She squeezed the cut, and more blood welled up. He slid his fingers down to clasp her elbow, inhaled the scent, then licked down the stripe of the cut.

"What do I smell like to you?" The feel of his tongue on her skin, tasting her blood, sent her shooting to heights of sensation that rivaled those she'd felt when his mouth had been between her legs the night before.

"Honey." Having licked the wound clean, Gavin swiped the back of his hand over his mouth. "Honey that's been warmed in the sun."

He noted her stare, which was focused on his neck. "You're thirsty, too."

Aubrey nodded.

"What do I smell like to you?" He hadn't offered himself, not yet, and she could think of nothing but thirst. But she could remember the taste of him on her tongue, of the scent that had filled her nostrils.

"Chocolate." Her eyes shifted to the throbbing pulse in his wrist, then to the firm length of thigh encased in fitted denim. "Melted chocolate. The good stuff, like from a real candy store."

Their stares met. Aubrey leaned in. She just wanted a taste… surely just a sip would take the edge off of her ever-growing thirst. But through her thirst she became aware of a knocking at the door.

"Are you expecting someone?" The moment was gone. Gavin leaned back so fast that Aubrey might as well have burned him as inhaled his scent.

"No." Aubrey frowned, looking from Gavin to the door and back. "No. No one should be here."

"Stay here." Gavin pressed down on one of her shoulders, urging her to stay seated on the couch. He stood and crossed the room to the door.

Aubrey was one step behind him.

"This is my home!" She grabbed him by the arm and tugged. She wouldn't use her new, extra strength unless she had to. "And you shouldn't be here. Malcolm will give me hell if he finds out I didn't wipe your memory right. And then he'll do it."

"He can try." Gavin set his jaw, but allowed Aubrey to ease in front of him. "Check who it is before you open the door."

She shot him an exasperated glance, but was too edgy to do more than that. Really, there shouldn't be anyone at her door.

A quick peep through the peephole told her that her visitor was no one she knew. A man and a woman stood on the other side. She'd never seen them before.

The innate stillness that surrounded them told her that her visitors were vampires, as did the lack of an audible heartbeat.

Knowing that if she didn't open the door for them they could quite easily just let themselves in, she signaled to Gavin to stand back, out of sight. Then she opened the door just enough to seem friendly yet cautious.

"Yes?" She knew now without a doubt that her visitors were vamps. There was no smell of fresh, living blood, no rushing noise as it flowed through slender veins.

"Ms. Hart?" The man spoke.

"*Dr.* Hart." She made the correction automatically, with the same surge of irritation that always accompanied the gaffe.

She'd worked bloody hard for the title. She wanted people to use it.

The man looked slightly taken aback, but smoothed over his features quickly and seamlessly. "My apologies. I am Blaine, and this is Valentina. We are here to discuss your new…circumstances. Might we come in?"

Aubrey eyed them warily. The man spoke with a thick accent, Eastern European, if her guess was correct, but his English was perfect. His suit was simple but fit him neatly, and was entirely black.

The woman's garb was similar. Both had pale skin like Aubrey's, but their hair was dark, identical shades of nut brown. They had similar features, too—shadowy eyes and prominent, straight noses.

Aubrey wondered if they were siblings. More, she wondered what they were doing here.

"I assure you, we come in peace." The woman—Valentina—spoke with an accent as well. "Not that you have reason to believe us. But you might prefer that we speak in your house, where others cannot hear." She motioned with her eyes down the hall, and Aubrey thought of Mrs. Newbanks, the snoopy divorcée who lived across the way.

"Come in." She stepped back and allowed them to enter. Both Blaine and Valentina moved with a grace that belied, at least to Aubrey's eyes, their lack of humanness. Both halted abruptly when they saw Gavin, standing with arms crossed belligerently, across the room.

"You have told someone of your new life?" Valentina turned to Aubrey and pressed her lips tightly together in disapproval. Aubrey watched, fascinated, as the little color that the woman' skin had faded with the pressure.

"Not exactly." Aubrey squirmed in place, feeling as if she'd done something very wrong. She also felt nervous, on edge. Something about these two unsettled her, but she couldn't have said why, exactly.

"Please…uh…sit? Can I…can I get you something to drink?" The words were automatic, and she cringed after saying them. Of course she couldn't get them something to drink. She didn't have any blood.

But she had no idea what vampire etiquette was.

"I would love some hot chocolate, if you have it." Blaine was excruciatingly polite as he seated himself—rather stiffly, in Aubrey's opinion—on the edge of the couch. She noticed that he was staring at Gavin without trying to seem as if he was doing so.

"Hot chocolate?" She was incredulous. "Can you—can we—" She stopped herself. They hadn't even admitted that they were vampires, though she knew bloody well that they were.

Blaine chuckled, and Valentina cocked her head at Gavin as if he was something tasty to eat. "Yes, we can. We can eat, we can drink. I would prefer a taste of your guest, here, but it's not polite to eat occupants in another vampire's home." He gestured at Gavin, who stiffened and reminded Aubrey of a cat about to pounce.

He was on alert, full alert. He was holding back for her sake.

Hmm.

"I don't have any hot chocolate." That was a lie, but she was uncomfortable leaving these two alone with Gavin—though she wasn't sure who was the danger, exactly.

"Well, then." Blaine patted the seat beside him, gesturing for her to come sit between himself and Valentina. Aubrey resented being asked to sit in her own home. Instead, she crossed the room and stood next to Gavin.

She found his warmth reassuring as it worked on her chilled skin. She didn't know what he was now—*he* didn't know what he was—but he made her feel safe.

There was the smallest tightening of Blaine's features, then they were again smoothed with apparent ease.

"That lack of knowledge is the reason we are here." He gave her a slow smile, one with enough flirtation in it that Aubrey was a bit startled.

Beside her, Gavin tensed, and his heart rate sped up. He may have been angry with her, angry and confused, but he didn't like another poaching on his territory.

"Your maker was…how shall I put this…a dreg." Both of the other vampires' faces reflected disapproval. "He barely followed our rules himself, and we certainly can't trust that he showed you the way properly. As it is, he abandoned you before he was allowed to, and for that he will be punished."

Even though these two were here to help out, a chill skated down Aubrey's spine.

"Well." She forced a smile to her face. "What do I need to know?"

Blaine and Valentina turned to look at each other, and then back to Aubrey. "It might be easiest for you to simply visit our council's headquarters." Valentina nodded at Blaine's words, but Aubrey got the distinct impression that that wasn't what he had been about to say.

"Council's headquarters?" Malcolm had mentioned a council—with distaste dripping from his words—but he hadn't said any more about it. The few conversations that they had had since he had turned her had been perfunctory, Malcolm telling her a minimum of information. "Where is that?"

Another quickly exchanged glance.

"Lviv, Ukraine." Valentina seemed unimpressed when Aubrey barked out a laugh and Gavin snorted in disbelief.

Blaine stood smoothly, and held out a hand to the woman. "Come now, Valentina, we are silly to expect her to just hop a plane with us and fly halfway around the world. Let us go get some dinner—a pleasant if unnecessary meal—and talk. Then she can decide."

"All right." That sounded reasonable, and Aubrey relaxed some. Gavin stayed tense at her side, and didn't move.

"The gentleman will come, of course?" It didn't sound like a question.

"It wasn't ever in question." Aubrey looked up into Gavin's face and was amazed at the ferocity in his expression. He touched his hand to the small of her waist, nudging her forward and indicating that he would follow.

"I need to change first." She looked down at her thin T-shirt and short boxers. Eyeing the group warily, she raced for her bedroom and grabbed the first thing that she saw, a little sundress that wasn't at all appropriate for the crunchy bite of the fall wind.

She didn't care. She wasn't going to leave Gavin alone with these two strangers. Besides, she no longer seemed sensitive to the cold, or to warmth, for that matter. Her flesh stayed chilled and firm, no matter the temperature of the air surrounding her.

Aubrey heard rustling from behind Mrs. Newbanks' door when they all exited the apartment and made their way down to the lobby.

"What are you, by the by?" Blaine dropped the question to Gavin once they were outside. The words were casual, but seemed deceptively so.

"A doctor." He was being deliberately obtuse, but Aubrey was wondering if he could see something that she couldn't—

he had jumped to her defense so quickly, even though she knew he was upset with her.

"Ah." That wasn't what Blaine had meant at all, and they all knew it.

If he didn't know what Gavin was, did they have any hope of finding out?

They walked down the street in pairs, Blaine and Valentina, Aubrey and Gavin. When they came alongside a parked, shiny black SUV the first pair stopped dead in their tracks.

Aubrey skidded to a halt. If she hadn't had her new speed, she would have found her nose pressed into Valentina's back.

While she was trying to regain her footing, which she could have done easily enough with her newfound grace, Valentina grabbed one of her wrists and clamped a bracelet on it.

Aubrey screamed. The bracelet was nothing special, apart from the fact that it was half of a pair of handcuffs, and the metal pressed against her skin was scorching her flesh.

She could smell the nauseating odor of her own tissue frying. The pain radiated up her arm and allowed Valentina to clasp her other wrist in her bony hand.

"Gavin!" The noise beside her said that he was fighting, himself. There was no one else on the street, unless they were hiding in the shadows. No one to help.

Aubrey was strong, but Valentina was stronger. And the pain from the cuffs was clouding her mind.

A blast of blue light hit her as she tried to kick Valentina somewhere, anywhere, to prevent being shoved into the back of the now-open SUV. The force of the glow sent her falling to meet the rough concrete of the sidewalk.

She smelled blood, her own blood, welling up from the areas where the ground had ruthlessly scraped her skin away. The air was hot wherever the blue light touched.

"Come on!" Her arm, the one with the cuff, was grabbed roughly and she was dragged to her feet. "Run!"

She smelled Gavin, and so she ran. She didn't look behind them, had no idea if the two were chasing them or not. Her entire being was so consumed with keeping up with Gavin—and with the pain that threatened to melt her bones.

Aubrey had no idea how long they ran, but she instinctively trusted that Gavin would get her to safety. She was no weakling who waited for a man to save the day, but she wasn't stupid, either. She was in excruciating pain, and her mind was fogged from it.

Finally Gavin pulled her into an alley, and she caught a glimpse of the coffee shop across the street where she'd met Malcolm. They were close to the hospital. Gavin pressed her into the wall, the rough surface of the brick pulling at her hair. Covering her mouth with his hand and cradling her wounded arm against his chest, he pressed her in, shielding her with his chest.

After a long moment, when he apparently deemed that all was safe, he let his hand fall from her mouth.

She was weak with thirst, dizzy from the burn, but otherwise all right, so she only needed a minute to gather her thoughts.

"What did you do?"

# Chapter Four

Gavin had no idea what he'd done, but he hated admitting it. Still, what choice did he have?

"I just…I was angry." Mostly he was angry that either of the deadly duo had laid hands on Aubrey, even though he was still angry with her himself, but he didn't see the need to mention that. "I wanted to get them off us." Off her.

"And then that blue light was coming from my hands again. But instead of healing, it pushed them away. It was like a blast. A big blast of…I don't know." He truly didn't. "It was hot. Dry. Like the air in a desert."

Aubrey stared at him as if she'd never seen anyone more strange. She bit her lower lip, and he saw that her fangs were fully extended.

Given the last few hours, the notion of a blood-drinking vampire didn't freak him out as much as he'd been when he first realized she'd bitten him and turned him into a vampire.

"You're thirsty?" Still, he wasn't sure he could let her drink from him. His own thirst had been fully abated by the small taste that he'd had earlier.

Her hunger seemed darker and deeper.

She licked her lips, then deliberately shook her head.

"I'll be fine." He suspected that she was just too proud to ask him for a drink. "But I don't know how much more I can take of this bracelet. I don't know why it's hurting me so badly."

Gently he lifted her wrist until he could see it easily. Her skin was raw and red, even peeling away in some spots, and when his fingers accidentally brushed it she winced.

"Sorry." As carefully as he could, he tilted the cuff until it caught a gleam of light from a streetlight shining golden just outside the alley.

The light showed him a marking carved into metal. Sterling silver. Huh.

He told Aubrey what is was. She winced again.

"Well, that myth is true, then." Her eyes were starting to look glassy, with a crystalline sheen overtop the sky blue. "Wonder if the one about garlic is, too. That'd be a kicker. I love garlic."

"Aubrey." He caught her chin in his hand and turned her face toward his. Earlier today she'd looked vital, strong. Like a high-definition version of her old self.

Now she looked as if she was on the verge of collapse. The physician, the man and the id in him all stirred at the sight.

The physician wanted to heal.

The man wanted to protect.

The id? It was connected directly to his cock, and he was abashed at the fact that just holding her in his arms, breathing her in, made his glans stir, even when she was so weak.

The first two made up his mind. He held his wrist in front of her face, and he saw her pupils dilate at the sight of his throbbing pulse.

"Do it." He was fascinated to see her fangs gleam white in the faint light from the street. "Quickly. It will help until we can get the bracelet off."

She hesitated, clearly considering. Then as she realized that she had no choice, she brought her lips to his skin and slowly bit.

He wasn't sure if it was because of how it had happened the night before, during sex, that the pain was so pleasurable. It was an odd sensation, the suckling, but her mouth was hot and wet and it turned him on unbearably.

He shuddered, let out a groan and pressed his body against hers, careful not to disturb the arm with the bracelet on it.

His cock rubbed against the denim of his jeans as he pressed Aubrey back into the wall. He wouldn't press if she was repulsed by his arousal.

But she made a small noise that vibrated through his wrist and ground her hips into his as she pulled deeper from the vein.

They didn't have time. He knew that. They'd run far, but he didn't know how long Blaine and Valentina would be incapacitated.

Then Aubrey abruptly released his wrist, having drunk her fill. She stared at him hungrily, but it was a different kind of hunger.

He felt it, too.

She had a trickle of his blood running from the corner of her mouth. He wiped it away with his thumb.

She ran her tongue over the digit, then closed her eyes, relishing the sensation.

He gritted his teeth, wanting nothing more than to reach up underneath her little dress and jam his cock into her waiting flesh.

He wouldn't take advantage of her while she was in so much pain.

Aubrey had other ideas. He found his lips plastered against

her own, tasted the salt and the sweet of himself on her tongue when she lunged at him.

"Now. Now." She pulled her lips away only long enough to murmur the words. He started to protest that they didn't have time, that it was too dangerous, that she was hurt. But her hands had undone his jeans, and she'd freed his straining erection, and then she'd guided his fingers under her sundress and to the slick, naked chasm between her legs.

"Fuck." He lost his mind, and whatever thoughts he'd been entertaining along with it. With a growl from down deep in his throat, he caught one of her legs over in the crook of his arm and lifted it to circle his waist.

A moment later he embedded himself in her, knowing from the look of bloodlust dancing in her eyes that she was ready for him. She cried out into the night at the sudden invasion, then rocked her hips toward him in search of more.

"Fuck," he cursed again, fighting her skirts with his free hand. His thumb found her clit and began to rub insistently, intent on making her come as fast and as hard as possible. At the same time he set a frantic pace, thrusting into her again and again.

They could be set upon at any moment. They both knew it. But they couldn't stop. Their bodies strained to get closer and closer still, as if their lives depended on it, until they each cried with ultimate pleasure, and Gavin felt the hot silky glove of her channel fist around him tightly.

Spent, he lowered his forehead to hers and closed his eyes. He needed a moment, just one moment to collect himself.

Having caught his breath, he moved back. Eyes on each other, they straightened their clothing. The air was thick with tension, and he wondered if he'd made a terrible mistake.

Following his gut, he caught her wrist, the one with the cuff, in his hand and kissed it before taking a good long look. The blood had done her good—the scorched skin was no longer peeling and had faded from an angry cardinal red to a neon pink.

He ran his finger between the cuff and her skin. She hissed in agitation at the pressure.

He wished that he knew how to pick locks. And as he wished, he was astonished to see that damn blue light surround the tip of his finger.

The light heated until Aubrey cried out in pain and he felt as if he'd pressed a finger to the lit element of a stove.

But he'd melted right through the silver of the cuff. One twist and it fell to the ground.

What *was* he?

Aubrey was slightly amused that it had taken being turned into a vampire to kick her coffee habit.

The smell outside the chain coffee store didn't repulse her, but the caffeine-laden air no longer held the same kick to her senses, either. She couldn't sense any trace of Malcolm in the night, either, and that *was* a problem.Though it was a long shot, Aubrey couldn't think of anywhere else to turn—she didn't know anyone else who could answer their questions.

"He's not here." She couldn't explain how she knew. There was almost an electrical charge in the air when her maker was near, alerting her to his presence.

Gavin growled and slammed his fists against the glass window in frustration. Aubrey could see several patrons inside the shop jump, startled, and she hastily took Gavin's hand and led him away and down the street.

"Easy." She tried to ignore the warmth that the feel of his fingers entwined with her own brought to her skin. They had other things to worry about.

"How can you say that? Look at your wrist!" His fingers

squeezed hers as if involuntarily, and she felt a warm glow despite the danger that they were in.

She didn't answer, though, because she didn't know what to say. Instead, she changed the subject.

"I know a place we can check." She noticed that although he was trying to give the outward appearance of their just being a couple out for a stroll, Gavin was subtly scanning the street.

She was chagrined. She was the one with the supersenses. She would see danger far before he ever would.

Or maybe not. He did have new, inexplicable powers that had proven invaluable.

"Where are we going? Is it far?"

"Just another block." They moved at a brisk pace that once would have left Aubrey breathless. "It's a magic shop. I think Malcolm lives somewhere close to it. He mentioned it a few times, and once I saw him coming out of the store."

"That's all we have to go on?" Gavin cast her an incredulous stare without breaking stride. "Do you have a better idea?" Aubrey snapped because she wished she knew more. But up until a few weeks ago, she'd lived a completely average, even boring life. Running from vampires who belonged to some kind of council was foreign territory. So was needing to find answers that might save her life.

It was all she could come up with.

They reached the shop quickly, but as they approached the small square structure, Aubrey felt something icy dance chilly fingers over her skin.

"He's here." Of that she was sure. "But something's not right." She felt the electrical buzz that she always experienced in Malcolm' presence, but it had a different…energy.

"Stay behind me." Gavin moved in front of Aubrey, shielding her with his body and accidentally jostling the cuff that still pressed against her skin. She winced and then scowled, nudging him in the small of the back.

"I don't need you to protect me." Once she might have, but not any longer.

"I know." Gavin stopped, flat against the building beside the smudged glass door. "But that doesn't mean I'm not going to do it anyway."

Aubrey furrowed her brow. That was one to puzzle out later.

"Are you sure he's in there?" Gavin's fingers twitched, and Aubrey saw a faint shimmer of light surround them. It was mesmerizing.

Tearing her eyes from the glow, she closed her lids and tested the air of the hazy purple night with all her senses.

"Yes." She was sure that Malcolm was close by, almost within touching distance, but she still sensed that something was wrong. "Be careful."

Gavin opened the glass door quickly, and they both slithered in. The store was full of shadows, odd for a retail establishment, and Aubrey was puzzled until she realized that the overhead lights were out.

She also heard breathing, a deep rasping that sliced the ears, and knew that they weren't alone.

The smell of blood hung heavily in the air, and it wasn't blood still contained within skin. No, this blood had been spilled, released from its prison.

But it was still fresh. Buttery sweet, it tickled her nostrils and made her throat dry.

"Who's there?" Her question was followed by a slight moan. With a sideways look at Gavin, she cocked her head in the direction that the voice came from to indicate that she was going to go see.

As she moved, she felt Gavin right at her back.

She saw the figure clearly as she rounded a wooden shelf stacked with glass bottles. The body of a woman, a plump woman with pale, pale skin and heavily hennaed hair was stretched on the black-and-white-tiled floor, shaking and, Aubrey could see quite clearly, bleeding from savage tears in her wrist.

"Darkling." The woman, who Aubrey now recognized as the owner of Esme's Magic Emporium, started when her eyes tried to focus. Aubrey felt as though her innermost secrets were being examined, even as the woman began scrabbling backward, trying to get away from her. "Darkling!"

"It's okay." Aubrey found herself shushing the lady quickly, repulsed that someone would be scared of her. "It's okay. I won't hurt you." If only she had the willpower not to drink, not to lap at the spilled blood with her tongue.

"Who did this to you?"

The woman again looked at her, her bottle-glass green eyes intent. "Witchling?" But her gaze wasn't on Aubrey. It was fixed behind her, on Gavin.

The two exchanged a look. Gavin moved closer. The woman seemed to relax with him in proximity, too.

"Here." Crossing his arms at the waist, Gavin stripped off his T-shirt and tore a length from the bottom. He wrapped it tightly around the woman's wrist, his movements brisk and professional. "You need to call an ambulance."

"Right." The scent of blood was dulling her senses, keeping her from focusing on the danger and on Malcolm. Dully she crawled to the shop's phone, which had been thrown from the high wooden counter.

"Why aren't you thirsty?" She felt as if she were trying to walk through water.

"He's a Witchling," the woman answered before Gavin could, her voice breaking as he propped her up on a satin cushion that he'd found on the floor. "He's a Witchling, you're a Darkling. That's why."

Aubrey and Gavin exchanged another look as Aubrey made the quick, anonymous call to 911. She crawled back their way, sensing a ripple in the energy that was Malcolm as she did so.

"Malcolm is here somewhere, Gavin." She tried to keep her voice to a whisper, because she was certain that the shop had secrets it hadn't yet told them. "We need to go. The ambulance will take care of her."

"I can't leave when I could help." He looked at her helplessly, clearly torn between leaving with Aubrey to find Malcolm and staying to help the woman.

Aubrey bit her lip, then gestured at him with her hand. "Hurry."

Gavin placed his hands on the woman's wrist. There was a crackle like static before the air began to hum with energy. The blue light emanating from Gavin's hands cast an ocean-tinted hue over his face.

Aubrey could feel her blood heat in response to his power. It made her want him in more ways than one.

How was he doing this? What was a Witchling?

What was a Darkling?

As if she'd spoken aloud, the woman turned her head to face Aubrey. She still seemed more apprehensive with Aubrey than with Gavin.

She also seemed not at all surprised that Gavin could shoot light from his fingers and heal her arm.

"Witchling. Darkling. Both vampire…but different." Her words gained in strength the longer Gavin hunched over her wound, but she still sounded weak. Aubrey inched closer. It didn't seem like the right time, but she needed to know.

"What do you mean?" The woman closed her eyes as

if gathering strength. When she opened them again, they glowed with a liquid sheen that told Aubrey she was something more than human.

"Darklings…most vampires are Darklings. They drink blood, they walk at night. They are stronger, faster." The woman sighed as Gavin stroked a final hand over the skin of her wrist. Aubrey could see that it was now smooth, no longer torn open, though the new skin was an irritated-looking shade of red.

Gavin sat back on his heels to listen also, looking drained.

"Witchlings… Witchlings are rare. Once plentiful. Now no more." The woman cocked her head to one side, listening. "They have the thirst, but only need a sip once in a while. They walk in the day, they live, they breathe."

Aubrey and Gavin exchanged a look. That explained a lot.

"Why… why can I do this?" Gavin gestured to the woman's wrist with hands that still glowed faintly.

"Witchlings…not stronger. Not faster. But they have powers. Different ones. You heal." Finished speaking, the woman made a shooing motion. "Now go. The ambulance is coming. But so will they. The Karpaty Council. I will be safe. They were already here. You will not be safe." With that she again closed her eyes, and Aubrey knew that their conversation was over.

"Let's go." Aubrey could hear the faint wail of the ambulance siren in the distance. She was still unnerved by the charge in the air that told her Malcolm was near, but they needed to leave.

Gavin nodded, then touched his fingers to the area between her shoulder blades, indicating that they should leave out the back of the store.

The charge electrified the closer they got to the rear door, and the fine hairs on the back of Aubrey's neck stood straight up. She slowed, suddenly reluctant to step through that door, but Gavin urged her onward.

A dark shape sprawled on the crunchy pavement outside the door. Hesitant though her steps were, Aubrey nearly tripped over the prone figure.

Bile would have risen in her throat if she'd had any left.

"Is that Malcolm?"

Aubrey nodded dumbly. She didn't need to look any more closely to know that he was dead.

She felt a spasm of grief shiver through her body, a grief stronger than she should have had over someone she barely knew, someone who had, in fact, killed her.

Frozen in place, she stared down at the body. Gavin stroked a hand quickly over the tangled mess of her hair before tugging firmly on her arm.

"We have to keep moving." His fingers squeezed hers, and the warmth helped to ease her chill. "There's nothing we can do for him now."

They walked, Gavin leading Aubrey, Aubrey paying no attention whatsoever to their surroundings, lost in her inner pain. The streets were eerily quiet, no yellow cabs, delivery trucks or other vehicles to be seen. Twice she thought she heard footsteps behind them, but when she perked her ears toward the sound to listen again, it was gone.

She blinked when they stopped. The garish neon light of a motel sign hurt her eyes.

"I want you to go in and rent us a room." Gavin pressed the cool, smooth leather of a wallet into her hand. "I'm going to stay here and watch. Come right back out when you're done, and we'll go to the room together."

Aubrey nodded automatically. Gavin grabbed her chin in his hand hard enough to catch her attention.

"Can you do this?" She nodded again, dimly thinking that

it was a dumb question. Of course she could. But deep down she knew that he was protecting her yet again, and while she didn't need it, she found that it brought a nice sensation flooding through her.

"I'll be right here." She felt an odd little flutter around her heart as he spoke, especially odd because that heart no longer beat. "Right here waiting for you."

Gavin cringed when the words left his mouth. They sounded cheesier than he'd intended them to.

But he was rapidly finding that Aubrey brought out a softness in him that few others saw.

He'd never allowed anyone close enough before to do the same, not even Aubrey.

He leaned against the dirty paneling that made up the outside of the cheap motel. His eyes scanned the street constantly, and he wished that he had the enhanced hearing that Aubrey had displayed.

Why was she so upset over Malcolm's death? He hadn't sounded like a real prince of a man. He could only assume her feelings had something to do with the fact that Malcolm had made her what she was.

No, that wasn't right. Malcolm may have turned her into a vampire, but Aubrey was who she was because she'd fought to be that way. She was a gifted doctor, one he'd pushed mercilessly both because of her potential and because he needed to deny the cosmic pull of his attraction toward her.

His desire for her hadn't been at all appropriate in the hospital.

Now that he'd tasted her skin, and she his blood, he wondered if there was any going back.

"Here." Aubrey shoved through the filthy glass door of the office and pushed a key into his hand. It was an actual jagged metal key, a throwback to the time before plastic, re-writable key cards.

She still seemed numb, but at the same time he trusted her.

But first she needed to rest. He could see her fatigue with every step she took. He was tired, too—using his power, or whatever it was, drained him—but he could and would wait until she'd rested. He couldn't explain why, but he felt the need to keep watch.

She also needed to drink. He wondered if he should be ashamed that the thought of her suckling from his neck made him hard.

Their room was number sixty-six, a fact that made him raise an eyebrow, but he refrained from commenting on it or from ruminating on any other meaning. Sixty-six wasn't six-six-six, after all, though the superstitious side that he tried to deny screamed at him in warning.

They key stuck in the lock, but after a few vigorous shakes they were in.

He squinted into the dim light, envying yet another of Aubrey's enhanced senses.

Then he found himself pushed back against the cool metal of the door, and he forgot all about the decor.

He hadn't thought that Aubrey would want to be touched at all, given her current state of mind. But she undid his pants with a hard yank, freeing the cock that was already hard and ready.

He knew that often death needed an affirmation of life. Though they would be better off using this downtime in another way, he wouldn't deny her that.

Not that it was hard for him to comply, at any rate. And it would distract her from worming out the fact that he was going to leave.

The council wanted him. He was a Witchling, whatever

the hell that was. If he left, Aubrey would be safe, or would at least be able to find her way.

With a groan he threw his head back against the door and let her slant her lips frantically over his own. His skull bounced off the metal, causing stars to dance in front of his eyes, but he didn't care.

He fisted both hands in her long silken hair when her lips slid down to caress his throat. Her tongue danced over his pulse, and he tensed, waiting for the sting of her fangs.

Anticipating it.

It didn't come. Though she lingered in that place where the blood rushed hot and fast, and though he heard her moan, she didn't bite. Instead, she dropped to her knees, still fully clothed, and pulled his pants down.

A strangled noise escaped his mouth when her mouth closed over the tip of his cock. It was a thrilling sensation, his hot flesh inside the cool cavern of her mouth.

It was even more thrilling when she began to suck. She pulled hard, her attention focused on making him shake. Her right hand held him firmly, stroking up and down slowly while her mouth suckled fast, and her left hand weighed the warmth of his testicles.

Within minutes he felt as if he would explode. He tried to draw back—he didn't want to end things yet. He wanted to be inside her when he came. But she had him trapped between her willing flesh and the door, with nowhere to go.

As he felt his cock and sac tighten and begin to draw up close to his body, Aubrey released him from the heaven that was her mouth. She pulled his low hanging globes away from his body lightly, and with her free hand tore the shredded remains of his shirt off his torso.

She took a strip of the cotton and tied it firmly around the erection that had never been so hard.

He wondered where on earth sweet Aubrey Hart had learned about cock rings, but he certainly wasn't going to complain.

It was the sweetest kind of pain imaginable.

Gavin watched through a haze as Aubrey sat back on her heels and looked up at him. He wanted to grab her, to throw her on the bed and lose himself in her again and again, but this was her time. He'd suppress what he wanted in order to let her explore.

She stood slowly. With her eyes fastened on his own, she clasped the hem of her dress and lifted it over her head.

When she was naked, she turned dreamily. With deliberate steps, she walked to the bed, then crawled onto the scratchy spread on hands and knees.

"Fuck me." Before today, Gavin never would have expected to hear those words out of her mouth. Today, they made his pulse race. He crossed the dubious carpet of the room and climbed onto the bed behind her, pressing his groin against the soft curves of her behind.

She moaned. He urged her up off her hands until she was seated against his lap and her back was pressed to his front. He took his time moving his hands over her waist, her ribs, and then finally her breasts. He cupped them in his hands, his movements firm, before pinching her nipples tightly.

Her gasp was one of pain, but also pleasure. She moved her rear in his lap until the friction against his cock brought him to the brink again. If she kept it up, he would lose it, so he pushed her back down on all fours.

"Hard." She was tense, quivering as she waited.

He obliged. Grasping his shaft in hand, he stroked once, twice against the cleft that was already wet, then pushed in with one hard thrust.

They both released unintelligible noises. He paused for

a moment, fully sheathed in her wetness, using all of his senses to fully appreciate the experience, but she pressed back against him, asking without words.

He began to move, thrusting as hard and deep as he could. Reaching around her slender waist, he moved his hand to her clit and strummed over the engorged flesh, enjoying the hitch in her moan when he did so.

He focused on holding himself back, not an easy trick while he gave her what she wanted. When he felt her shudder around him and heard her breathy exclamation of pleasure, he pulled back, easing out of her tightness.

She protested, but he wanted to look into her eyes when he came.

He turned her over slowly, her limbs pliant in the aftermath of orgasm. She squinted up at him curiously as he straddled her, then knelt back on his heels.

Slowly, gaze fastened to hers, he undid the makeshift cock ring. It had done its job. Now he wanted to feel every inch of her.

Slowly, so slowly, he eased back into her tender flesh. She bit her lip, and he saw pearls of blood bead.

Dipping his head, he licked them away, then offered her his right wrist.

She froze for a moment, then slowly reached for the offered hand. She licked over his pulse, then kissed.

Then she sank her teeth in, slowly, almost tenderly, mimicking the way that he was moving inside her.

His entire body clenched as he felt her begin to pull blood from his veins. He shuddered, pleasure racking his frame.

Trying to hold out just moments longer, he turned blindly to stare at the rickety table beside the bed. A nearly gutted red candle sat on it, and he had a momentary image of pouring heated wax over the pale skin of Aubrey's breasts.

He closed his eyes, loving the feel of her teeth in his flesh and his cock in her heat. When he opened them again, the candle was lit, looked as if it had been lit for hours, with wet wax pooling all around the base.

His skin emitted that faint, eerie blue glow.

Caught in the moment, he reached for the candle. Aubrey's eyes widened, but she didn't say a word, didn't protest as he held it over her torso.

Caught in the most sensual experience he'd ever had, he slowly tipped his wrist until a drizzle of hot wax fell down to paint itself on Aubrey's skin.

Her hips bucked against his. He waited for her to protest, ready to stop if she didn't like it, but the pain brought a frenzied look to her eyes.

She released his wrist, blood smearing his skin and hers. It mixed with the red wax until the two were nearly indistinguishable.

"More." Her voice was a growl. Muscles tense, he poured again, letting the wax pool on her rib cage and abdomen. Her hips pistoned faster and faster with the sensation, catching him in the rhythm, until he could no longer control himself. The candle fell, gutting itself out and splattering scalding wax over them both. Holding his weight on his arms, he matched her pace, welcoming the impending orgasm.

They came at the same time, him with a hoarse shout and her with a sigh of satisfaction. He felt himself melt down on top of her, their flesh glued together. Rolling so that he didn't crush her, he pulled her tightly against his body and shuddered through the aftereffects of their lovemaking.

How could he leave knowing that he'd finally found what he'd always been looking for?

## Chapter Five

When Aubrey opened her eyes, she saw the bare skin of a well-muscled back and fitted denim cupping a tight ass.

The owner of the back and the ass was peering through the slatted blinds of their window, and the noise of the metal hitting glass had awakened her, as had, she thought, the tension emanating from him.

"What is it?" She sat straight up when she noted his tense demeanor, untwisting the fabric of her dress that had wrapped itself around her body in sleep.

They'd already had a shower. Aubrey had been all for a group shower, but Gavin had insisted that they bathe one at a time, with the other keeping watch. He'd also insisted that they dress again, in case they had to move quickly.

Practical, Aubrey knew that. Practical, but not at all what she'd wanted.

But perhaps he'd been right. He turned away from the window and moved toward her, tension in his frame.

"How do you know?" Aubrey asked, pulling at the cheap fabric of the bedsheets in agitation.

Gavin paused before replying.

"The morning after you bit me, I woke up in the back of

my van. I remembered what had happened, and I was angry. While I was sitting there, pissed off and not sure what the hell was going on, I blasted a hole in the floor with that blue light. It seemed logical to assume that it had something to do with you biting me, though I suppose we'll never know unless we go with Blaine and Valentina—which we're not going to do." He raked a hand through his hair, making it stand on end, and Aubrey imagined how he must have felt. She felt dreadful.

There was no way that she could have known that her mind wipe wouldn't work, but it was still her fault.

Gavin continued to speak. "That was the first introduction to my powers. The second part came when I was at your apartment, when those goons were on the other side of your door. I just… I just knew that something was wrong. I don't know how to describe it. It was like electricity in my veins. Right now it's a low hum, like static. Something's coming."

As his words faded he jolted as if being shocked with that same electricity. "It just ramped up. Something's wrong." He strode to the window, peered out into the night, then turned back to Audrey just as fast.

"We have company." Aubrey scrambled to extricate herself from the sheets, but Gavin scooped her up and had her on her feet before she could.

She pulled at the twisted fabric and it ripped. She left it on the floor where it fell in shreds.

The door exploded inward in a shower of metal fragments. Gavin moved to shield her with his body, but she still felt slices carve through her flesh.

There was yelling, and Gavin pushed her back again. When she regained her footing she saw a giant of a man filling the doorway. In front of him stood Blaine and Valentina, and behind him were the shadows of more.

Her hope sank. There were so many. How could they get away from so many?

She'd rather die than let them take Gavin away from her.

"There is no point in trying." A shard of metal had caught Blaine on the cheek, and he wiped the dripping blood from the gash away dispassionately.

He looked at Gavin. "If you come with us and cooperate, we'll let her live."

In front of her, Aubrey felt Gavin begin to shake. After hearing the beating of his heart speed up and detecting an increase in his scent, she understood that it was with rage.

As long as she'd known him, he'd never taken kindly to orders.

"You won't touch her. I'll kill you all before you do."

His fury was for *her* sake?

The realization made up her mind. Though it hadn't been her choice, this life was hers now. She was a vampire. So was Gavin, and though they were different, they were perfect for one another.

They'd fight for the right to be together, or die trying.

Her fangs were out and she was flying across the room without ever consciously deciding to. When she was only a whisper away from raking Blaine's surprised face with her teeth, she was yanked back and she screamed in frustration.

Then there was a solid wall of blue light dividing her and Gavin from their attackers. She froze in astonishment when she realized that the energy radiated from Gavin's outstretched hands.

"You won't touch her." His words were carved in steel. "You won't touch either of us."

Through the wall of light, Blaine snarled, "We'll kill you both." He launched himself at the light.

Aubrey gasped at the audible sizzle when his flesh met

the light. The acrid stench of burning flesh filled the air a split second before the Darkling's body exploded into a shower of ash.

Valentina remained as she was, but her face showed noticeable fear.

"Tell your council that they can't have me. They can't have Aubrey. And I'll kill anyone who tries to take us." He flexed his fingers and the light pulsed toward the group of Darklings, who flinched.

Gavin glanced at Aubrey, then grinned, a feral smile that made her insides clench with inappropriate desire.

"Know what? I'll tell them myself." He again flexed his fingers, and the light pulsed, then moved in a solid sheet until every Darkling but Aubrey was engulfed in it.

Screams tore through the night and the blue became a blinding force. Aubrey winced as the disgusting smell of charred flesh and ash filled her nostrils.

And then they were alone.

Gavin collapsed onto his knees, drained from the fight. Aubrey followed him down, wrapping her arms around him and sobbing with relief.

"How did you—how did you know—" Her words were swallowed into Gavin's mouth as he rained kisses over her lips.

He drew back for a breath and grinned at her. "I have no idea. Well, I sort of do. They threatened you and…it just exploded out of me." He buried his face in her hair.

"But it sure clarified something for me."

"What's that?" Aubrey could hardly speak, since Gavin was pressing her so tightly against him.

"I've known it since I met you. You are mine." Before Aubrey could reply, another voice chimed into their conversation.

"What the hell happened here?" Aubrey recognized the nasal voice of the desk clerk that had given her the room key, and also his smell.

He smelled like stale, like he hadn't showered for a day too many, and he looked astounded as he stood in the shattered doorway gazing around at the wreck of the hotel room.

Gavin drew Aubrey into his lap, clearly euphoric in the aftermath of the battle.

"I don't know, man." He grinned up at the scrawny young man while clamping a possessive arm around Aubrey's waist. "But since we're staying together—staying together forever—I think we're going to need another room."

\* \* \* \* \*

# HER VAMPIRE LOVER

## Caridad Piñeiro

**Caridad Piñeiro** is a multi-published and award-winning author whose love of the written word developed when her fifth grade teacher assigned a project—to write a book that would be placed in a class lending library. She has been hooked on writing ever since.

When not writing, Caridad teaches workshops on various topics related to writing and heads a writing group. Caridad is also an attorney, wife and mother. For more information, please visit www.caridad.com.

# Chapter One

Lost luggage, weather delays and a missed connection were not how Sonja Dubcek had planned to start her dream vacation. Luckily, she had caught a flight that still got her to Amsterdam in time for her overnight train ride to Prague. It was almost antiquated to use the railroad instead of hopping on another plane, but Sonja was rather old-fashioned.

Or at least that's what her ex-boyfriend had said to her when she caught him in bed with one of her girlfriends.

"Sunny," he'd said, because everyone called her Sunny. "You're just too uptight. Join the twenty-first century, for God's sake."

He'd been casually leaning against the pillows in their bed, her former friend beside him. When he'd suggested a threesome, it had taken all her control not to lose it.

That had been nearly two years ago and in all that time, Sunny had rebuilt her life, found better friends and promised herself a grand adventure because she knew she wasn't as boring and predictable as her ex had insisted.

This trip to Prague was just that. Her grand adventure. If a little romance happened to come her way, all the better.

Hopefully, once her luggage finally showed up.

She boarded the train with the small overnight bag she had thankfully packed with the essentials, and the conductor guided her to her sleeper. The room was a well-designed and modern bed/bath combo, but barely bigger than her closet at home. Because she had no luggage to speak of, it was perfect.

Grungy from the nearly twenty hours of traveling, Sunny treated herself to a hot shower in the tiny corner cubicle. Washing away her troubles brightened her mood, until she creamed her elbow on the edge of the shower stall. Pain radiated through her arm and she wondered how anyone a bit bigger would be able to use the facilities. At five foot five and a size six, she barely fit.

Rubbing at her elbow as she finished washing, she then dried off and switched into the spare set of clothes she had packed: a button-down Oxford shirt, black jeans and a rather tiny lacy bra and panty set to which she had treated herself at Victoria's Secret. She could be just as daring as the next girl when she wanted to be.

As a precaution, she hand-washed the T-shirt and undies she had been wearing, all the time hoping the airline would deliver her things to her hotel in Prague as promised.

Too excited to just sit in her sleeper car, and with hunger starting to gnaw at her innards, she headed out to the dining car.

She'd heard that Europeans ate later, but you couldn't prove that from the nearly full restaurant and the line of people waiting to be seated. Sunny positioned herself at the end of the queue and patiently waited, occasionally scoping out the area to see if any tables had freed up. Impatiently she wondered why one booth capable of seating at least four remained empty, considering the crowd and the delays.

Those having supper seemed in no mood to rush and

nearly an hour passed before Sunny was finally the next person in line.

The host in the foyer to the car arched a brow and said with an almost-disdainful sniff, "Table for one?"

Biting back annoyance, Sunny nodded. "Just one."

With a flare of a hairy eyebrow, he said, "That'll be another half an hour or so. We've just seated quite a few tables."

Sunny pointed to the still-empty booth. "What about that one?"

Flailing his hands as if she had just suggested something sacrilegious, he said, "Oh no, no, no. That is the count's table and it is reserved."

Sunny glanced at the table again. "It's been vacant for at least an hour. Surely you have a limit for how long you hold reservations?"

"For the count, we always make an exception. Just in case he decides to drop in." The host tilted his head up at an angle that had him looking down at her as if she was a bug under a microscope.

If Sunny was one thing, it was persistent. With a determined glare, she said, "Are you telling me that you don't even know if the count is going to dine here tonight?"

The man blustered for a moment under her withering stare, but then finally confirmed her understanding. "As I said, it is tradition to hold the spot."

"In my home we have a tradition as well. We don't keep guests waiting." Without a pause, she walked into the dining car and to the empty booth set for one.

*Interesting.* She apparently wasn't the only one who dined alone.

The host, who had raced after her, stammered a protest as she reached the booth.

"Madam, you cannot sit there," he said quietly so only she

would hear. He glanced around the room nervously, as if half expecting the count to materialize out of thin air.

"Watch me." She slipped in the booth and sat, admiring the rich patina of the leather covering the seat, so unlike the more pedestrian cloth on the other booths and chairs in the room. The booth itself was made from mahogany and intricately carved with a pattern of twining vines and roses.

The host realized she would not be dissuaded and after another quick glance around the room, as if to decide if he might stuff her somewhere else instead, he raised his hand and snapped his fingers.

One of the waiters immediately hurried over.

"Give her your full attention. We need the table clear in case the count arrives."

Without another look at her, the man dashed back to his podium, his manner supercilious.

"I'm so sorry, miss. Henri can be a little full of himself. What can I get you?" the waiter asked with a polite bow and a welcoming smile.

Grateful for the change in attitude, she smiled and sank back into the comfortable bench. "A glass of cabernet and a menu would be nice."

"Certainly, miss." With a nod, her waiter rushed away and Sunny peered out the window. Dark shadows mingled with occasional bursts of lights from a passing station or the more muted glimmers from distant homes and towns. Not much to see of the countryside because it was night, but her return trip in a week would be during daytime and she looked forward to viewing it then.

The waiter arrived with her wine and menu, and hovered nearby as she perused it. Clearly he intended to honor the host's request to move her along quickly. The menu had a nice selection, but given the prices on some of the items and the fact she had a budget to keep, she ordered the simplest and cheapest dish—the roasted chicken. Besides, some of the other choices were items she would not normally eat. Dining-wise, the adventure she had promised herself would have to wait a bit.

The waiter scurried to place her order, and Sunny picked up her glass and toasted the empty seat across from her. "To life and love."

It was the way her parents had toasted each other for as long as she could remember. A drunk driver had taken their lives just last year and although she missed them every day, she was glad that they had gone together to their next adventure.

She sipped the wine. Dry, it had the barest hint of vanilla and berries. She placed the glass on the table, hoping that if it breathed a bit, the flavors would mature. As she turned to peer out the window again, she picked up on the growing silence in the room until it became unnaturally quiet, like the moment before a storm hit.

A second later, a low murmur grew and seemed to rush toward her like a tsunami bearing down on the shore. From the corner of her eye, she caught a glimpse of the host as he approached and of someone in a dark, impossibly black suit following immediately behind.

Preparing for the worst, she picked up her glass of wine and took a sip. Then she buried her attention on the dark, blurry images rushing past her window, until the reflection of the host standing beside the booth marred the view.

She turned to find him there, along with a man who could have been in one of those ads for expensive Swiss watches. Tall, lean and lethally elegant, she had no doubt that this was the count for whom the table had been reserved. Everything about him screamed rich and royal, from the perfect fit of what she now realized was a blue-black suit, to the snowy shirt with the perfectly knotted tie and the hand he held just so before him. His wrist boasted a large and obviously expensive gold watch. Swiss, of course.

"I'm sorry, miss. I warned you this table was reserved for the count. You'll have to move," the host said, but there was no hint of real apology in his voice. If anything, it had a nasty bite of "there, I told you so" in its tone.

While she tried to decide whether to cave and leave, or fight and maintain her ground, the count silenced the host with a polished and almost-careless gesture.

"Thank you, Henri, but that may not be necessary."

The pitch of his voice was low and her toes curled as she imagined that voice in the dark, whispering the proverbial sweet nothings in her ear. Her gaze fixated on his lips, harshly masculine but full. A devastating smile came to them along with a hint of a boyish dimple at odds with his otherwise manly and proper appearance.

That dimple propelled her gaze upward. Her heart did a little flip-flop as she detected the glimmer of masculine interest. The curl that had begun in her toes at her first sight of him worked its way dangerously upward.

She licked suddenly dry lips and said, "I'm sorry, Count—"

"I prefer Gregori," he replied smoothly and then gestured to the booth.

"Would you mind if I joined you for supper?"

# Chapter Two

A bright stain of color worked its way across her cheeks and Gregori had a hard time deciding if it was from embarrassment or something else. He hoped it was something else, although there was a vibe about the woman that struck him as almost virginal. He couldn't quite say why, because she was beautiful. Toffee-colored hair with streaks of sunlight framed a heart-shaped face with deliciously full lips. But it was her eyes that snared his attention the most. They were the dark violet-blue of the happy-faced pansies his father had used to plant to cheer up Gregori's ailing mother.

That violet-blue gaze had been almost demure as it traveled over him at first glance.

He was used to women with a more direct approach and the kind of perusal that left no doubt about just what they wanted, which was fine with him. It was usually just what he wanted anyway. Especially because it gave them that bright taste of desire as he sank his fangs in for an after-sex bite.

But not this woman, he thought again, as he waited for her answer, anxious. He hadn't felt that way in a long time.

"I wouldn't mind."

Funny response. She'd not said she'd like it or love it or any of the other expected replies.

Henri immediately jumped into the discussion. "She's already ordered, Count. The roast chicken." His nose twitched with obvious disapproval.

"A wonderful choice. The same for me. I'm sure it will be as delicious as always," he replied with a glare at the host.

Holding out his hand, he introduced himself more properly. "I'm Count Gregori and you would be…"

She slipped her hand into his. It was warm, smooth and slightly moist from nerves. A skitter of desire worked through him as he imagined that hand trailing over his body.

"Sonja Dubcek, but everyone calls me Sunny."

He held back a shudder at her nickname. Nothing sunny held an attraction for him. But as he brought her hand to his lips and her excited pulse registered against his vampire senses, he realized he'd be lying to himself if he didn't acknowledge his interest in her.

"Sonja," he said, enjoying the way her name fell from his lips. "If you wouldn't mind indulging me yet again, I'd love to add a few of my favorites to our meal."

"Of course. It's not a problem." She withdrew her hand from his overly long grasp and lowered it to her lap.

Inclining his head down to Henri's shorter height, he rattled off his selections and after the host hurried off, he eased onto the bench beside Sonja.

His actions surprised Sunny. She had expected him to sit across from her. The booth seemed cramped with him beside her. He had seemed lean at first glance, but she realized now that he was a big man and broad across the shoulders. Although she scooted over as far as she could, his arm brushed against hers as well as against the side of her breast—until he turned a bit to face her.

"Tell me about yourself, Sonja."

She almost didn't want to talk because hearing him speak intrigued her more than it should. His baritone voice was deep and smooth, like a well-played cello. An upper-crust English accent bore traces of another, more subtle inflection. One she couldn't place. She humored his request, intending to hear more from him during the course of their meal.

"I'm a high school math teacher in New Jersey on vacation. My flight was supposed to leave last night, but there were delays, so I only landed this afternoon."

"You must be tired after such a long trip."

"I am, but I'm also excited about visiting Prague and seeing where my grandparents were born. How about you, Count?"

"Gregori, please. I should have guessed you were Czech from the last name." He motioned to the waiter, who immediately brought over a bottle and two wineglasses, and whisked away her half-full wineglass.

"I wasn't done with that," she said, slightly annoyed at his high-handed actions.

He surprised her by leaning in close. In a conspiratorial whisper he said, "I don't like to complain, but the wine choices here are usually a bit limited. This one is from my private stock and I think you'll enjoy it more."

He poured them both a taste, but when she reached for her glass, he snared her hand and tucked it into his. "Let it breathe a bit while you tell me a little more about yourself."

Sunny hesitated and examined his features. Ruthlessly handsome would have been a good way to describe him. His face was all strong, powerful lines, but as he smiled and cocked his head to the side, the boyishness returned and his dark brown eyes glittered with amusement.

Did he find her humorous somehow? she wondered and called him out on it.

"Do you find me funny?"

He shrugged and the blue-black wool of his suit stretched tight against those wide shoulders. "I guess you could say I'm used to women who won't shut up about themselves. You're a refreshing change."

His candor tempered her anger. "Maybe you should stop hanging out with all those princesses."

His grin broadened, awakening that delicious dimple on one side, and he brushed his thumb across the knuckles of the hand he continued to hold. "Maybe. So tell me more, Sonja from New Jersey."

"Not much to tell. I teach. Work out on occasion. Visit with my friends and family."

"No boyfriend?" he asked with an inquisitive arch of his brow.

"Not right now," she admitted, unsure of why she had. Although she had considered she might find a little romance on this trip, she wasn't sure the count was what she had in mind.

"American men must be quite foolish not to snatch up such a beautiful woman."

She couldn't help but laugh. "Does that pickup line work often?"

To her surprise, he laughed as well and shook his head. "Poor Sonja. Sometimes a compliment is just a compliment."

His chastisement stung a little, but then he leaned forward until his warm breath spilled against her lips and her heart did that funky flip again. In a low, sexy whisper that sent a wave of heat through her, he said, "When I seduce you, believe me, you will know."

Before she could respond, he released her hand and picked up his wineglass, urging her to do the same. "Close your eyes and open your senses," he said and she watched as he did so while taking a sip of the wine. After he swallowed, that engaging smile returned to his lips and he focused his gaze on her as he waited.

Sunny brought the glass to her lips and Gregori held his breath, imagining his lips there instead. She closed her eyes as he had asked and took a sip, holding the wine in her mouth a moment before swallowing. When she opened her eyes and faced him, her lips were moist and smiling.

"Delicious."

He couldn't resist. He tucked his hand beneath her chin and swiped his thumb across those luscious lips.

She drew back, but barely. A brighter flush erupted on her cheeks and her eyes darkened to nearly purple. As he slowly withdrew his hand, he touched his thumb to the small indent in her chin in a final caress. Maybe even as a promise of what could come, if she let it.

A second later, Henri and a waiter approached. The waiter set the covered plates before them and then whisked away the lids with a flourish. Henri immediately stepped in and poured a glass of another wine for each of them.

Sunny shot Gregori a questioning glance, but he quickly explained. "The foie gras is in a reduction with bits of pear. This Sauternes is on the sweet side and will mesh well with the fruit."

Sunny stared down at the grilled piece of goose liver delicately drizzled with a brown sauce. Toast points and more sauce with bits of caramelized pear completed the presentation on the plate. Not knowing what to expect because she had never eaten foie gras, she followed Gregori's lead, cutting off a small piece to taste.

As soon as she closed her lips over the morsel, an assortment of flavors exploded in her mouth. The sweet of the fruit and the slight tang of the sauce. The buttery smoothness of the liver, like nothing she had ever tasted. She couldn't quite hold back the slight moan of pleasure.

"I guess you like it," he teased and took a sip of the Sauternes. She did the same, experiencing the perfect balance of the slightly sweet wine against the earlier tastes.

She polished off the foie gras and Sauternes way too quickly, almost greedily, caught up in the sheer luxury of it and the decadent feeling it had roused in her.

Gregori was slightly slower, and when he had only a bite left, he lifted his fork and offered to share it with her.

As her gaze met his beyond the tempting tidbit, she understood he intended for them to share that, and more.

Closing her mouth over the morsel, she tasted all of the earlier flavors and one more.

She tasted Gregori.

Between her legs a low throb pulsed with each chew and after she swallowed, her mouth was dry with want. She reached for her glass, but it was empty.

Instead of refilling it, Gregori offered up his own, turning it so that she would drink from the exact spot he had. As he tilted the glass and she sipped it, the wine was still sweet, but the taste of him was far more enticing.

After he moved the glass away, she licked her lips, wanting more. Determined to take the leap, she decided to explore this unexpected adventure that had presented itself.

She leaned forward, prepared for another taste of him. Bringing her lips to within an inch of his, she asked, "Would you mind sharing something else?"

# Chapter Three

Gregori sucked in a breath and rethought his earlier statement about seduction. If anyone was being seduced, it just
might be him.

"Not at all," he whispered and closed his eyes, expectant.

Her mouth skimmed over his, soft and warm. Mobile, as
she traced the edges of his lips, sipping like a bee might sip
nectar, before she opened her mouth on his, tasting him with
a quick lick of her tongue.

He groaned and tangled his fingers in the silky strands of
her hair, holding her close as the kiss deepened.

Remnants of the wine lingered, sweet, but beneath that was
the subtle flavor of Sonja, clean and welcoming. Inquisitive,
as she responded to him with a hesitant touch of innocence
that was so at odds with the sensuality he sensed deep inside
her and the daring that had initiated the kiss.

They broke apart at an abrupt and almost-condemning
cough from beside them, both breathing heavily.

As Gregori turned slightly, he realized it was Henri. For
a moment, he considered ripping out the man's throat for in-
terrupting such a delicious interlude. He restrained himself,
especially when fear crept into the host's eyes. It occurred

to Gregori that his desire for Sonja had allowed a bit of the vampire to become visible.

"What is it, Henri?" A low rumble tinged his voice, confirming that the demon had to be controlled.

Henri glanced down at the tray in his hands. "Just some lemon ice to clear the palate."

And hopefully to cool him down, he heard in the subtle condemnation of the other man's tone.

Gregori nodded and the host placed the ices before them along with some clean spoons. As refreshing as the ices were, he regretted that they did cleanse him of the taste of Sonja. As he glanced at her from the corner of his eye, he wondered if she felt the same.

They had barely finished when the waiter returned with a cart loaded with the fixings for the Caesar salad he had ordered. When Sonja craned her head forward to watch, Gregori shifted, draping his arm across her shoulders and tucking her tight so she might have a better view.

A mistake, he realized as her hand dropped to his thigh and the side of her breast brushed against his chest. Between his legs, arousal clawed into him, making him so hard that it was almost painful. He sucked in a breath and fought it, fought the demon who wanted to come out and slake that desire in any way it could.

Beneath Sunny's hand, Gregori's body trembled and it was impossible for her not to notice the way the fabric of his slacks stretched against an impressive erection. The pulse that had been beating between her legs became more insistent and her body grew damp with need as she imagined taking that long, thick, hard length deep into her body.

She took a shaky breath to quell that need and instead smelled him, smelled his masculine scent beneath the light, and probably very expensive, cologne. Her nipples tightened in response and she shifted a bit on the bench. That brought her breast against the muscled wall of his chest.

As her gaze skipped across his for a moment, it was impossible to miss that he was as affected as she was.

He had draped his arm across her shoulder, but as she leaned forward, he dropped his hand until he could dip beneath her arm and cradle the side of her breast. She shook as she imagined him moving his hand just a little more to touch her tight nipple. Instead, he just brushed his hand back and forth tenderly, almost pleading for her touch as well.

She moved her hand on his thigh, a slow caress as they sat silent as the waiter prepared the salad. Their attention was barely on the man's actions as with one light stroke after another, desire grew between them.

After the waiter placed their salad plates before them, Gregori moved his arm, bringing instant regret, but she kept her hand on his thigh, stroking. Loving the feel of the hard, tight muscles beneath her hand and the slight tremble in his body.

The salad might have been excellent, but she was so caught up in the feel and smell of him, in the want that he roused, that it was tasteless as she ate it.

When Gregori pushed away his half-eaten salad and turned toward her, draping his arm back around her shoulder to once again touch her, she sighed with pleasure.

He leaned toward her and nuzzled his nose against the shell of her ear and whispered in that rich baritone, "Touch me."

"Here?" she nearly squeaked.

His answer was the tug of his lips on the lobe of her ear before he dropped a kiss just beneath, on the sensitive skin of her throat.

Her heartbeat raced, sending blood rushing through every part of her body. Making her clitoris swell and rub against her panties and the seam of her jeans.

When he nipped at the tender flesh of her throat before dropping another kiss there, she glanced toward the center of the dining car and realized that his big body and his position hid her from the view of the patrons.

Answering his plea, she worked her hand up his thigh and grazed the length of his erection with her pinky.

He jumped beside her and groaned again. "Please, Sonja."

His response shook her to the core. She suspected he wasn't a man used to begging.

She covered him with her hand, stroking the long length. Finding the head of him beneath the fabric and circling it, which had him almost visibly shaking.

A movement over his shoulder snared her attention and she jerked her hand away just as the waiter arrived with their dinner plates.

Gregori's lips tightened with displeasure at the intrusion, but surprisingly, he remained calm. As he met her confused gaze, he said, "I'm a patient man, and I know you must be quite hungry after your long day of travel."

She appreciated his thoughtfulness, but their little interlude had excited her and awakened her adventurous streak.

"Maybe I'm not a patient woman."

He dropped the fork in his hand and it clattered noisily against the fine china. Looking around at the other diners, whose number was finally growing sparser as the night wore on, he picked up the fork and shot her a strained grin.

"Anticipation makes the satisfaction all the more sweet."

She supposed it did, and in reality, she was hungry. Famished for food and for him. The sooner they finished their meal, the sooner they might find a way to explore the desire sizzling between them.

Gregori, however, took his time, eating the perfectly roasted chicken with leisure. His strong hands sure as he cut and ate, buttered a roll and offered her up a piece. Just to be sure he remembered where they had left off, she nipped at his thumb when she took the piece.

"You're not playing fair, my love," he warned, his eyes darkening.

"Really?" she teased and because the intensity of his look was causing heat to pool between her legs and rise upward, she slipped free the next two buttons on her shirt and tugged the fabric open slightly in hope of some cooling.

Gregori's vampire senses picked up on the rising temperature of her body and the musky smell of her desire. His erection tightened and jumped in response, and, at his core, the heat of the demon coalesced and pushed to be free. It struggled to be loose to taste her flesh and her blood.

Those same senses picked up on the heartbeats from the few patrons still lingering in the dining car. Not more than half a dozen. An easy enough number for him to handle.

Pushing out with his vampire powers to the other diners in the car, he offered them a suggestion about the kind of desire that awaited them outside so they might leave him and Sonja alone. Then he returned his attention to Sonja, but as he did so, he caught sight of Henri's reflection.

The host approached with a chilled bottle of champagne, while the waiter immediately behind him scurried around to serve them dessert.

After Henri had poured the champagne, he stood there, hands clasped before him, patiently awaiting further instructions.

"Please clear the dining car and make sure we are not disturbed for the remainder of the night," Gregori said.

The two men hurried away and after a murmur of voices as they shooed the last couple from the space, the solid thunk of the door attested to the fact that his commands had been followed.

"Do you always get what you want?" Sonja asked.

He faced her and laid his hand on her thigh, stroking the buttery soft denim covering the firm muscles beneath. "It depends on what I want," he answered honestly.

"So what do you want right now?" She spooned up some of the chocolate mousse and whipped cream and paused with it halfway to her lips.

"I want you to feed me."

Sonja diverted the spoonful she had been about to eat to his mouth, but as she did so, he reached out and, with one hand, slipped free another button on her blouse. His action exposed the lace-edged silk bra beneath.

"Beautiful," he said and popped open another button.

"You're very sure of yourself, aren't you?" She didn't stop him, however, as another button popped free. Instead, she scooped up another bit of dessert and brought it to his mouth, her hand a little shaky.

He met her gaze over the bit of chocolate and cream on the spoon. Easing his hand beneath the pale blue cotton of her blouse, he cupped her breast and circled his thumb around the hard point.

Her hand jerked, smearing some of the cream and chocolate on his upper lip. Before he could clean it off, she leaned forward and licked his lip free. She whispered a quick kiss across his mouth before she spooned up more, and he took her nipple between his thumb and forefinger, tweaking it gently.

A breath shuddered in and out of her body at his caress and he pushed on, quickly undoing the front clasp to free her breasts. Cradling her soft flesh, more silky than the fabric, with his hand, he pleasured the sensitive nub with his fingers.

She fed him again, and he greedily ate the dessert, but knew she possessed something far tastier.

Leaving his ministrations for only a moment, he pulled the blouse free of her jeans and eased the fabric aside. He bent his head and licked her tight nipple, dragging a soft gasp from her before he deepened the pleasure by sucking it into his mouth, alternately licking and teething the hard point.

His mouth was sheer heaven, Sonja thought, threading her hand through the heavy strands of his short hair. Wanting to give him pleasure as well, she covered him with her other hand and stroked his arousal. She imagined what it would be like to have that hard flesh deep inside her and damp flooded from her body, soaking her panties and jeans.

He wrapped his arm around her waist and pulled her forward as he shifted off the bench and dropped to his knees before her.

She experienced a pang of hesitation, worried about someone walking in as he cupped her breasts with his hands and strummed his thumbs across her nipples.

He must have sensed her momentary lapse, because he rose up and skimmed his lips across hers. He whispered, "No one would dare come in."

No one would, she knew. He was the count and used to having his way. And now he intended to have his way with her. If she let him.

As he kneeled before her, his gaze tilted up at her, inquiring, she realized he was hers to command. A thrill of excitement flared through her at that insight. She was the one in charge.

"Kiss me," she said and then dipped her gaze down to her breasts. "There."

He smiled and the dimple winked out at her, acknowledging the little game they would be enjoying.

"As you command," he said before playfully dropping a quick peck at the tip of each breast.

"So stingy?" she teased and laid a hand on his shoulder, applying gentle pressure to urge him toward her breasts again.

"How can I pleasure you, Sonja?" His gaze slipped over her breasts, as potent as any caress. Between her legs, a deep pulse throbbed with need.

She knew then what she wanted him to do.

"Make me come, Gregori. Right here. Right now." She sank her fingers into the thick strands of his hair and drew him forward.

Excitement rose sharply in Gregori, but so did the demon who wanted a bite of her luscious flesh. He fought back the vampire, wanting to experience the pleasure she brought to him. It had been too long since he had experienced this myriad of emotions and satisfaction with a human woman. He wasn't about to waste such uniqueness by draining it dry.

He leaned forward and sucked at her breasts, shifting between the two while also caressing her with his hands.

She held his head tight to her, urging him on with her soft cries of pleasure and the trip hammer beat of her heart, which sounded close to his ear as he made love to her. His own heart, normally slow as death, answered, picking up speed as his excitement grew.

When she parted her thighs, cradling him between them, the sharp smell of her arousal ensnared him. He brought his hand to her center. Dampness greeted him even through the thickness of the denim. He pressed his thumb there and she moaned, clutching him ever tighter. He rubbed harder, using the seam of her pants to create ever greater friction. Biting down roughly on the puckered tip of one nipple, he, too, began to lose control.

That sharp nip and another stronger stroke of his thumb pulled her over.

She arched her back and called out his name, her eyes closed against the pleasure. Her position exposed the flush across her breasts and the mad pulse at her throat.

Beating, beating, beating. The blood rushing all throughout her with the force of her climax.

Gregori lost it.

The vampire surged forward, fangs bursting from his mouth painfully. His eyes gleamed neon and focused on just one thing.

That luscious, very alive pulse.

He sank his teeth into her throat and she cried out, the pain of the bite melding with the pleasure. Her blood spiced by her passion, made him ache to possess her body as well.

With a deep pull, he drank from her and she shuddered in his arms, whimpering. The sound was innocent and condemning, but a second later she wrapped her arms around him, pulling him tight and murmuring his name again.

From deep inside him, something roused. Something alive and different.

As he took yet more from her, his mind was suddenly filled with images of his past interspersed with new and different memories. Her memories, he realized, so shocked by the exchange that he ripped away from her.

She met his gaze, her eyes half-closed and slightly unfocused from his feeding. The wound at her neck still bled, staining the pale blue of her shirt. Accusatory.

"Gregori?" she asked, pain and confusion coloring her words as she shook her head and focused on his monster face. Then she shocked him yet again by reaching up and running her thumb across his bloodstained lips and down his sharp white fang.

"I don't understand," she said, but before he could respond, she passed out.

Gregori didn't understand either.

# Chapter Four

Gregori gently laid Sonja back against the bench, ripped off his jacket and wrapped it around her. He licked her throat to seal the wounds from his bite and bundled her into his arms, hurrying from the dining car and to his sleeper.

His keeper waited at the entrance to the ornate sleeper, and as Gregori approached, his man opened the door, stone-faced except for the barest arch of his brow.

Gregori normally didn't bring dinner home with him.

Inside, he hurried to the massive wooden four-poster bed and laid her on the silk comforter. She was still unconscious as he undressed her, but she roused as he propped her up against the pillows and tucked the sheet up to shut off his view of her nakedness. He wasn't sure how long he could fight off the temptation to taste her again.

With a low moan, her eyes fluttered open and she grasped her forehead with one hand, rubbing there as if to wipe away the fuzziness from his bite.

"Just give it a minute," he said and rose from the bed. He filled a glass with some fortified wine for her and another with brandy for himself. He needed something strong to wipe the memory of her deliciousness from his palate.

When he returned to sit on the bed, the sheet had dropped down, exposing her breasts. Perfectly round and lush, her nipples were still tight from the remnants of her passion and his bite. His mouth watered at the thought of kissing her there again and his still-erect cock twitched with anticipation.

He raised the glass to her lips. "Try this. It will help strengthen you."

Sonja took a first, hesitant sip and wrinkled her nose. "Sweet," she murmured, still too wobbly to manage more than a single word.

"There's honey and some other things to help you recover." There was chagrin in his voice as he spoke.

"Recover from your bite because you're a vampire," she said in a rush before her energy failed her. As if sensing what it had cost her, he urged the glass to her lips again and she took another, bigger sip. As the sweet liquid traveled down her gullet, warmth spread through her body and with it desire.

"Why am I feeling like this?" she asked and drank from the glass yet again, feeling the surge of power and something else: his memories, flooding her brain with a collage of disjointed images that somehow made sense to her.

"I don't know. I'm feeling it, too," he admitted and with a shaky hand, gulped down a goodly amount of whatever he was drinking.

"Is this a vampire thing? The way I'm feeling?" she said, surprising herself with the calmness the images brought. She should be afraid of him. Afraid of the violence of which he was capable, but the images swirling through her brain were so different, holding her fear at bay.

He shrugged those broad shoulders she had admired earlier. "I've heard tales of vampires who found their soul mates. They shared everything with them through a bite. I thought they were just urban legends."

"You were a hero." The images had told her his story. Shown her how he had sacrificed himself during the Holocaust to save his ailing Jewish mother and Catholic father. She reached out with her hand, grasped his and turned it to reveal the tattoo along the inside of his wrist.

"I did the only thing I could."

He had done more, she thought, as his memories settled beside hers in her head. Another sip of the sweet wine seemed to clear away the last vestiges of weakness and lack of focus. She opened her eyes and met his gaze, realizing that just as she now knew so much about him, he likewise had her story.

"He was a fool. No man who had you in his bed should stray." Anger roused in Gregori at the idiot who had acted so foolishly and cruelly.

"I'm in your bed."

A shudder shook his body as he thought about just what he wanted to do with her. To her. But despite her provocative statement, he smelled the traces of her fear. He knew that deep inside, he was afraid as well. Afraid of what was happening between them. Afraid of what he might do to keep her with him because he wasn't sure he could let her go.

"I want to make love with you," he confessed and downed the rest of the brandy in one big gulp. It burned its way down his throat, as bitter as the thought that she might refuse him.

She didn't.

"What's stopping you?" She pulled down the sheets and exposed her breasts to him. The flush of life and desire pinked her skin, tempting him as both man and vampire.

"I don't trust myself." As he said it, he leaned forward and jerked off one of the satin ropes holding back the drapes around the bed. Reaching beyond her, he yanked off a second rope and then held them up for her to see.

Her gaze skittered from the ropes to the thick, carved bed posts. "You want me to tie you down?"

He nodded and didn't wait for her response before fastening the cords around the bedposts. Then he stood by the side of the bed and held out his hands like a prisoner waiting to be cuffed. "You'll have to do the rest."

Heat rushed through her body and wetness pooled between her legs. Heeding his request, she kneeled on the mattress, took hold of his hands and urged them to the side so she could undress him. With a jerk, she opened his tie and tossed it aside. She yanked his shirt free of his pants and quickly undid the buttons while he toed off his shoes and socks.

She hesitated as she parted the rich linen and revealed his magnificent body. His pale skin and chiseled muscles were like a finely sculpted statue, but unlike chilly marble, pleasant heat warmed his flesh.

As she swept her hand across the thick muscle of his pectorals and cupped them in her hands, she said, "So the part about being cold as death—"

"An old wives' tale." He mimicked her actions, cradling her breasts and teasing her puckered nipples with his fingers.

"How about the stake through the heart and decapitation?" She slipped her hands to his shoulders and eased his shirt off, revealing the breadth and strength of his upper body.

"We're more human than most think, which means you better tie me up soon because I can't resist you for much longer." He once again held out his hands to be bound.

She grasped one wrist and urged him to lie on the bed. She straddled him as she tied first one wrist and then another to the thick and ornately carved posts of the bed. For good measure, he pulled hard on the bindings, his muscles straining, but her ties held.

Between her legs, his erection pressed up into her as she

sat astride him, only the fabric of his pants separating them. He was thick, hard and massive—too much for her to resist. She dragged herself across him, needing something.

He raised his hips, increasing the pressure of him against her and she closed her eyes, rode him a few more times, the friction of the cloth erotic against her nether lips and mons. But it wasn't enough.

She slipped down his legs and quickly undid his pants, dragging them and his briefs from his body. He had beautiful legs, long and lean. His cock…sweet Lord, his cock was a sight to behold.

"Touch me, Sonja," he said, a low rumble in his voice.

As she met his gaze a glimmer of otherworldliness brightened the dark brown of his eyes. The vampire, she assumed, and a little tingle of fear crept into her until she reminded herself that he was the one at her mercy right now.

Skimming her hands up his legs, she encircled his erection in one hand and cupped his balls with the other. She stroked and massaged him until he was arching off the bed, wanting more.

She wanted more as well, but not yet. She was rather enjoying being the one in charge. Bending, she licked the head of his cock. He jerked off the bed and growled, the sound wild and uncontrolled.

"I guess you like that," she teased and offered up another lick as he moaned her name. The wooden posts creaked as he fought against them.

Between her legs, her clitoris throbbed and her vagina clenched on emptiness. Her breasts tingled as they skimmed the soft hair on his thighs.

As she bent and took him into her mouth, swallowing him as far as she could, she reached up and tweaked her own breasts, pushing for her own climax. Moaning around his dick, she sucked and licked him until they were both shaking.

Gregori barely held back his release as he watched her play with herself. Somehow he managed, but he needed her on him. Needed to taste those sweet breasts and take her over the edge with him.

"Ride me, love. I want to come inside you," he urged.

She sat up then and covered him with her body. She grasped his cock and held it to her center. She was so wet, her juices dripped on him as she slid the head of his cock into her vagina.

He bucked up, wild with the need of her, and drove himself deep inside.

She gasped and sank down on him, grinding her hips roughly as she continued to play with her breasts, her head thrown back in ecstasy.

Gregori lost control to the demon then. With a loud roar, the vampire emerged.

Sonja stopped then to look down at him. The fear was there again, but also something else. Something dangerous. His innocent little teacher wanted to dance with the demon.

"Come here," he commanded and yanked at the ties, wanting freedom.

Sonja leaned forward and surprised him yet again. She nipped at his lower lip, biting him before moving to offer up her breasts for his kiss.

Gregori latched on to her nipple, sucking and licking and grazing the sharp points of his fangs across the tip, which dragged a ragged gasp from her.

"Do it again," she said, offering up her other breast for his love bite.

He did as she commanded, lost in the pleasure of her body as she began to move her hips, riding him toward completion. She cradled the back of his skull in her hands to keep him close as he tasted her over and over again until his climax exploded over him.

Groaning, he shoved his hips upward, pumping into her until she hoarsely shouted his name and dropped down onto him. Her lips met his, breaths rough until sanity slowly returned.

As it did, the demon retreated, leaving him to savor the heat and wet of her surrounding him. Her body bonelessly draped over his as her weight bore him down into the mattress. Her full breasts crushed against his chest. The smoothness of her belly tucked along his hard abdomen.

He sighed with the wonder of the moment and she propped her elbow on his chest, stared down at him, a sexy satisfied smile on her lips.

"You didn't bite me."

He dipped his gaze down to her breasts for the briefest moment.

"Only when you begged," he teased and grinned.

Embarrassed heat flashed through Sonja along with the need for humor as his dimple winked at her. "It wasn't really begging. Just a request."

His smile broadened and his eyes twinkled with delight. "Then how about this request? Please untie me."

She arched a brow. "Untie you? Why?"

He glanced down at her breasts once more. "Because I need to touch you."

Her insides clenched with the thought of his hands on her. Deep in her vagina, his dick twitched and began to harden. Gingerly, to keep him tucked inside her, she undid the tie on one hand and, as promised, he dipped it down to play with her breast.

A sigh escaped her as she undid the second tie and he

rolled until they were lying side-by-side. He tucked her thigh over his, driving himself ever tighter into her.

"You feel so good," he murmured, skimming the back of his hand across her breasts as she lay with her head pillowed on his arm.

"So do you." In truth, it felt perfect to have him inside her, beside her, his hard parts fitting perfectly to all of her soft spots. His large hand and gifted fingers tenderly exploring and rousing desire as she circled his hard male nipple with her finger.

For long minutes they lay there, caressing each other. Desire was banked so the pleasure of being together could take center stage.

"Where do we go from here?" she wondered aloud, not sure she would ever find anyone who could make her feel this good.

"The train reaches Prague in a few hours," he said, almost wistfully, and slowly rotated the hard tip of her breast between his thumb and forefinger.

"Do you live there?" She tweaked his puckered nipple and his dick jumped inside her. She grinned at her discovery. "I'm glad you like that."

"I live in Prague and in the countryside." He increased his caress, tightening the pressure against her breast as he admitted, "I like a lot about how you make me feel."

"I like you also," she confessed and laid her forehead against his. She whispered a kiss across his lips and shifted her hips to try to satisfy the growing need created by his caresses.

He seemed to understand she needed more. He dipped his hand down between their bodies and parted her curls to find her clit. Applying gentle pressure, he caressed her and each little rub caused an accompanying squeeze of her muscles against his thick, unyielding cock.

The action dragged a pleased sigh from her and a request from him. "Tell me what else you'd like."

A thousand things flitted through Sonja's brain, but then suddenly she settled on one. "Talk dirty to me."

He stilled his caress and arched a dark brow. His grin turned wicked and his gaze settled on her breasts as he said, "On one condition."

## Chapter Five

If he would keep on touching her, she'd agree to almost anything. Except possibly another bite. "What condition?"

"You talk dirty back."

She shook with the thought of what she might say. What he might say. Then she plunged ahead.

"I love the way your cock feels in me. The way it fills me. Comes alive when I do something like this." She tweaked his nipple again and his dick swelled and jerked inside her, dragging a moan from her and from him.

Gregori barely controlled himself, but he wanted to play her little game. It had been too long since he'd frolicked and enjoyed a beautiful woman who had wit and humor. "Your pussy is so hot. Wet. When you hold me inside…"

He ripped his hand away from her clitoris and moved it back to her breast. "Your tits are amazing. So sensitive."

As if to prove his point, he only touched his finger to the center of her nipple and she jumped.

"So not fair," she murmured, but there was little complaint in her voice, only the humor he was coming to realize was an inherent part of her.

"What would you consider fair?" He pressed forward, taking the hard tip between his fingers and making her bite her lower lip.

"Fair?" She scrunched up her face while she considered his question. When her features finally relaxed, he realized he would have his answer and hoped he would like it.

She moved her hand from his chest to trace the edges of his lips with her index finger. "You have a great mouth, less the fangs, of course."

"Of course," he said although he nipped her finger with his human teeth just to prove a point.

"I want that mouth to make love to me." She looked downward to where they were joined and he nearly came at the thought of tasting her release, of feeling her come against his lips.

"I live to obey," he teased, but she protested his withdrawal until he shifted lower, kissed her breasts and eased his hand between her thighs to rub her clitoris as he licked and kissed his way down her body.

Her skin was salty-sweet. The indent of her navel was ticklish, he discovered as he dipped his tongue in before continuing downward.

He settled his body between her thighs and gently parted her legs before reaching in and spreading her nether lips to find the swollen and flushed nub buried in her dark curls.

She raised her hips, inviting him close.

Kissing her, his brain exploded with her scent and taste, nearly overwhelming him and dragging forth the vampire. He would let the demon loose, but not yet. For now, he wanted to savor her.

He flicked his tongue cross her clitoris and eased two fingers into her slick vagina, stroking them in and out to build her passion, increasing the pressure of his mouth against her clitoris and at her vagina until she came.

The release punched through Sonja with the force of a locomotive. Her body shook and arched to him as wave after wave rolled across her body and his mouth and hands kept her release alive.

As his hands left her and grasped her hips, she protested— until she realized his intent. Gently he helped her onto her stomach and she came up on all fours, opening herself to him. She wanted the drive of his thick cock into her, pushing her ever higher.

With one forceful shove and his hands on her hips, he impaled her with the length of his dick and stilled, a growl of pleasure escaping from him and rumbling through her body.

She waited for him to move again, but instead he shifted one hand toward her ass. He slowly worked a finger into her anus and she cried out in surprise. The pressure of that sole digit increased the feel of his erection moving in and out of her. It brought her yet another long, powerful climax that had her almost screaming his name and begging him for more.

He gave it to her, pumping into her with barely controlled violence and stretching her with yet another finger until she was almost light-headed from the passion.

Gregori was lost in the feel of her, so tight around him, so tight around his fingers as the pressure of them inside her had her vagina so wonderfully tight against his dick. But as her passion mounted and he stoked it with the powerful shift of his hips, the connection between them warned he would lose her soon from the strength of her release.

He wanted one more thing before *la petite mort* took her away.

Releasing the demon, he leaned forward and grazed his fangs across the side of her throat.

A shiver racked her body and a hint of tension pulled her from her climax. She turned her head slightly and looked at him, her eyes heavy-lidded with passion and with a hint of fear.

"I need to feed. I will not hurt you and the pleasure…"

With the barest graze of his fangs, he scratched a faint line across her shoulder, but even that little bite was enough to bring the vampire's desire to her. It dragged her eyes closed as her body shook roughly beneath him and her vagina vibrated all around him, creating a ball of need in his gut that he had to assuage.

"Sonja, please," he pleaded, determined to have her consent to his bite.

"Yes," she hissed and moved her hips, drawing herself along his length as she, too, sought yet greater passion.

He groaned and controlled the urge to rip his fangs into her throat. More gently he brought his mouth to where her pulse was beating so powerfully; her blood was a rushing river through her body. His head swam with the remembered taste of her and he lost a little control, spilling the first hint of his seed.

As she shifted her hips again, urging him on, he finally bit down.

Her head reared back and she screamed his name as the pleasure/pain of his bite swept through her, lifting her release onto another plane. Flooding her brain with not only more images, but also with what he was feeling as he made love to her.

He moved then, driving his cock in and out of her as he sucked at her throat until she was moaning and writhing beneath him, but then with another rough call of his name, her body tensed and shattered beneath him.

Sonja collapsed onto the bed with him on her. He was still working his fingers and dick in her, seeking his own release as she grew even more light-headed from the sensations he was creating. Even as her release ebbed through her, the strong pull of his mouth was rousing yet another climax, which she wasn't sure she could endure. Already her body and mind were not her own; they were connected to his in ways she could not have imagined.

He finally moved his hand from her ass and eased his fingers against her belly, splaying them there to hold her to him as with one final push he came.

He pulled free of her throat and growled her name. Inside her, the heat of his seed warmed her and a moment of panic seized her.

No condoms. Not this time or before.

Did she even need condoms with a vampire? she thought and laughed out loud, earning a confused grunt from him as he withdrew from her.

She protested the loss of him until he tenderly turned her to face him and then slipped inside her once again.

"I cannot have enough of you," he admitted with his human face.

"Nor I you," she also confessed, but laid her hand on his chest to steady herself because she was still feeling a little light-headed and almost giddy.

"Easy, Sonja. It'll pass."

Only she didn't want it to end, she thought, tucking herself tight to his chest. Laying her head there and hearing a slow, steady beat. His heart, she thought, placing her hand there. A heart that was still alive.

As the aftermath of her passion faded, peace seeped into her as he held her, lazily stroking a hand up and down her back. She had never experienced such harmony with a man before. She had never felt so complete.

"I feel the same," he said, clearly in tune with her feelings.

"Is it because of the bite?" They had shared so many images with each other and yet?

"Possibly," he answered, leaving her unsatisfied. It was like having all the pieces of the puzzle before assembling it. You knew they would eventually form a picture, but you needed more information to put all the pieces together.

She wanted to have that complete picture of him, needed it—to try and explain why she was here in his arms, not wanting to leave them. And as painful as giving her the complete picture might be for him, she knew there was one thing she needed to understand more than anything else.

"Tell me how you became a vampire."

## Chapter Six

Where to begin? Gregori thought. He knew she had scattered bits and pieces of the stories from the exchange of memories that had happened with each bite. But putting all that together into his story?

She couldn't have picked a more painful episode in his life.

She rubbed her hand across his chest in a gentling motion, trying to ease the unrest she sensed in him. She was apologetic as she said, "It's okay, Gregori."

"No, it's time. I haven't shared that story with anyone in a long time." And never with a woman, he thought, but kept that to himself, afraid that she already had too much power over him.

"My father defied his parents by marrying my mother. She was Jewish and sickly. They worried about both, I think, although I think my grandparents were a bit relieved when I came along."

"They had their heir," she filled in for him and he confirmed it with a grunt.

"There had sometimes been trouble in the cities with the Jewish citizens, so my father chose to keep us in the countryside. Especially after the Nazis arrived."

She tensed beside him and met his gaze. He realized the images were coming together to form the story in her mind. "You had to come to the city because your mother was ill."

He nodded. "We got caught when we visited her Jewish doctor and were soon on a train and on our way to a concentration camp."

"That's where it happened."

The memories raced through his brain, vividly alive despite the passage of time. "They knew how to cull out the weak. They pulled my mother aside as soon as we got there. Cracked my father's skull open when he fought to keep her with us."

"But he didn't die then," she said and reached up, cradling his jaw to offer yet more comfort. "You did what you could."

He had. He had volunteered himself for their experiments in exchange for his parents' lives. Thanks to him they'd had a few more months. Hard months. He often wondered if he had done them a favor or only prolonged their agony.

"I would have given anything to have more time with someone I loved."

Her words eased one heartache, but awoke another: the thought of losing her. He would, he knew. No woman would want to spend her life with a vampire. No one as young and healthy as Sonja would willingly give up their human life for that of one of the undead.

"Don't be sad, Gregori," she said, her touch calming and loving. He would take it for now and keep the memory of it for once she was gone.

"Rest, Sonja. We only have a couple of hours until we reach Prague."

"So soon?" she asked, giving life to hope within him. So much so that he couldn't stop himself from asking, "Will you come home with me?"

He didn't want to leave her. Didn't want her to leave him, but he wouldn't use his vampire powers to keep her with him even though he could. He wanted her to make that choice freely.

Her quick "yes" filled him with joy.

With a smile on his face, he said, "Sleep, my love."

She murmured a sleepy goodnight and closed her eyes, tucked tight to his chest, his softening cock still pleasantly nestled in her warmth.

The night was his time, so it was impossible for him to rest. That would come in the morning as the rise of the sun stole his strength and forced him to sleep.

For now, he simply enjoyed the feel of her, so trusting in his arms, so filled with passion as they made love. Just the memory of that had him growing hard again, something he hadn't thought possible considering how well he had been satisfied.

She was too tired and drained by his bite to notice right away and so he let her rest, content to lie tucked inside her until an hour passed and she slowly awakened beside him. As she opened her eyes, they were dilated with sleepy desire and he knew that this time, their loving would be slow and tender.

He lazily played with her breasts and she reached down to cup his balls with a deft hand, massaging them until he was the one shaking against her.

"Let go, Gregori. Come for me," she urged and then surprised him by dipping her head and biting the hard nub of his nipple.

A groan ripped from his throat and she smiled against his chest and bit him again, a little higher, a little rougher, until she was at the sensitive crook between his neck and shoulder. Tightening her hold on his balls, she deepened her caress and had him moaning and quivering from the pleasure of it.

Then she bit his throat and sucked on it. He cupped the back of her head and held her to him as he finally moved in her, a slow shift that dragged a throaty growl from her.

He retreated and entered again. She held his balls tight in her hand and moved her mouth to his lips. She took his bottom lip between her teeth and nipped at him again.

It was all that she needed to bring his release. He ground his hips into her as he came and took her over with him. Her muscles milked him as the release rocked their bodies and the motions ebbed slowly as their satisfaction lingered long beyond that burst of pleasure.

He could have remained in her arms forever, but the loud knock on his door brought reality crashing down on their interlude.

"Count, we are almost in Prague," his keeper warned through the door, his voice slightly muffled by the thickness of the wood.

Gregori looked down at her and, despite her earlier decision to come with him, he gave her yet another chance to change her mind.

"Are you sure you wish to come with me?"

Her bright and certain smile chased away his fears. "I'm sure."

It was like being with a rock star, or at least how Sonja imagined a rock star might travel.

They exited Gregori's sleeper car into a service tunnel that led out of the train terminal. Directly beyond the building, a Rolls-Royce limo with heavily tinted windows waited for them. After Gregori's man opened the doors, they dashed inside, and after her bag was tucked in the trunk, they were soon on their way through the streets of Prague.

Although the windows were dark, Sonja was able to see

out and eagerly took in the sights of the beautiful city. It had a gothic look to it and even from the streets, the spires of the cathedral were visible.

It didn't take long to reach Gregori's town house, not that she would have called the large stone building a town house. It was the size of at least three Manhattan brownstones and surrounded by an ornate wrought iron gate. Center steps were flanked on either side by gardens filled with a riotous bloom of flowers and carefully manicured boxwoods along the edges.

As had happened before, a servant opened the gate and front doors and only then did Gregori make a dash inside to avoid the early morning sun. She followed at a more sedate pace, wanting to absorb all that she could, including the slightly disbelieving looks from each of Gregori's people. Judging from their glances, he was not one to bring anyone home.

She tried not to let that please her too much. After all, they'd only just met and in a week she'd be gone. She held back the disappointment that thought provoked.

As she entered, Gregori was speaking to a middle-aged woman. The woman glared at her, but then nodded as Gregori whispered something to her.

He took Sonja's hand as she approached and introduced her to the sour-faced woman. "Sonja, this is Vanesa, my housekeeper and a family friend. I'm assuming you may be ready for breakfast before heading out to explore the city. Vanesa can prepare something for you and give you some ideas of where to visit."

"What about you?" She had supposed he wouldn't be able to go with her during daylight, but loathed the idea of leaving him alone.

"I have some…things to do. I'll see you tonight." Before

she could utter another word, he kissed her hard and with such need that she responded and clung to him, but then he abruptly ended the kiss and hurried away.

She watched his retreating back until he turned the corner of the center hall and then gave her attention to Vanesa.

"Do not toy with him," the older woman warned, clearly uneasy with Sonja's presence.

"This isn't what you think," she replied, although in truth, Sonja wasn't really sure what it was.

"He's a good man," Vanesa replied, hesitantly stumbling over the word *man*.

"No need to play games, Vanesa. I know what Gregori is."

The housekeeper eyed her carefully, her hands folded primly before her as they rested on her spotless white apron. "You know and yet you are here."

"Yes," she answered without hesitation.

A change came over the woman then. With slightly more warmth, she held out a hand in invitation. "Then let's get you settled."

Armed with her guidebook and Vanesa's instructions, Sonja spent the early part of the day exploring the city, but by mid-afternoon she was dragging. The night of making love with Gregori had drained her as had his bites. But as she tiredly made her way back to his town house, she also acknowledged that she was eagerly looking forward to spending another night in his arms.

When she arrived, Vanesa was passing through the foyer with a covered silver tray in her hands. She paused and craned her neck back haughtily because Sunny was several inches taller. "Back so soon?"

"I was hoping Gregori would be up."

Vanesa lifted the tray in emphasis. "*The count* is awake,"

she said with some formality. "I was just bringing *the count* an afternoon snack."

Sunny gestured to the snack. "Mind if I take it up to Gregori?"

Vanesa hesitated, clearly still dubious of Sunny's intentions, but then relented, holding the tray out for her to take and offering up a warning. "If you think you can stomach it. Third door on the right at the top of the stairs."

For a moment Sunny wondered if she wasn't making a big mistake, but at the sly gleam in the other woman's eyes, it occurred to her that this was a test of sorts. With an aplomb she hadn't known she possessed, she whisked the tray from the woman's hands and dashed up the stairs, eager to see Gregori.

At the door to his room, she paused and took a long inhale, trying to control the flare of desire that had her insides skittering in anticipation. A rush of blood brought heat to her cheeks and other points south.

Gregori would surely pick up on that, but what was she to do?

With her tote tucked tight beneath one arm, she balanced the tray in one hand and rapped sharply on the door.

"Come in, Vanesa," he called out, the rich baritone of his voice vibrating within her.

She managed to open the door and enter at a sedate pace, intent on showing some control.

That good intention flew out the window the moment he turned in her direction.

Weak afternoon sunlight bathed one side of his face in red-gold light, casting the other in shadow until he stepped into the center of the room. The amber light from an assortment of table lamps and sconces played over his features.

The sight of him took her breath away again. He was as handsome, maybe more so, than she had remembered. As she had walked around all day, she had wondered if maybe she had been mistaken, but there was no doubt now.

His features were totally masculine, except for that boyish dimple that emerged the moment he laid his eyes on her and grinned.

"I wasn't expecting you home so soon." Such a normal-sounding comment in a far-from-normal situation.

"I was tired," she said, which was a half truth.

He swaggered toward her, took the tray from her hands and placed it on a small table in the sitting area adjacent to his bed. His large, rather inviting-looking bed.

"Was that the only reason?" His smile broadened and he raised one dark brow in challenge.

"If I told you the truth, you might get too cocky."

"Too late," he said and glanced downward, drawing her gaze to where his erection peeked from beneath the edge of the robe.

He had a beautiful cock, long, perfectly straight and so responsive, she thought as she touched his head with her index finger and he swelled just a bit larger with her caress.

She raised her head and locked her gaze with his as she let her tote drop to the ground. She used that hand to sweep open his robe and reveal the rest of his perfection. But she gripped the velvet lapel tightly, trying to show some restraint even as she encircled his erection with her hand and stroked him.

"Why do you hold back?" Gregori was puzzled by her restraint and because of that, he contained himself from reaching out to touch her.

She shook her head, obviously puzzled as well. "I wish I knew. I mean, I want you, but want isn't always a good thing."

He stepped closer until the tip of his dick brushed against the smoothness of her jeans and the feminine softness of her belly. Cradling her jaw, he skimmed his thumb across the stain of color on her cheeks, trying to understand.

"Why is this not a good thing? We are so wonderful together." In fact, he could never remember a woman who pleased him so much both in and out of bed.

"It's too fast. Too sudden," she confessed and he couldn't argue with her. Because of that, he moved away from her grasp and belted his robe around himself tightly.

"Why don't we sit, then, and share a snack? I'm always famished when I first rise." He gestured to the tray on the table.

Sunny's eyes widened with undisguised disgust and he chuckled, well aware of what she thought. He walked to the table and whipped off the cover, revealing the platter of assorted cheeses, bread and fruit.

"I'm going to have to speak to Vanesa about teasing you."

"It's almost like she's testing me," Sunny said as she sat at the table.

"She's very protective." Gregori strode to a small dry bar and poured two glasses of wine. He returned to the table and sat beside Sunny, his thigh brushing against hers and her side tucked to his as he wrapped his arm around her back.

Sunny was about to ask why, but then a slew of images whirled around in her brain. A young girl, gray eyes wide with fear, jogged through her mind and morphed into the features of the woman who guarded Gregori so well.

"You saved her also. During the invasion by the Russians."

He shrugged casually, as if it had not been any big thing. "A tank and a young girl are no match. I did the only thing I could."

Her heart swelled inside her as a fickle emotion grew within her some more. She didn't dare yet admit she was in love with him, but it was impossible to ignore what her heart was saying.

He had given so much to so many, she realized as they sat together, eating the snack Vanesa had prepared and talking about all that she had seen earlier that day and her plans for her remaining time in Prague before she took the train back to Amsterdam.

It was after that discussion that he grew silent, his features hardening while the light dimmed from his eyes.

Wanting to restore his earlier joy, she brushed a kiss across his lips and said, "Would you show me around the city tonight?"

## Chapter Seven

The last thing Gregori wanted to do was to waste a precious second of their time together out in public. Yet he knew it would please her and so he acquiesced, but with a request.

"Let's share this snack and then we can go. I even believe that my man was able to get your bag from the hotel where the airline delivered it, in case you want to change."

While he loved her in the faded jeans whose softness clung to her curves, her patience for wearing the same two outfits had likely worn thin.

"I'd love that." She plucked a piece of cheese from the plate and brought it to his lips. He accepted the tidbit and then returned the favor, pulling a grape from the bunch and popping it into her mouth.

They exchanged several servings like that until Sunny accidentally smeared some goat cheese along the side of his mouth. As her gaze settled on the dab of white, Gregori had no doubt about just what she intended.

She licked off the cheese and then settled her mouth over his, coaxing him to respond.

He couldn't resist her and answered her plea, opening his mouth to hers and tasting her, sweet from the grapes and a small sip of wine. As they kissed over and over, she dropped her hand to his thigh and moved upward to where his erection had come alive again.

She encircled him, but he reached down and stopped her. "You'll unman me if you keep this up."

Despite his hold on her, she moved her hand up and down his dick and he grew harder. Sucking in a breath, he braced himself to look down and watch. She continued until a glistening pearl escaped his tip.

She worked that bit of moisture all around the head of his penis and it was cool for a moment before she covered him with her hand, stilling her motion.

He met her gaze and, without words, he understood.

Rising, he led her to his bed and shucked off his robe. She was on him immediately, licking and biting his nipples. Stroking his erection with the forceful movement of her hand.

Somehow he managed to undress her, and as he fell back onto the bed, he dragged her with him, pressing her down into the mattress. He left her after a hard kiss, reversing his position so that she could take him into her mouth and he could pleasure her with his lips and hands.

She eagerly worked him, sucking and nipping at his dick until his head swam from the passion she roused. It took all his focus to keep from coming and to offer her the same satisfaction she was providing.

But that she was feeling the same satisfaction was evident from the wetness of her against his lips. Her rough exhortations stoked his own climax as he sucked on her clitoris and drove his fingers into her pulsing vagina.

She tensed for a moment beneath him, but then her body sang with her release. Against his cock came the explosion of her breath, creating both chill and warmth. When she massaged his hard, tight balls with her hands, he finally came.

Spent, he reversed his position so he could hold her in his arms, gentling her.

They lay together, tucked tight to each other, caressing tenderly until they eased down from the pinnacle they had reached.

Gregori had never experienced such want and satisfaction with another woman. He had never had peace such as he was feeling now, wrapped in Sonja's arms. Her legs tangled with his and her hair spilled across his chest as she rested her head there. He inhaled deeply, taking in her scent. Clean, but with a hint of something floral.

He memorized that scent for when she would leave him.

Beneath Sunny's cheek, his almost nonexistent heartbeat registered, more slowly than it had right after they had made love.

Made love, she thought, unable to deny that somewhere in just a day or so, she had developed feelings for him.

Propping an elbow on his chest, she leaned her head on it and gazed down at him. She imagined doing that every day for the rest of her life. He would always look this way, young and handsome.

But she wouldn't.

Tension crept into her, and he sensed it. When he met her gaze, she couldn't miss the sadness in his eyes. She understood it. He knew, as well as she did, that this was but a vacation interlude and she would soon be on her way home.

She raised her hand and brushed her fingertips along his cheek. "I care for you, Gregori. I don't wish to hurt you."

"Nor I you," he said, stroking his hand along the column of her throat and down to the tip of her breast. He rubbed the back of his hand there and her body instantly responded despite the satisfaction she had experienced just a short while earlier.

Against the softness of her belly, his erection came to life, hardening between their bodies.

"We can't spend all our time like this," she teased, but couldn't stop the moan that escaped her as he took the tip of her breast between his thumb and forefinger and tweaked it.

"Your tits are a wonder." He rotated the tip just a little harder and between her legs, wetness erupted in anticipation.

He had to feel the heat of her against his thigh as it rested between her legs and as he pressed upward with it, up against her swollen mons, she knew that he did.

"Gregori," she protested and covered his hand with hers. If he didn't stop, they'd soon be making love again. For the briefest moment, she wondered why that was a bad thing, but then reality came roaring back.

"Please, I need something more than just this." The words exploded from her mouth, shot out from the logical part of her brain that understood just how crazy this all was.

He stopped, reluctantly, but nodded. "You said you wanted me to show you around the city. How about we both clean up and then we'll go."

He didn't wait for her answer before bolting from the bed and into his bathroom.

She lay there for a long moment until the sound of running water drifted across the room. She had to leave and get ready for the night. A night that was sure to end right here again, she acknowledged, smoothing her hand across the fine sheets on his bed.

And after that, what? asked the logical part of her brain once more.

Only she didn't have an answer.

The water ran in the shower, but Gregori stood at the wash basin, hands braced against the cold porcelain. He stared at the mirror that didn't stare back, his body heavy with need and another hunger stalking the edges of his awareness.

A need for blood.

In a vampire, sex and blood were irrevocably bound and although he had sated that desire with some blood bags, it wasn't the same as fresh blood, hot and pulsing with life.

It wasn't Sonja's body and blood, so refreshing and lush.

The dual hungers attacked him, and he almost howled his frustration at not being able to satisfy them as he wanted.

Instead, he stalked to the linen cabinet to one side of the bathroom that also held a small refrigerator he kept stocked with blood bags.

Yanking one from within, he brought the blood bag to his mouth, grimacing at its coldness and resistance as his fangs pressed to the plastic. He bit down and the metallic saltiness filled his fangs and mouth. Between his legs, his erection swelled with the infusion and he grabbed hold of his cock. He stroked roughly while finishing off the blood and jerking yet another bag from his store of nourishment.

With each suck of his mouth and pull of his hand he climbed ever closer to a complete release until a slurpy second-best appeased his blood hunger and he came all over his hand. His seed was slick and slightly warm as he pumped himself again and again, eyes closed and images of Sonja filling his mind.

Inhaling shakily, he dropped the empty blood bag to the floor and stepped into the shower. The warm water spilled over him, washing away the remnants of his passion and the blood along his lips. He lingered there for several minutes, enjoying the heat as it seeped into his body.

It wasn't as pleasant as the warmth from Sonja, but it would do until later, when he intended to satisfy at least one of his hungers while keeping the other at bay. He had fed from her too recently, but worse, he feared that with the emotions he was feeling, he might lose control and not stop his feeding.

He already cared for her too much to deny her the life she was meant to live. So, for now, the blood bags would have to do.

# Chapter Eight

Gregori had been a delightful companion, showing her around a number of sites in the city before taking her to an elegant restaurant for a sumptuous meal. But as charming as he had been, she had sensed something lurking below that pleasant surface. Something dark and dangerous that she somehow found exciting.

Maybe it was the way his dark gaze settled on her and followed the vee of her little black dress down to her cleavage. Her nipples puckered in response as she remembered his mouth on her breasts. Between her legs, an insistent throb awakened and she shifted against her seat, trying to find a comfortable way to sit as they finished the last bite of dessert.

"Are you okay?" he asked and she nodded.

He leaned close, his nose brushing the shell of her ear. A low and exciting rumble tinged his voice as he said, "Liar. I can smell your arousal."

He bit her earlobe and she shuddered, grabbing hold of his thigh to steady herself as images of them making love pummeled her brain. He groaned in response to that simple touch, laid his hand over hers and guided it to his hard erection.

"Will it always be like this?" she wondered aloud, glancing around the restaurant to see if anyone had noticed the indiscretion.

"I do not know," he said and his gaze locked with hers. "It has never been this way before with anyone else."

A waiter was coming their way, but with a flick of his hand, Gregori used his vampire powers to shoo him away.

"You've not used that on me," she said and stroked her hand up and down his cock, growing wetter with each passing second.

"I want you to come to me freely, Sonja. I want no deceptions between us."

She wanted that as well, even as jumbled as her emotions where about what she was doing with him. About what would happen with them as the week drew to a close and it was time for her to go home. But even with those doubts, she knew one thing at that moment.

"Can we go home now?"

He shot up from the chair and offered her his arm, a veneer of politeness sheathed over barely checked desire.

She tucked her arm in his and they hurried from the restaurant to where his limo waited at the curb. The driver, who had been lounging there, snapped to attention and swung open the door.

"Take us home," Gregori instructed as she climbed in and he followed.

She faced him on the long leather bench seat and shot a quick look at the privacy screen.

It was up, and Gregori wasted not a second scooping her into his arms and settling her across his lap, her legs straddling him. Her center nestled over the hard ridge of his erection.

Sonja trembled as she imagined taking him deep within

her, but Gregori swept his hand down her arm in a calming gesture.

"Not yet, my love. There is still much to explore."

He shifted his hand to the vee of her neckline and eased aside the fabric to expose her breast. She had gone braless in anticipation of his touch and all night long the soft brush of the crepe satin had teased her nipples and kept her desire kindled.

"You are so lovely. So perfect," he said, his gaze fixed on her breast while he rubbed his thumb back and forth across the tip. The touch was oh so delicate and yet it still had her shaking in his arms.

"We don't have long before we're home." But despite his warning, he dipped his head to touch his tongue to that sensitive tip.

She cupped the back of his skull and held him to her. He answered her unspoken plea, sucking the tip into his mouth and teething her until she moaned aloud with her need and rocked her hips against him.

The fine wool of his suit rasped lightly on the tender skin of her thighs and the desire-drenched silk of her thong panties. As she rode him, the thong bit deeper into her cleft, creating delicious friction against her clitoris.

Gregori was barely restraining his need to be sheathed in her and to have the rush of her blood feeding him. With her so close, the beat of her heart pounded against his senses as he sampled her breasts. The pulse of her passion throbbed against his erection. The dual beats warred with each other and with his heartbeat until the hungers twined together.

The heat of the vampire exploded throughout his body just as the car slowed. He reached forward and slapped at a switch. He growled into the intercom, "Keep driving."

Sonja looked down at him then and her eyes widened as the first telltale hints of the vampire blurred onto his features.

"Gregori," she said tenderly and cradled his cheek, no fear within her.

But she should fear, he thought as he pulled away the other shoulder of her dress, baring her upper body. She should be very afraid because he wasn't sure that this time he would be able to hold back.

He shuddered as the need for blood and sex snaked together through his body. The pain in his mouth warned his fangs were revealing themselves, but Sonja bent and brushed her lips against his.

Did she know the demon might not stop this time? he thought, but he was powerless as she dropped her hands and shifted back just enough to free his erection. When she moved back over him, the wet heat of her undid the last vestiges of his control.

He pulled aside the thin strip of silk separating them and plunged upward just as she drove down. Their combined gasps filled the air along with the smell of their passion.

He set his mouth on her breasts, his fangs scraping her tender skin, leaving bright pink streaks across her fairness, but she didn't protest. If anything, she urged him on with the sharp movements of her hips, driving them both ever closer to release.

He was lost in the feel of her, all womanly softness and allure. But as the faint smell of blood teased his nostrils, he pulled back and noticed the tiniest drops along the scratches on her creamy skin. Regret filled him at marring her and he licked his way across the scratches. His vampire saliva would heal all evidence of the wounds.

But as he did so, those tiniest sips of her blood shattered what little control remained.

He reared forward and sank his teeth into her throat. Hot, lush blood gushed into his mouth and fangs. Unlike before, his feeding this time was rough and almost violent, his need was so great. He kept on sucking and drawing her life force into him, too lost in her to stop.

Sunny pushed against him, protesting as she sensed the difference in this bite. She tried to break free, but he held fast and swept his arm down around her hips to keep her near.

With another long pull, her defiance weakened as the passion of the vampire's bite insinuated itself into her body. Instead of pushing him away, her arms twined around his shoulders to hold him close, to caress him as he continued to feed. Her hips took up their seductive motion once more, riding him. Fulfilling his other hunger as he took her blood again and again until he was nearly drunk on the rush of life singing through his veins.

But even as he found himself restored by her vitality and passion, her body softened in his arms.

He yanked away, fangs and mouth wet with her blood. He met her slightly unfocused gaze, fearing he had taken too much.

"Why?" was all she said as her eyes slipped closed and her body melted against his.

Pained panic roared through him. Gently he laid her on the bench seat, leaned forward and licked at her throat to seal the wound. After he did so, he took her pulse, only slightly relieved by the thready beat. He couldn't fail to notice the chill on her skin and its paleness.

She was in shock, and he had to care for her.

Engaging the intercom, he barked at the driver, "Take us home." Then he reached into his pocket for his cell phone and dialed Vanesa. When she answered, he said, "I need you to prep an IV."

"You didn't turn her, did you?" his housekeeper accused.

No, he hadn't, but a little more feeding and he would have had no choice but to turn her to keep her alive.

"I didn't, but she's in shock. I need to get some fluids into her." He snapped the phone shut before Vanesa could say another word, not needing her censure. God knew he had enough of his own guilt and disgust festering inside of him at that moment.

Jerking off his sport coat, he wrapped Sonja into the jacket and drew it tight around her to build some warmth. After rearranging his clothing, he picked her up in his arms and rocked her the way one might a baby.

It wasn't long before the car stopped and the door popped open. He flew up the stairs to where Vanesa waited in the foyer, her lips in a condemning slash.

Ignoring the equally accusatory glare in her gaze, he took the steps two at the time and rushed to his room.

As he had requested, a bag with plasma hung from a metal IV stand beside his bed. He gently laid Sonja on the covers, removed her soiled clothing and then tucked her in. Lifting one arm from beneath the bedclothes, he grabbed hold of the rubber tourniquet and wrapped it around her arm. He flicked at a vein at the crook of her elbow and as a vein came to the surface, he inserted the IV needle.

She flinched slightly but remained quiet. After taping the needle and tubing in place, he rose and found Vanesa standing a few feet away.

"I see you haven't lost your touch."

It had been a long time since he'd doctored anyone or even himself. Not since the days of the resistance to the Russian invasion.

"Do you still have that old electric blanket?"

Vanesa nodded. "I'll bring it up."

Gregori stalked to the bathroom where he yanked off his bloodied shirt and washed his face and mouth clean of any remnants of Sonja's blood. Returning to her side, he pulled on a black sweater and then dragged one of the chairs from his sitting area close to the bed. As much as he wanted to hold her, he had to keep his distance because the memory of the satisfaction he had taken from her was still too fresh in his mind and too tempting.

Vanesa bustled in a few minutes later, the blanket and an extension cord in hand. With his assistance, she quickly covered Sonja and had warmth bathing her chilled body.

"Do you need anything else?" she asked when Gregori settled himself back into the chair.

"What I need no one can provide."

With a knowing dip of her head, Vanesa left, closing the door to give him privacy.

Gregori leaned back in the chair, elbows braced on its arms as he steepled his hands before him. Watching her. Listening to the lub-dub of her heart grow stronger as the minutes passed and became an hour. The IV bag ran dry, and he removed it now that her pulse was stronger. As he did so, her eyelids fluttered open. He sat by her side and poured a glass of the fortified wine he normally only kept in his sleeping car on the train.

Sonja had been the first woman he'd brought home.

Sonja would also be the last.

As she fully opened her eyes and her head flopped in his direction, he eased a hand behind her shoulders to help her sit up and brought the glass to her lips. She laid a shaky hand over his and drank the wine down greedily.

When not a drop remained, he eased her back onto the pillows and met her sleepy-eyed stare.

"Why?" was all she managed to say again and yet it was all that was needed.

He shrugged, uneasy with what he was about to say, but more certain of it than he had been of almost anything else that he had done during the course of his long life.

"Sex and blood. The two are meshed together irrevocably in a vampire." He locked his fingers together and squeezed them tightly until they were white from the pressure.

"As much as I want you, want what we could have together, I almost failed in keeping the demon inside me from draining you dry."

Sonja reached for him, then pulled back, clearly afraid. "I'm trying to understand."

Could she ever really understand? he wondered. Did she comprehend what it meant? What he had to do for both of them?

"I'm leaving in the morning. Going to the country. You can stay here as long you'd like. Vanesa will see to your needs."

Tears silvered her eyes and she bit her bottom lip. "Will you be back?"

"Will you?" he countered, finally laying on the table the question that had been there from the first. From the moment it had become something more than just a one-night stand.

"I don't know."

He nodded and shifted back to the seat by the side of the bed. "Rest," he urged and she closed her eyes, but he knew she didn't sleep right away. It was there in the uneven breaths she took—she was battling her emotions.

Eventually her breath slowed and her pulse settled into a regular, reassuring beat.

Inside him, pain wrapped its fingers around his heart and gut and squeezed. The emotion was so great, strangling anything else in his mind, that his vamp awareness almost didn't sense the dawn approaching. Warning him that it was time to seek safety from the sun.

Funny really. Sonja, his Sunny, had already taken what little life was left in his heart.

Rushing from her side, he nearly threw himself down the stairs in his haste. The ever-capable Vanesa was in the foyer waiting.

"The car is ready. I've called ahead so the house will be anticipating your arrival."

He shot a look back up the stairs, hesitant. But then he hugged Vanesa hard, aware there was no going back. "Take care of her for me."

"I will."

## Chapter Nine

Sunny stood on the steps of Gregori's town house. The lights beside the door flipped on as night came to life in the city.

It was hard to believe it had been only two months since she'd been here. Since he'd left her lying in his bed, her neck feeling as if a dog had chomped on it and her heart in pieces.

She had fallen in love with him in those few days they'd spent together. Whatever that weird connection was that had sprung up between them, she had come to know his honor and his soul. A soul that could still love even though he was a vampire.

Granted, she wished he didn't come with the whole bitey thing, she thought and ran her hand across the spot on her neck that was still sensitive. As she did so, need awakened deep inside her, but so did something else.

She laid her hand over the barely noticeable bump and pressed against her belly, wondering if she was only imagining the movement. The doctor had told her it might be some time before the baby was big enough to feel, but Sunny could sense it growing inside her.

Would Gregori be aware of their child through whatever connection they shared?

For a moment she considered turning around and heading back to New Jersey. After all, single moms were not all that uncommon, but she had never pictured herself in that role. She had always imagined herself married and with a home in the suburbs. Maybe even with more than one child.

Was that even possible? But then again, clearly part of her vision for herself had come to pass.

*Would the child be human like her or a vampire like him?*

So many questions, but before she asked those, there was one question she needed answered.

*Would he want them?*

Before she changed her mind, she took the first step up the stairs and kept on going until she was at the door. She was about to knock when the door swung open.

Vanesa stood there, a broad smile on her face. "I'd hoped you'd be back."

"I had to wait until the school semester was over," she explained and stepped into the foyer.

A sound at the head of the stairs drew her attention.

Gregori stood there, dressed much as when he had left her. Black slacks and a black sweater that hugged his muscled arms and chest. His face severely pale against all that midnight and his blue-black hair. His dark eyes traveled over her, filled with a mixture of disbelief, hope and love.

"I should leave you alone," Vanesa said and hurried from the foyer.

Gregori walked down the steps slowly, almost as if afraid she might disappear, but she held her ground and waited for him.

When he stood before her, the first hint of a smile came to his lips. "You came back."

"I couldn't stay away. I love you, Gregori." For over a

month she had wondered how to say it, but it had been easier than she had ever imagined.

Gregori's heart actually stopped for a moment, but then began its slow, barely there beat. He had been ready to accept that those few days with her were all the happiness he would ever have. But now...

"I love you and I'm sorry for what I did. For hurting you," he said and cradled her cheek. With that first touch, awareness flared through him at the change in her body. At the life growing deep within her. A life he had helped to make.

"I never thought..." He shook his head and dipped his hand down to splay it across her belly.

She laid her hand over his and pressed it tight to her still nearly flat abdomen. "How is this possible?"

He grinned then and that boyish dimple she had remembered in her dreams emerged. "I would think you would know the how, my love."

Chuckling, she ran her index finger along that dimple. "So vamp sperm—"

"I'm young in vampire years. It takes time before everything that was once human disappears, but this...I had thought this was no longer possible for me."

He wrapped her in his arms and peace settled inside him as she returned the embrace and whispered in his ear, "I love you, Gregori. Will you take me as your wife?"

He imagined her in his bed, wearing his ring. Her belly growing larger with the child they had made. Making love to her every night. Maybe even forever, although for now he'd find a way to curb his need for her lifeblood.

Easing away, he cradled her face in his hands and so that there would be no doubts, he said, "I would be honored to have you as my wife. To share my life with you."

Her sexy smile was bright and her eyes glittered with love. "How about we start the sharing right now?"

He covered her mouth with his and she answered him wholeheartedly, opening her mouth to welcome him in, pressing her body to his and shifting her hips across his growing arousal.

He growled and dropped his hand down to her buttocks. "I've missed you so."

"Then what are you waiting for?"

With a surge of his vamp power, he carried them up the stairs and to his bed in a blast of speed. As she stood in his bedroom, he had to resist every impulse to rip the clothes off her body. His hands shook as he unbuttoned her blouse and drew down her jeans to reveal the new lushness of her body.

He covered her fuller breast with his hand. She sighed and her nipple immediately tightened against his palm.

"Make love with me, Gregori." She reached out and cupped his cheek, ran her thumb across his lips.

"With pleasure," he replied and urged her into his bed. Hastily he pulled off his own clothes and then joined her in the center of the mattress, covering her with his body, tasting and touching every inch of her until she writhed on the bed.

He wanted to plunge his cock into her hot, wet depths. Drive her to completion, but he tempered the roughness of that desire because of the baby. Their child, he thought with wonder. Instead, he rolled to his back and allowed Sonja to do the taking. He let her guide them with the gentle roll of her hips and the eager cries of pleasure that slipped from her lips as he caressed her breasts with his hands.

The climax built slowly, almost magically between them. It pulled them higher and higher until they were both trembling and breathing roughly.

Sonja bent then and took his mouth with hers, biting and

kissing the edges of his lips, slipping her tongue inside to dance with his and trace the straight, and very human, line of his teeth.

Smiling, she rolled her hips one last time and drew them both over the edge.

After, they lay twined together and kissed some more, unable to keep away from each other. As Sonja opened her mouth on his and experienced his humanity once more, she whispered against his lips, "You kept the vampire away."

For nearly two months he had been working on controlling the vampire, learning to curb his hunger and feed only when he could control how much he took. It hadn't been easy to avoid those feedings as soon as he woke or the cravings that came as he walked the streets at the dead of night.

But he had because of one thing.

"I wanted your love more than the blood, Sonja. I knew I had to learn in hopes you would come back."

"I love you enough to take the risk, Gregori."

She kissed him again and desire rose up swiftly as it did with her. He tempered his need to join with her, taking his time, building her passion. He savored every nuance of her response in a way he could not before because now he knew one thing: Love had tamed the vampire and brought him the happiness he had once thought impossible. As long as they had love, nothing could drive them apart.

\* \* \* \* \*

# THRESHOLD OF PLEASURE

VIVI ANNA

A bad girl at heart, **Vivi Anna** likes to burn up the pages with her original unique brand of fantasy fiction. Whether it's in ancient Egypt, or in an apocalyptic future, Vivi always writes fast paced action-adventure with strong independent women that can kick some butt, and dark delicious heroes to kill for.

Once shot at while repossessing a car, Vivi decided that maybe her life needed a change. The first time she picked up a pen and put words to paper, she knew she had found her heart. Within two paragraphs, she realised she could write about getting into all sorts of trouble without suffering the consequences.

When Vivi isn't writing, you can find her causing a ruckus at downtown bistros, flea markets, or playgrounds.

# Chapter One

"Do you believe in monsters, Eden?"

Eden Swain ran a hand through her tangled blond hair as she shifted the phone from cradling it between her shoulder and head to her hand. Sitting up and leaning forward, she no longer felt drained. The woman on the other end of the line had her full attention.

"I don't know. I believe in evil, if that's what you're asking."

"The devil inside?" the woman asked.

"Yes, something like that, I guess."

"I'm not talking about the evil inside men. I'm talking about the forces of darkness. Demons and the like."

Cold tendrils of air caressed Eden's neck and face like a lover's touch. Instantly, goose bumps rose on her arms and shivers raced down her spine. She looked around the office, seeking the source of cool air, but no windows were open. Glancing up, she searched for air-conditioning vents. There were none.

"Do you mean scaly red skin, black horns and a forked tongue?" Eden joked, trying to lessen the tension she could feel rising through the phone line.

The woman sighed. "Don't be stupid, Eden. You know better than that."

Gripping the handle tightly, Eden pleaded into the phone. She didn't want to lose this one. For some reason, the woman had opened up to her. She couldn't let her fondness for sarcasm ruin the effort the woman had obviously made to pick up the phone and call the suicide help line.

"I want to understand. I want to help you."

There was a long pause. Eden could hear the woman's heavy breathing on the other end. It was labored, as if she had been running—or was scared out of her mind.

"I know you do, Eden. You tried before but I just don't know if you can."

"What? When? Do I know you?"

The woman disconnected.

"Hello? Hello?"

There was no answer—only silence. Slowly, Eden set the handset down in its cradle. Rubbing a hand over her face, she cursed under her breath. She'd blown it again.

From the moment she'd answered the call, Eden had sensed a real opportunity to help the woman. It was as if the woman had phoned *her*, not just the help line. And maybe that was true, considering her last few words. Before the woman had started talking about monsters, Eden had felt she'd made a connection. A real one. However, it had snapped once the woman started rambling about evil and demons.

Maybe she had been on drugs and needed someone to talk her down. It was just that she'd seemed so lucid when they'd first started speaking. She'd sounded like an intelligent and very together person. Eden knew too well the dangers of drugs and drug users—they were unpredictable and potentially dangerous. She'd learned that the hard way.

Reaching for the glass of water on the desk, Eden noticed the tremble in her hand. She needed a real drink. It was getting harder to stay sober. She'd promised herself that she would not drink on the job, but with each desperate call from one person to another, her thirst had become nearly insatiable. Each time she picked up the phone, she imagined a glass of scotch in her hand instead.

The self-induced torture was killing her, which was probably what she was hoping for. Masochism 101.

"Why don't you go home?"

Eden looked up at the shift supervisor, Allison, and nodded.

Putting a hand on Eden's shoulder, Allison squeezed gently. "You've been here for five hours—that's enough for one night. Go home and get some sleep. Some *real* sleep."

Allison's meaning was clear. *Get some sleep not induced by alcohol.* Eden couldn't remember the last time she had fallen asleep sober. Maybe before the shooting.

Standing, Eden grabbed her leather jacket from the back of the wooden chair and slipped it on. She bent down, retrieved her bike helmet from under the table and slid it over her mop of disheveled curls.

"Be careful on that thing, hon. It's supposed to rain later tonight."

Eden witnessed the uneasiness in Allison's eyes and winced inwardly. "No worries, Allie. I'm good."

Saying nothing, Allison just nodded and went back into her little office in the corner.

The moment Eden opened the back door to the alley, the cool crisp air surrounded her and elicited shivers up and down her spine. A cold mist peppered her face. Glancing up into the dark sky, she hoped that she got home before the rain was unleashed. By the fresh tang in the air, they were in for a good downpour.

As she stepped on the metal stairs, she looked down the alley toward her bike. Good. It was still there. Since she'd started volunteering, she'd been parking behind the building, and so far, to her surprise, her motorcycle had remained untouched. The downtown neighborhood was high on crime. During her two years with the police force, she'd been on more calls in the area than she could count.

The last one ending her short-lived career.

She went down the steps and toward her vehicle.

Closing her eyes briefly, Eden swung her leg over her bike. The voices were getting stronger, as they did every day. She hoped she would make it home before the screaming started. If she could get home quickly, the scotch would soften the voices to a dull ache, an ache she'd been living with for the past year.

Eden kicked the bike over and revved the engine. Before she shifted into gear, she had a distinctive feeling of being watched. Her skin crawled as if a long, slimy snake was slithering over her body. She hated snakes—it was her only phobia, most likely developed by having two older brothers who'd loved to torment her with dead things tucked neatly in her bed at night.

Turning her head, she glanced down the alley. There was nothing there except an old green BFI bin, and discarded trash swirling around on the dirty cracked cement. She looked back to the opening of the alley. Nothing there either, not even the obligatory alley cat yowling into the night.

Eden released the brake and coasted out of the alley. She stopped at the opening and glanced down the street. At the late hour, it was nearly deserted, except for the few homeless bums picking through garbage cans for pop cans and bottles. After one last look, she revved the bike and roared onto the road.

Speeding down the street, Eden kept glancing in her side mirrors. Every once in a while she thought she saw something pale and quick like an animal behind her. But when she turned her head, the road was empty. As she zipped through the sporadic traffic, Eden was completely aware of her surroundings. She noted each vehicle, its color and make as she passed. When she glanced in her mirrors, she saw them behind her just as they should be.

Fifteen minutes on the road, and the sky opened up and sheets of rain poured down. She slowed her bike so she wouldn't skid, but the urge to speed up itched at her hands. She wanted to be off the roads and safe in her apartment. As she zipped down each street, she felt open and vulnerable. She felt exposed.

As she turned onto her street, she spied a giant white wolf in her mirror. When she glanced over her shoulder, it disappeared. However, as she looked in her mirror again, it was there, stalking her a few car lengths behind. Fear wrapped around Eden, squeezing her with prickly, icy tendrils. Swallowing the bile that rose in her throat, she turned down the alley instead of driving to the front of her apartment. She pulled out onto the parallel street and doubled back. What the hell was a wolf doing in the city?

As she turned another corner, she glanced in her mirror. Nothing was following her. To confirm, she slowed and looked over her shoulder—still no animal or anything. Maybe she'd imagined it, had to have. Breathing a sigh of relief, Eden rounded the next corner back onto her street. She was obviously more tired than she thought. The rain must have produced weird shapes on her mirrors—with the lights reflecting off the slick black asphalt, it was no wonder she was seeing things.

After one last glance over her shoulder, Eden pulled to a stop in front of her apartment building. She parked, got off the bike and pulled off her helmet. She lifted her face to the rain and let it cascade over her sweaty skin.

If only it was that easy to be cleansed, she thought.

Wiping at the water as it flowed over her eyes, she spied a shape atop the roof of the building across the street. When she looked again, it was gone. Could just be kids out for some fun. Cautious, she eyed the building as she unlocked the front door of her complex. Satisfied that she was only delirious, Eden went inside.

Taking the stairs two at a time, she was out of breath when she reached the third floor and her apartment door. Quickly unlocking it, she went inside, turned on the lights, and tossed her helmet and jacket onto the floor by the door. Not bothering to take off her boots, Eden wandered into the kitchen and grabbed the half-empty scotch bottle on the counter. Putting it to her lips, she went to take a long pull, then stopped. It was too easy to take a drink. She needed to stop with the easy way out.

Cradling the bottle against her chest like a life preserver, she wandered back into the living room and collapsed onto the worn sofa. She put her boots up onto the scarred wooden coffee table and looked at the bottle. It tempted her but she battled the urge down. Her therapist had told her to take it one day at a time. Sometimes an hour at a time. This was one of those hours. Sighing, she wiped her mouth with the back of her hand and let her head fall back against the cushions.

She felt jittery and unnerved. Being inside the sanctity of her apartment did not make her feel safe. She still sensed that she was being watched, being followed. Jumping up, Eden walked to her bookshelf and picked up the small handgun she had stashed there behind a ripped copy of *Pride and Prejudice*. It had been over four months since she'd touched it. The last time, she had been drunk and in the middle of one of her furies. She gazed down at the snub-nosed Beretta, enjoying the feeling of it in her hands.

Squeezing her eyes shut, Eden set the gun down and returned to the sofa and talked herself down. Soon the voices in her head softened. They were now only inaudible mumbles.

Still carrying the bottle like a security blanket, Eden walked to the window overlooking the street. She glanced out and up at the neighboring building. Rain poured down in thick silver sheets, but she thought if she squinted hard enough, she could see movement on the roof. There was one last thought in her head before everything went numb.

*He's coming for me.*

# Chapter Two

From his perch on the opposite rooftop, Mikhail watched her through the window. The curtains were not drawn so he could see her quite clearly. It also helped that his eyesight was superior to most.

He'd followed her home from her work, his intentions two-fold. He had been told to keep an eye on her, to make sure she kept her distance from Threshold. And he was also curious about her. Which was why he'd taken to watching her most days now.

When he'd first been given this assignment, he'd done a lot of research on Eden Swain. He knew she'd been a police officer for only two years before the incident in the alley-way. He also knew that she'd had a breakdown afterward.

She'd left her position, although he wondered if it had been forced, and she regularly saw a therapist. He also knew she drank to forget. On many occasions, he'd followed her to a liquor store or to a small hole-in-the-wall bar, where she would sit on her own, not talking to anyone, and drink.

He also knew she was alone.

And this, he thought, was why he'd taken to her so quickly. Because of his own loneliness. It was difficult to be what he was, even in his world, which was so different from this one. He was an outcast as much as Eden was in her own way.

Her face turned in the window, her gaze tracking him on the rooftop. He knew she couldn't possibly see him, as he was too far away and cloaked in darkness, but he ducked anyway.

He waited for a few minutes, then peered over the roof's edge. She was gone from the window. He imagined that she'd gone to bed. This was confirmed when the lights went off in the living room and went on in what he suspected was her bedroom. Unfortunately the curtains were drawn so he couldn't see her.

He knew she was in for the night, but he couldn't force himself to get up and go home. So he settled on the gravel, sitting cross-legged and resting his arms on the edge of the roof. Since he barely slept, fatigue would not come for a long time. He'd sit and watch and wait. And make sure she was safe.

Although he'd been given the task to keep Threshold safe from her, he knew it was she who needed his protection.

## Chapter Three

*Once more the dream came.*

Although adrenaline raced through her body like wild-fire, the gun was sure and steady in Eden's hands. A call had come in about screams in a downtown alley, the second call in three weeks in the same area. Before, it had been some kids playing around in the Dumpster.

This time it was a man holding a young woman hostage by knifepoint, and she was on her own until backup showed up.

The man appeared agitated, unhinged, likely high on something. He had his arm around the woman's neck, and held a knife to her throat. There was already blood on the blade and running down her neck. The front of her light-colored shirt was stained red. She was crying silently.

"Let the girl go," Eden said, her gun trained on him.

"Never!" he shouted, then giggled. "She's mine forever and ever. Master told me so."

The woman made a whimpering sound that put Eden's back up. Then her head lifted and she caught Eden's gaze, pleading in her eyes.

"It's going to be okay, ma'am."

"Of course she's going to be okay," the man said, "She's been chosen."

It was then that Eden noticed the blood on his teeth and around his mouth. He'd been biting the woman and tasting her blood. Eden's stomach lurched at that.

"We can all walk away from this. Just let her go."

"No one gets out alive, bitch."

The tip of his knife dug into the woman's throat. She tried to get away but couldn't, the blade sliding even more across her skin.

Without flinching, Eden took the shot. Everything moved in slow motion after that.

The bullet ripped through his cheek, knocking him sideways. His hold loosened on the woman and she dropped to the ground.

Eden rushed to the man's side to make sure he was down. She pressed her fingers to his throat. No pulse. Vacant eyes stared up at her and he wasn't moving. She holstered her weapon and crouched next to the injured woman.

"I need an ambulance stat," she barked into her radio. A siren could already be heard in the distance.

Whipping off her jacket, Eden pressed it to the wound in the woman's throat. The knife had definitely nicked a major artery—blood bubbled out of the hole with every breath the woman took.

In reality, Eden had stayed there administering pressure to the wound until the EMTs arrived. But the woman had died on the gurney and they'd been unable to resuscitate her.

However, the man Eden had shot and killed had disappeared. The only evidence of him was another blood pool in the alley.

In her dreams, the woman always smiled up at her and begged, "Save me."

She did this now, then lifted her arm and reached for some unseen entity.

Glancing around, Eden noticed a dark shape materializing through the veil of tears. She rubbed at one eye with her bloodied hand, but the shape was still blurry. In awe, she watched as a tall, dark figure approached her.

It was a man dressed in black, with longish dark hair and pale skin. As he neared, she noticed the rugged features of his face and his full, sensuous mouth. Why she noticed these things as the woman died at her feet, she didn't know. Eventually, the dark man stood over her, staring down, his eyes shining with emotion.

As he smiled, he held out one long, elegant hand toward her. "I can make the pain go away, Eden. Just take my hand."

She wanted the pain to recede. Too long had she lived with the emotional turmoil that the woman's death had induced. Daylight hours brought too many sobering feelings, and the night brought agonizing nightmares, just like the one she replayed almost every night.

Eden wasn't sure how long her mind could survive her inner torment. Not much longer, she was sure.

Raising her head to meet his gaze, Eden felt a sexual tug. The man invoked sensations she had long ago dismissed as unimportant. She wanted him to take her pain. She wanted him.

He grinned as she raised her arm. But before she could touch his hand, Eden saw red flames dance in the black of his eyes....

"Eden." His voice was a caress, touching her in places she hadn't been touched in far too long. "You want to forget." He smiled and she spied a pair of fangs jutting from his upper jaw. It sent a shudder down her body, but she didn't pull away.

"You want so many things. I can give them to you. Will you let me?"

Her hand moved toward him as if it wasn't her hand at all. *No!* She shook her head and snatched her hand back. Frantically, she looked around. Everything was wrong. Where was the woman she'd been unable to save? Where was the blood?

Where was she?

She was no longer in the alley surrounded by death and carnage—she was in a room, a bedroom, facing a bed with red satin sheets and candles. Hundreds of candles. Candles everywhere.

Someone stood behind her—she could feel his presence and she both wanted to lean back into that solid mass and surrender to him *and* she wanted to spin around and shove her gun beneath his chin.

"Eden."

It was him. The dark man. The one from the alley. She'd have recognized that voice anywhere. Deep, potent as the smoothest scotch, faintly accented. He had the kind of voice that spoke to her on more than one level.

"Eden, I want you. Please, let me touch you, for both of our sakes."

His voice didn't just sound like scotch—it had the same effect on her. Numbing her senses, dulling her inhibitions. She turned around to face him, fully intending to tell him off, but one look at him and all intentions evaporated.

She'd been with men before but never with one who looked like him. He wasn't real. He couldn't be. He was too perfect, standing there with his silk pajama bottoms riding low on his hips and nothing else. His feet were bare. His chest was bare and smooth and sculpted like that of an elite athlete. But it was his face—his rugged jaw, his patrician nose, his dark, dark eyes—that pierced her with desire and longing, that affected her most.

And those fangs. They weren't long—were almost invisible among the rest of his teeth—but she saw the curve of them, and the sharp tips.

"You want me, too. I can see it." He approached her with the fluid grace of a panther and Eden was mesmerized by the unconscious play of muscles across his torso as he neared.

It took effort to lift her eyes, but she somehow managed, and when she met his gaze, she caught her breath. The intensity of his stare stole the air around her.

"How badly do you want to forget?"

"Very," she whispered.

He touched her face, the softest of caresses. "Will you permit me to help?"

"How?"

"Like this."

Up until that moment, everything had been happening as if in slow motion. But the minute the dark man said *like this*, time sped up. His hand whipped out to circle her neck, pulling her closer. His other hand lifted her chin, tilting her face toward him.

One second he was looking down at her, the next his lips were on hers. No, not on hers—they were a part of her.

If what he was doing was kissing her, it was like no kiss Eden had ever experienced. His kiss was hungry and desperate and controlling and possessive. She responded in kind, needing his mouth and his tongue and all of him. As if her life depended on it.

Her tongue laved across those fangs, and it sent another pang of lust between her thighs.

No amount of scotch could compare to the effect one kiss from this man had on her. She was drunk from him.

"More," she whispered against his lips. "I need more."

She could feel him smile against her lips.

He picked her up and carried her the few feet to the bed

and ever so gently set her down on the cool silk before joining her.

"You are so beautiful." He stroked her cheek, the edge of her jaw, down her neck to the base of her collarbone. "You have no idea how much I want you." With a hand behind her neck, he pulled up as he lowered his head to kiss her.

It had been too long. That was the only explanation for the effect this man was having on her. His touch, his lips, his words—all of him made her forget everything else.

Was this what he'd meant when he'd said he'd help her forget?

"Tell me how. Tell me how to forget," she said breathlessly.

He stopped kissing her neck and raised his head so that he could meet her gaze. "You need only give yourself to me."

This time, when she saw the fire leap into his dark pupils, she didn't care. She'd give anything to forget.

"I want to, but..."

"Lie down."

He gave her a little nudge and Eden fell on her back. She didn't even bother to wonder what had happened to her jeans, her shirt, her bra...her gun. The only thing she had on was her panties and that was it.

Lying there, with her hands above her head, she had never felt more desirable than she did at that moment—not even when she'd been with Charlie—as the dark man's gaze devoured her from head to toe and back up again.

"Do you give yourself to me?"

Eden didn't even hesitate. "Yes."

His smile was as dark as his bottomless pupils, and he leaned across her and kissed her. First her lips, then her throat, then lower.

"Please," she sighed, arching toward him. "Please."

He moved lower until his mouth found her breasts.

"Yes!"

The second his tongue grazed her nipple, Eden jolted with the fiercest arousal she'd ever experienced. Holy hell, if that was what he could do with a mere touch of his tongue, what would it feel like if he touched her between her thighs? Kissed her there? Made love to her?

Eden wanted to find out.

She needed to find out.

With fingers threaded through his dark hair, she pushed him lower. He didn't need coaxing to leave her breasts as his tongue sampled and tasted all of her—her rib cage, her navel—until finally he hovered between her spread legs, his breath cool and sweet against her thighs.

"Eden?"

"Yes." She lifted her hips. "Please. Yes."

One side of his mouth turned up in a smile, one lovely curved fang flashing at her, before her perfect, dark stranger hitched his thumbs beneath the waistband of her panties and tugged.

The silky material slid over her hips and down her legs.

"Open yourself. Give yourself to me."

Never had Eden been so brazen. Never had she been so uninhibited. She let her thighs fall open and reveled in the hungry expression of the man with the fierce black eyes.

With a long finger, he touched her exposed flesh. "This is how you will forget." Then he lowered his head and engulfed the most sensitive part of her with his mouth.

It was like being caught between pleasure and pain, ecstasy and torture. Heaven and hell.

Eden's hips shot skyward. "More," she screamed. "I need more!"

Then there was another voice in her dream, a deeper one....

"*Get away from her!*"

Gasping, Eden jolted from her sleep and sat up in bed. What the hell had just happened?

Cold sweat slicked her face and body.

A dream. A fucking dream, that's all it was. But it had felt so real.

She rubbed her face. Then again, lately all of her dreams had felt real. She shivered in the cool morning air. Her bedroom window was open and the breeze floated in, ruffling her gauzy blue curtains.

Staring at the window, Eden frowned. She couldn't remember opening it before she'd passed out on the bed. But her mind was so muddled lately that it was possible she had done it.

Rubbing a hand over her sweaty face and into her tangled nest of hair, Eden tried to push the dream out of her mind. It was the same one she'd been having for the past year, except for the dark man. He was an unsettling new addition.

Swinging her feet over the bed, Eden stood on quivering legs and stumbled down the hall to her bathroom. After filling the sink with icy water, she submerged her face until the bite of the cold liquid stung her cheeks and her lungs burst with the need for oxygen. Behind her closed eyes, the comely face of the man in black flashed before her. He was smiling. And blood dripped from his wide, inviting mouth.

Gasping, she flipped her head up. Water ran down her neck and soaked her sweat-stained tank top that she always wore to bed. Shivers racked her body as she grabbed a towel and wiped at her face and throat.

Who was this man? Why was he invading her mind? And why did she find him so alluring? Was she attracted to him because he seemed to be offering her a way out of her consuming guilt?

If only there was a way out.

After drying off, Eden took the robe from the back of the door and wrapped herself in it. Even after seven months she could still smell her ex-lover Charlie's cologne in the blue terry cloth. She had washed it several times since his departure, but still his scent remained to taunt her.

Just another thing to attest to her past failures.

Eden shuffled down the hall and into her kitchen to make coffee. Strong black coffee. Opening her refrigerator, she took out the white pizza box, opened it up and grabbed the last slice. Taking a bite, she poured a mug of coffee, then took it and her breakfast into her living room. Plunking down on the sofa, she grabbed the remote and clicked on the TV.

There usually wasn't a hell of a lot on during a Thursday morning, but the background noise was all Eden was looking for. Something, anything, to drown out the incessant thoughts and images bombarding her mind. She only had an hour to kill before she had to head out to work anyway. Flipping through cooking programs, ridiculous talk shows and infomercials was just the mundane sort of distraction she needed.

After she'd folded the last of the pizza into her mouth, Eden flipped to a news station and paused. On screen was a picture of a young woman with black hair and blunt-cut bangs, dark eyes, and a thin, unsmiling mouth. Something about her made Eden shiver. Somehow, she knew that face.

The picture panned back to the newscaster, and he went on about how the woman in the photo, identified as Lilith Grae, had been missing since yesterday afternoon. A phone number flashed on the screen. Eden recognized it as the number for the missing persons' division.

*You tried before...*

The woman's voice echoed in her ears. Eden had no reason to believe that this was the same person, except for the churning and gurgling in her gut telling her it most definitely was.

Eden reached for the cordless phone on her coffee table and dialed a number.

A man answered on the third ring. "Moser."

The timbre of his voice made her shiver even after seven months apart. Clearing her throat she said, "Hey, Charlie."

There was silence for a moment, and Eden thought for a second that he might hang up on her. "What's up, Eden?"

"What do you know about the missing Grae woman?"

"Not much. Twenty-one years old, troubled home life, last seen two days ago, no note, no phone call, no nothing." He paused, and Eden imagined that he was popping a piece of gum into his mouth. He'd quit smoking years ago and replaced the habit with gum-chewing. "The question is, what do *you* know about the Grae woman?"

"I don't know. Nothing probably."

"Spill it, Swain. You wouldn't be phoning me otherwise."

Eden pinched the bridge of her nose. Her headache was getting worse, likely Charlie-induced; he possessed an innate ability to give her one. "I think I talked to her last night on the help line."

"Are you shitting me?"

"I don't know for sure. The woman on the phone didn't give me her name, but there was something in her voice that told me she was scared, maybe even running from something."

"Look," he said, and she could hear the exasperation in his voice. "There's nothing I can do with that. You know how this works."

"Yeah, I know."

"You have anything else? Anything I could use?"

"No." Eden didn't want to mention the conversation about the devil and demons—for some reason she wanted to keep that to herself. "Maybe I just related the two because I was bothered by her call last night."

He sighed and she could hear the rustling of paper. "What time was the call?"

"About midnight."

"From a cell phone, do you think?"

"No, it sounded like a pay phone. It had that hollow echo to it, you know?" She chewed on one of her fingers, nerves zinging through her. A sense of urgency jolted her mind. Something was happening. And it was happening now. "Where did she work?"

"Why do you need to know?"

"Just humor me, okay?"

More rustling of paper. "Some club called The Gate. Does that ring a bell?"

"No." The feeling of urgency increased. Eden felt as if her heart was going to burst out of her mouth. "Charlie?"

"Yeah?"

"I think she might've been the woman from my shooting."

There was a long pause, then a sigh. "Eden, you know that's impossible. Lilly Cain died, remember?"

Eden dragged a hand through her hair. "I know. I know. She just looks exactly like her. And her name...so similar."

"Have you been seeing Dr. Clarkson?"

"Yes." She hated when people brought up her therapist as if she was going mental. Who knew? Maybe she was.

Eden jerked forward on the sofa, her fingers itching to grasp the cool glass of a bottle of scotch. "I got to go. Sean's here to pick me up," she lied.

"Yeah, I heard you were working for your brother."

"It's a job." Eden stood. "I'll talk to you." She pressed the end button on the phone and tossed it onto the sofa. Pacing the room, Eden mulled over what Charlie had told her. Not much information, but enough that she could do her own investigation.

The urge to do something, to track down this woman, munched on Eden's insides. Her gut told her something was seriously wrong. For some reason she was certain that Lilith Grae had called the help line to talk to Eden specifically. That the woman somehow knew her.

*Fate.* Normally, she didn't believe in it. But it seemed as if fate was starting to believe in her.

# Chapter Four

The heat was unbearable as Eden drove home from work. Sweat trickled down her back and pooled into the dip of her pants. She rolled down the window and took in some deep breaths of the smog-tainted air. She didn't care—she just needed to feel some sort of breeze on her face. She was overheating from the inside out. Panic raced through her. Black spots started dancing in her eyes.

She rubbed her face hard, digging her knuckle into her eye to try and erase the dark dots. Something was wrong. She felt light-headed, dizzy even. She'd drunk water most of the day and she hadn't hit her head at the job site. So what was the problem?

Gripping the steering wheel tightly, Eden wished for a drink. Scotch would calm her down, soothe her nerves. Just a little sip to take the edge off her anxiety.

Ahead on the right, the word *liquor* jumped out at her in red neon. Swerving, she cut across two lanes of traffic to take the turnoff. Car horns blared. Tires squealed. But all Eden could concentrate on was the cool, calm feel of a bottle of scotch in her hand and the way it would numb her tongue and throat on the way down to warm the hollow pit inside.

Screeching to a stop in front of the liquor store, she swung open her door and rushed in. She went straight to the back, knowing instinctively where the scotch was kept. She reached for a bottle, then stopped. This wasn't right. She had to fight the urge. Instead, she snatched a bottle of Gatorade and rushed down the aisle to the checkout. A man in a black hoodie cut in front of her and set his purchases on the counter.

The clerk quickly put the man's items into a plastic bag and rang him through. Eden tapped her foot impatiently as she waited, when all she wanted to do was run back and grab a bottle of booze and guzzle down half the amber liquid.

Finally, it was her turn. Setting the drink down, she tossed in a couple candy bars—chocolate soothed her urges sometimes—and slid a twenty across the counter.

The guy in the hoodie still hadn't left. He had moved over to give her space, but was busy putting the change back in his wallet. Eden glanced over at him. She couldn't see his face because the dark hood obscured it. He was tall, though. Lanky like an athlete.

The clerk handed Eden back her change, smiling at her the whole time. His fingers fumbled against her hand and all her coins scattered onto the counter and floor. Swearing, Eden bent down to retrieve them. Tucking the money into her pants pocket, she stood up to get her bag.

The tall stranger had left. Funny. When she was down on the ground she didn't recall seeing him leave. He had been there, but then he was gone.

Obviously more tired and upset than she realized, Eden grabbed her purchases and left. Once home with a glass in her hand, she'd feel better. Maybe then she could figure all of this out. Maybe then, she wouldn't feel so disjointed and confused.

It took her only a half hour to return to her apartment. The second she walked through the door, she went into her kitchen and grabbed a glass and ice. Sitting down on her sofa, she slid the Gatorade out of the bag, already feeling the panic subsiding with the expectation of the sugary drink.

Except it wasn't Gatorade in her hand, but vodka.

She never drank vodka. Angry, she set the bottle down on the table and looked in the bag. Her candy bars weren't in there either. Just a newspaper. An alternative arts magazine by the looks of it.

"Damn it." Sighing, she leaned back on her sofa. The guy in the hoodie must've taken her bag by accident, and now she was stuck with his stuff.

It just wasn't her day.

Rotating her stiffening neck, Eden leaned forward and screwed the cap off the vodka. Well, she couldn't let the ice go to waste. She filled her glass to the rim. Lifting it to her mouth, she took a healthy swallow. It burned on the way down. At least it was better than panic and anxiety drowning her in its swirling vortex.

She drained the glass and filled it again. Taking another big swallow, she absentmindedly flipped through the newspaper. Nothing but industry music news and club dates. Not something she was into. She liked her music hard à la Metallica, not with Mohawks and facial piercings.

After draining the glass a second time, she turned a few pages. That's when she saw it.

The Gate.

While she stared down at the advertisement, her heart skipped a few beats. Hands sweating, the glass nearly slipped from her fingers. Setting the drink down, Eden leaned close to read the ad.

The Gate was a club downtown. A hip, alternative place that catered to all-night ravers. Chills ran down her spine. This was too much of a coincidence.

Something wanted her to follow the clues.

* * *

After eating Chinese takeout, Eden found herself standing in line to get into The Gate.

Among a motley collection of Goths, punks and bohemian chic, she stood out like a pimple on a perfect, pale face. With her black tank top, worn jeans and black combat boots, she appeared more grunge than subculture, which wasn't really all that cool since grunge had officially died with Kurt Cobain.

As she waited, she searched the crowd in front of her and behind for Lilith Grae. Although there were plenty of girls with long black hair and pale complexions, she didn't see Lilith.

The line moved and Eden found herself at the front. Two beefy bouncers manned the door like sentries to an army base. One of them glared at her when it became her turn to go through.

"No cops allowed," he grunted.

The people pushing at her back suddenly moved away as if they'd been told she had an infectious disease.

"I'm not a cop." She added softly, "Anymore."

The bouncer looked her up and down, then held out his hand. "Wallet."

Digging into her back jeans pocket, she slid out her leather billfold and handed it to him. She ground her teeth as he rummaged through it, inspecting her driver's license, then glancing at her. She could've taken him down in a matter of seconds if she had wanted. She'd taken down bigger and faster men during police training. She was a firm believer in *it's not the size of the dog in the fight, but the size of the fight in the dog.* And she had a lot of fight inside.

After sliding two twenties out of it, the bouncer tossed her the wallet. He stuffed the money into his pocket and unhooked the rope from the line, gesturing her forward.

"Go ahead, sweetheart."

She muttered a few choice curse words as she passed him.

The club was a massive, raucous menagerie of strobe lights, neon and writhing bodies. Eden could smell the sweat from the doorway.

The place was packed with wall-to-wall tattoos and metal studs, and she had to push her way through to the bar, which was up on a platform away from the throng of dancers. Two large birdcages hung on either side of the bar—girls in skimpy leather outfits danced and gyrated inside. Despite the view, it would provide a good position to survey the club.

After shoving through, she realized there were no available stools at the bar and absolutely no room to maneuver to get a drink. After several attempts to push through, she was about ready to give up when a rail-thin girl with pink cornrows fell off her stool and landed on her back right at Eden's feet. Eden stepped over her and slid happily onto the seat.

One of three bartenders gestured to her. "What do you want?"

"Scotch, rocks." Then she groaned. "No wait. Cranberry soda."

The bartender smirked, then grabbed a short glass, slammed some ice into it, and poured in the juice and soda. He handed it to her. Instead of putting money into his waiting hand, Eden gave him a picture. The picture of Lilith Grae she'd downloaded from the missing persons' website.

"Do you recognize her?"

Glowering at her, the bartender didn't look at the photo. "No."

She glared right back. "Just look at the damn picture, please. I'm not asking for anything but that."

Slowly, he glanced down at the photo. Eden knew he was really looking. Not like some people who just glanced and never really saw.

"She used to work one of the cages."

Eden took the photo back and gave him some money. "What happened to her?"

"She quit obviously." He yanked the money from between her fingers.

"You better be back with my change."

The bartender scowled at her but did return with a few bills and some coins.

Satisfied, she took a sip of her drink and swiveled on her stool to survey the crowd. It was like looking for a grain of sand on a beach. Lilith would blend well with the pack. Eden would never be able to pick her out among the dyed black hair and pale complexions.

Obviously, this had been a wasted venture. What was she thinking? She wasn't, was the issue. Draining the rest of her drink, Eden decided to just let the police do their job. They were good at what they did. They would find the woman.

"Are you looking for someone?"

Startled by the booming voice, Eden jumped in her seat. A man sat next to her. A huge man. The stool looked as if it would break any second under the strain of his enormous mass. He wasn't obese by any means. Just big. Like a body-builder on massive doses of steroids.

He was wearing a black T-shirt and camouflage cargo pants and was holding a cigarette. The seams on his pants and shirt looked as if they'd rip open at any moment.

"I'm sorry? Are you talking to me?"

He tapped the ash off his cigarette and turned his head to look at her. "I'm looking at you, aren't I?"

Her heart slammed in her chest so hard she had to gasp for breath. His eyes were as black as soot, the pupils red. Eden looked up at the lights overhead. It must've been a reflection off something, like a cat's eyes glowing in the night.

"I'm just sitting here having a drink," she said as she picked up her glass and jingled the ice.

"Ahuh." He tapped the ash from his smoke again. "I haven't seen you here before."

"It's my first time."

He grinned and gray tendrils of smoke curled out of his nose and mouth. "I like first-timers."

Bile rose in her throat. She hadn't seen him take a drag off his cigarette, so where was the smoke coming from? Parched and shaky, she instinctively reached for her glass, then remembered that it was empty. But as she clasped it in her hand, she felt the cool, refreshing liquid inside. Her glass was full again. Shivers rushed down her spine.

"I have a message for you, Eden Swain."

Fear wiggled its way into her body, like a worm burrowing into black soil. Her throat tightened. "How do you know my name?"

"Go home, get drunk and forget everything you think you know about Lilith Grae." He stood to leave. "If you don't, you'll be sorrier than you've ever been in your life."

"Wait. Where is she?" Eden grasped his arm before he could turn away. His flesh burned like a hot plate against her skin. She yanked her hand back and swore. "Fuck me!"

Cradling her hand to her chest, she looked down at it. A black scorch mark covered her entire palm. Smoke was actually rising from it and the stench of burned flesh invaded her nose.

She looked up at the huge man with a renewed sense of awe and fear. It wasn't normal for skin to sear; he wasn't normal.

Leaning down into her face, he said, "You can't help her, Eden Swain. You're not worthy." More smoke snaked out of his nose and mouth as he spoke, as well as the putrid smell of rotten eggs.

Eden's stomach roiled and she had to bite her lip to stop from retching.

With the pain of her burn still registering, she watched as he walked away. He moved through the crowd easily. She supposed that didn't surprise her since he was such an enormous man, easily seven feet tall, but it wasn't as if people were consciously moving out of his way. In fact, it seemed as if nobody even acknowledged his presence.

They didn't stare or gawk as he moved past, but just sort of drifted out of the way as if pushed gently by an unseen breeze.

Eden couldn't let him walk away—she had too many questions. Even though fear coursed through her, she had to try. For the woman. For herself.

Leaning over the bar, she snagged a cotton rag, put the ice from her drink into it and wrapped it around her hand. It hurt like a bitch, but she sucked it up and jumped off her stool to follow the mammoth.

Because he was so tall—easily head and shoulders, maybe even nipples, above everyone—it was easy to track where he was heading: to the washrooms.

Leaning against the wall outside the men's room, Eden waited for him to come out. Other men gave her strange looks as they brushed past her, but she ignored them. She was beyond caring what anyone thought of her, or question what she was doing.

She was even more determined to locate Lilith Grae. The giant's warning just affirmed her decision that she was on the right track. Obviously, there was more going on than simply a missing woman.

After ten minutes, Eden was through waiting.

She pushed open the door and marched in. There were two guys at the urinals. Ignoring their indignant protests, she continued on to the three closed stalls.

Eden peered through the crack in the first door. A young man in leather nearly fell off the toilet. She moved to the next one. This time there was a couple, a man and woman, getting their jollies—they didn't even notice her intrusion. The third and final stall was empty.

"Where the hell did he go?" Eden spun around the room, looking for another exit or a utility door or employee entrance. There were none. She glanced up and saw a small barred window. No way that anyone could fit through that, especially not a man weighing at least two hundred and fifty pounds of solid flexed muscle.

"Damn it!" she yelled.

The washroom door swung open again. Two beefy bouncers stomped in; she recognized one of them from the front door.

He grinned. "It'll be my pleasure to show you the way out, sweetheart."

# Chapter Five

The bouncers escorted Eden out of the club, but they couldn't force her off the street. She stood on the other side of the road, leaning against someone's car, and kept watch on the place. Something was going on inside the club, something nefarious or something unnatural. Either way she'd wait here all night to find out. She couldn't let this lead disappear.

After two hours of sitting, Eden stood and flexed her legs. Her ass had gone numb. As she walked around, the prickly sensation radiated over her butt and down the backs of her thighs. She hated that feeling.

Something stirred in the alley a block over. A pop bottle rolled out of the mouth and onto the street. Vigilant, Eden watched, waiting to see if someone emerged. A flash of something pale rushed into the lane. She couldn't be sure, but it had the look of a man, although it could have just been dogs rummaging through the garbage bins.

Big dogs the size of humans?

A sudden urge to make sure crept over her. What if it had something to do with the giant from the club or with Lilith?

After looking both ways to make sure no one was observing her, Eden sneaked along the sidewalk and ducked into the alleyway. It was practically barren except for a big green garbage bin that stood against one wall about halfway down.

Keeping her eyes forward, she bent down and unsheathed the knife from the strap on her calf just above her boot. She flicked the blade open and stepped down the alley, her back to the brick wall opposite the bin. She didn't know what she was expecting, but she was of the motto *forearmed is forewarned*—with *armed* meaning literally with weapon.

As she crept, she listened for any out-of-place sounds, except she could barely hear over her own labored breathing and pounding heartbeat. Dread was pumping through her veins like a toxin. Maybe coming down the alley hadn't been a very bright idea.

A sudden breeze whipped through the alley, sending pieces of papers and trash into a swirling dust devil. Eden shut her eyes as it whirled around her, peppering her face with dirt and debris. Almost as soon as it formed, it was gone, entombing the alley with dead silence.

Eden's skin crawled. Someone or something was staring at her—she could feel it on her flesh like a thousand scurrying cockroaches. With her thoughts working overtime, Eden decided to turn and go back the way she'd come. There was nothing here. Even with the minimal light, she could see down to the end. At least, that's what she kept telling herself as she rushed along the wall to the opening of the lane.

Glancing once more behind her, she stepped out of the alley and onto the sidewalk with a sigh of relief. She flicked her blade closed and tucked it into her pants pocket. Shaking her head at how foolish she'd just been, Eden started to walk back to the car to continue watching the club.

She managed two steps before she was quite literally swept off her feet.

A black hood was thrust over her head and she was picked

up under the arms and yanked into the air. Her feet flailed, seeking anything solid to touch on, but found none. She was being carried somewhere high.

As pure terror surged over her, she clawed at the felt hood over her face. She couldn't get enough air. She was going to suffocate.

"I wouldn't do that if I were you." The dark-chocolate-rich voice came at her ear.

"I can't breathe."

"Yes, you can."

His voice was soothing and she could feel a little of her panic leak away. Slowly, she let her hands drop. As she did, they brushed against the arm holding her around the chest. Wide and strong. And hairy?

"Where are you taking me?"

"We need to have a little talk." The second he literally growled the last word, he tossed her.

She landed on her ass.

Which was probably a blessing since she couldn't see. If she had tried to land on her feet she might have twisted her ankle or worse.

Cursing, she yanked off the hood and looked around to get her bearings. She was on the rooftop of a building. A high building by the looks of it.

Gravel bit into her palms as she gained her feet. Dizzy, she stumbled sideways and nearly landed on her butt again. A pair of strong hands held her up. Not the same hands that had dropped her to begin with—these were not hairy.

Shrugging off his hold, she swung around to give him a piece of her mind. The words lodged in her throat. She nearly choked on them.

He was beautiful. There was really no other way to describe him. Not in the effeminate way some men were pretty, but flawless like a statue of pale marble carved by the most talented of sculptors. His skin seemed to glow, as did his eyes.

Oh, and he was naked.

"What is going on? And who the hell are you?" She tried to not look at his other amazing parts. "And why the hell are you naked?"

"None of those things matter." He walked around her as he spoke, and she got a glimpse of his extraordinary ass. "What matters is that you listen very carefully to what I say to you now, Eden Swain."

"You know you're the second asshole today who's tried to tell me what to do."

He stopped in front of her and arched a brow. "Who else has spoken to you?"

"Some big dude in the club." She lifted her hand, the one still wrapped in a dishrag. "He gave me a little souvenir to remember him by."

"What did he tell you?" His eyes fixed on hers and she had the sudden urge to fall into them, to surrender herself to the fortitude in them.

"To go home and forget about Lilith Grae."

"Considering the source, those are wise words." He began circling her again. "After tonight, do not concern yourself with this matter. Go back to your life. Do not get involved."

"And what if I tell you to take a flying leap off this building and continue to do what I want?"

He smiled but there was no joy or humor in it. "You talk tough, but you would not be able to handle the consequences of your actions." His eyes glinted like stars in the night sky. "You think you live in hell now? You have no clue what that truly is like."

Without thinking, Eden used her injured hand to snag his arm as he walked around her. Pain seared through her and she grimaced. "You don't know me. You have no clue about my life and what I've had to deal with."

He covered her hand with his own. "I know more than you realize, Eden Swain. Your soul bleeds all around you."

Tears sprang to her eyes with the description of the emotional torment she'd been going through. How could this stranger see right through her, to the very essence of her being?

He was no ordinary man—it was evident in everything about him.

"I do not tell you these things to hurt you. I say them to keep you from more harm." He squeezed her hand, then let his own drop. "Searching for Lilith Grae will only bring you more pain." Giving her his back, he walked toward the edge of the building.

As he walked away, she noticed his long bone-white hair fluttering in the breeze. He had a graceful way of walking, majestic like an animal. Which of course was crazy. When he reached the edge, he turned and looked at her once more.

"Heed my words. Save your soul."

"Wait!" She rushed after him. "Is she safe? Can you at least tell me that?"

He paused as if pondering whether to give her the information or not, as if it wasn't a good idea. "Yes, she's safe."

He stepped up onto the ledge and jumped off the roof.

Eden ran to the edge. When she looked over, he was nowhere in sight. Not falling to his death, not gliding down with a parachute or hanging from a helicopter. He was just gone. Evaporated into mist.

But there was movement in the street below. It looked like a giant dog striding down the road. A dog or a large, pale wolf. Exactly like the one she'd seen trailing behind her the other night. Which was impossible, wasn't it?

Vertigo made her head swim and she stumbled back. But

it was more than the fear of heights that made her mind muddled. Her whole life she'd been able to figure things out. Algebra equations and word anagrams were as easy to do as playing tic-tac-toe. She'd always been skilled in solving problems. But now, she had no clue how to figure this one out.

Everything she'd experienced since the woman's disappearance was beyond her scope of logic and reason.

Eden rushed across the rooftop to the door that led to the levels below. When she wrapped her hand around the metal handle and tugged, she realized that her injured hand didn't hurt anymore. Her throat constricted as she stared down at her hand. Unraveling the cloth, Eden took in slow, measured breaths. She wasn't prepared for what she saw. Or didn't see.

The black burn had completely vanished. Her palm appeared pink like new skin.

Flexing her fingers, Eden recalled Lilith's words on the phone. She had talked about demons and evil, but what she had failed to mention was the other side.

# *Chapter Six*

Eden didn't sleep much that night. Her dreams were filled with smoke-blowing demons and wolves with startling, pale eyes. And a man so perfect and pale she thought she'd go mad with wanting him.

*Eden Swain.*

Her name echoed between the buildings, joined by thousands of soft voices murmuring, as if every leaf on every tree was calling to her.

*Eden Swain, Eden Swain. Over here, Eden Swain.*

Eden looked around. She was no longer in the city but in a forest filled with towering trees and a heavy mist.

A shadow crossed her path.

"What do you want?" she called, spinning toward it, only to feel as if the shadow was behind her and not in front of her. "Where are you?"

*I'm here. Come to me, Eden.*

"Why should I listen to you?"

*There is only one way to save your soul.*

A white wolf appeared, the biggest wolf she'd ever seen. Its eyes glowed in the moonlight. Its teeth were bared but it wasn't growling. No, an animal growled out of fear. This animal wasn't fearful; it looked hungry, and if Eden wasn't mistaken, she was going to be supper.

Eden's hands flew to her waist where her gun should have been holstered. It wasn't there. Looking down at herself, she saw that she wasn't dressed in her usual street clothes—she was wearing some billowing white gown, the kind of thing a Victorian virgin would wear on her wedding night.

The kind of thing that was impossible to run in.

But Eden had no choice. Without a weapon her only chance for survival was to run. She turned and fled, racing through the forest, dodging trees and jumping over fallen logs. The stupid nightgown she wore got caught on bushes and branches that tugged on her like tiny malevolent hands, tearing the fabric, making her stumble.

At first she could hear the animal's loping strides behind her, but panic and exertion deafened her senses so that the only sounds she heard were her own panting breath and the pounding of her heart. She dared to glance behind her—a mistake because she didn't see the root until after her toe got caught. She fell so hard the air got knocked out of her and she writhed on the ground, gasping to get it back.

When she was able to breathe again, she jumped to her feet, crouching in a defensive position, prepared for the inevitable attack, but the animal was gone. There was nothing there. The forest was silent.

Eden turned three hundred and sixty degrees, searching and listening for any telltale sign. *Thank God.* She leaned against the nearest tree, closed her eyes, and focused on slowing her breathing and her heart rate.

When she opened her eyes, he was there. Not the wolf, no. The pale man. Naked and glorious. He approached her with silent footfalls, his pale eyes glowing in the dim light.

"Go away," Eden shouted, feeling every bit the trapped prey and hating herself for it.

*Do you fear me?*

She laughed. "Not likely. I'm just not in the mood to be eaten."

*That's a shame.*

He came nearer still, close enough to touch, and the closer he came, the harder it was for Eden to breathe.

His pale-eyed gaze swept across her body and Eden shivered. She looked down. Her tattered gown lay in a puddle at her feet and she stood completely naked with nothing but her fists to protect her.

*You nearly gave yourself to him, yet you stand in fear of me. Why?*

"I don't know what the hell you're talking about." She inched a teeny step to the right, hoping to distract him so she could make a break for it. "Do me a favor and open your mouth when you talk to me."

*Can't you hear me?*

"Of course I can hear you. I'm speaking to you, aren't I?"

The man smiled and Eden expected to see fangs behind those sensuous lips, but she saw only the gleam of straight white teeth.

He leaned toward her and whispered, "Is this better?"

He was within striking distance. "Yes," she said through gritted teeth before driving her knee up, hard, and feeling a sense of satisfaction when it connected with something both soft and solid.

But it wasn't the part of him she'd hoped to nail. He'd moved so quickly she'd missed her intended target and now her knee was firmly grasped in his huge hand while he regarded her with an unreadable expression.

"Let go of me."

He shook his head and hoisted her leg up higher, driving it to the side and stepping up to the opening he'd created. With the weight of his body leaning into her, he no longer needed to hold on to her leg, and he grabbed her wrists and forced them high against the tree above her.

"What do you want from me?" she bit out.

"What do you think?"

"If I knew the answer, I wouldn't have asked."

He smiled slowly. "You, Eden. I want you." To illustrate his point, he moved his hips, adjusting the point where his arousal pressed against her naked body.

She sucked in a breath, appalled by her unconscious response to this stranger. Her sex dripped for him, her heart pounded for him, yet her mind recoiled.

"You want me, too. Don't fight it."

*Don't fight it?* If there was ever a phrase that made Eden want to fight, that was it. She writhed inside his embrace, trying to kick herself free, trying to wrench her hands out from his steely clasp. But it was no good. The bastard was too big, too strong.

His head ducked down until he was right beside her ear. "I won't force you, Eden." He lingered there, as if smelling her hair. "Tell me to let you go and I will."

It was so distracting, his sweet breath against her cheek, his heart pounding against her breast, his cock wedged so close one little adjustment and he'd slide right inside her. She bit down on her lip intending to tell him to back off, but no words would come. The heat between them was too intense, too fierce. She didn't want it to end. So, she moved ever so slightly, adjusting her leg up higher on his waist, and felt the head of his cock at her opening.

He needed no more encouragement. Grabbing onto her ass with one hand to hold her against the tree, he thrust inside her. She moaned as he filled her fully. It was more than just a physical sensation but a mental one as well. He filled her in places she'd forgotten were so empty.

Her hands streaked over his shoulders, digging her nails into the hard flesh of his back. She held on as he drove her hard, pushing her closer and closer to the edge of pleasure.

As he stroked hard between her legs, he nuzzled his face along her neck, licking and nipping his way up to her ear, then back down along her jawline. With each raze of his teeth on her skin, a twin sensation blossomed inside her. Heat, brutal and fierce, built like a wild fire deep within her sex. Her whole body flushed with the intensity of it.

He moved faster and harder, bucking against her. Every stroke of his cock sent a ripple of pleasure over her. She couldn't stop the mewls escaping her lips. The intensity of what he was doing to her body was almost too much to bear.

The tree bark scratched at her flesh as he plunged into her again and again, cresting her body up and down. But the pain was nothing compared to the pure sweet agony deep inside her slick warmth. Eventually they became one thing and she couldn't even form a rational thought.

"Oh God," she panted, her heart racing so hard she could barely breath. "Harder."

Wrapping his hand around her ass cheek, his fingers brushed against her sex and he pulled her to him just as he buried himself inside her. All her muscles twitched and seized as an orgasm nearly shattered her into pieces.

She cried out, clamping her eyes shut against the onslaught of pleasure that surged from inside and cascaded over every inch of her flesh. He kissed her then, swallowing each moan she made. It was hard and hot and wet and fierce and made her head swim even more. Then she felt him surge between her thighs.

When he was finished kissing her, he pulled back and looked her in the eyes. "He will try to have you, but know this. You are mine."

She opened her eyes and expected to find herself staring into the man's hungry eyes, but instead she was staring at the numbers on her clock radio. It was 6:00 a.m.

Eden rolled onto her back and blinked up at the ceiling of her bedroom. A dream. That's all it was. Another crazy dream. She touched her lips. So why were her lips swollen as if she'd just been kissed within an inch of her life? And why did her thighs ache and her insides burn?

Eden groaned and crawled out of bed, itching to fire up her laptop in order to do some research on The Gate nightclub. She wanted to know exactly who owned it and how long it'd been in business. Something was going on at that club and every instinct she had screamed that it had everything to do with the missing woman, Lilith Grae. Maybe even with the man she'd shot a year ago. Someone at the club knew Eden was looking for Lilith, and by the way Eden had been treated, it was obvious that person didn't want the woman found.

And Eden needed to know if the man who'd taken her for a wild ride onto a roof of a building was connected to the club. She thought that he was for sure.

He knew her, that much was clear, but how and why?

After finding zero references to the club on the net, Eden closed the lid on her laptop and looked around her apartment. She had lots of time to kill. Several hours before she went back to the club to investigate further. Come hell or high water she was going to find out how that big-ass, fiery son of a bitch had disappeared through a solid wall.

Eden wasn't operating under any assumptions that the bouncer was going to let her in through the front door. She had no doubt he'd recognize her even if she went in disguise. So she had to find another way in.

Every business had a back entrance. She'd learned that the hard way. She just had to find it and exploit it to her advantage.

By the time 2:00 a.m. came Eden was more than ready to go. She'd dressed all in black and had packed a blade in her ankle sheath. She needed to be prepared if big, bad and stinky attacked her. Because she had a strong feeling that if she came across him, he wasn't going to give her a warning. He'd given that to her the first time. She didn't believe in second chances.

Eden parked a couple blocks away from the club. Instead of heading down the main street, she took a detour down a side street, then crossed, intent on finding an alley behind the building. The kitchen staff had to have a way in and a way out, especially to take the garbage out.

After taking a wrong turn, she found the alleyway. As stealthily as she could, Eden walked down the lane, counting down the doors from the end of the street. She knew that the club's main door was four businesses down from the main street, so it was logical that their back door would be four down, as well.

When she reached the fourth door, she pressed her ear to it. She could hear the telltale thump of techno music—she definitely had the right door.

Eden ran her hand down the door to the handle. She turned it—it was locked. She hadn't expected anything different. Reaching around to her back, she slid out her lock-picking kit from her rear pocket. She unrolled it and plucked out the tools she needed.

It took her about five minutes to pick the lock. It was something she'd learned during her short-lived career as a cop. Sometimes to catch a criminal a cop had to think like one, and sometimes even act like one.

Putting her tools away, Eden slid her pack into the small of her back, then carefully opened the door. There was no one in the immediate area. She crept inside, hoping no kitchen help decided right there and then to toss out any trash. She was in a small corridor and she walked it pressed against the wall, mindful of any noise that she made.

The corridor opened up into a storage room. This was

where all the extra napkins and straws and little pink um-
brellas were kept until they were needed. She crossed the
floor to the door and peered through the small window into
the kitchen.

There were two people manning the grills and deep fry-
ers. Eden slowly pushed open the door and walked in. Their
backs were to her and she quickly moved across the kitchen
to the swinging door. She'd just touched the door to push
through when a voice sounded behind her.

"What are you doing back here?"

She turned and, feigning ignorance, looked around. "I was
looking for the bathroom."

"Well, this ain't it."

"I noticed. Sorry to disturb you. I'll just go out and find it."

That made the little kitchen man grin and he shook his
head as she pushed the door open and went through.

Now she was in another short hallway, and Eden walked
it quickly, hoping not to come across any waitstaff along the
way. At the end of the corridor, she could see club-goers mill-
ing about the hall in front of the washrooms. She recognized
the scene from the other night. She stepped out and pretended
to be part of the crowd. No one noticed her as she sidled up
to a group of three women insistently chatting about some
guy who'd bumped into them on the dance floor.

One of the girls glanced at her. Eden gave her a quick
smile, then passed them to near the men's washroom. She
stopped before the door, looked around to make sure no one
was paying much attention to her. With her blond curls tucked
up into her black wool hat maybe she'd be mistaken for a guy.
She could only hope as she took a deep breath and pushed
open the door to enter.

Thankfully there was no one at the urinals. She couldn't
be as sure about the three stalls. Leaning over, she looked
for feet under the doors. She found none, and, taking a final

big breath, she pushed open the last cubicle door and went in, shutting and locking it behind her. Now she had the privacy she needed to really inspect the wall.

On first look, she couldn't see any indication of a trapdoor or slide-away. She ran her hands over the whitewashed brick, searching for anything out of the ordinary. She didn't find anything. No latches or buttons or cracks in the mortar. Nothing to show that the wall would or could move at all. It seemed 100 percent solid, so how had the bastard gone through it?

Eden leaned against the cubicle side and stared hard at the wall. She was missing something. But as she stared, something happened. Her visions wavered in and out as if looking through a wave of extreme heat. The solid bricks didn't appear so solid anymore—they looked languid, viscous like a thick white fluid. It had to be a trick of the fluorescent light in the bathroom, but she dared to hope otherwise.

Tentatively, she reached out with her hand and pressed her fingers to the wall right were she could see it shimmer. Her fingers didn't hit anything solid, but something gushy and malleable. She kept pushing and her fingers went through the material and disappeared from view.

Panicked, she pulled her hand back and looked down at it. It was still solid; her fingers were still there. But they glimmered with what looked like something shiny and wet. She rubbed it between her fingers—it was like liquid silk.

Taking a deep breath, Eden stepped forward and pushed both hands to the wall—they sunk into the impossibly mysterious substance. She followed it through, unsure if she was delirious or if this was truly real.

As she walked through the gelatinous wall, her body tingled. It was as if a thousand pins had pricked her flesh, from the top of her head to the bottoms of her feet. There wasn't exactly pain, but it wasn't a pleasant feeling either.

The sensation lasted only a few seconds, and then she was through the barrier. Blinking, Eden looked around. She was no longer in a cubicle in the men's washroom but in a back alley someplace else. She whipped around and stared at the brick wall behind her, the wall she'd just come through. It looked solid, formidable even. She placed her hands against the brick and pushed. Nothing happened. It was as unyielding as it appeared.

She glanced down at her hands and her body and noticed the same type of glimmer from before. It clung to her skin and her clothing. She ran a finger over the back of her hand—it came away damp with a glittery substance that reminded her of gelatin.

Eden turned back around to face the alley she was in. It didn't appear to be the same one she'd come down to get into the club. She didn't recognize it offhand, but then again, most alleys looked the same.

Filled with trepidation, she walked down the lane. Every now and then, she stopped and listened. There were sounds in the vicinity. Most were ordinary city noises—cars whizzing by, ladies in high heels clicking down the sidewalk, the bark of a dog—but there were also other sounds. Ones she couldn't quite put her finger on. Odd noises like the clacking of something heavy, and shuffling as if someone was dragging something big behind them as they walked.

Before she even stepped out onto the main street, Eden knew she wasn't in the city she lived in any longer.

# Chapter Seven

It was the smell that alerted Eden to the danger long before she saw it lumbering down the street toward her.

A combination of musk and mothballs, the smell reminded her of wet, dirty dog. Which, by the size and shape of the creature walking toward her, might not have been such a bad description.

Eyes wide, heart pounding, Eden watched pressed up against the brick wall as a dog, upright on two feet, with a very scruffy muzzle but bright green eyes, strode on by her as if on his way to an important meeting, or date by the swagger in his back end. He glanced briefly at her as he passed and gave her a derisive sniff, then continued on as if nothing was amiss.

Eden stayed pressed against the wall for another ten minutes, trying to get her bearings. She was also struggling for breath because she swore she saw a half man-half snake slither down the center line of the road. It almost got sideswiped by a horse and buggy going the opposite way. Thankfully, the horse yelled "move it" at the last minute and the snake creature slithered off to the right.

Eden wasn't quite sure she could handle a man-snake/

horse/buggy mashup right now. She was barely hanging on to her sanity as her gaze darted everywhere at once, trying to take everything in. The street looked like any other average downtown city street at night. There was concrete beneath her feet and buildings made out of brick and cement and glass in all four directions. She read neon restaurant signs for the best Chinese food in town and pawn shop displays in windows. It could've easily been any street downtown.

But it clearly wasn't.

Because Eden would've known if there were—what she could only guess were—Satyrs living in her city. Two of them walked past her; one of them winked.

"Hey, baby, looking for a good time?"

Scared, she just shook her head and kept her lips pressed together and her gaze glued to the sidewalk.

They moved on, chuckling at her obvious nervousness and ignorance.

Finally, after another few minutes of agonizing confusion and fear, someone took pity on Eden. That someone was a four-foot-high mottled green goblin named Durt.

"Are you lost, lady?"

"You could say that."

"What I want to know is if you're saying it."

She nodded eagerly. "Yes, I'm definitely lost."

"Come from the other side, have you?"

She nodded again.

"Well, for the right price, I could be your Threshold tour guide." He smiled, revealing two gapped rows of razor-sharp yellow teeth.

"Threshold?"

"Yup." He lifted his stubby arms out to the sides. "Welcome to Threshold. Where anything goes."

"Okay?" she drew the word out, looking around trying

to decide her next step. "What is this place exactly? How does it exist?"

"I don't know, lady. Do I look like a scientist or a theologist?"

"Theologist? Are you saying this is...like hell or something?"

He snickered. "This ain't hell. It's better than that. It's the world between the worlds. The place where anything and everything can exist and does."

As if to prove his point, two female werewolves walked by, both dressed like Lolita Goths, resplendent in short plaid skirts, black knee-high socks, four-inch wedge Mary Janes and tank tops. They each sported pigtails, accented with big pink bows.

Eden looked back at Durt. "How much do you charge?"

"For you, ten even."

"Ten dollars an hour?"

He shook his bald head. "No, not dollars. Your paper is useless here."

"Then ten what?" Eden really had a bad sense that she shouldn't have asked and she didn't really want to know.

"Rats."

"Excuse me?"

"Rats. I love them. They taste so darn good. And I can't get them here. Well, not the eating kind anyway."

"What kinds are here?"

"The talking kind. And they don't ever shut up."

"Well, I don't seem to have any rats on me at the moment."

He snickered again. "I know that. I'm not an idiot. I want you to get them for me when you go back. We'll make a deal. I'll show you around, help you navigate, and when you go back you have to get me ten dead rats and send them through to me."

She shrugged. She figured she didn't have much of a choice. "It's a deal."

Durt gobbed on the palm of his right hand and held it out to her. "To seal the deal."

She spat on her palm and then shook his hand. It was disgusting but she tried to keep her face still—she didn't want to insult the little creature. He seemed to sincerely want to help her, and she didn't have any other contact in this world.

"Okay, so what's your pleasure? Food, booze, drugs, sex, whatever it is, you can find it here." He leaned closer to her and said behind his clawed hand, "And just so you know, I don't judge. We all got our vices. Whatever depraved thing you want, I can direct you to it."

"I need information."

"Ah, now I see. You're looking for someone."

She nodded. "He's big, dumb, looks like he's been built from stone and stinks to high heaven of sulfur."

Durt snorted. "You just described half the population. But I know of a place where you can ask questions freely without fear of being shot, stabbed, eviscerated, bitten or blown to bits." He stared down the sidewalk. "Come on. It's not far."

Eden followed the little green goblin down the street, careful to avoid bumping into a man-lizard with glowing red eyes and talons walking the opposite way. Its elliptical pupils narrowed at her as she passed. Shivers rushed down her spine and she pulled her leather jacket in tighter around her body.

She had a feeling that being in this place was going to give her permanent chills.

They walked, Durt in the lead, about five blocks until they came to a desolate, dilapidated-looking building on the corner of two wide streets. Eden glanced around and noticed that it was smack in the middle of a crossroads of sorts. A screaming pink neon sign hanging over the door read *The*

*Chained Heart.* Durt pushed open the banged-up pink door, and Eden followed him through.

Eden didn't know what she had expected at The Chained Heart, but it definitely wasn't what she saw. It was a tavern, an old-school medieval-type place. There were wooden tables and chairs and a long bar, all standing on a gray stone floor and leaning somewhat from excessive use. Various types of people sat at the tables drinking what she thought to be beer by the frothy tops in large pewter steins.

She would've thought she'd walked onto a movie set for a historical film if it wasn't for the vampires, werewolves, Satyrs, centaurs, lizard people, one haggard-looking Cyclops and others that she couldn't even begin to name taking up the wooden chairs and drinking the ale. It was like watching a cheesy B movie except with stellar special effects.

Durt crossed the room toward the bar. Eden followed him. Several patrons greeted the little goblin, most with pleasant "hellos" and handshakes, but there were a few steely-eyed gazes thrown his way.

When they reached the bar, Durt slammed his hand down on the counter. "What can I get you?"

Everyone seemed to be drinking the same thing, so she decided that was probably her best bet. The easiest way to blend in. "A pint."

He nodded at the ogre-looking bartender. "Two pints, Larry."

Larry shuffled over to the taps and pulled two frothy-looking pints. He set them down on the counter in front of Durt. He didn't look at Eden. "Seven."

Durt dug into his pants pocket and came away with a leather pouch. He opened it and upended seven gold pieces onto the counter. Larry took them in his beefy, hairy hand and ambled away again.

Durt handed Eden the beer. She nodded to him as she took

a tentative sip. Surprisingly, it was really good. She drank some more, then set it down on the counter.

"So, where can I get that information I'm looking for?"

He eyed the other patrons over the rim of his mug. "I'll feel them out for you. Some of them can be really surly."

Which was punctuated by the Cyclops punching a lizard-man in the snout. Lizard-man went down, falling under his table, and the rest of the patrons went back to their drinks and conversation.

But Eden wasn't concentrating on that. No, she was look-ing at the huge smoking demon walking out from where the washrooms were located. He had a cigarette in his mouth and a mug of beer in his hand. And he still wore the same clothes as before.

She marched toward him, ignoring Durt's grunt of alarm. "Hey. I want to talk to you."

The smoking demon glanced at her, then took up a stool at the bar, promptly giving her his expansive back. He took a healthy gulp of his drink.

Eden slid in next to him at the bar. "I said I want to talk to you."

"I heard you," he grunted, then blew smoke into her face. It had the stench of sulfur through it. "And I suggest you get lost, or you're going to get hurt. I already warned you once. I don't give second warnings."

Durt pushed himself between Eden and the demon. "Just a mistake, Bif. Nothing to get angry about." He nudged Eden away.

But she wasn't going. She had questions for *Bif.* "I want to know where Lilith Grae is. I know you know, asshole."

An uncomfortable hush settled over the bar. It was so quiet it was palpable—Eden could feel the silence on her skin. She swallowed audibly and glanced around. It was obvious she had said the wrong thing.

Durt gaped at her and was about to say something when his gaze landed on something, or someone, behind her. He immediately dropped his gaze and bowed his head.

Eden swung around. And there he was. The dark-haired man from her dreams.

"I have a private room. We can talk freely in there." He didn't wait for her response, but crossed the tavern floor as if he was floating. She looked around and everyone was staring at her; some were gasping. She straightened her shoulders and followed the man to the far side of the room where there was an open door.

She stepped through, and it shut of its own accord behind her. The man was standing by an intimate round table set for two. He gestured to one of the chairs. "Please sit."

She did.

He picked up a decanter filled with what looked like red wine. "Would you like wine?"

She nodded, still unable to find her voice.

He poured her a half glass in the jewel-encrusted goblet in front of her. He then filled his own cup. After setting the decanter down, he sat and picked up his glass. He lifted it toward her.

She picked hers up and tapped glasses with him. He drank, watching her over the rim. She brought the glass to her mouth and tilted it back carefully. The second the wine hit her tongue there was an explosion of zesty flavor in her mouth. And something else. There was an explosion of images in her mind.

She, naked on the table, spread out like a buffet, and he between her thighs, feasting on her.

Gasping she shut her eyes against the carnal picture of desire.

"Are you all right?" he asked, a small, knowing smile on his face.

"Yes, I'm fine." Although the sudden pulse of heat in her sex told her otherwise.

"Do you like the wine? It's over four hundred years old."

Eden clutched her glass. "It's quite good."

He nodded, his smile broadening. It made her thighs tense.

After another careful mouthful she set the cup down and regarded the man seated across from her. "Who are you?"

"My name is Bael."

"Okay, that's your name, but *who* are you?"

He chuckled and leaned back in his chair. "That's what I've always liked about you, Eden. You're always so to the point."

She flinched a little at his use of her name in such a familiar way. "You talk as if we know each other."

"We may not have met in person, but we certainly do know each other. I've been with you," he tapped his head, "for months."

"So you're saying you are a figment of my imagination?"

One perfectly sculpted eyebrow rose at that. "Don't be obtuse, Eden. You know perfectly well I'm real. And you also know perfectly well where you know me from."

She sighed, not wanting to accept the truth. "My dreams," she finally breathed.

He nodded, satisfied, then drank from his cup again. A server took that moment to enter the room with their food. Steam rose from the covered trays and a delectable scent wafted to her nose.

The server set a covered plate in front of her, then with a flourish unveiled it. On the plate was a thick piece of meat—wonderfully bloody, just the way she liked it—vegetables and some kind of rice mixture. It smelled and looked delicious. Her stomach rumbled in agreement.

Bael waved his hand toward the meal. "Eat, and you can tell me why you are here."

She picked up the fork and knife and cut into her meat. It

was like slicing butter. She put it in her mouth and groaned as it literally melted in her mouth. She'd never tasted anything like it.

"Good Lord, that's an amazing piece of meat."

Bael smiled. "I'm sure he would thank you for that, but I'm pretty sure the Lord had nothing to do with it."

She didn't know what to say to that, so she continued eating, moaning every so often at the deliciousness of the meal. She couldn't help it. It was like having sex. But in her mouth.

As she thought that, more sordid images flashed in her mind.

She on her knees in front of him, his engorged cock in her hand. She was licking the length of it and sucking eagerly on the knob.

She shook her head to clear the image. The ache between her legs intensified, and she squirmed a little on her chair to ease the discomfort.

He was watching her when she did this as if he'd known what she'd seen in her mind. As if he'd sent her the thought.

With the steak finished, she picked at the vegetables and watched Bael as he ate. She watched the movement of his mouth and found it mesmerizing and arousing. He had full lips and they looked soft. She couldn't help but wonder what they would feel like on her skin.

The second that thought crossed her mind, he smiled, and his gaze lifted to meet hers. The look in his eyes slammed her right in the gut and threatened to venture lower. She crossed her legs to try and stop it.

"I'm looking for someone," she said, trying to get her mind off how devastating he was and back on the reason she'd come to this place.

He lifted that eyebrow again. "Who?"

"A woman named Lilith Grae."

She watched his face, looking for signs of recognition.

There weren't any, but that didn't necessarily mean anything. He could be an accomplished liar. She'd met many before.

"What makes you think she came to Threshold?"

"Instinct," she said. "And I followed that big, dumb stonehead out here from a club that I believe she frequented. Plus, he mentioned her, and the fact that I should forget about it."

"So naturally that made you even more curious."

"Naturally."

He smiled at that, then leaned back in his chair. "What does she look like, this woman?"

Eden took out a folded picture of Lilith from her pocket and slid it across the table to him. He didn't look at it, but said, "Leave it with me, and if I see this girl or hear of her, I'll get in contact with you."

"Thank you."

He inclined his head. "Of course. Do you know where you are staying?"

She shook her head. "No."

"Well, if you are so inclined, I have an empty room in my home. You'd be more than welcome to stay."

There was a little gleam in his eyes that came with the invitation and it made her belly and thighs tense again. He was potent, this man. More potent than any person she'd met before. It was obvious that he'd had a lot of practice in seduction and in the act itself. It rippled around him like an aura, taunting her, tempting her.

"That's kind of you. I'll think about it."

"I'm sure you will."

Eden took that as a cue to leave. She stood, her knees weak, and set her napkin on the table. "Thank you for the meal."

He inclined his head. "It was my pleasure."

She turned to go, then paused and glanced over her shoulder. "If you see her..."

"I will find you, be certain of that."

She nodded her thanks, but put a hand on her gut where it churned and rolled unpleasantly. She didn't like his last statement one bit. It was a veiled threat—she was certain of that. It scared her a little. And aroused her at the same time.

Bael wasn't a man to be trifled with, that was obvious. He'd been warm and pleasant and seemingly helpful to her, and she had to admit she found him extremely attractive, but she instinctively knew he was bad news. Especially for her. And that just made her desire him all the more.

Durt was at her side the second she stepped out of the other room. "I thought you was a dead woman."

"Don't worry. I'm good at taking care of myself." Eden looked around and noticed that the tavern was empty, save for the barkeep wiping down the counter and putting up the bar stools. *Closing time already?* She didn't think she'd been having supper for that long.

Durt tsked at her. "That may be, but Lord Bael is one bad dude. If he wants to talk to you alone, that usually means you is dead."

Eden gestured to the empty bar. "What's happening here?"

"Time to go, it is."

"But I have more questions to ask."

"Will have to wait until morning." Durt grabbed her arm and escorted her toward the door.

"Where am I supposed to go until then?" she asked as the little goblin pushed open the wooden door and hustled her out.

"I find you a place. Cheap but safe."

She stepped out into the chilly night. Durt came out behind her, chatting incessantly about the place where he was going to take her.

"Good place, don't you worry."

She hadn't taken but four steps when an imposing figure stepped out of the shadows in front of her.

"I told you to leave this alone."

He grabbed her before she could protest. By the time she took in a breath to scream, she was being carried through the streets by a large, hairy white wolf.

## Chapter Eight

Eden dropped to the gravel in a back alley. This time, though, she didn't land on her ass. The second her feet touched ground she was swinging at her kidnapper. But she twisted the wrong way and turned her ankle. Pain seared up her calf but she didn't let it stop her from attacking.

"You son of a bitch!"

He dodged her foot easily, dancing just out of reach of her leg. She tried again, but the animal was too nimble. He regarded her with those pale eyes as if he wanted to play. She shook her head and turned to limp away.

"Screw you."

"I warned you, Eden."

She whirled around and stared at the gorgeous, naked man.

"What are you?" she asked, having difficulty not staring at his impressive manly parts.

"What do you think?"

"A werewolf," she said.

"I'm a shape-shifter."

"There's a difference?"

"Of course."

He said it with a look as if he was appalled that she'd suggested otherwise. She turned away, still having a hard time not looking directly at his endowment.

"Could you put some clothes on?" she asked.

"Why? Does it bother you?"

"I'm just having a difficult time not talking directly to your penis."

He guffawed unexpectedly and the sound sent a rush of shivers over her body. There was no discounting the surge of heat between her thighs. She was still achy from her encounter with Bael, and now sexy, naked shape-shifter had to come along and ramp things up again. Images of her sex dream with him flashed in her mind and liquid heat pooled between her legs.

"What do you want? Why did you kidnap me again?"

"I know you think you are doing the right thing by looking for the girl, but you put her in more danger by being here."

"So she is here?"

"Talking with Bael just proves my point about the danger." His jaw tightened.

"He seemed nice enough. At least he was willing to talk to me."

The shape-shifter quirked an eyebrow. "Nice? You think Bael is nice?" He shook his head in disgust. "What is wrong with you?"

"Where do I start?" She laughed, then wiped a sweaty hand through her tousled hair. "Tell me your name."

"Why?"

"Because I asked nicely. And I want to know who I'm being threatened by."

He stared at her for a long beat, then tilted up his chin. "Mikhail."

"Okay, Mikhail, I take it this Bael is what?"

"A vampire."

She laughed. "You mean like Count Dracula? I've come to suck your blood?" she said in an accent.

"No, like a vicious, soulless seducer of the night who will rip out your throat and drink your insides, then ring for tea."

She shuddered at the thought. But deep down she'd known he was something like that. The dark allure of him, the seduction, the fiery flare in his beautiful eyes.

"He's not to be trifled with."

"He offered to help me find Lilith."

Mikhail smiled, and it was cold and calculating. "Of course he did. That is what he does. He makes offers—offers a person can't refuse. Then he owns you for eternity."

"I didn't sell him my soul, if that's what you're insinuating."

"Not yet you haven't."

"Do you really believe I am that awful, that ruined?"

He moved toward her. Eden had a raging urge to retreat, but she stood her ground. She didn't want him to know how afraid she was of him.

"*Damaged* would be a better word. Your soul has holes punched through it. It's torn and ragged, in need of repair. I fear that you will trust in the wrong person to do the mending."

The hair on her arms stood to attention as he neared. There was an electric current in the air and it sizzled over her skin. His presence was almost too intense, too powerful, as if she should drop her gaze and not look upon him.

"I didn't realize I needed saving." Her voice was not as steady as she'd hoped.

He took another step closer. "You are a strong woman, Eden. There is no doubt. But this is a fight you cannot win, a fight you shouldn't even be involved in."

"It's too late for that now. I'm involved. The girl called me, Mikhail. Do you understand? She called *me*."

He sighed, and it was the first real sign of humanity that she'd seen in him. "I understand."

She met his gaze and kept it. "So you'll tell me where the girl is?"

"No, I won't."

"But I thought..."

"You thought wrong." He crossed the last few feet between them and took her arm. "But I will take you to a safe place for the night, and afterward you can find a portal back to your home."

"I'm not going home. You can't force me to."

"We'll see about that."

He came toward her and instantly transformed into the wolf. With one step he was a man, and the next he was a majestic animal. Eden couldn't wrap her head around it.

And she didn't have time to before he grabbed her, tossed her onto his back and bounded down the alley. She had to wrap her hands in his fur to hang on or be thrown off. The thought of letting go did cross her mind but the inevitable painful tumble she'd take on the cement changed her mind.

As Mikhail ran through the streets, Eden tried to keep note of the twists and turns and landmarks along the way in case she needed to get back in a hurry and on her own. However, she wasn't too keen on maneuvering the dangerous creature-filled streets on her own. If the little goblin hadn't found her to begin with, she wasn't sure she would've made it past the first city block unscathed.

After a fifteen-minute ride, Mikhail stopped in front of a dilapidated housing complex. The place reminded her of the stacking-box-like structures in the poor districts of Jakarta, Indonesia, when she'd visited years ago. The smells and the sounds were very similar, as well. Not that she minded. She'd felt at home in Jakarta, so this was a bit like a welcome back.

Mikhail nudged her off his back and returned to his human

form. As Eden followed him, her attention was drawn to one balcony where a couple were having sex. Loudly and in public view. But the odd thing was they were both catlike. Their skin was spotted and their faces triangular with luminous eyes and whiskers. She tried not to watch, but it was fascinating and a little bit arousing.

Once inside the building, Mikhail directed her up a flight of broken-down stairs to the second level. There he led her to a door painted blue and opened it. He gestured for her to enter. She did, although with reservations.

Once Eden was inside, he shut and locked the door, with several dead bolts and a metal slide bar. Nothing was coming through that door unless it was a giant. And she didn't rule that out considering where she was.

Eden took in the small apartment, noticing the sparseness of it. It reminded her a little of her own place. There were three rooms: a small kitchen, a bathroom, and an area with a bed along one wall and a sofa and table along the other. There were no other comforts such as a TV or computer. Maybe such things were pointless here.

"This is where you live?"

"Sometimes. It's not my main abode but I use it for emergencies." He pointed to the bed. "You can sleep there. I will use the sofa."

"Can I shower first? I feel like I've rolled down rabbit holes."

"Of course." He turned on the light in the bathroom for her. "Then I'll tend to your ankle."

She nodded and limped into the bathroom, closing the door behind her. After all that had happened she'd almost forgotten about the pain radiating from her ankle. But now that the adrenaline had ceased racing through her bloodstream, the throb had intensified.

Eden stripped off her clothing, turned on the water in the

stall and stepped into the hot spray. The relief of the scalding water pounding on her skin was almost instant. Sighing, she lifted her face to the spray and let it wash away the grime of the strange city and the anxiety she was feeling. She still wasn't sure this man didn't mean her harm.

When she turned from the spray and opened her eyes, he was standing in the bathroom, watching her. Her first instinct was to cover herself but she was too tired and she figured it was too late for that. He'd already seen her body, and from the size of his erection, he'd obviously liked what he'd seen.

Eden shut off the water. "Something you need?"

She was trying hard not to stare at him, at the beauty of him. He was a tempting distraction and it had been a long time since she'd had any real male contact. Just in her dreams. With him. She desired the real thing, and he was definitely the real thing. More magnificent then she'd fantasized.

He held out a towel for her. "Here."

She took it, rubbed it over her face and hair. Then, almost as an afterthought, she wrapped it around her body, though she had the urge to wrap herself around him instead.

"Sit." He pointed at the toilet. "I'll look at your ankle. I have healing abilities."

She flipped the lid closed and sat on the cool plastic. Mikhail went to a knee in front of her and took her foot in his hands. They were strong and rough on her skin as he moved her foot back and forth, trying to gauge her injury.

She winced when he flexed it to the right. "Ahh. That hurts."

"Hold still." He placed her foot gently on top of his bent knee, then cupped his hands around her ankle.

She wanted to ask him what he was doing, but all rational thought abandoned her as heat from his hands rushed into her flesh. It was as if a fire had been ignited inside. It wasn't painful but a bit uncomfortable as the surge of heat swept up her calf, then to her thigh. Heat waves caressed her skin and molded her flesh until she was flushed and panting.

When next she looked down, her towel had fallen away and her legs were spread. A trickle of moisture lined the inside of her leg. In all her life, she'd never felt this heated, this wanton. The urge to trail her hand down to her sex to ease her suffering dug at her mind. She had to grit her teeth to hold it at bay.

"What did you do to me?" she asked, her voice strangled by desire.

"Healed you."

"You did more than that." Her muscles quivered with need. Her heart thumped hard with want. "I can't leave this room without having you."

"Be careful what you ask for. I will not take you kindly."

She sat forward, placing a hand on his face. She ran a thumb over his full lips, wishing they were on her body right now.

"I don't want kind."

"What do you what?"

"You. Now. However."

He stood, his hard cock level with her face. She reached out to touch it, dragging a fingernail over the tip. Mikhail groaned, then, grabbing her by the hair, he dragged her up to his eager mouth.

He kissed her. It wasn't soft or gentle, but hard and rough, possessive. As if he was claiming her as a prize for a game he'd just won.

After thoroughly kissing her, he turned her and walked her backward to the wall. He pressed his body against hers, mashing her breasts tight to his chest. His erection dug into her belly, an iron rod jabbing her softness.

Without any effort, he picked her up and pushed her legs apart to settle between them. Eden spread her thighs as far as they would go, bracing one foot against the shower door and the other on the sink counter. There was no seduction here. None needed as she was already hot and wet and ready for him.

Using only one hand to hold her captive against the wall, he used the other to guide his cock to her opening. With one long, smooth, yet hard, thrust he was buried inside her moist channel.

"Oh, God," she whimpered, as he began to move between her thighs. Her dream paled in comparison to the reality of his hard cock inside her.

At first he just thrusted in and out, hard and forceful. Then he started to twist his pelvis until he was grinding on her. With every movement he rubbed against her mound. She was so open that the base of his cock knocked against her clit with every stroke.

As he fucked her raw, he bent his head and feasted blissfully on her breasts, tongue and teeth torturing each nipple. It wasn't long before the heat building in her belly became unbearable. She writhed against the wall, moving her body to end her suffering. She wanted it to last and be over at the same time

She dug her nails into his back as he drilled her hard, holding on while he rutted like an animal between her legs. His fingers dug into her ass cheeks as he thrust himself, balls deep, into her sex.

Eden cried out as an orgasm exploded deep inside and radiated outward all the way down to her toes and up to the top of her head. Her whole body flushed with heat, and every muscle convulsed with the power of it.

He pushed her against the wall and followed. His climax forced a low growl from between his lips. She felt him tense then tremble as he came.

She'd had good sex before, but had never experienced an

orgasm so deep inside that when he set her down, her legs shook so badly she had to sit or collapse to the floor. Mikhail remained braced against the wall, his back to her, breathing heavily. Sweat slicked his entire body, making him glisten. Eden had to fight back the urge to run her own slick body over his.

"Um, that was..."

But she didn't get a chance to finish her sentence before he turned around and looked at her. His face was hard, his eyes were slit like a wolf's and he was still hard.

"I'm not done with you."

He reached for her, picking her up as if she weighed nothing. He tossed her over his shoulder and crossed the room in two strides to lay her on the bed.

The look on his face had her scrambling back on the mattress. Fear and arousal mixed together into one potent elixir. She didn't get away, though. He grabbed her leg, yanked her back to the edge of the bed and flipped her over onto her stomach, all within a few seconds, and with little fuss on his part.

Before she could utter a protest, he had her bent over the bed and was parting her legs. He pressed a hand to her back to hold her down and pushed his stiff cock into her slick opening once more.

Her orgasm had barely subsided when it started building up again. This time she could feel the first tremors of desire deep inside her vagina. It was like a hard ball of quivering heat vibrating inside her belly. The vibrations in her sensitive nerve endings were almost unbearable. She grabbed the blanket on the bed to scramble away but Mikhail held her firm, intending to pleasure her into submission.

Which was what he was doing now, thrusting deep into her. Gripping her tight around the hips, he pulled her back as he thrusted forward. The sounds of their moist flesh slapping together filled the room. As did the cloying scent of their mingled juices. Saliva and sweat and come.

Eden wallowed in it, unable to do anything but surrender to it and the delicious torment he was inflicting on her body.

Clenching her fists in the blanket, she closed her eyes and succumbed to the tsunami of pleasure that coursed over her, through her. It was so intense she bit down on her bottom lip as her insides exploded.

She cried out, unable to keep anything in anymore. Tears streamed down her cheeks as she climaxed again and again. Juices from inside soaked her thighs and the blanket beneath her.

"Oh, fuck," Mikhail groaned as he rammed his cock in hard and tight and came.

He collapsed on top of her. She could feel his hot breath on the back of her sweaty neck. His heart beat so hard and fast against her skin that she thought it was her own.

For a long moment they lay like that. He on top, still inside her. Both just trying to catch their breath, trying to restart regular brain function. After another few minutes, Mikhail straightened up and pulled out of her. Eden crawled a little farther onto the bed and collapsed face-first, too exhausted to even roll over.

Her brain was a muddled mess as was her body. She thought the only decent thing to do now was sleep. She would figure things out in the morning.

She didn't look up to see what Mikhail was doing, but she felt him next to her on the bed. A blanket was draped gently over her, and right before she fell asleep, he brushed a few curls of her hair from her cheek and muttered, "You are safe now. I will always protect you."

## Chapter Nine

Mikhail watched her sleep. For once her face was relaxed. She'd lost that usual furrow of determination and worry. He knew it would return the moment she woke. Eden was a woman with single-minded purpose. She was a pit bull with the taste of blood in her mouth.

He admired her tenacity. Even if it did interfere with his job of keeping her out of Threshold business.

Eden moaned and rolled over onto her back, the blanket sliding off one perfect, plump breast. He liked that she was curvy. More to bite into. He wondered what she dreamed of. Their recent bout of incredible sex or was Bael visiting her again in her dreams? He wouldn't put it past the vampire to invade her thoughts especially now that she was in his territory and with Mikhail. It was just he didn't understand his endgame. If Bael truly wanted Eden to stay away, why was he beckoning her forward? Taunting her to find him and consequently Lilith Grae, the woman Eden had watched die.

He couldn't let her find the woman. If Eden truly knew what had happened to the woman, she'd never let it go. She'd never keep quiet. And Threshold's secrets had to be kept. That was part of his job.

In the morning, he'd take her back to the portal and send her through. Then he'd block that entrance so no one could ever use it again. Eden would have a hell of a time trying to find another one. They were few and far between and cleverly veiled. Bif had been careless with his threats and had completely underestimated Eden's drive and motives. Mikhail should never have sent the demon to do his job. It had been a grave error of judgment on his part, a mistake he never planned on making again.

Although he might never see Eden again, she had to go back. Back to her home and forget about this place and all its inhabitants. It would pain him to do so, more than he wanted to admit just now, but it had to be done. For her own safety if anything.

Mikhail's stomach grumbled and he got up to go into the kitchen. He needed a constant supply of food because his metabolism was ten times faster than a human's. Shape-shifting took a lot of energy. And their sexual romp had been quite the workout, as well. He had many voracious appetites, food and sex being his top two.

He opened the freezer and took out a packaged steak. He preferred fresh meat but he couldn't be picky at this point. He'd defrost it and eat it. He rarely cooked his meals—raw was always best and contained the most nutrients.

He was about to open the microwave and toss the meat in when he heard a noise outside the apartment door. Someone was coming up the stairs to his floor.

Mikhail crossed the room and unlocked the door in seconds. He stepped out on top of the landing just as Bael and three of his goons were approaching.

"What do you want?" Mikhail asked, not happy at all to see the vampire at his door.

"I knew you'd bring her here. It's so tortured hero of you."

Bael grinned and his cronies chuckled along with the joke.

"What do you want, Bael? I told you I would take care of this."

Bael took in Mikhail's naked form. "Yes, it looks like it. Is she as tasty as she looks? I certainly hope so. Or this would be a wasted trip."

"You said you wanted her gone. So I'm doing that. Tomorrow she'll be back in her world with no way of returning."

"Well, I've changed my mind."

"What?"

"Now that I've met her in person, I've decided that Eden would be a delightful addition to my court. You can't really tell that stuff in dreams."

Before Mikhail could take a step forward, Bael's henchmen were on him. One grabbed him around the neck from behind and the other two restrained his arms. He was strong but three vampires were stronger. And it looked as if they had just fed.

Bael glided toward him as if he floated on air. He patted him on the cheek. "We always knew this was going to happen, brother. You didn't really think she was going to fall in love with you and want to make little wolf babies with you?" Bael threw is arm up in the arm dramatically. "Especially not when she could have me."

The vampire nodded to the goon holding Mikhail around the neck. He started to squeeze and soon everything spun, then went black. The last thing Mikhail saw was Bael entering his apartment with the swagger of a conqueror.

# Chapter Ten

Eden rolled over onto her side, gathering the blanket tight to her chin, but her eyes snapped open when she noticed the silk beneath her naked body. She had not fallen asleep on soft, silky sheets.

Gathering the blanket to her breasts, she sat up to survey her new surroundings. She was definitely not in Mikhail's run-down apartment but in a large, opulently furnished suite.

The four-poster bed she lay in was huge, dressed in red silk sheets and velvet pillows. One long wall was a bank of windows and she could see the lights of the strange new city. Across the room a fire crackled in a large fireplace made from stone. In front of the hearth was a thick throw rug laid over the dark hardwood floor. There were also two golden Queen Anne chairs in front of the fire. A man sat in one, reading a book and sipping a glass of wine.

He closed the book and, setting his glass down, he turned to look at her. Bael's smile was warm and inviting and it sent a shiver down her back.

"Did you sleep well?" he asked.

"Is this one of my dreams?"

He stood and approached her. "I assure you, it isn't."

"What am I doing here? How did I get here?"

"You're a guest here in my home. I thought you'd like to see the true beauty of Threshold."

"Doesn't explain how I got here."

"Doesn't it?" His eyebrow lifted in amusement.

"Where's Mikhail?"

"Oh, I suspect he'll be along shortly." Bael walked to a table in the corner, where several covered dishes were laid out. "He's working for me, did you know?"

She didn't know, and she tried to keep the surprise from her face, but by his widening smile, she hadn't managed to.

He lifted the lids. "First you should eat." Delectable smells rolled over to her. "I had the cooks prepare several dishes I thought you'd enjoy."

"Thank you," she said, thinking it best to be polite. Unlike the way she could be with Mikhail, she didn't know if she could push this man and not be hurt. "Where are my clothes?"

Bael walked over to a large armoire and opened it. "There are clothes in here for any occasion." He took out a slinky black dress. "You're a size six, are you not?"

She indeed was a size six, but didn't want to know how he knew. So she didn't say anything.

He brought the dress over to the bed and laid it out. "Lingerie is in the drawers." He smiled then. From his close proximity she could clearly see his fangs peeking between his lips. "Or you may prefer to go without. Which is what I imagine you'll do."

"Why is that?"

"Because it will be much easier for me to fuck you that way." He ran his fingers over the dress. In response, shivers rushed through her body and heat blossomed between her legs.

She was embarrassed by her reaction to him. Especially

after just having sex with Mikhail so fervently only hours before.

"You assume I want to have sex with you."

"Don't you?"

He smiled as little licks of pleasure wound their way up her parted thighs and over her breasts. It was as if he'd touched her with just his thoughts.

"Stop it," she said, pulling the blanket higher to her chest.

"Stop what? I haven't done a thing.

"You know what I'm talking about. You're in my head. You've been in my dreams."

"If I am in your head, it is only because you want me there. The power is and always has been yours, Eden.

"That's not true."

"Sure it is. You wanted escape from your guilt. You called me to deliver you from it."

Eden thought about that. It was true she'd been suffering day after day from guilt and anger and despair. She had wished to be saved from it. In her dreams, Bael had eased her suffering. And it had felt good.

"You can be free here, Eden. In this world, in this place." He opened his arms to indicate the room, the apartment, the city. "You'd never want for anything. All your desires, all your pleasures would be fulfilled." He sat on the bed beside her. "Food, drink, clothing, amusements, sex. Whatever your imagination can dream up, you can have it. With no judgment. No one to censure you." He reached over and touched her face, feathering his fingertips across her cheek to her mouth.

Her lips parted on a sigh she hadn't meant to give as his thumb ran over her bottom lip. In her mind, she imagined kissing him. Imagined his mouth nibbling at her neck and venturing lower to her breasts, where his tongue swept over a nipple, and a fang scraped oh so cleverly against her sensitive bud.

Gasping, she pulled away from his touch. "Stop."

His hand dropped to his lap. "I could give you such pleasure, Eden. More than you could even imagine."

She could imagine a lot and she suspected Bael could and would give it to her if she asked. But she still didn't trust him. He'd invaded her dreams and now her conscious mind. The control was not hers—it was his. And she didn't like that one bit. With Mikhail she knew he'd allow her control if she asked for it. She had a sense he'd give her even more than that.

"And what would I have to give you in return? Because I know this wouldn't be for free. Nothing in life is."

"You don't trust me. I understand." Smiling, he stood. "Get dressed and I will give you a reason to."

"How?"

"Lilith Grae. You wish to see her, yes?"

"She's here?"

"Yes, she's here. And in good health." He moved toward the door. "She's eager to see you. I told her you've been looking for her." He opened the door. "I'll be back in an hour to fetch you."

"Bael?"

He stopped and looked in earnest at her.

"Where's Mikhail? You didn't hurt him, did you?"

"Of course not. Why on earth would I ever hurt my own brother?" With that he left, shutting the door behind him. Eden heard the distinctive click of a lock. It would seem trust didn't run either way.

Bael and Mikhail, brothers? She never would've suspected that. They certainly didn't look alike and their personalities were polar opposites. Bael was warm and inviting, Mikhail cold and unyielding. One opposed the other. And she seemed to be stuck in between them.

* * *

As promised, Bael returned to fetch her. She'd dressed in the garment he'd laid out for her, but she did put on some underwear. She didn't want to prove him right. She'd also nibbled on the provided food, and found all the dishes to her liking. In fact, they'd all been her favorites. Once more Bael must've invaded her thoughts to get that information.

"You look lovely," he said.

She felt lovely. The silky fabric of the dress clung to her curves. She'd never worn anything so rich and elegant before. And with her hair swept up—she'd found hairpins in the bathroom—she could've walked a red carpet and been able to hold her own.

It was a shame that Bael also looked lovely. His dark hair was pulled back from his perfect chiseled features and he filled out his suit like a man who frequented the gym regularly. Eden imagined a lean, chiseled frame underneath his expensive clothes, an image that wasn't helping her to quell her attraction to him.

He offered her his arm. "Shall we?"

"Where are we going?"

"I want to show you the city. What Threshold can offer."

"I thought you were taking me to see Lilith Grae?"

"I am. You'll see."

She didn't see but really had no recourse to argue. So far, he'd treated her very well. She was under no illusion that she could just walk out of his building freely, but she didn't necessarily feel like a captive either.

Once she saw Lilith and heard her story, she would decide what to do. Flee or stay.

The tour through the city was conducted from the back of a stretch limo. The streets seemed not much different from her own, except for the presence of strange but beautiful creatures walking them. This part of the city was mostly high-rises, high-end shops and popular nightclubs. Not at all like the area Mikhail had taken her to.

Eden thought about Mikhail and wondered if Bael had been telling the truth about not hurting him. Not that the shape-shifter needed her worry. She imagined it would take more than Bael to keep him down and wondered if he was trying to reach her. Or if giving her to Bael had been his plan all along.

She hoped it hadn't been, as she'd started having feelings for him. More than just lust. She sensed he cared more for her than he let on. She'd heard meaning in those words he whispered to her when he'd thought she'd been asleep. At least she hoped there had been meaning.

The limo stopped in front of a club. It had no name that she could discern but the lineup to get in stretched for a block or two. The door opened and Bael slid out, then reached in a hand to help her out. The second she was out of the limo with her hand wrapped around Bael's arm, camera flashes blinded her in a flurry of activity. It was the oddest thing to have supernatural paparazzi taking her picture and shouting at her to "smile" and "look here" as she and Bael walked to the club entrance.

A huge man, who looked much like Bif and smelled the same, unhooked the velvet rope and allowed them entrance.

"Good evening, Lord Bael," he said as they passed.

Before they entered, though, Eden heard a voice out on the street calling to her. When she turned her head, she saw Durt, her little goblin friend, being ushered the other way by two large catlike creatures.

# Chapter Eleven

Mikhail paced in front of the Inferno building. Three burly demons with rocklike skin stood guard in the foyer, glaring at him every time he looked over. They had kept him from going up to see Bael, from rescuing Eden. He'd tried every entrance and had been blocked on all sides. Bael was using all his resources to stop Mikhail from reaching her—he had to think of another way. Eden was a strong woman but Bael was a master of seduction. He had many gifts, and giving pleasure was at the top of that list. Mikhail had seen ruthless dignitaries and bloodthirsty warlords succumb to Bael's charms. The longer Eden was with him, the harder it would be to break his spell, if it could be broken at all.

He had to destroy it though. For her sake and for his own. It would ruin him to see Eden with Bael. He would not be able to withstand that kind of torture.

Mikhail was considering mounting another attack, this time from up top, when something caught his eye. That something was a little goblin hobbling his way from down the street. He was waving his little green arms.

"Sir! Sir!" he was shouting.

He remembered the goblin from when he'd grabbed Eden in front of the tavern.

The goblin reached his side, heaving heavily for breath. "Sir."

"What do you want?"

"I..." he started, gulped in air, then continued, "saw the lady."

"What lady?"

"The one you stole. The pretty one from the other side."

Mikhail grabbed the goblin's bony shoulder. "Where?"

"At the club." He turned to point from where he'd just come.

"Which one?"

"Club Anything."

Mikhail grimaced. Of all the places that Bael would take her, it would have to be there. A place where everything and anything was on the menu. Any pleasure, any perversion, could be had at the club.

He'd known of those who'd gone into the club and had never come out. Word was, some languished inside, caught so deeply in their fantasies that they never wanted to leave. Some, especially those who couldn't pay for long, became part of the establishment. Employees to work off their debt. Paid in things only they wanted. More salacious fantasies.

Bael owned the club as he did most things in Threshold.

Without any idea of how he was going to get in, Mikhail ran down the street toward the club, hoping he wasn't too late to save her.

## Chapter Twelve

The club was like nothing Eden had seen before. It was a cross between Coyote Ugly and French boudoir. There were scantily clad women of varying species behind the bar, spinning bottles and serving drinks, and saloon-looking gals swinging from the ceiling on velvet swings. The rooms were done in rich reds and golds. There were curved settees about the area; patrons perched on them sipping martinis and other assorted drinks. The music was a curious blend of heart-wrenching strains of Mozart and the *thump thump thump* of Dubstep. She took it all in with wide-eyed curiosity as Bael led her across the room to a private, roped-off area along one side.

After they were seated on one of the velvet-covered sofas, a waitress showed up with a tray of drinks. A full glass of rich red wine for Bael and a scotch on the rocks for her. She took the offered drink and wondered if that was truly wine in Bael's glass and not something else red and thick. She watched him as he took a sip and shuddered.

He smiled at her over the rim of his glass. "So, what do you think so far?"

She shrugged. She'd been expecting Caligula but had gotten Moulin Rouge instead. "Not as scandalous as I was expecting."

"Oh, the scandals go on in the private rooms in the basement. You could swim in a pool of chocolate sauce and have twenty little fairies lick it off your body if you wished."

She winced at that.

He laughed. "Oh, you'd be surprised how incredibly arousing that can be."

Eden took a drink, reveling in the way the scotch burned her throat on the way down. It was like a welcome friend to her. She drank more until her glass was empty.

"Delicious, isn't it? I don't know why you've denied yourself such a simple thing."

"My therapist says I rely on drink too much. That I need to learn to deal with life soberly." She said it matter-of-factly but she felt a little bitterness when she said it, of always having to explain herself.

Bael shook his head. "Foolish sentiments. Why not enjoy life to the fullest? Why wallow in guilt for craving these things? Makes no sense to me."

As soon as she set her empty glass down, there was a full one next to her hand. She picked it up and took another healthy drink. Already she could feel the effects of the alcohol. She was warm and calm inside.

"When can I see Lilith?"

"Now, if you wish."

"She's here?" Eden looked around the room, searching for the woman.

"She's in the basement."

Eden flinched a little, nervous about what she was going to see in the rooms in the basement of the club. She was afraid she'd see something that she craved so deeply she'd never want to leave. Thoughts of Mikhail filled her mind then, and she wondered if that had already transpired.

Bael stood and offered her his hand. "I'll take you down."

She took his hand and together they walked the club to a door painted red near the DJ booth. There was a burly werewolf in jeans guarding it. He bowed his furry head when Bael and Eden approached.

"Good evening, Lord Bael."

"Good evening, Franklin."

Eden tried not to snicker at the werewolf's name. It just seemed like such a normal name for someone so irregular. She averted her gaze as they went through the open door. But she felt Franklin's gaze on her the entire way. He sniffed at her as she passed him.

When they were through and the werewolf shut the door behind them, Bael chuckled. "I think Franklin likes you."

She shuddered. "Lucky me."

This made Bael laugh, and he patted her hand. "I like your ballsiness."

Before them the stairs descended in a steep decline. Candelabras lined the stone wall downward, candles flickering from within. When they reached the bottom, they turned to the right into a stone corridor that reminded Eden of a medieval castle. The dungeons, in particular. There were closed painted doors on either side of them as they walked the hall.

Sounds of ecstasy and agony emanated from each room.

Her grip on Bael's arm involuntarily tightened. Heat blossomed in her belly. Arousal quickly started to take root inside her, and she was embarrassed by it.

Which obviously Bael picked up on, because he said, "We are all primal animals. We want and need and crave. And here in this club you can get all that and more. Everything here is consensual. Nothing is forced."

He stopped at a green painted door and opened it. He pulled her inside. The dark seemed to swallow her whole. When her eyes adjusted to the dim candlelight, she could make out a round platform in the middle of the room. On top a naked woman was laid out, legs and arms spread, strapped to the table. There were several people, both men and women, crowded around the table. Then one spun the platform.

The woman went around and around, then stopped. Eden noticed a red arrow painted on the platform's surface, and it pointed to a young woman with long blond hair and pointed ears. She stepped forward and pressed her mouth to the woman's leg, on the thigh. Then she in turn spun the platform. It was like an erotic version of spin the bottle. And the woman was the bottle.

They watched for a few more minutes, as each person took a turn kissing, licking, or biting different areas of the naked woman's body. Every time she moaned and groaned, writhing in obvious pleasure on the platform. Then Bael took Eden's hand and led her out of the room.

Out in the corridor, Eden ran a hand over the back of her neck. She was sweating and it wasn't because of the heat in the room, as it wasn't all that warm. It was what was going on around her—it had an obvious effect on her. It seemed since being in Threshold she'd been in a constant state of arousal.

Bael opened another door and ushered her in. There was no gentle candlelight in this room. Instead, several strobe lights flashed on and off. The heavy bass of music thumped through wall speakers. At first it was disorienting and Eden had to grab onto Bael so she didn't run into something or someone.

The room seemed to be filled with people. Some naked, most in varying stages of undress and all engaged in sex of some kind. There were couples and trios and higher numbers together. Looking at it all, taking it all in, was dizzying.

Bael guided her to the side, to a bed, where a woman was laid out and two men were servicing her. The woman was Lilith—Eden recognized her immediately. When Lilith saw

Bael and then Eden, she pushed her playmates away, then grabbed Eden's hand.

She pulled Eden down to the mattress. "Hello again."

"Are you okay?" Eden asked her.

Lilith smiled, and it was lazy and giddy, as if she was drugged. "Hell, yes, I'm okay. Do I not look okay?"

Eden looked her over. She was not entirely naked, but wore stockings and a garter. And that's when she noticed the marks along the side of her neck, where Eden had seen a knife dig into her flesh.

She lifted a hand and drew a finger over the two round scars. "What are these?"

"My birthmarks." Lilith grinned, and Eden saw the fangs in her mouth.

"I saw you die," she said. "I held you until you died."

Lilith grabbed her hand in hers. "I know. I'm sorry if you thought that I was truly dead. You didn't get a chance to see my rebirth as Lilith Grae."

"You're a vampire?"

"Yes. Isn't it wonderful?"

"And the man with the knife, the one that had you in the alley?"

She nodded. "Yes, he was my maker. But he's truly dead now. Bael ended him."

Eden looked over at Bael who had been sitting nearby, listening.

"You see, everything is fine, Eden. Lilith is happy. And the man who did this to her has been punished. He should never have turned her in your world."

Eden just looked at him, trying to assimilate all that she'd seen and heard. She was trying to find a way to accept that the girl she'd watched die, the one she thought she'd failed, hadn't truly died. She'd found new life as a creature of the night, a vampire. And the man Eden thought had gotten away with murder had in fact been punished, just as he should've been.

Bael slid in beside her on the bed. "You see, you can release your guilt. There is no reason to hang on to it. Let go, Eden. You can be free here. For as long as you like. Forever, if you wish it."

His words were like silk across her skin—they caressed her and soothed her. He put an arm around her and drew her closer. He settled his mouth at her ear and whispered, "I can give you all that you desire. You just need to let go. You just need to give yourself to me. Entirely."

She leaned into him. His words seduced her. She wanted to be free of all her guilt and worry and sadness. She didn't want to have to face those who would look upon her with pity and sympathy because of her situation. No more therapy, no more obligatory calls from family members wondering how she was getting on. No more knowing looks from her old partner down at the station. She could leave it all behind and succumb to Bael. To what he was offering her.

She wanted to. She was tired of fighting to stay sober, to stay happy, to stay.

Bael stroked a hand down her neck to her shoulder and then ventured lower. He cupped her breast in his palm. "You are exquisite. I want you to belong to me."

He leaned in and captured her mouth with his. He kissed her passionately, sweeping his tongue into her mouth, over her tongue. She responded in kind, then his fangs nipped at her and she pulled back.

She remembered how she'd felt in another man's arms. She had felt all the things Bael was offering, and Mikhail had asked for nothing in return. Plus he'd made her feel safe and secure. Two things she hadn't felt in a very long time. He also didn't demand her submission—she'd given it to him willingly.

He didn't quest for her soul as Bael did.

Eden shook her head. "I'm leaving. This is not what I want." She went to stand, but Bael held her firm.

"You lie to yourself, Eden. I can smell your desire. You want me. You want this."

"Let me go."

"It's too late for that."

Opening his mouth, his fangs distended, he leaned toward her throat. She tried to push him away but he was too strong. She looked at Lilith to help her, but the woman was watching with eagerness and glee.

She smoothed a hand over Eden's back. "It's all right. It will only hurt for a little while. Then euphoria."

Although Eden wanted to get away, her body betrayed her by reacting to Bael. To his nearness, to the heat radiating off his body, to his delectable scent that lingered on his skin. It smelled good enough to lick.

She hated that heat swelled between her legs. That her sex throbbed, seeking release. Her nipples hardened as the vampire pressed against her. A little moan escaped her lips when he brushed his fangs across her skin.

But it was all fake. It wasn't real. He was in her head, tricking her, seducing her from the inside out. It wasn't the same with Mikhail. Eden knew she felt those things for real with him. He didn't need to deceive her to illicit true feelings.

Right before Bael sunk those teeth into her flesh, she saw flames dancing in the black of his eyes. Then everything became a vivid, colorful blur of sight and sound.

She thought she heard Mikhail's voice in her ear. And felt his hands on her body, but surely she must be dreaming for that to happen. Because she had given herself foolishly to Bael and was now his slave.

## Chapter Thirteen

When Mikhail saw the trickle of blood down Eden's neck, he nearly went ballistic. He wanted nothing more than to eviscerate Bael with his claw, but he knew he had to save her first. And time was of the essence. His healing capabilities had their limits.

He'd fought his way into the club and down to the basement rooms and had burst into each room to search for her. He'd seen her in the strobe lights almost the moment he'd opened the door. He'd crossed the room in two strides and had Bael by the neck. But it was too late—he could now see the bite marks in her neck.

After tossing the vampire across the room, he scooped Eden up in his arms and ran out of the room and the club. There was so much rage on his face, in his eyes, that no one dared stop him from leaving with her.

Durt met them outside in the back alley. The goblin had commandeered a car, and he opened the back door the second he saw them. Mikhail settled Eden on the seat and climbed in beside her while Durt got behind the wheel.

The goblin drove to Mikhail's apartment, ignoring all rules of the road. And Mikhail was thankful for it. When they arrived, he took Eden out and ran her up the stairs to his place. He kicked open the door and rushed her to the bed. She was barely breathing when he laid her down on the mattress.

He stripped off his clothes, and hers. For this healing he needed no barriers between them. He settled on the bed and drew her into his lap, cradling her head in his hands. Closing his eyes, he settled his palms around her throat, where the wound still wept blood.

His chi filled his hands. The heat of it drew across his flesh, burning him from the inside out. But he felt no pain. He suspected he would in time, given the nature of her wound. He let it saturate him, then he spilled it into her.

He opened his eyes and watched her face, looking for signs that his healing was working. But her face remained slack, lifeless. As if she'd already become one of *them*.

He drew more power from his reserves. His flesh now seared with pain. It was as if he'd placed his hands in a great fire until his skin sizzled and split open. But his skin didn't burn, just turned red with strain. He pushed more into her. More than he'd ever used on anyone before. More than anyone could likely bare.

She took it in, greedily.

He watched her face and saw the first glimmer of hope in the fluttering of her eyelashes. Then her eyes opened and she stared up at him. Mikhail saw awareness in her eyes. She had not passed into darkness. She was still here. She was still Eden. His Eden.

He released his hold on her neck. The bite marks had closed and the skin around them was freshly pink, like brand-new skin. She would have little scars but at least she hadn't died and been reborn into the night.

"Mikhail?"

He smiled down at her and swept stray hair from her face. "I'm here."

"Am I dead? Did he turn me?"

"No. You'll be fine."

Eden brought a hand to her neck and ran her fingertips over her wounds. She winced as she touched them. He suspected they would hurt for a few days until the toxicity of Bael's bite left her system.

"I nearly lost myself to this place. I should've left when you told me to."

He ran a hand over her hair. "It's not Threshold that is the problem. It's Bael." He captured a curl in his fingers. "There are other things in Threshold worth staying for."

She looked at him, tracing a finger down his cheek. "I don't know what to do. I feel so lost right now. I've been pushed by my guilt for so long that I'm almost empty without it."

"You need to fill yourself up with other things."

"Like what?"

Mikhail placed his hands around her waist, lifted her up and then settled her into his lap. He was already hard just from looking at her.

"Like sex."

She laughed and wrapped her legs around his waist. Reaching down between them, she guided him into her. She was soft and wet and open for him. Like silk, she wrapped around his cock. He groaned as she moved ever so slightly on him.

"And what else?" she asked.

"And love."

Her eyebrows went up at that. "Love? I'm not sure I even know what that means anymore."

"I could show you if you let me."

He spread his hands across her back and held her still for one moment while he studied her. With his gaze on hers, he leaned in and kissed her. It was simple and sweet and perfect.

When he was done kissing her, he leaned back and looked

at her. Really looked at this woman who had somehow captured him and tamed him. If only a little, and if only for a
short time.

"I want you to stay here with me."

"For how long?"

"For as long as it takes for you to never want to leave."

Smiling, she wrapped her arms around him and kissed him
until they were both breathless and on the threshold of more
pleasure than either of them had ever hoped for.

\* \* \* \* \*

# MILLS & BOON®

**Power, passion and irresistible temptation!**

The Modern™ series lets you step into a world
of sophistication and glamour, where sinfully
seductive heroes await you in luxurious
international locations. Visit the Mills & Boon
website today and type **Mod15** in at
the checkout to receive

## 15% OFF

your next Modern purchase.

Visit **www.millsandboon.co.uk/mod15**

# MILLS & BOON®

## Why not subscribe?

Never miss a title and save money too!

Here's what's available to you if you join the exclusive **Mills & Boon Book Club** today:

+ *Titles up to a month ahead of the shops*
+ *Amazing discounts*
+ *Free P&P*
+ *Earn Bonus Book points that can be redeemed against other titles and gifts*
+ *Choose from monthly or pre-paid plans*

### Still want more?

Well, if you join today we'll even give you
***50% OFF your first parcel!***

So visit **www.millsandboon.co.uk/subs**
**or call Customer Relations on 020 8288 2888**
to be a part of this exclusive Book Club!

# *Snow, sleigh bells and a hint of seduction*

## Find your perfect Christmas reads at
**millsandboon.co.uk/Christmas**